Scattered Like Seeds

Scattered Like Seeds

| A NOVEL |

Shaw J. Dallal

With a Foreword by John B. Harcourt

SYRACUSE UNIVERSITY PRESS

This book is part of the Mohammed El-Hindi Series on Arab Culture
and Islamic Civilization and is published with the assistance
of a grant from the M.E.H. Foundation.

The paper used in this publication meets the minimum requirements of American
National Standard for Information Sciences—Permanence of Paper for Printed
Library Materials, ANSI Z39.48-1984. ∞

Library of Congress Cataloging-in-Publication Data
Dallal, Shaw J.
Scattered like seeds : a novel / Shaw J. Dallal : with a foreword
by John B. Harcourt. — 1st ed.
p. cm.
ISBN 0-8156-0553-6 (alk. paper)
1. Palestine—Exiles—Fiction. 2. Palestinian Arabs—Fiction.
PS3554.A4333S23 1998
813'.54—dc21   98-8761

With love and humility,
this novel is dedicated to my parents
and to the Palestinian people,
who inspired it

By the [Winds] Sent Forth
One after another
[To scatter seeds]

Which then blow violently
In tempestuous Gusts,

And scatter [people]
Far and wide;

Then separate them,
One from another

Then spread abroad
A Message . . ."

—*The Holy Quran,*
Al-Mursalaat Surah, LXXVII, 1–5

Shaw J. Dallal teaches Islamic culture in the Honors Program of Syracuse University and international business management and international law and economics at Utica College. He is a trained lawyer and a businessman turned professor and novelist, who has served as the chief legal advisor for the Organization of Arab Petroleum Exporting Countries (OAPEC) in Kuwait.

Contents

Foreword | John B. Harcourt

There was something truly unusual about the young man who arrived at Ithaca College in 1953. He had spent two years in the College of Engineering at Cornell University. Now he was double registered, having also enrolled as an economics major in a small, struggling institution just beginning to venture into the humanities. Virtually all of his classmates were men and women from communities in upstate New York; he was a Palestinian, yet he was most closely linked to his fellow students by poverty. Like so many of them, he would combine a standard academic program with full-time employment, working from 4 P.M. to midnight in a local industrial plant.

I soon came to know Shaw Dallal. He was an English minor and a member of the Canterbury Club, for which I was faculty adviser. He told us of his childhood in his native Palestine. We learned of his father's struggle against the Ottomans in World War I and of his bitterness against the British when the Balfour Declaration was announced. We heard of his education in the schools of Palestine during the British Mandate in that country and of his meeting an American priest while working in a hospital in Kuwait. This mentor had persuaded him that only in the United States could he obtain a first-rate education without significant financial resources. Thus encouraged, he had applied to several distinguished U.S. col-

Dr. John B. Harcourt is Charles A. Dana Professor of English Emeritus, Ithaca College.

leges and universities and had chosen Cornell University because of the scholarship grant it offered him.

Shaw married a young American woman, a fellow student
at Cornell, while still an undergraduate, and managed to graduate from Ithaca College in 1956. Still combining the academic
program with a heavy workload, he went on to complete his
law studies at the Cornell Law School, from which he received
a J.D. For many years, we heard little of him. Then one day
he reappeared as the eminently successful businessman—owner
and chief executive officer of a multimillion dollar conglom-
erate in the Middle East—and was now in a position to make
substantial gifts both to Ithaca College and to Cornell University. We had lunch together several times a year. On one of
those occasions, he arrived with a bulky typescript in hand.

In semiretirement, Shaw had written his first novel.

Like most first novels, some parts of it were unabashedly
autobiographical. General Ayoub Allam is an idealized, though
modified, portrait of Shaw's father. The tense encounters with
Israeli soldiers are faithfully delineated. The move to the United
States and the decades of Americanization follow the broad
outlines of Shaw's career. The pattern is shattered with the
Arab-Israeli War of 1967; both author and his fictional surro-
gate feel the strong tug of Palestinian nationalism. After read-
ing the novel, I called Shaw's attention to Franz Werfel's novel,
The Forty Days of Musa Dagh, in which a young Armenian,
apparently fully assimilated to Parisian culture, was drawn
back into the world of his ancestors when their losing struggle
against the Turks began.

A Palestinian, a Middle Eastern student at Ithaca College
and at Cornell University, a U.S.-trained lawyer and a Persian
Gulf businessman, husband to an American wife, father to an
American family—Shaw seems always to have been straddling
two worlds, two worlds in an uneasy, perhaps irreconcilable,
tension. His novel crackles with these two tensions. Writing
it was not only a catharsis, but also a struggle to understand

the fullest implications of his own life's underlying contradictions; each revision gained in understanding of the human concerns that transcend partisan loyalties.

Scattered Like Seeds is unusual for a "modern" novel. For one thing, it consists almost entirely of spoken words—words in dialogue with others, words in inner dialogue with self. In this respect, it resembles a play or a film scenario. It is also "traditional" in form, concerned to tell a gripping story as directly and clearly as possible. The reader may at first be taken aback by its lack of portentous symbolism, trendy ironies, and studied indirection. But Shaw seems to have realized intuitively the advice offered by Malcolm Cowley many decades ago: "If it isn't real it isn't a symbol. If it isn't a story it isn't a myth. If a character doesn't live he can't be an archetype of modern life."*

To be sure, *Scattered Like Seeds* is a political novel, though hardly a simplistic one. The wrongs done to the Palestinian people, both by Israel and by the Arab states, darken every page; the great powers, including the United States, fuel the regional hostilities. The larger conflict becomes intensely personal in Thafer's humiliation at the Allenby Bridge as he attempts to enter Israel to visit his aged mother.

Yet outrage at U. S. support of Israel is tempered by Thafer's profound attachment to his adopted country, even though his own and others' various attempts to distinguish between the American people and the U.S. government sometimes ring hollow, even to himself. Israel is the enemy, yet the brief encounter with the Jewish woman on the plane reveals a common humanity deeper than any nationalism or ideology or even religion. Shaw mercilessly exposes Arab weakness, both in individuals and in states. Feudalism, autocracy, the gap between the indolent, decadent rich and those living in direst

---

*Malcolm Cowley, "The New Critics and the New Fiction," reprinted in the *Saturday Review Reader* 3, 126.

poverty, the refusal to admit error, the inability to achieve significant united action—all these are things Thafer discovers as he attempts to live and work in this strange world to which he has returned. Human, all too human—the failures on every side bring bitterness too great for tears.

Shaw's novel will be roundly condemned by those who see the Middle-Eastern situation in simple black-and-white terms, whether they be pro-Israel or pro-Palestine, but *Scattered Like Seeds* is far more than a fictional presentation of opposing points of view. The larger issues have been distilled into Thafer's personal conflicts; in the final analysis, he is any divided soul, trapped in the ambiguities of history.

Acknowledgments

The first few pages of *Scattered Like Seeds* were prompted by a genealogy that my late father-in-law, Kenneth W. Fuller, compiled and distributed to his children and grandchildren. Becoming aware that my children and grandchildren are descendants of the Pilgrims, I wanted to record for them something of their Palestinian heritage, but the form would be different, a short story about the Palestinian people. The first to read it was my secretary at the time, Loretta Koehler, to whom I am deeply indebted. "This should be a novel," she commented after typing the first draft of the original short story. "You should continue."

I am also grateful to the following friends who were kind enough to read earlier drafts and who made helpful comments: Ayman Alami, the late Howard C. Alexander, William G. Andrews, Trudy Ash, the late Rabbi Elmer Berger, Pasquale and Jacqueline Ciaglia, Robert Cimbalo, Melvin and Marion (Upty) Clouse, Diane Cook, David Coryell, Robert N. Davis, Robert and Maralynn Dowell, Esther Doyle, Sally Ann Edwards, Robert Duncan Enzmann, Traci Fordham, Jeremy Gelb, Frank and Frances Giruzzi, John B. Harcourt, Aref and Rosemary Hinedi, Joseph Karam, John and Doris Kavouksorian, Kevin M. Kelly, Mark Levi, James C. Mills, Hobart and Lois Morris, Eugene Nassar, Walter Oczkowski, John D. Ogden, Mansur Rafizadeh, Andrew Rock, Kathi Rodgers, Mary Rossi, Eric Schmidt, Michael Spath, Jean Stanton, Michael and Joan Stephenson, Joseph and Claire Sturr, Ludwig Tamari, Evelyn

Tudhope, Michael Wall, Abdul-Qader A. Yousuf, M. Bashar Yousuf, and John Zogby.

I would like to thank my friend Melvin Clouse for urging me to write this novel, for his willingness to read its various drafts, and for his unwavering support and guidance.

I thank Mehrzad Boroujerdi for his special guidance and support.

I would like to express deep gratitude to Professor John B. Harcourt for his invaluable friendship and support. In particular, I would like to thank him for writing a foreword for the novel. I thank my high-school classmate and life-time friend, Muhammad Hallaj, for writing the introduction.

I would like to thank my friend and countryman, Ahmad Mohammed El-Hindi for his generous financial grant.

I want also to thank the staff of Syracuse University Press, especially Cynthia Maude-Gembler, the executive editor, for their continued support and professionalism.

Yet the greatest gratitude must be reserved for my wife, Diana, who toiled endlessly in editing the various drafts of the manuscript and whose continued support and encouragement were vital to its completion.

The following historical, political and cultural sources have influenced my thoughts about, or composition of, this book: 1) on the Middle East in general. Daniel C. Diller, *The Middle East*, Congressional Quarterly (1985–94); 2) on the 1947–48 Arab Israeli War and related matters, Simha Flapan, *The Birth of Israel: Myths and Realities*, Pantheon Books (1987); 3) on the 1973 Arab Israeli War and the oil embargo that ensued, Mohamed Heikel, *The Road to Ramadan*, Fontana/Collins (1975); 4) on the conflicts between Iraq and Iran as well as between Iraq and Kuwait and related matters, Micah L. Sifry and Christopher Cerf, Editors, *The Gulf War Reader*, Times Books (1991); 5) other subjects, Abed Al-Samih Abu Omar, *Traditional Palestinian Embroidery and Jewelry*, Al-Sharq Arab Press (1986).

Introduction | Muhammad Hallaj

This historical novel faithfully narrates the extraordinary Palestinian experience. To Palestinian Americans, such as the writer of *Scattered Like Seeds* and myself, the narrative reads like a personal diary that contains the triumphs and agonies of every Palestinian. More than the story of one Palestinian, *Scattered Like Seeds* is the biography of a people who, when for the first time in their history they came close to realizing the principle of self-determination, tottered instead on the edge of extinction. Their struggle to cling to survival and to share the universal ideal of national freedom, much misunderstood in the West, is a saga unique in this century—full of pain and promise, tragedy and heroism.

In the end an irony has proved to be fateful. The collective tragedy, the displacement and scattering of Palestinian society, has created unprecedented opportunities for individual Palestinians to become educated, prosper, and persevere in the struggle for Palestine's national independence.

Scattered Like Seeds is a work of fiction. Its authenticity, however, can be easily verified by reference not only to documented history but also to the life experiences of countless Palestinian Americans who can see themselves in the story of Thafer Allam.

Dr. Hallaj is a political scientist. He has taught at several universities in the United States and in the Middle East. He served on the Palestinian delegation to the Arab-Israeli Peace Negotiations and is a member of the Palestine National Council.

| PROLOGUE |

I | June 5, 1967

"What's the matter, Thafer? It's still too early. It's not yet six."

"I know, Mary Pat," Thafer Allam says, tossing in bed, waiting for the newscast. "I can't seem to go to sleep."

"What's on your mind, dear?"

"The trouble in the Middle East."

"I know, but you have to get some sleep. They'll always have trouble over there."

Then memories of his early childhood sweep over him.

Mama, he lisped, soldiers.

Where? his terrified mother asked, interrupting her lullaby. At the door.

His youthful mother stopped her rocking, knelt on the floor, and murmured a prayer. Stay with baby Salwa. Rock her gently. I've got to answer the door.

No, Mama! Don't go! I'm scared!

Rock baby Salwa, Thafer dear, please. Don't be scared. You're a big boy.

I want Papa. Don't go to the door, Mama, they have guns!

The pounding at the massive outer door of their Jerusalem home grew louder. Open! the stern, abrasive voice shouted.

His mother went to the outer door while he tugged at her skirt and left his younger sister crying. Her hands began to shake as she unlocked the outer door and faced four British troopers.

Your name?

Jihan Atiya Allam, his mother said, not looking at the trooper and pressing Thafer to her side.

3

Is Ayoub Allam in?

No, he isn't.

Where is he?

At the farm.

Is he your husband?

Yes.

Where's the farm?

West of Tulkarm, near the sea.

How long have you lived in Jerusalem?

All my life.

What weapons have you in the house?

None.

Are they buried in the yard?

I have no weapons.

Who's in the house with you?

My little boy and baby daughter, just three months old.

How old's the boy?

Four, almost five.

Where are the weapons?

I don't have any.

How many terrorists are hiding here?

No terrorists are here.

What's your name? the British trooper asked Thafer.

He had hid behind his mother and did not answer.

Thafer Ayoub Allam, his mother said, pressing him closer to her side.

We're going to search the house. You and the children go to the kitchen until we call you.

His mother, still shaking, rushed and snatched baby Salwa from the cradle as Thafer trailed behind, still clinging to her skirt. Come to the kitchen, Thafer dear, come, come. You're a brave boy. Of course you are.

Why do they want to search our house, Mama?

Because the British are wicked. They don't fear God, dear. They want to give our country to the Jews.

Why?

I can't tell you now, Thafer. Wait until they leave.

Are they going to search my room?

His mother did not answer.

Mama, will they search my room?

Let them search it to their heart's content.

Will they take my wheely duck?

Let them take it. Papa will make you a new one.

"Full-scale war breaks out in the Middle East," the radio announces at 6:00 A.M. that Monday morning in 1967. "Conflicting reports have reached here about the outcome of the fighting. Stay tuned for a special report in our 7:00 A.M. newscast."

At once, Thafer Ayoub Allam and his wife, Mary Pat Connally Allam, sit up. "What do you make of that?" Mary Pat asks.

"I don't know," Thafer replies, as bewildered as his wife.

"Do you think your mother got your telegram?"

"I hope so."

"Do you think she got to Amman?"

"I don't know," he says again, feeling completely helpless.

Thafer sent a telegram to his mother on the advice of the Tunisian UN ambassador, whom he represented in a traffic violation case two weeks earlier. He wrote her that the Middle Eastern situation was tense, that she should leave the West Bank town of Tulkarm and go to Amman, where his older brother and his family live. He does not know if his mother received his telegram. And even if she has, he doubts that she will heed his advice.

Finally, Thafer gets up, shaves, showers, and dresses. He knows Mary Pat is concerned, and he also knows that her concern is because of him, but he doubts that she has any idea how worried he is.

Still in a daze, he walks to the kitchen. Mary Pat is helping the children get ready for school.

"Mom, what's bothering Dad?" asks Kathleen, their twelve-year-old daughter. With her long dark hair and big brown eyes, Kathleen most resembles her Palestinian father. Her complexion is a little lighter than her father's, but darker than her mother's.

"War broke out in Palestine this morning," says Mary Pat. Her fair face wears a worried expression. Tall, thin, and beautiful, she is also dignified and imposing despite always mischievous blue eyes.

"War, Dad?! Is Grandma OK?" asks Andrew, their fourteen year old. He is tall like his father, but fair like his mother. He looks anxious too.

"I hope so, Andrew, but I don't really know," Thafer says, trying to maintain his composure. He is obviously preoccupied. His dark eyes look distant, as if he is far, far away.

"Mom, could Dad go there?" asks Kathleen.

"No, stupid," says Andrew.

"Don't talk like that to your sister, Andrew," Mary Pat says sternly.

Colleen looks at her stepfather nervously. She is tall like her mother and has her mother's fair complexion and dark blue eyes, but she does not look like any of the other Allam children.

Sean, the youngest, grabs his lunch bag and gets ready to catch the early bus. He has dark brown hair and a dark complexion, almost like his father's, and his mother's dark blue eyes.

The 7:00 A.M. news report is more complete. It tells of violent fighting on three fronts—the Egyptian, the Jordanian, and the Syrian—of fierce air battles on the Egyptian front, and of bitter street fighting in Jerusalem. Claims and counterclaims make the picture unclear, but Thafer has an uneasy feeling about the outcome as his children leave for school this late spring morning. Privately, he hopes and prays for an Arab victory.

As Thafer drives to his office in Osaga, New York, a few miles from their home in Ashfield, he listens to the radio. Somber music plays as he waits for the 8:00 A.M. news, and once again he remembers.

Four British troopers nearly knocked down our door with their bayonets this morning, his mother told his father that day in 1938. They were looking for you. Thafer and I were petrified. That's why the place is torn apart. They found the black wooden pistol you carved for Thafer. Who made this? their leader asked. My husband, I said. He looked and looked at the black toy, almost in disbelief. It looks real, quite real, the Englishman finally said. Then he slipped it under his belt.

How long did they stay?

They seemed to stay forever, but maybe two hours.

I wonder if they went to our house in Tulkarm. Have you heard from the boys?

No, but I know that Saleem and his family are still at the farm with your nephew Muneer and his family. Kamal and Rassem are either at the house in Tulkarm or at the farm too.

I hope they're all safe.

I'm sure they are. How long is this going to go on, my dear?

I have no idea, but as long as it takes. Our rebels now control 80 percent of the country, but the British are bringing in reinforcements.

That doesn't sound good.

It means bloodshed, but we're determined to liberate the homeland from the monstrous British Mandate, and rebel morale is very high.

Is it possible to win?

I have to believe it is, my love. The alternative is disaster.
How?

More Jewish immigration to Palestine, more land taken from our farmers by the Jews, which we'll never get back. We have no place to go if we lose our land.

Why can't we share with them? We've always lived with Jews.

It won't work. They want our land. They want to drive us out of the country. Our people will be scattered like seeds, far and wide. It's a matter of life and death for us.

But Thafer and Salwa are so little. The older boys can at least take care of themselves.

If anything happens to me, the good Lord and our older sons will care for the little ones. I'm fighting so that we won't lose everything. Do you think I enjoy spending week after week moving from cave to cave in the hills?

What about our young children?

The good Lord will look after them.

It's December. You've spent more than two years with the rebels. Isn't that enough?

"Israel claims that it has destroyed the Egyptian air force," the radio announces at 8:00 A.M. "The reports are still inconclusive and conflicting, as Egypt denies Israel's claim." Thafer shakes his head in disbelief. He gets out of his car and walks to his law office at Tucker, Carpenter, and Vale. The firm is located in downtown Osaga, a city of about three hundred thousand in central New York State.

"The Israelis are going to beat the hell out of those camel drivers," a man riding the elevator with Thafer tells him.

"You may be right." Thafer pretends not to be disturbed by the man's remark.

II

"Full-scale war rages on. Both sides claim victory," broadcasts the 10:00. A.M. news report. Sitting in his office, Thafer is restless, tuning from station to station.

He paces the floor of his office. I'm going to go home, he decides, as he walks out to his secretary. "I don't feel well, Maureen. I'm going home. If anyone asks for me, would you kindly tell them I've taken the day off?"

"Certainly. I'm sorry you're not feeling well, Thafer. I hope the war is not upsetting you."

"Not too much," he smiles.

"You're home, Thafer!" Mary Pat greets her husband. "I'm glad you came home, dear. Take off your suit and put on something relaxing. That'll make you feel better."

He throws himself into her arms. "Oh, Mary Pat."

"Try not to think about the war, please Thafer. Is that possible?"

"No. I need to talk about it."

"Then talk to me about it."

She takes his hand and leads him to their family room.

He looks up at his parents' portrait on the wall in front of him. It is an old picture of his father in his early fifties and his mother in her late twenties. His father wore a white Arab headcloth and a western suit. The expression on his handsome moustachioed face is quite serious, befitting his years. Thafer's more youthful, smiling mother wore the traditional Palestinian dress, a white mantilla partly covering her brown hair.

He stares out the window at their apple tree in full bloom and the lush green of their neatly mowed lawn. The scent of wood smoke and images of his family farm with its fields fill his head. He sees his father and mother, his brothers and sister working in the fields, neighboring farmers working happily on their land in the distance, and others making their way to work.

"Do you think Israel started the war, Thafer?"

"No doubt about that."

"Then why does everyone blame Egypt and Syria?"

"The Egyptians and the Syrians are damn fools. Egypt forced the United Nations observers to leave the Straits of Tiran in the Red Sea."

"What does that have to do with Israel?"

"Israel, Mary Pat, considers these straits its only access to the Iranian oil it needs and assumed that Egypt would enforce a blockade against Israeli shipping. Israel began to mass troops on the Egyptian border. Egypt responded by massing troops in the Sinai."

"Why did the United Nations have to listen to Egypt's request?"

"The United Nations observers were stationed in the Red Sea at President Eisenhower's request after Israel participated with England and France in the 1956 attack against Egypt. That was after Egypt nationalized the Suez Canal Company. Israel occupied the Straits of Tiran and Sinai during that war. President Eisenhower insisted on Israel's withdrawal from Sinai and from the Red Sea. In order to expedite its withdrawal, he proposed that United Nations observers be stationed on the straits. To maintain its sovereignty over the straits, Egypt agreed to allow the United Nations observers to be stationed there on condition that they leave when asked by Egypt to do so."

"So Egypt had a perfect right to ask the UN observers to leave the Red Sea."

"But they shouldn't have."

"Why?"

"Because the Egyptians should have known that when the UN left, Israel would start a war."

"Weren't the Egyptians prepared?"

"If you listen to their propaganda, you'd think that they were, but in reality they have never been a match for the Israelis militarily."

"The Egyptians are clumsy."

"They don't understand U.S. politics."

"It sounds like Israel was looking for a fight."

"It was."

"Let's hope that the United Nations stops the fighting."

"The United Nations can't stop the fighting because the United States doesn't want it stopped."

"But why?"

"Because the United States wants to pressure the Soviet Union to stop helping Vietnam. Egypt and Syria are Soviet clients, Mary Pat."

"So, we want to humiliate the Soviet Union in the Middle East the way the Soviet Union is humiliating us in Vietnam."

"It looks that way."

"Oh boy! What a mess!"

"I'm also surprised and alarmed by my own feelings. I just hadn't realized that after living so many years in the United States, married to you and with four Yankee children, I would still have these passionate feelings about my homeland and my people."

"But that's understandable! Is something else bothering you, Thafer?"

"When I went to visit my dying father in 1959, Mary Pat, he begged me to return. I had no desire to go back, and I stayed only ten days after his death. I didn't belong anymore. My mother pleaded, my brothers pleaded, our relatives and friends pleaded, but I just couldn't. That was eight years ago. I don't know what it is, Mary Pat. Maybe it's the war, maybe it's some other thing, but I have this strong yearning to return to the land of my birth."

"What are you saying, Thafer? What about your family here? What about your career, your practice, your teaching, your life? You're emotional and upset now, dear. We need you here. Stop thinking like that. You're an American now. I mean a real American. This is your home, your town, and your country."

"You're right, and I love you, and I love our children."

Thafer lays his head on Mary Pat's breast like a child, and she strokes his hair and kisses him.

"Let's wait until the dust settles. Then we should think of some way to bring your mother here."

"She won't come. You know she won't leave her home, even for a visit."

"But why, Thafer? Why?"

"It has to do with the way my family left Jerusalem in 1948. My mother was the one who wanted the family to leave. My father was against it, but he was getting old and finally agreed with my mother. So we moved to Tulkarm and never returned to our real home in Jerusalem. My mother blames herself and is determined never to leave Palestine, even if it means her life."

"Let me go fix us some tea," she finally says.

"Thank you, Mary Pat." Then he begins to remember again.

There was a massacre in Deir Yasseen, said his older brother Rassem, his face full of anxiety as he rushed into their home in Jerusalem in early April of 1948.

What happened? his mother asked.

The Jews went into Deir Yasseen and killed everybody—women, children and men, everybody.

Are you sure? his elderly father asked.

Look outside, Father.

A column of dark smoke hovered over the quarry of Deir Yasseen. Jewish trucks carried the dead victims to Jerusalem's Jewish quarter, not far from the Allam home, and put them on display.

We should all move to Tulkarm, his mother screamed.

Let's find out what happened, his father said, trying to calm her.

Jewish armored cars drove by their home, announcing with loud speakers that all Palestinians who didn't leave would face a fate similar to that of the inhabitants of Deir Yasseen.

I don't think we should leave, his father said, pointing out that there was a British police station around the corner. They are obligated to come and defend us. We're defenseless civilians.

The British won't intervene, his mother cried. They'll look the other way.

Then let's die defending our home.

How?

With our bare hands! With anything else we can lay our hands on!

Let me take Salwa and Thafer to Tulkarm. I can't let them die. We'll come back.

If you go, we all go, but I don't want to leave.

I won't go, Father, his brother Rassem said. I'll guard our house.

No, we all stay here together or leave together.

The unarmed inhabitants of the village of Deir Yasseen, their hands tied behind their backs and their eyes blindfolded, were driven from their homes by armed Jews. They were lined up and executed. Pregnant women's stomachs were stabbed and cut open. Children were slashed. Screams, the explosion of grenades, and the smell of gunpowder and smoke filled the air of the defenseless village on the outskirts of Jerusalem. Fleeing men were shot, pleading women were raped, and helpless children were stabbed. The village was then looted and turned upside down. The bodies of the victims—old men, women, and children—were carried to the rock quarry of the village, laid out on the stones, doused with gasoline, and set ablaze. The odor of the burning corpses lingered over the village's almond trees in full bloom and filled the air of Deir Yasseen on that clear spring day of April 9, 1948.

III

For all six days of the 1967 war, Thafer stays up nights listening to the news, hoping to hear something reassuring, but to no avail. Finally, it is clear that Israel has the upper hand. The Arabs have suffered a stunningly quick defeat.

On the last day of the war, he again stays at home. Bitterly disappointed and emotionally exhausted, he watches the evening news on television that day while thousands of Jews stamp and swirl the hora on street corners in New York and in

Washington. Arm in arm, they march through the streets singing. They embrace and kiss.

He wonders where his aging mother is. He imagines her walking helplessly between the hills of his war-torn native country, thirsty and hungry under the blazing June sun. He imagines her drained and exhausted, clutching a few belongings in a sack or suitcase, trudging aimlessly with nowhere to go.

"What are you thinking about, darling?" Mary Pat asks, looking through the kitchen door at her husband.

"It's all over, Mary Pat."

"At least the strain and the anxious waiting will be over, Thafer."

"That's right."

"We'll sit down and eat in just ten minutes, gang," she says, walking back to the kitchen stove.

"Smells good, Mom." Colleen joins her mother in the spacious, neat kitchen. "What're you cooking?"

"Lamb, your father likes lamb."

"I have a date tonight, Mom. Can I leave early?"

"Go ask your father."

"He's changed. The war must've shaken him up. I don't dare go near him."

"Don't be silly. Go tell him."

Colleen walks toward her stepfather. "Dad, I have a date tonight. Can I leave early?"

"When will you be home?"

"About eleven."

"Just be careful."

"I have baseball tonight, Dad," says Andrew, "You think you'd like to come and watch?"

"I don't feel like doing anything tonight. I'm sorry."

"I'll go with you, Dad," says Sean.

"You have homework, Sean," says Mary Pat.

"I'm sorry about the war, Dad," says Colleen guardedly in a low voice.

"I am too." Thafer feels the strain of the sudden change in himself. "I'll be back to normal soon, Colleen." Suddenly he is frightened of the change. Once the smoke clears, I will return to my old routines, playing baseball with my sons after school, tutoring my daughters in math and science, and helping Mary Pat with chores about the house, he muses.

"Dinner is ready." Mary Pat sits down at the dinner table. "Sean will thank God for us tonight."

"Our Father, we thank you for this food. We thank you for our parents. I hope Grandma, Dad's mom, and Dad's family are safe. And I hope Andrew wins tonight. Amen."

"Amen."

"I have a meeting tonight, Thafer," Mary Pat tells him after supper. "I'll be back about 10:00."

"What meeting, Mary Pat?"

"It's the Women's Association. I'll be back just as soon as I can, sweetheart. I know you're still upset about the war, but I shouldn't miss this meeting. I've already missed two in a row. I won't stay long, I promise."

"I'll be all right. Kathleen and Sean will keep me company."

"I won't be long, dear."

"Have you heard from the gynecologist?"

"No, dear. And don't worry about that now. You have enough on your mind."

"I can't help it, Mary Pat."

"I'll be all right," she says, kissing him. "I'll be back soon."

As he sits watching his wife walk to the door, he now remembers the summer of 1952, following his first academic year at Cornell University. As that summer advanced, he became more and more lonely. The letters from his parents were slow in arriving, and the long hours of work were wearing him down. He used to work at a nearby farm, five miles from

Ithaca, and bicycled to and from the farm daily. After the stint at the farm, he worked at a hotel waiting tables. After that, he worked at Cornell's Main Library as a page—on Tuesdays and Thursdays under Mrs. Connally, the widow of a former graduate student who had been a Ph.D. candidate in the physics department and was killed in the Korean War. She and her one-year-old infant daughter, Colleen, lived with her grandmother, the landlady of the rooming house where he too lived. From the beginning of the summer, Mrs. Connally had been a considerate, compassionate, and gentle supervisor. She knew that he had three jobs and was a poor Palestinian student working his way through college. She probably thought him an orphan.

Instead of making him run up and down the stairs, Mrs. Connally often gave him clerical work, such as sorting cards in the stacks of the library. And as he sorted cards, she would come and converse with him in a gentle, almost motherly way. She had deep blue eyes and loose blond hair. She was tall and attractive, probably in her middle twenties. He was barely eighteen.

Thafer remembers how his mother braved the intensifying violence, taking him and his baby sister to Tulkarm in April 1948 and leaving his father and brother Rassem in Jerusalem. When his father and brother finally joined them in Tulkarm, the fighting had spread to Tulkarm.

We should all have stayed in Jerusalem, his mother told his father when he joined his family in Tulkarm, the small Palestinian town forty miles northwest of Jerusalem.

Anyway, here in Tulkarm we'll be closer to the farm, his father said.

Thafer remembers how terrified he was of the air raids on Tulkarm. His father sheltered him with his body as they both lay on the floor while Jewish planes dropped bombs on the town. Thafer! Thafer! his father shouted at him. Get down! His mother covered his younger sister on the floor with her own body. His cousin-stepbrother, Muneer, and his wife and children were all down on the floor.

One of his cousins, a twenty-six-year-old schoolteacher, was badly wounded in that raid. His legs were amputated in an attempt to save his life, but he later died anyway. Thafer's aunt was deranged after her only son's death and was sent to a mental hospital, where she died chanting her son's name.

Hundreds of thousands of Palestinian refugees swarmed into Tulkarm and neighboring Palestinian villages. They came from Jerusalem, Jaffa, Haifa, Ramla, Lydda, and other Palestinian cities, towns, and villages. Mothers looked for their children, husbands searched for their wives, and families slept in the open fields. Every time he went to sleep, Thafer feared he would not awaken again. He shivers in a cold sweat as he relives the horrors of those days.

An elderly farmhand entered their home in Tulkarm two weeks after his father arrived from Jerusalem.

What is it? Thafer's father asked the farmhand, whose face was ashen and his voice weak.

Saleem was martyred last night. He and his wife and two children. I'm very sorry. What can I say?

As Thafer saw the pain spread over his father's face, he began to cry.

What is it? What is it? his mother screamed, looking at his father as if she herself knew there was bad news.

Tears rolled down his aging father's cheeks.

What is it? What is it? Please tell me, his mother begged.

Saleem and his family. His father choked on the words.

Oh, my God! Oh, my God! That's what I've been dreading.

IV

"Dad," asks Kathleen, joining her solitary father after she finished her homework, "do you like Israel?"

His daughter's question startles him. At first he is unable to respond. "Why do you ask?"

"Mom doesn't like Israel, but our teacher says that Israel is our friend. I want to know what you think."

"I don't like Israel either."

"My friends like Israel, and they're glad Israel won the war. The teacher is too."

"Don't let this upset you."

"I'm back, darling," says Mary Pat. "It's quiet."

"The two younger ones have gone to bed. Colleen and Andrew aren't home yet."

"The game will be over at about 10:30."

"Andrew will be home soon then. What about Colleen?"

"She'll be home soon too."

"How did your meeting go?"

"The usual stuff. We have two women who are really extreme. I'm for women's rights, but I want to get them in a calm way."

"I bet."

She laughs.

"What do these two women want to do?"

"They want to change the social structure. They want equality, now. They want women to be equal to men in every-thing."

"I like rebels. I admire them. This country was built and defended by rebels."

She smiles at him. "That's the Palestinian in you, Allam."

"It's the Irish influence, Connally."

"Is it?"

"Why shouldn't women be equal to men in every respect? Why should women continue to take our rubbish?"

"Do you mean it?"

"I do."

"Then you stay home tomorrow, clean the house, change the beds, wash the dishes, buy groceries, fix dinner, and set the table."

"Wait."

"There's no waiting," she laughs.

"Mary Pat," Thafer asks his wife before they go to bed, "what did the gynecologist say? I want to know."

She pauses, looks pensive at first, then smiles. "Don't worry about me, I'll be all right."

PART ONE

I | March 1972

"Mary Pat," Thafer murmurs, facing his wife's fresh grave. He has stopped to put flowers around the plot on his way home from his office. "I'm here again. I never realized how lonely it would be without you. I'll always come, Mary Pat, I'll always come. I miss you, my love." He bows his head.

"I've got to go now, Mary Pat. I have to get dinner for our children. That's what you would want me to do, wouldn't you? Colleen and Andrew are home. They have their midterm recess."

He stands silently at his wife's grave, unable to leave, acutely feeling the loneliness.

"So long, Mary Pat," he finally whispers, then walks dejectedly to his car. He drives out of the cemetery, passing the old eagle sculpture at the entrance. All the way home he sings softly as Mary Pat often did when cooking or doing chores around the house. He continues all the way home.

> Stand beside her, and guide her,
> Through the night, with the light from above.

"I'm home, Colleen," Thafer calls as he enters the quiet house.
"Hi, Dad."
"Where's everybody?"
"They're upstairs. They'll come down soon."
"Do you think they'll feel like going out to eat?"
"I doubt it, but we can ask them."

"Andrew, Kathleen, Sean," he summons the clan.

The children all come down, and he asks if they'd like to eat out.

"Why don't we order a pizza or something. Sean and I will go get it," says Andrew.

The others agree.

"That's fine with me, then."

.   "Oh, Dad, Mr. Tucker from your office called about an hour ago," says Colleen. "He wants you to call him back at his home. He said it was important."

"Not another emergency now," Thafer mutters. "All right, Andrew, call for the pizza. I'll see what Jim Tucker wants."

Now seventy, James Wilson Tucker, the senior partner in his firm, hired Thafer when he was fresh out of law school, and Thafer has a great deal of affection and respect for him.

"Colleen said you called, Jim."

"I hated to call you now, knowing what you and your family have been through, Thafer, but after you left the office this evening, I got a call from Velour. They would like our firm to represent them in a transaction they are trying to conclude with a group from Mexico City. The Mexicans apparently want to build an offshore nuclear plant in the Gulf off Veracruz. There's going to be a crucial meeting in San Antonio on Thursday, and I would like you to be at that meeting, Thafer. I have asked Claudia and Bert to go too, but I want you to head the team."

"I'll be glad to go, Jim. You want us to leave tomorrow, then?"

"Yes. I thought if you went a day ahead, you'd have time to relax and get ready. What do you think?"

"That's fine, Jim."

"What about the children? Edna and I thought we could have them stay with us for a few days. Have Colleen and Andrew gone back to college yet?"

"Andrew will probably go back Sunday. I haven't talked to Colleen about her schedule yet."

"Or, if it will make the children feel more comfortable, Edna and I could stay with them until you come back. If in the meantime Colleen and Andrew go back to college, we can take care of the younger ones until you're home."

"That's really great of you, Jim." Thafer knows that his children would be uncomfortable with that arrangement. "Colleen is a big girl now. I'm sure she'll manage until I come back."

"I'll go ahead, then, and have the office make reservations for your flight and your hotel."

"That's fine."

"Thank you, Thafer."

"You're welcome, Jim. See you in the morning."

"What's that all about, Dad?" asks Colleen, her face showing some anxiety.

"I guess I have to make a trip to San Antonio tomorrow."

"By yourself?"

"No, with Claudia Sheppard and Bert Stevens."

Colleen looks upset. "Not Claudia Sheppard, Dad! Mom never liked that woman. She's divorced and can be very nasty, Mom always said."

"Well, she's a smart lawyer who's been with the firm as long as I have. Jim Tucker has a lot of respect for her and for her legal ability. So what if she's divorced? Her personal life is none of our business."

"Just be careful of her."

"She's not really a bad woman. She has a young daughter whom she worships. She only becomes abusive when she drinks. That's apparently what ended her marriage."

"I know you like Bert Stevens, so that should help."

"Bert's great."

"Boy, Dad, old man Tucker is pretty tough to take you away now."

"He's also a very thoughtful and decent man. I know that he'll never do anything to hurt me."

"He knows you've had a death in the family. It's been barely a year."

"I know, but we have to go on with our lives. Your mother is not with us now, so let's do our best to live our lives and be what she would have wanted all of us to be. Jim Tucker and the whole firm have been very good to me. They didn't bother me for six months. Now I have to go on with my work, Colleen."

"I know," she says, hugging him.

Thafer and his four children eat quietly that night. After supper, he goes up to his bedroom to change his clothes. He can hear his children's conversation in the family room below.

"Do you think that old goat Tucker is trying to fix Dad up with Claudia Sheppard, Colleen?" Kathleen asks.

"I never thought of it, to tell you the truth."

"You're always thinking someone is fixing someone up with someone, Kathleen," Andrew says. "Will you get off it? Dad's a lawyer and also a nuclear engineer, so the office needs him on these technical things whenever they come up. Something came up, and they had to call on him. Maybe this will occupy him and get Mom's death off his mind. Maybe it'll be good for him."

"You're always jumping on me whenever I open my mouth. Is this ever going to stop?" Kathleen pauses. "Look, all my friends think that Dad is young and handsome, and he has just lost his wife. So he's available. Old man Tucker thinks he's doing Dad and his family a favor by getting him together with Claudia Sheppard. Otherwise, why send her on a trip with Dad now?"

"Because she's another smart lawyer in the firm," Andrew says. "Dad even says so. Anyway, suppose she is a decent woman that Mr. Tucker wants Dad to get to know better, what's wrong with that? Dad is still young. He's not even forty. Mom was much older than him."

"Not that much older, Andrew," Colleen says. "Only seven years."

"Whatever. Don't expect him to remain a widower the rest of his life."

"We don't," says Colleen, "but not so soon and not Claudia Sheppard. Besides, we don't want to lose Dad to someone else. We just lost Mom."

"Who says he's going to get married soon? You're both just making up these things in your own minds. I think that's crazy." Andrew is upset. "Look, I think this is getting out of hand. It's crazy. Dad is hurting as much as all of us are, if not more. This is not the time to worry about something silly like this. Why don't we just drop it?"

"All right, let's drop it," Colleen agrees sullenly.

"I tell you," says Kathleen, "I'd prefer it if Dad goes back to his homeland to visit his mother and family there and meets a nice Palestinian woman, someone who's as nice as Dad."

"Yeah," says Sean.

"You have some imagination, Kathleen," Andrew says.

"What's wrong with that?" Colleen asks.

"Nothing," Andrew replies angrily. "Didn't we say we're going to drop it? Then for God's sake drop it."

The Allam children are quiet for a moment. Thafer comes down to join them in the family room.

"Do you need me to help you pack for your trip tomorrow, Dad?" Colleen asks.

"I'll manage, Colleen, thank you. I won't be taking much with me. This will be only a three-day trip, I imagine."

"Dad," Sean asks, "do you like Claudia Sheppard?"

"Hush, Sean," Kathleen shouts.

"Kathleen!" Thafer silences her, then turns to his younger son. "Why do you ask, Sean?"

"Just wondering." Sean looks sad and bewildered.

"I hardly know Mrs. Sheppard, Sean," Thafer assures him. "She's a smart lawyer and a colleague. She has some personal problems, but we have to make a business trip together to-morrow. That's all there is to it. That's not so unusual these days. We will have another young man with us, who is single and is actually closer to her than I am. Is anything else on your mind, Sean?"

"No."

"Colleen, will you be able to manage until I come back, sweetheart?"

"Don't worry about us, Dad. Everything will be fine."

"I think I better get back to New Haven tomorrow," Andrew says.

"That's fine," Thafer agrees.

"As soon as you're home, Dad," Colleen says, "I'll go back to Boston."

"If you feel you need to go back sooner, I'm sure Kathleen and Sean can manage for a couple of days, Colleen."

"I want to wait until you come back, Dad."

The two boys say good night quietly and go up to their bedrooms.

"I couldn't help hearing your lively discussion," Thafer says to his two daughters. "I just want you to know that I'm not interested in Claudia Sheppard or in any other woman. I am not interested in marriage, period. I don't know that I can be, after your mother."

The two girls look at their father and seem embarrassed. Neither says a word.

Thafer stares out the window and wonders if the flowers he placed on Mary Pat's grave that evening will survive the late March cold.

II

"These people are not Mexicans," Claudia Sheppard says as she, Thafer, and Bert Stevens seat themselves for dinner at the Holiday Inn where they are staying. She arrived at the table a few minutes earlier and has already started her drink.

"Velour's representatives say they are," Thafer says.

"What difference does it make?" Bert Stevens asks.

"All the difference in the world," Claudia continues. "Suppose these people are communist agents. Suppose they are from Eastern Europe or from some other hostile quarter. Do you think it's good for national security, to let Velour continue dealing with them? I'm just not comfortable with the whole thing. This business of a nuclear plant offshore from Veracruz sounds fishy to me."

"Claudia," Bert says, "we're lawyers. We've been retained by Velour to protect their interests in the details of the contract. As long as the transaction is legal, it's none of our business who these people are. We haven't been asked to investigate Velour's customer. Velour already did that and got its export license. If national security were involved, it wouldn't have been able to obtain the export license. We can't tell Velour to watch out for these people because they may be communists. Furthermore, I don't think national security is an issue. This is purely commercial."

A waitress appears. "Would you like something to drink before dinner, gentlemen?"

Quickly emptying her glass, Claudia immediately asks for another bourbon on the rocks.

Thafer and Bert exchange glances, then order drinks.

"You were saying, Bert, it's none of our business who these communists are?" Claudia resumes.

"Claudia, why do we have to assume they're communists?"

"I'm just telling you, they are not Mexicans." Her thin, attractive face becomes red. "And why do they want to install a nuclear plant offshore Veracruz? Suppose the plant ends up in Rumania or in Albania or in the Middle East?"

"Suppose it does," Bert says. "Do you think Rumania and Albania can't get one from the Soviet Union or from Europe for that matter? As far as the Middle East is concerned, you talk to Thafer about that, but Israel has acquired a nuclear plant from France, and I think Iraq has contracted to buy one, also from France. Why shouldn't these people buy their plants from us? The plants are not for military use; they are for civilian purposes, for the production of energy. Am I right, Thafer?"

Thafer, quietly sipping his gin and tonic, hasn't been paying attention to his colleagues' discussion, and Bert's question takes him by surprise. "Did you say something about the Middle East and Israel and Iraq?"

"Where have you been, Thafer?" Claudia snaps. "I think that's rude. You've been in outer space since we left. You've been avoiding me like the plague. Do you think I'm some sort of bimbo?"

"No, Claudia, I don't think you're a bimbo," says Thafer in a very low voice. "I think you are a perfect lady and a smart lawyer. Please, let's not make a scene. Take it easy, Claudia."

"Oh, shut up! Why haven't you been paying attention to our discussion, then?"

"For God's sake, Claudia!" Bert says. "If you're going to behave like this after one drink, then I'm going to leave," and he stands up.

"Please sit down, Bert." Thafer turns to Claudia. "Claudia, I didn't mean to be rude to you, but I have a lot on my mind."

"You have a lot on your mind?" she asks sarcastically. "Why don't you share some of that with us? Maybe we can help you."

Thafer begins to see some crude humor in the outburst. "Let's have dinner first. That'll make us all feel better." He calls the waitress.

"Do you wish to see the wine list?" the waitress asks, taking the menus.

"No wine, Miss," Bert says.

"Thafer said we'd have wine with dinner," Claudia insists.

"We'll skip the wine, Miss," Thafer says. "Thank you."

"You know, Claudia," Thafer resumes, "I think I'm going to go back to the Middle East."

"That's stupid," she says.

"The other day," he says, "I was visited by a Tunisian UN diplomat whom I represented five years ago on a traffic violation. He introduced me to his companion, who turned out to be a Saudi diplomat at the United Nations. They offered me a job in the Middle East."

"How can you work for those people, Thafer?"

"What people?" His face becomes grim.

"Those Arabs. They're Jew haters. They're barbaric."

"Claudia, I really thought you were more intelligent than that. How can you condemn a people you don't know?"

"All right, all right, I didn't mean to offend you, but frankly that's the general perception. People look at Thafer Allam as the exception. You got lucky and came to the United States; then you met and married, very young at that, a devoted and warm Irish Catholic American widow."

Thafer rubs his eyes. "I did all that," he says, "but the world doesn't really know my side."

"I'm sure," she says.

Thafer has just entered his room, taken off his coat and necktie, and closed the curtains in his spacious suite when his phone rings. He looks at the phone suspiciously, hesitating to pick it up, but feeling the excitement it triggers in him.

"Hello, this is Thafer Allam."

"Thafer, I'm upset. I don't want to be here by myself."

Thafer remains wide awake, feeling troubled. He wonders if tough old Jim Tucker knows that what he wants is not Claudia, but his homeland, where his heart and soul belong. He thinks he should tell Tucker about this longing—that he needs a leave of absence from the firm for a year or two to settle his feelings once and for all and that he needs Tucker's support. He wonders if he will get the position he has applied for. He has a feeling that he will. Then he begins to think about his children. He remembers what Kathleen suggested to her brothers and sister about his going back to see his mother and bringing a nice Palestinian woman back with him. The idea of his return will not be too strange to his children, he thinks. But he wonders if old man Tucker can be helpful. He wonders whether Tucker and his wife, decent and kindly people though they are, have any idea what is tormenting him. He also wonders if Claudia knows.

III

At first, Thafer hesitates to approach Tucker, fearing that his sudden decision to accept a new job in the Middle East, about which Tucker knows very little, would be too shocking. But he finally musters his courage and goes to Tucker's office unannounced. He sits and faces the older lawyer and looks into his piercing blue eyes. He remembers that intensity, undiminished from the first time the two of them met. Tucker had invited Thafer to come for a job interview during his last year in law school.

"What's on your mind, Thafer?" James Wilson Tucker finally asks as Thafer sits in his spacious cheerful office and hesitates in starting the conversation.

"Jim, I need your advice and council," Thafer decides to plunge right in. "About four months ago, I was invited to apply for the position of chief legal counsel for the Organization of Arab Petroleum Exporting Countries, OAPEC, at their headquarters in Kuwait. Ever since Mary Pat's death, Jim, I've been restless and have wanted to go back to the Middle East. This morning, I received a very attractive and interesting offer for the job. They want me there for two years. I'm torn. I would like to accept this opportunity, but I'm also concerned about leaving my children behind less than eighteen months after Mary Pat's death. Of course, if I accept their offer, I'd like to come back to the firm after the two years are up."

"What is OAPEC? Does it do any nuclear business?"

"Not that I am aware of. It's an economic organization of Arab states that are oil producers. My understanding is that they pool their economic resources and build large-scale industrial projects in order to industrialize the Middle East."

"It's not really important whether they are in the nuclear plant business or not. I'm just curious about why they're interested in you."

"I'm sure that my fluency in both English and Arabic, as well as my American legal training, have something to do with that."

"Must be. As far as your coming back to the firm is concerned, Thafer, I don't expect any problem whatsoever. You're a valuable member of the firm. You just take a leave of absence for a year or two, do your thing, and come back." The older man pauses, then looks at Thafer. "I know you have a family over there, your mother and so on. You've lost Mary Pat, and that's been a shock to all of us. What I don't know is whether this would be good for you and for your children now. I'm not saying it is or it isn't, Thafer. I don't know. I'd like to think about it. Have you discussed this with your children? How do Colleen and Andrew feel? Kathleen will be going to college next year, but what would you do with Sean? Possibly Edna and I could persuade him to stay with us for a year, but how would he feel about that, Thafer? These are the things that come to mind. I can see how you would be attracted to an opportunity like this. If I were your age, and I had an offer to be legal counsel for an international organization of this stature, I wouldn't say no easily. Maybe something good for the firm could come out of this. So, Thafer, let me give it some thought. I'd like your permission to kick it around with Bill Carpenter and Bob Vale."

"Certainly, Jim."

"When do they want you over there?"

"By April 15, Jim."

"Oh boy! That soon?"

"I'm sure I can ask for a delay if I need to."

"If we decide to go ahead—I mean, if you and your family decide this is what you want to do—then you shouldn't ask for a delay. I tell you what I want you to do, Thafer. Your children are home for the weekend. Why don't you discuss it with them, feel them out, and get back to me. In the meantime, I'll do some thinking of my own, and let's confer again."

Thafer goes back to his office, closes the door, and begins to debate with himself.

Why do I want to go to the Middle East? It's an almost irresistible impulse. Something keeps making me want to go. Yet I have a great career ahead of me here. I have cordial relations with my partners. They all respect me. I make good money. I have a nice home, lovely children, and I think Claudia would marry me in a minute. So what is it? Something within me urges me to return to the Middle East—not to visit, but to live there.

The Middle East is not stable, he tells himself. Those people over there have problems, big problems. Do you think you know them? Do you think they're your people? Wait until you go there. Besides, you're an American; you've spent more years of your life here than you have there. Do you want to go see your mother? That's fine; go visit her. Take your children with you. She's been aching to see them. You've been a good son and send money to her, but having her see you and your children will be worth more than all the money you send. Go see your brothers and their families, your sister and her family. But to return to the Middle East—

You won't be returning for good, he tells himself, just for a year or two.

After supper, Thafer decides it is time to talk to his children.

Colleen, his oldest daughter, is listening to a Mozart symphony, and the first side of the record has finished. Andrew and Sean are about to go out.

"Please wait, Colleen; don't turn the record over yet. I need to talk to all of you. Tell Kathleen to come down. Andrew, Sean, I want to talk to all of you before you leave."

The children seem surprised, but join him in the family room.

"What is it, Dad?" Colleen asks.

He hesitates.

"What is it, Dad?" Andrew urges.

He begins to feel heat going through him. "I want to talk to you about an opportunity I have to work in the Middle East."

"Oh boy! Am I relieved! I was afraid you were going to say Claudia and you are going to get married."

"Kathleen!" says Colleen.

"Dad," Andrew pushes, ignoring the girls, "what opportunity in the Middle East?"

"I have an offer from the Organization of Arab-Petroleum Exporting Countries to be their chief legal counsel."

"What do they do?" Sean asks

Thafer explains that it is an organization of Arab states that produce oil and that they plan to cooperate in their industrial projects to avoid duplication and unnecessary waste.

"Would they build nuclear plants?" asks Colleen.

"They might," he says.

"Would we go with you?" asks Kathleen.

"You can if you want to."

"How long is this for?" asks Andrew.

"Two years."

"Have you discussed it with the firm?" asks Colleen.

"I discussed it with Jim Tucker. He will bring it up with the senior partners and discuss it with me tomorrow. He thinks that the decision should be mine and my family's. I agree, and that's why I am discussing it with you."

"I'll support anything you want to do," Andrew says. "I think that you should go."

"Yes," Colleen agrees, "you should go if that's what you want to do."

"I think it's a great idea." Kathleen is most enthusiastic. "I want to visit in the summer, but I'm not sure about college over there. I kind of have my heart set on college here. I'd want to spend the summer with you, though, and go see Grandma and our other relatives. Would we keep the house?"

"Yes, of course. Remember, the move is temporary, just for two years. I'll probably be granted a leave of absence from the firm."

"I want to come with you," Sean says, "but I really don't want to miss out on baseball, and I don't want to go to private school here. Can I stay in the house, here, with Kathleen?"

"Yes, Sean, but I'll have to get someone to stay with both of you."

"When will you have to go, Dad?" asks Colleen.

"About April 25, but if we have to, we can delay that."

"I'll be back from college by the end of May," says Colleen, "so we only have to worry about one month when Kathleen and Sean will have to have someone stay with them."

"Actually, Jim Tucker offered to have Kathleen and Sean stay with them." Thafer looks around for their response.

"I don't want to stay there," Sean says.

"Then you don't have to. We'll think of something that you like."

"I don't either," Kathleen adds.

"I want to go to see you this summer too, Dad, and visit my cousins and Grandma," Sean says.

"I'm going to have all of you go over there in the summer," Thafer tells them. "OAPEC will provide housing for all of us."

"I'm going to be sixteen next month," says Sean. "Why can't Kathleen and I stay in the house by ourselves for a month, until Colleen and Andrew come home?"

"Don't worry about it now, Sean. We'll find a way."

IV

On the morning of April 30, 1972, Thafer and his children are up early. He is packed for his trip to Kuwait. Andrew drives his subdued father to the Osaga airport, as the other three children sit silently in the back seat of their station wagon. At the airport, the scene is different.

"Please call us as soon as you get there," says Colleen, embracing her stepfather and weeping quietly.

"I will, sweetheart."

"As soon as you get yourself settled, we all want to visit," Kathleen reminds him.

"I know you do, sweetheart," he says. ·

"I don't mind coming there to live with you, Dad," says Sean.

"I know, but I prefer for you to stay here and finish high school, Sean."

"Don't worry about us," says Andrew. "We'll all manage, Dad."

"I'm counting on you, Andrew. Take care."

"You take care, Dad," says Andrew, hugging his father.

On the short flight from Osaga to the city of New York Thafer Allam tells himself that returning to the Middle East will be the greatest challenge of his life. Now he will be returning to his source, where he wants to light a few fires of hope for his people. He looks down at the village of Ashfield, where he has left his deceased wife resting eternally and his four anxious young children. The peaceful village already seems distant. Dotted with small white houses, it is surrounded by spring green meadows and pastureland. He is unprepared for this glimpse of the splendor and serenity from which he is so determinedly distancing himself.

He begins to remember his first day in the United States—September 14, 1951—when he arrived in New York City on an Air France four-engine plane with $27.00 in his pocket. An African American showed him to the bus that took him to the Greyhound station, where he waited for hours with his two small bags, afraid to buy food because he then might not be able to pay for the bus ticket. At 2:00 A.M. on Sunday morning, September 15, 1951, he finally arrived at his destination—Ithaca, New York—where he knew no one. He was almost seventeen and had not even taken his last year in high school because of the strife in his native country from 1947 to 1949.

Do you have any relatives in Ithaca? the bus driver asked him.

No, the frightened sixteen year old answered.

What do you want to do in Ithaca? the bus driver persisted.

I came to attend Cornell University.

Do you have any money? the bus driver asked.

Twenty dollars.

You come with me, the bus driver said. Let's find a place for you to spend the night.

The bus driver walked with Thafer to a small hotel in Ithaca. Can you put this young man up for the night? he asked an elderly desk clerk at the hotel. He's a foreign student and doesn't have a whole lot of money.

Why don't I take him to Willard Straight Hall up on the campus, where he could stay for the night. It's less expensive, the elderly man confided.

Will you take care of him? He doesn't know anyone here.

I will, the elderly man said. Don't worry about it. I'll take him in my car to the campus.

Can I count on that? the bus driver asked.

You bet.

Do you want something to eat, young man? the elderly man asked Thafer as he drove him to the Cornell University campus. Can I get you a sandwich?

No, thank you, sir, Thafer said, feeling frightened.

The elderly man then took him to one of the buildings on campus, carried one of his small bags, and entered the quiet building with him.

This young man is a foreign student. The Greyhound bus driver from New York brought him over to our hotel, but he hasn't got much money. Can you put him up for the night?

Sure, the student at Willard Straight Hall said.

Can I count on that? the elderly man repeated.

Sure, you can!

Thafer slept without eating. The next morning he went to see the counselor of foreign students and told him that he, Thafer Ayoub Allam, a native of Jerusalem, had arrived in the United States of America the night before with twenty-seven dollars, that he had paid seven dollars for the bus from New York City to Ithaca, and that he now had twenty dollars left.

Have you had breakfast? the counselor asked him.

No, sir.

Let's go have breakfast.

After breakfast, the counselor took him to the treasurer's office and obtained a loan of one hundred dollars for him.

He then confirmed a free tuition scholarship for Thafer at Cornell University, arranged a modest room for him at the home of an elderly woman and her recently widowed granddaughter, Mary Pat Connally. He also found a part-time job for Thafer at Cornell University's Main Library, where he worked until he graduated from law school.

There are tears in Thafer's eyes as he remembers his earlier days in the United States.

What do you think? he asks himself.

I don't know how I made it. He is overwhelmed.

He remembers his family's orange grove and the gentle hills of his native country, the stone terraces that circle the hillsides, the twisted trunks of the olive trees, the high steeples and colorful minarets, the sweet scent of jasmine, and the houses made of hand-hewn stone.

His mind zigzags in puzzlement.

In no time, the small airplane circles over New York. He looks down at the city that twenty years ago welcomed him as he sought refuge from the turmoil in his native land. Now he is about to return to the turmoil.

After his plane lands, he walks into the terminal, looking for the flight that will take him across the Atlantic.

He senses an extraordinary change in his disposition. He shakes his head as he looks at the mammoth airliner that will take him to London.

"This is always scary," the elderly woman who sits next to him says. As the plane speeds faster and faster down the runway, she looks frightened.

He looks at the terrified woman, feeling frustrated and helpless at first, then almost instinctively he reaches for her hand.

Closing her eyes, she holds his extended hand tightly. As they soar high above the Atlantic, she lets go of his hand. "Thank you," she says, not looking at him.

"You're welcome," he says.

He loosens his seat belt and sits forward eagerly as he begins his voyage halfway around the world.

"This isn't your first flight across the ocean?" the elderly woman asks, seeming to regain her composure.

"It's the first in many years."

"I get nervous every time the plane speeds down the runway, but I get over it when we're airborne."

"I get edgy myself."

"You speak English beautifully, but do I hear a slight accent?"

"I was born in Palestine."

Her face turns white. She pauses and looks at him tentatively. "Do you have a family there?"

"My mother lives on the West Bank."

"Are you going to see her?"

"I am going to Kuwait first, then I'll go to see her."

I am on my way to assume a position that may give me an opportunity to help my people.

"When was the last time you saw your mother?"

"In 1959."

"That's a long time. I hope you find her in good health."

"Thank you, thank you very much."

She continues to look at New York City below. "There's a lot of oil in Kuwait," she says.

"Yes, there is."

She pauses again. "Oil is very important. It's given that part of the world new opportunities."

"Yes, it has." It's changing the course of history.

"That situation over there is tragic. Do you think they'll ever have peace there?"

"I hope so."

"Do you think the Arabs want peace?"

"I'm sure they do."

"I'm not so sure, but I know why."

He looks at the woman closely, then begins to think of the devastation of Palestinian towns and villages in 1948. Intoxicated by their astounding victories over the corrupt Arab armies in 1948, the Israelis forced the exodus of more than seven hundred thousand Palestinians, evicting them from their homes and farms. They took over hundreds of thousands of acres of Palestinian-owned land—including olive and orange groves, vineyards, citrus orchards, and tree gardens. They seized Palestinian dwellings, shops, workshops, and storerooms, and confiscated bank accounts totaling tens of millions of Palestinian pounds. Hundreds of thousands of Jewish immigrants began to come to Palestine, to take over Palestinian property and to settle on Palestinian land. Israeli officials disclaimed responsibility for the exodus of Palestinians and embarked on a public relations campaign claiming that the exodus was voluntary. Chaim Weizman, Israel's first president, described the exodus as an answer to Israel's need for land and a miraculous simplification of its own problem.

Thafer remembers how the Palestinian urban disintegration was planned and implemented by Israel under the leadership of David Ben Gurion. On January 15, 1948, six months before the Arab armies entered Palestine to rescue the Palestinians from the Jewish Haganah, Ben Gurion wrote in his *War Diaries* that the strategic objective of the Jewish forces was to destroy the Palestinian urban communities, which he described as being the most organized and politically conscious segment of the Palestinian population.

"Excuse me," the elderly woman says, "can you hand me a pillow?"

"Certainly."

"Thank you."

She looks at him searchingly again. "Did you learn English in Palestine?"

"Right."

"What's your business here?"

"I'm a lawyer."

"Good for you. My late husband was a lawyer. Do they teach law over there?"

"They do, but I studied law here."

"Now you're going back?"

"Just for a year or two."

"Do you have a family here?"

"Four children."

"No wife?"

"She passed away fifteen months ago."

"I'm sorry. You seem like a nice young man. You'll get another one over there, I'm sure. I have to say that I sympathize with Israel," she then says abruptly. "I just don't like to see it get hurt. Do you understand how I feel?"

"I do."

"Do you?" she asks, looking at him.

"Yes," he says.

"That's good. It's a difficult situation, I know."

"Yes, it is."

"I'm Jewish, you know, but I am nonobservant."

"I'm not exactly observant myself," he says awkwardly.

"That doesn't really matter. What matters is one's character and one's code of conduct. My husband was not Jewish, but he was a good man. Two years after he died, I went to Israel for a holiday to discover my 'roots'—you know, repressed aspects of my own ancestry. I even thought of living in Israel and practicing medicine there. I'm retired now, but I was a pediatrician for more than forty years. Have you been to Israel?"

"Not since its creation."

"You should go; you'll be amazed at what they've done with what they have. I must confess that when I went there the first time, I was skeptical, but I soon learned that the conviction of the Orthodox that God has given them the land of Palestine and that Jerusalem must be Jahweh's Holy City goes back to the visions of the early prophets. I learned for the first time how the nightmares of nineteen centuries of homelessness, pogroms, ghettos, and then the Holocaust can burn themselves into a Jewish soul. These things make the creation of a secure homeland for the Jewish people a necessity, something so terribly urgent for them."

He listens attentively.

"For the first time," she continues, "I began to feel a great sense of identification with Israel. In a way I never thought I would, I felt a commitment to seeing that it endured safely. Then I began to see the ugly side of Israel. The tragedies of the Palestinians' experience have left me very disturbed. 'Next year in Jerusalem!' has ceased to be a joke for me. 'This year peace!' is what I want to hear. Both sides can denounce one another, can demonize one another, can paint the United States or the Soviet Union as the Great Satan, but in the end both sides must get beyond all that. Both sides must realize that neither an Israeli victory nor an Arab or Palestinian victory can ever be a victory for mankind. My hopes for Israel's security and endurance won't change," she continues, "but I still see Zionism as one of the greatest disasters of our century, not just for the Palestinians, but also for the Jews. But, of course, Israel is simply there and will continue to be there in the foreseeable future. Neither the Arabs nor the Palestinians will drive out the Israelis, nor can the Israelis make the Palestinian problem go away. They cannot drive the Palestinians out. Some kind of accommodation has to be found. Do you see what I mean?"

"Yes," he says.

"You and I can resolve the problem, but it's the stubborn leaders who have to be convinced. You work on your side, and I'll work on mine," she smiles.

"That's a deal," he says.

Resting her head on the pillow he handed her, she then pauses and looks at him with dignity, her eyes peaceful. "Thank you for holding my hand," she says.

V | Beirut

At about 5:00 that evening the jet hovers over Beirut, then lands. The clear sky and the blue Mediterranean remind him of an earlier time, long forgotten. It is an odd sensation that sends a chill over his body. Holding a small handbag and not knowing which direction to take, he descends from the plane into the warm and disorderly airport. He follows a few passengers into an untidy building.

He is beckoned by two men whom he has never seen before; they smile and call his name. He is puzzled.

"Thafer," shouts one of them from behind the glass partition. "Clear through customs. We'll wait here."

Not knowing what else to do or say, he nods his head, prompting them to smile broadly in amusement.

After clearing customs, he walks toward them. They embrace and kiss him as if he is a brother.

"We are good friends of your family. I am Hani Amri, and this is my brother Adnan. You look like your brother Kamal. The minute you entered the building, we spotted you. We immediately knew who you were."

"Thank you for coming." Thafer tries to recover from his surprise.

"We'd like to have you stay with us."

"Thank you."

"We have a small old car," says Hani Amri. "If you don't have much luggage, I'm sure we can manage."

"I have one suitcase and this small handbag."

Thafer feels strange driving through the wide, clean streets of Beirut with the two Palestinian brothers. A modern and beautiful city, Beirut seems carefree. Leisurely strolling at sunset, men and women fill the sidewalks. Tourists and visitors with their cameras fill the streets, but Thafer feels far removed from the scene.

Suddenly, he is uneasy. There is an abrupt change as they enter a rubble-strewn street. Decaying, crumbling buildings appear. Some are charred.

"Where are we going?" the anxious Thafer finally asks.

"To our home," says Hani Amri. "We're about to enter Sabra."

He is appalled as they enter the refugee camp. He looks at the shacks of the Palestinian refugees, at the people, the elderly men and women, the children, the cars, and the animals in the narrow, dirty streets. The smell is sickening.

This is the stench of poverty and deprivation, he thinks.

"We're almost there, Thafer," says Hani Amri.

"I didn't think our people were still living like this."

There is silence. Hani Amri drives on slowly.

Thafer looks at the older brother and feels some comfort in the serenity and dignity of his presence.

He looks again at the veiled women, the begging children, the poor workers jamming the dirty restaurants and the filthy streets. The smell makes him sick.

"You seem subdued, Thafer," says Adnan Amri, the younger Palestinian.

"I'm saddened and overwhelmed."

"Do you plan to go back to the United States?"

"I don't know."

"The United States is the real enemy."

There is silence again.

"The United States is the staunch and faithful supporter of our enemy," Hani Amri finally says.

"That makes it our most contemptible enemy." There is anger in Hani Amri's eyes.

Now Thafer's unease is mixed with fear. He gazes at the young Palestinian and tries to assess him. His youthful face seems agreeable and harmless.

"The American people don't know about the tragedy of our people," Thafer says guardedly.

"Why don't they?" protests the young Palestinian, fire in his eyes and passion in his voice.

"Because we have not been able to talk to them and have not been able to get their attention. Israel is smarter than we are."

The two Palestinians look at Thafer with obvious surprise. There is a long pause.

"Thafer," says Hani Amri, breaking the frightening silence, "why do you think Israel is smarter than we are?"

"Because the Israelis have displaced our people, destroyed our towns and villages, usurped our land, and made it appear to the world that they are the victims."

"That's not smart," says Adnan Amri. "That's malicious!"

"We should work very hard to tell the world the tragic story of our people. We should go directly to the American people and tell them what Israel has done to our farms, to our villages, to our towns and cities."

The brothers listen.

"There are six million Jews and less than fifty thousand Palestinians in the United States," says Hani Amri. "There are also more than three hundred thousand Israelis there. The Palestinians haven't got a chance. The Jews rule the United States."

"I agree that Israel has tremendous influence in the United States, but the Jews don't rule the United States. More than three million Arab Americans live in the United States, and more than four million Muslim Americans. They should try to influence the policies of the United States."

"Do you think the American people are interested in knowing what happened to our people?"

"If they are not now, the Arabs have what it takes to make them interested."

"How?" asks the older brother.

"They have a trump card."

"What's that?"

"Oil."

"They will never dare use it."

"I'm not so sure of that."

"Let me be frank with you," says Adnan Amri. "When we have the bomb, then and only then will we have a trump card.

Those who don't have the bomb will always be at the mercy of those who have it."

Thafer just looks at the young Palestinian. His heart is beating hard.

When they arrive at the Amris' home, Thafer notices a portrait of Yasser Arafat on the wall.

"Do you like it?" Adnan Amri asks.

"It's a nice portrait."

"Do they in the United States still consider him a terrorist murderer, with hate in his heart?" asks Hani Amri.

"That's more or less the way they look at him."

"As you said in the car, Thafer, Israel has been clever in creating myths. One such myth is that Arafat is determined to finish the ugly job started by Adolf Hitler. Yet Arafat is one of the very few leaders, Arab or Jew, who firmly believes in a comprehensive peaceful settlement, without bloodshed, of the Palestinian-Israeli conflict."

"Then why is Israel scared of the PLO?" asks Thafer.

"Israel is not scared of the PLO as a military force. It can crush all the military units of the PLO with its hands tied behind its back. It is scared of a PLO that wants peace and that advocates the political and civil rights of our people. Israel wants all Palestinians, including you, Thafer, to disappear from the face of the earth. We are the rightful owners of the lands they have taken from us. Our continued existence is not only a threat to them, but a constant reminder of the ugly deeds they have committed against our people."

"Israel," says Adnan Amri, "will try to have our people disappear from the face of the earth. We have no other alternative. We have to defend our existence. We will defend our existence when we obtain what they already have—the bomb."

"Do you prefer a chair or a cushion, Thafer?" asks Hani Amri.

Thafer hesitatingly looks around and does not know what to say.

"We usually sit on cushions."

"That's fine, sir."

"Why don't you rest a while," says Hani Amri. "Adnan and I will go help the family get something ready to eat. You must have had an exhausting trip."

"That would be nice. Yes, it was a long and tiring trip."

"I hope you didn't mind the discussion."

"Not at all."

The Amri home is in an old and neglected building on the edge of the refugee camp. Thafer stays in the small living room, where there are a few dilapidated chairs and worn out cushions on the floor. They have brought him an old mattress to sleep on, a pillow, and a blanket, but no sheets.

As he lies on the worn out mattress in the Amri home in the refugee camp in Beirut, he wonders about the two Palestinians who have just entered his life. He feels both kinship and aversion, trust and apprehension. He is uncomfortable with himself. He feels badly about seeming insensitive, yet he is frightened and fascinated by that young Palestinian, Adnan. Thafer is touched by his brash anger and even finds himself identifying with that anger. Maybe that's why he frightens me, Thafer muses.

Then there is the small, decaying house in the refugee camp, which deeply saddens him. It's good for me, he tells himself. I've lived in an affluent suburb in central New York. I've become a callous American. I've forgotten my roots. Now I know how my people live.

He hears children crying. How many people live here? he asks himself. Perhaps they don't have enough room. That's why I have to sleep on this old mattress on the floor of their tiny living room.

Yet the tour of the refugee camp is the greatest shock of his journey. He is haunted by the sight of the blackened buildings, by the faces of the Palestinian women behind their thin veils as they walk with their children through the silent narrow streets littered with garbage. The stench still makes him queasy.

How would Mary Pat have reacted to this? he asks himself. Would old man Tucker have stomach for any of this? What about Claudia? What about his children? He wants his children to see this. They should know that the world is not just central New York: they should see hungry people, miserable people, people who are victims of man's inhumanity.

Then he wonders about Adnan and the bomb, and he shudders.

Is he serious about the bomb? Thafer asks himself.

Dead serious.

These people are very angry, he finally tells himself as he tries to get some rest. They're bitter and suspicious; they have lost everything, and I mustn't go around trying to teach them how to be rational and good.

"Are you up, Thafer?" asks Adnan.

"Yes, I am, Adnan."

"Did you have a good night's rest?"

"Yes, I did," he lies. Tell him you're humbled.

"The bathroom is vacant now, Thafer," says Adnan, gently opening the door of the small living room where Thafer has spent the night. "Would you like to follow me?"

"Thank you," Thafer says, leaving the stuffy room and following the young Palestinian to a tiny, dark room containing a small washbowl and a toilet, but no bathtub or shower or mirror.

Adnan hands him a small white towel.

"Thank you." He enters the room and latches its makeshift door.

In Ashfield, he muses, I would've been able to have a nice shower or a nice tub bath in a beautiful bathroom, all brightly lit and mirrored, next to my own bedroom. I wouldn't have had to use this filthy, dinky little hole. He feels guilty. Maybe this is where I belong after all. How am I going to shave? I can't even see.

He keeps the door ajar, but there is no hot water.

"Do you need anything, Thafer?" asks Adnan Amri.

"No, thank you, Adnan. I'm almost through."

The young host is placing dishes on sheets of newspaper laid on the floor of the living room when Thafer returns from his brief visit to the dark bathroom.

"I apologize for our facilities, Thafer," says Hani Amri, entering the living room.

"Please don't apologize. It's an honor for me to stay with you in your home, sir."

"Thank you, Thafer. There are thirteen of us living here, between Adnan's family and mine."

"I understand." He does not know what else to say. "It won't be very long."

"We just have to be patient," says Hani Amri. "We have to endure, that's all."

It is a simple Palestinian breakfast—pieces of unleavened flat bread, chickpeas, homemade white cheese, and tea to drink. They say very little while they eat.

After breakfast, the older man is anxious to talk. His younger brother clears the floor.

"Your father, Thafer, was a great man," starts Hani Amri. "He devoted his life to defending the homeland. He was a military genius, one of the best of his generation. I know that because my father, who fought under him, told me."

Thafer is moved by the man's words.

"Your father's strategies confounded the British army between 1936 and 1939. They were confused and didn't know how to cope with him. Your father had fewer than four thousand men fighting under him, but he outmaneuvered the better-equipped British army and succeeded in dislodging it from most of the homeland. Then more British reinforcements were rushed from the Suez Canal, and the 1936 rebellion was crushed mercilessly by England."

Thafer listens with feeling . . . *You have fought the good fight, his mother said to his father. That's enough, she pleaded . . .*

"Your brothers, Kamal and Rassem, and I did our share in 1948, Thafer. Now you and Adnan must carry the torch."

As Thafer listens, he is uncomfortable. He wants to say something gracious, but doesn't know what.

"That's all I have to say, Thafer" says Hani Amri.

"Thank you." Thafer feels unhappy with himself. He wants to say more. He wants to say that he'd be honored to carry the torch to free their homeland, to follow in his father's footsteps, to do everything he can, and to fight the good fight. But he only looks down.

"You seem uncomfortable, Thafer," continues the older brother.

"I'm just moved by your kind words about Father," he finally says. "Thank you very much."

"Well, Adnan will take you to the airport this morning. I'm sorry I can't go. I teach this morning."

"Where?"

"Here at the camp."

"Are there schools at the camp?"

"Yes, we're all volunteers."

"How many people live in the camp?"

"About fifty thousand."

"How many Palestinians are there in Lebanon?"

"About four hundred thousand."

"Do they all live like this?"

"More or less."

The three men pause.

"I don't want to keep you, sir," Thafer finally says, moving closer to shake the older man's hand.

"I don't want you to miss your flight, so perhaps we should say good-bye for now."

"Thank you for your kind hospitality."

"This is your home." The older Palestinian opens his arms to Thafer and embraces him warmly.

That's my home, he muses. Indeed it could have been!

VI

"Maybe your brother Kamal has told you, Thafer," says Adnan as he drives Thafer back to the Beirut airport, "that I'm an officer in the military section of the PLO."

"No, he hasn't."

"Yes, I started training when I was twelve. It's been nearly twenty years now."

"Is my brother Kamal connected with the PLO?"

"He's not part of the armed struggle." Adnan looks at Thafer. "You know, Kamal and Hani did their share in 1947 and 1948. Now it's our turn, yours and mine."

Thafer squints.

"Do you think that you might join the armed struggle, Thafer?"

The question terrifies Thafer. He feels heat radiating through his body.

Adnan Amri glances at Thafer Allam and must see the terror on his face. "I suppose, Thafer," he says with a steady voice, "that after one lives away from the homeland as long as you have, one becomes terrified at the idea."

"It isn't just living away from the homeland, Adnan; it's that I personally don't believe that armed struggle is the answer."

"What do you think is the answer?"

"I believe in resistance based on nonviolent struggle."

"That'll never work," says Adnan Amri, his voice more strained.

"Has it been tried?"

"I can tell you it won't work, not here. The enemy is too depraved and spiteful."

Adnan calms down, making Thafer feel a little more comfortable. "How can you be opposed to armed struggle? I can't believe they preach that in the United States."

"I'm opposed to armed struggle because it only breeds more violence. It hasn't worked."

The young Palestinian is scornful and looks at Thafer disdainfully. "They call this pacifism. It's surrender. I don't believe in it, and you shouldn't." He is angry.

He drives on, not looking right or left and not speaking. "Tell me," he finally says in a low voice, "how's the race problem in the United States?"

"Well, there is a problem," says Thafer uneasily, "but it isn't as bad as it used to be. I think that the people and government recognize that they have a problem, and they're working on it. It'll take time."

"You learned about pacifism from the African leader, Martin Luther King."

"Not only from Martin Luther King, but from Gandhi also."

"Interesting. Look what happened to them. If they had not believed in nonviolence and had armed bodyguards, they might not have been assassinated. Neither Gandhi nor King was able to carry on his pacifist struggle for his people."

"Yet each ignited flames for his people that will not be extinguished."

"Pacifism, Thafer, does not suit the human race. Nonviolence can't stop racists who are willing to kill you and kill your family and throw you out of your country because of your religion. Look what happened to your brother and his wife and his two children."

Thafer winces and does not respond.

"I'm sorry, Thafer."

"I was surprised to hear that Hani is a schoolteacher," Thafer says to change the subject.

"He teaches at the refugee camp. We are refugees because of the United States, you know."

"I want to say, Adnan," says Thafer, trying to keep the discussion low key, "that there's a difference between the policies of the U.S. government and the way the people look at conflicts in remote parts of the world."

"How?"

"On the whole, the people of the United States are good people."

"They are racists."

"I can tell you that I never encountered discrimination in the United States as I was warned I might before I went there. The race problem is a little exaggerated abroad."

"You never encountered discrimination because you're not too dark, but if you were darker or Black, you would've. Many dark Middle Eastern people who have lived in the United States have told me that racial prejudice is everywhere."

"I'm not saying that there's no racial problem there . . . "

"I suppose," interrupts Adnan Amri, with a scornful smile, "that you'll never settle in the Middle East. You're too attached to the United States."

"I'm attached to both, to the land of my birth and of my ancestors, and to the United States, the land where my children were born."

"If all Palestinian youth were to do what you did, then Palestine would lose its best-educated people at a time when it needs them most. There are thousands like you in the United States. It doesn't need you. We don't have anyone like you, and we need you."

Thafer is speechless.

"The land of your birth is calling you. It needs you. It needs you more than the United States. You should give a part of yourself to it and to your people. We all must."

"I intend to," says Thafer. "In my own way and as long as I live, I'll always serve the land of my birth and its people." He is visibly shaken. He does not know what to think. This is just the tip of the iceberg; I haven't seen anything yet, he muses. But he now knows his countryman better. He is sure of that. He is surprised how touched he is by the young Palestinian's passion. This young man is a warrior. He thinks that I take after my father. He doesn't know the job Mary Pat has done on me. Yes, she tamed and refined me. She made me gentle and kind. She turned me against violence and wars. I hope, for my own sake, that the Middle East won't change me again.

"Here we are, Thafer," says Adnan, pulling his car up to the curb next to the airport building.

"How can I thank you, Adnan?"

"Don't mention it. I'll carry the heavy suitcase."

"Thank you very much."

The two Palestinians walk toward the airport building.

"I have a job waiting for me in Kuwait," Thafer confides. "I hope that in this way I'll be able to serve our people and the land of our birth."

"That's good," says Adnan Amri in a low voice as he stops to put Thafer's suitcase down. He holds Thafer's arm firmly and looks at him with determination. "You're a nuclear engineer, Thafer. That's how you can serve the homeland best. Good luck in Kuwait."

"Thank you, Adnan."

"Take very good care of yourself."

"Thanks for everything, and you take very good care of yourself."

They embrace warmly. Thafer then boards his flight to Kuwait.

VII

The Kuwaiti airliner circles over the city of Beirut, then flies on to Kuwait. The plane is almost empty. Thafer sits by himself, staring at the clear blue sky and wondering what Kuwait will look like. A quiet little village, sandwiched between Saudi Arabia and Iraq, it was a tiny settlement of men of the desert when he lived there between December 1949 and July 1951, before he went to the United States. It was all his mother's idea to go to Kuwait. He had been sitting in his room in their Tulkarm home and had overheard his parents' conversation.

My dear, his distraught mother said to his elderly father, we have to get Thafer out before there's more fighting.

Where would we send him?

To Kuwait. My nephew Khalil works in Kuwait. Thafer always liked Khalil, and my sister will help us get Thafer to him.

Do you think Thafer would go?

If we do it right, he will.

I'm all for it, but he's too young.

Let's do it before any more fighting breaks out and before the Jordanians take him into their army.

I don't think there'll be any more serious fighting.

Dear, we lost a son. Kamal is still in the Syrian army in the north. Rassem is in the Iraqi army a few miles from here. We certainly don't want Thafer to be taken by the Jordanians. You know their king is the one who sold us down the river.

They all did. They were all afraid to come in in the first place, and they hardly fought. Actual fighting lasted less than four weeks. They were on the defensive from day one. Their hearts weren't in the war. We would've been better off without them.

Why did they come if they weren't going to defend us?

They came to prevent a scheme between the Jews and the king of Jordan, Abdullah, to create a Greater Syria under the Hashemites.

Unbelievable!

History will one day prove what I've just said.

That traitor, Abdullah!

Before the Arab armies entered, Abdullah had several meetings with the Jews. He told them that he would pretend to be hostile to them, but that his deal with them would stand.

Why is Abdullah doing this?

He wants to rule all of Syria. He thinks the Jews are going to help him financially so that he can invade Syria, but the Jews have different plans.

On the early morning of November 29, 1949, when Thafer was barely fourteen, his parents gave him ten blue Palestinian pounds and put him on a bus to Nablus. From there, he took a bus to Amman and arrived at noon that day. Then at 5:00 in the evening, he took another bus to Baghdad, Iraq, which he reached the next morning. The bus ride to Baghdad in the middle of the night was frightening. From Baghdad, he took a seven-hour train ride to Basra, as his father had instructed him to do. From Basra, he traveled by bus to Zubair near the Iraqi-Kuwaiti border, where he stayed three days waiting for a bus to Kuwait. The three days in Zubair seemed like an eternity. He stayed in a small hotel in the tiny Iraqi village, eating hardly anything for fear he might run out of money. On December 5 the bus left Zubair at noon and reached Kuwait at 5:00 that evening.

Kuwait looked desolate. There were no tall buildings and no minarets or towers. Its tiny mud houses, scattered over the desert, were little more than shacks. He carried one small suitcase with him. He asked the bus driver about the public security building where his cousin worked. That's the building, the bus driver said, pointing to a small mud house. He walked to the house and asked for his cousin. His eyes teared when he saw his cousin Khalil, who embraced and greeted him warmly.

The obscure, quiet village where Thafer lived more than twenty years earlier has become a busy commercial center. The once tiny settlement of men of the desert, lost to the world at the northern end of the Arabian Gulf—otherwise known as the Persian Gulf—is now at the heart of one of the major oil-producing countries of the world. OAPEC, whose chief legal advisor he is about to become, has its headquarters there.

A few miles from the center of Kuwait there is a small, bustling airport. The Kuwaiti airliner approaches, circles over the expanded modern city, then descends. He sees a big sign with large, bold Arabic letters: KUWAIT.

After the plane lands, a black limousine speeds from the adjacent building, pulls up, and stops near the plane. Two men with white umbrellas get out of the limousine, one quite distinguished with his white headcloth and flowing white robe. Over the robe he wears a light brown garment of camel hair trimmed with gold braid. The other man is dressed in a light gray uniform.

The day is very hot. Thafer winces when the furnace-hot wind blows in his face. He has forgotten how hot Kuwait gets. He carries his small handbag and tries to ignore the intolerable heat as he descends. He remembers not to touch the scorching hot rails of the plane's stairs.

"Dr. Thafer Ayoub Allam," calls the man in uniform now standing at the bottom of the plane's stairs.

Thafer raises his hand.

The man in the gray uniform puts his white umbrella over Thafer and carries his handbag. The distinguished-looking man in the white robe approaches the stairs. "Welcome to Kuwait, welcome, Dr. Allam," he says, extending his hand to Thafer in a warm handshake.

"Thank you, thank you very much, sir. It's very nice of you to come, sir."

The traffic through the city of Kuwait is quite heavy, the ride slow and leisurely. Thafer looks with amazement at the modern city. Cars, pickup trucks, men, women, and children jam the wide thoroughfares, as they did in Beirut. Some of the people wear Arab attire, others Indian or Pakistani clothing, and still others Western clothes. Wholly absorbed in the sights of the city all around him, Thafer is quiet on his way to the Kuwait Hilton.

The wind is shrill, and the sea below is turbulent. The air conditioning roars in his room as he turns from side to side, desperately trying to sleep this warm April night. The scene at the Osaga airport, where his four children bade him farewell, will not let him rest. It does not let go. He gets up, turns on the light, and opens the curtain. Glittering lights move slowly in the distance, and the wind continues to whistle. He returns to his bed, once again trying to sleep.

What on earth am I doing here? he asks himself. This isn't where I should be. He reaches for the arm of a chair close to his bed, turns the chair toward the window, and talks to his deceased wife.

Mary Pat, I'm scared. I'm confused. I'm driven, but I have no idea where I'm going. I'm worried about the four children I left in Ashfield while I pursue my dreams. I'm sorry, Mary Pat, I'm out of my mind. I'm trying to go to sleep in this empty room here in Kuwait, eight thousand miles from our children. Do you believe I'm doing this? The waves of the Bay of Kuwait are breaking on the shore below. The night is disturbing. I can't wait for the dawn to break. I'm tired, very tired tonight, Mary Pat.

But he knows Mary Pat can't help him, and he can't afford to be weak, not now. He thinks of calling Colleen to tell her he has arrived and that everything is fine. But everything isn't fine. He thinks he should get out of bed, shave, shower, and dress, but it is still too early. He hates the monotonous sound of the horrid air-conditioning. Well, he knows Kuwait is a very hot country. He wonders about a peculiar odor in the room, but he soon remembers that it is from those very tiny particles of sand finer than dust, seeping through the cracks around the window. He knows that this smelly sand dust seeps in around the most tightly closed doors and windows. He knows that's life in Kuwait, but he wanted to come back and even now wants to live with the powdery dust that settles on everything.

The shrieking wind blows harder and harder, and the air conditioning roars as though in competition.

Finally, he sits up, walks around the room, looks at the Western decor, and observes the furnishings. His eyes catch the picture of the emir of Kuwait on the wall. The expression of the handsome moustachioed emir is subdued, perhaps suggesting that he is not the master of his own destiny. He gazes silently, and Thafer gazes back. The emir's Arab attire adds to the irony of the moment. His unblinking eyes challenge Thafer to a stare-down, but admitting defeat, Thafer blinks away in amusement.

Now, Thafer paces the room quietly, feeling more relaxed, wondering about the next day. He is curious about his new place of employment and his new colleagues. He thinks about Uncle Muneer. He wants to look for him and wonders if he will be able to find him. He knows that Uncle Muneer lives in Hawalli, a section of the city of Kuwait. And he thinks of his mother. He wants to see her. He thinks of his children and wants to call them in the morning.

He wonders what really awaits him in Kuwait and doesn't have the slightest idea. Now he thinks he is crazy to have come—that he's forgotten the Middle East and that he's in for a big surprise.

Wasn't that brief stay in Beirut a clue? These people expect something from me that I will be unable to give. They want me to be as crazy as they are. They want me to share their passions without hesitation or reservation. And they want me to stop being an American.

I'm already as crazy as they are, he assures himself. I do share their passions without hesitation or reservation. And they'll like the American in me.

He hesitates. Maybe I'm as crazy as they are, maybe I share their passions without hesitation or reservation, but they'll resent the American in me.

VIII

The public relations official and Saeed, the driver who brought Thafer from Kuwait's airport to the Hilton, take Thafer the next day to the OAPEC offices. It is a hot, windy day.

OAPEC has its offices in the center of the city of Kuwait, next to the building that houses the Kuwaiti Ministry of Foreign Affairs. Thafer and the public relations official enter through the gate of the six-story, white stone building. A police guard stands at attention at the entrance. The official leads Thafer to the elevator, and they ride to the fourth floor, where the official then takes him to a spacious reception room adjacent to the office of the secretary general of OAPEC.

"Welcome to OAPEC, Dr. Allam," says a tall moustachioed man, extending his hand for a warm handshake. "And welcome to Kuwait. I'm Ziyad Ghassan, the secretary general."

"I'm honored to meet you, sir," Thafer says, standing.

"I want to say," the immaculately dressed man remarks, leading Thafer to his plush office, "that this punishing weather does not reflect the way we feel about you. We're delighted that you're here. How was your journey?"

"It was uneventful." Thafer is aware of the man's scrutiny.

"Did you stay overnight in London?"

"No, I took a flight from New York to London, which continued on to Beirut, and I stayed overnight there."

The distinguished-looking, gray-haired man speaks flawless English with a slight British accent. He has a thick, graying moustache, tranquil brown eyes, and a dark complexion. "I like Beirut. I grew up there, and we still have a home in Beirut." He pauses, then looks at Thafer again. "Where did you stay in Beirut, Dr. Allam?"

"With friends in West Beirut."

The secretary general's eyes are steady, and he listens with great interest. "Travel between Kuwait and Beirut used to be a hardship. Now I go to Beirut twice and sometimes three times a month."

There is something comforting in the reserved manner of the middle-aged secretary general.

"Are you all set to work for us?"

"Yes, sir."

"We worried about you for a while. We knew you were having problems making arrangements for your children. It wasn't easy, I'm sure."

Thafer feels heat going through him.

The secretary general momentarily swings his chair away from his new legal advisor. "Your predecessor, Dr. Allam, was a capable young man." Then, swinging his chair back toward Thafer and finding him composed again, he continues. "We were sorry to see him go, but this is the way it is. He was with us three years. I know you'll like it here, Dr. Allam."

"I'm sure I will."

"Beirut is a good place to break a long journey." He pauses. "Now, let me tell you a little about the office and about the staff. I have two assistants, one in charge of the economics division and one in charge of the administrative division. Both are quite capable and professional. You'll like them."

Thafer listens attentively as the secretary general's face becomes more serious.

"As with any newcomer, the staff may be curious about why you would leave the comfort of the United States for this desolate place."

"I wonder about that myself."

The secretary general laughs.

Thafer remains reserved.

"Do you have anything you'd like to discuss with me before I bring my two assistants to meet you, Dr. Allam?"

"Yes, Mr. Ghassan."

"Just call me Ziyad, Dr. Allam."

"And I am Thafer. Yes, as we agreed before I accepted the position, I need to make a trip to the West Bank to see my mother before I become heavily involved here. I haven't seen her since 1959."

"When would you like to go, Brother Thafer?"

"In two weeks, if possible."

"How long would you stay?"

"A week."

"I'm sure that can be arranged."

The secretary general pushes a button, then picks up a phone. "Would you come in, Lemya?"

A slender young woman armed with pad and pencil walks in.

"Lemya, I want you to meet Dr. Allam, our new legal advisor."

"How do you do, Dr. Allam," the shy woman murmurs.

Thafer stands up. "How do you do."

"Would you ask Hamdan and Mukhtar to come and meet Dr. Allam, Lemya?"

"Certainly."

"Now, Brother Thafer, you'll of course head the legal department, and for the most part you'll be working with me, but you'll also work with one of the assistants, Mr. Hamdan Mishaan, and with Dr. Suhaila Sa'adeh, his deputy. The lawyers in your department are consultants for their respective governments. They rarely come to OAPEC's offices. They will work with you in matters pertaining to the affairs of OAPEC, but their primary obligation is to their respective governments. So, as far as the legal department is concerned, you're it. You can have all the help you need, however. For assistance in matters relating to our relations with Kuwait, our host state, you can call on a private law firm here in Kuwait that represents us in such matters. I'll eventually arrange for you to meet the lawyer assigned to us."

Hamdan Mishaan, the assistant secretary general for economics, comes first. He wears a long white Arab robe and a checkered red and white headcloth. A man in his early forties, he is attractive and gracious. He has olive skin, a youthful face, and he is short and clean shaven.

"Dr. Allam, I would like to introduce Sheikh Hamdan Mishaan, the assistant secretary general responsible for the economics division. Sheikh, this is Dr. Thafer Allam, our new legal advisor."

Smiling, Hamdan Mishaan walks toward Thafer, extends his hand, and gives him a warm embrace and handshake. "Welcome, Dr. Allam, welcome, welcome."

Surprised by the warm encounter, Thafer blushes. "Thank you, thank you, Sheikh Mishaan."

Then Mukhtar Alian arrives. A little older than Hamdan, he is tall and slender and has a thin black moustache and a very dark complexion. He is less at ease. He wears a long white Arab robe and a white headcloth. When he is introduced, the shy man cautiously walks toward Thafer, his head stiff, and shakes Thafer's hand. "Welcome, Dr. Allam, welcome."

"Thank you, Sheikh Alian."

"Would either of you like to show Dr. Allam around, or would you like me to do that?" the secretary general asks.

"I'll be glad to show Dr. Allam around," Hamdan offers.

"Thank you, Brother Hamdan."

"Please call me Hamdan or Brother Hamdan. We don't actually call each other sheikh in the office, and we are not real sheikhs."

"And please call me Thafer."

"I'll call you Dr. Thafer or Brother Thafer."

"I gather that I will be calling the secretary general Brother Ziyad."

"Everybody calls him Brother Ziyad."

"What should I call the administrative assistant secretary general?"

"You can also call him Brother Mukhtar."

Hamdan introduces his secretary, Reem Makram, a dark, pretty woman, as they enter Hamdan's office, which is slightly smaller than that of the secretary general, but almost as lavishly furnished.

Hamdan then takes Thafer to a spacious office a little distance across the hall from his own. It is more elegant than Thafer expects. Overlooking the Bay of Kuwait, the office is quite cheerful.

"Of course, this used to be your predecessor's, Brother Thafer, but if you find that it needs anything, please let us know."

"Thank you, Brother Hamdan." Thafer tries to conceal his astonishment at the splendor of the office he will be occupying.

Then Hamdan takes Thafer to the office of the senior economist, Dr. Suhaila Sa'adeh. He knocks gently at her door.

"Come in," says a gentle voice.

Motioning for Thafer to follow him, Hamdan walks in. It is another luxurious office, almost identical to Thafer's and only a little distance from it.

Turning to Thafer, Hamdan says, "This is Dr. Suhaila Sa'adeh, our senior economist. She is also my deputy."

The tall, thin, distinguished-looking woman is probably in her middle thirties. She wears a long, light blue unfitted dress and a checkered black and white mantilla that partly covers her light brown hair and frames her pretty face. Retiring, almost shy, she wears no makeup on her fair skin. She stands up, extends her hand to Thafer, and greets him with reserve. "Ya marhaba, Dr. Thafer, ya marhaba," she says in a low voice.

The familiar Palestinian greeting and the woman's Palestinian accent send shivers through Thafer's body.

"Did you have a pleasant journey?"

"It was quite pleasant, Dr. Suhaila."

"Would you like to sit down a moment?"

"Just for a moment," says Hamdan. "We still have to make the rounds."

"I hope you will like it here," she says as she walks toward Thafer. "This is a terribly windy day, but it'll soon calm down. Is this your first trip to Kuwait?"

"No, as a matter of fact," he says, a slight catch in his voice, "I used to live and work in Kuwait."

"You did?!"

Hamdan looks surprised.

"Where did you work?"

"I was a young boy, and I worked as a messenger boy for the Kuwait Oil Company from late 1949 to the middle of 1951. I went to high school at night."

"Then you went to the United States?"

"I went home first."

"I'm sure the two of you will have a lot to talk about," Hamdan says, moving toward the door.

"I'm sure," she says.

As Thafer's eyes meet hers, he immediately senses the woman's awareness of something they share.

Hamdan then takes Thafer to the office of Dr. Suhaila's junior assistant.

"Hello, hello," says the young economist. "I bet this is our new legal advisor from the United States."

"Yes, Zaher, it is." Hamdan does not offer a formal introduction.

"It's great to see you, sir," says the young economist.

"It's nice to see you, sir," says Thafer, feeling the awkwardness of the encounter and noticing the man's captivating smile. Zaher, perhaps in his early thirties, is short and slim. His swarthy face sports a thick black moustache and a constant childlike smile. He is high-spirited and a bit unruly. If the annoyed Hamdan had not called him Zaher, Thafer would not have known the young man's name. He still does not know his family name. But there is something strangely appealing about him. The dignified white robe and white headcloth do not seem in keeping with his nonchalant, irreverent manner.

Finally, Thafer is introduced to Dr. Suhaila's senior assistant, Mahmood Abdul-Khaleq. Thafer admires the man's thick dark beard and moustache. His attention is caught by the sadness in his eyes and face. The man is quite reserved, almost unfriendly. His handsome dark suit adds to his somber appearance. Thafer is intrigued.

Hamdan and Thafer then return to Hamdan's office.

"That's enough for today," says Hamdan, reflecting a moment. "I'm sorry about the sandstorm, but you might as well be reintroduced to the reality of Kuwait. I guess you're familiar with its sandstorms."

"I don't remember their starting this early."

"Did you have a family here?"

"I had an older cousin the first two months I was here, but he left Kuwait to work in Saudi Arabia, and I remained here by myself for almost two years."

"How did you end up in the United States?"

"While going to night school, I met an American Anglican priest. He took an interest in me. When I told him I wanted to pursue my education and study in the United States, he helped me get the names and addresses of a few colleges and universities there. I made several applications and ended up going to Cornell University in New York.

"This is a wonderful story," Hamdan says, then pauses a moment. "I'm a self-made man, too, but I never went to college."

"That's not always important."

Hamdan then calls the secretary general, who comes to join them.

"Your villa, Dr. Thafer," says the secretary general, "should be ready in a week. In the meantime, you can stay at the Hilton or at any other hotel you may wish at OAPEC's expense. The Hilton is closer. It's probably more cheerful."

"The Hilton is fine, Brother Ziyad."

"Very well," says the secretary general, smiling broadly. "Welcome to the family, Dr. Thafer. We're delighted that you could join us."

IX

I should've done that last night, Thafer muses after he calls his children from his new office at OAPEC. Then he walks around his office, enjoying its comfort and the quiet of the central air-conditioning. A large picture of the king of Saudi Arabia is hung on the wall behind his desk.

Why does the king's expression suggest that he has smelled something rotten? he asks himself. He then moves to the other end of his office, where a map of the Middle East hangs on the wall. He notices the tiny state of Kuwait squeezed between Saudi Arabia and Iraq along the Persian Gulf. He also notices his native country on the map. The word *Israel* is printed over it, but it has been crossed out and replaced with "Occupied Palestine." Yet the globe in the corner next to that map still identifies the land of his birth as Israel. He walks back to his desk and sits in the maroon leather swivel chair, trying it for comfort and wondering about the new people who have just come into his life.

"May I come in, sir?" says a young man who enters the office with a tray and two cups of tea after gently knocking at Thafer's door.

"Please do," says Thafer.

"Brother Hamdan would like to join you for tea, sir. Where would you like me to put these, sir?"

"On the table on the other side of the office. And what's your name, young man?"

"Khaled, sir."

"Where are you from, Khaled?"

"I'm from North Yemen, sir."

He carries the two small cups of tea to a little table on the other side of Thafer's office and stares at Thafer for a moment before he leaves.

I wonder what's on Hamdan's mind, Thafer asks himself as he feels the fatigue of traveling and the anxiety of the uncertain future before him.

A knock at the door.

"Please come in."

"Where would you like us to sit, Brother Thafer?"

"Let's sit on the other side of the office."

"I want to continue our conversation, but I would like first to assure you that I want to be helpful in whatever way I can. I know it's hard when you come to a strange place like this, leaving your children behind and not knowing anyone, so please consider me a friend and a brother. I want you to feel you're among friends."

"Thank you, thank you very much, Brother Hamdan."

"Ziyad and I thought that one of us should have a reception for you. I was elected, but Ziyad will join us. We can do it in either ten or fifteen days, whichever you prefer. We'll invite some of the staff and their spouses, as well as a few friends and business people you'll enjoy meeting. How does that sound?"

"That sounds great. Thank you kindly. It doesn't really make much difference whether it's in ten or fifteen days, whatever is more convenient for you and for Brother Ziyad."

"Suppose we do it in fifteen days? That'll give you time to rest after your long trip. By the way, our working hours are from 7:00 A.M. to 2:00 P.M. We don't take a lunch break, and we don't come back in the afternoon. Thursdays and Fridays are holidays."

"That's fine."

Hamdan then pulls his chair closer to the table, as though he wants to confide something. "Ziyad will most likely go to Beirut in a few days. His wife hates it here. He'll probably stay in Beirut a week or ten days, and I'll take his place."

Thafer listens.

Hamdan pulls his chair closer. "Dr. Suhaila is a smart woman. She has a strong personality, and I'm sure you'll like her. Her husband was an officer in the Egyptian army and was martyred in the June War of 1967. Her junior assistant, Zaher, has a lot of money and he is a playboy. Her senior assistant, Mahmood, is living in exile here in Kuwait. He's a member of the Muslim Brotherhood. We call him Sheikh Mahmood because he wears a thick beard, but he's not really a sheikh. He's always frowning and will tell you with brutal frankness what's on his mind. If he doesn't like you, he won't talk to you, even when you greet him. He's a devout Muslim and prays five times a day."

Thafer thinks Hamdan has finished.

"Ziyad's secretary, Lemya," Hamdan continues, "is treacherous. She reports everything to him, whatever she hears or sees; even when he phones her from outside the country, she tells him everything."

Thafer continues to maintain a polite attentiveness. He looks tired and does not respond.

"Do you mind my telling you all this, Brother Thafer?"

"Not at all."

"Now, Brother Thafer, tell me something. What is it, frankly, that attracts you to this place? I hope you don't mind my asking you, but many here are wondering."

Thafer looks at Hamdan and tries to think what to say. The secretary general warned him that this question is on the mind of some of the staff. "What attracts me to this place?" Thafer repeats. "Well, as I said this morning, when I was a young boy, I lived in Kuwait for almost two years. It was here that I planned my journey to the United States, so I've always had a special feeling for the place. Naturally, I've been curious about its becoming a center of attention. Remember, I'm Palestinian. I want to give something of myself to the Arab people. I guess it's to compensate for the feeling of guilt I've had, rightly or wrongly, for leaving. I left for something more glamorous and more attractive." Thafer smiles.

"You know, some people here at OAPEC assume that you work for the American CIA."

Thafer suddenly feels hot and begins to perspire. "Brother Hamdan, I just want you to know that I don't work for the CIA. I don't believe that I ever knowingly met anyone who works for them."

"I didn't say that you do. I just want to tell you what's in the minds of many here. I guess I shouldn't have said anything." Looking troubled, he stands up self-consciously. "I should go back to my office. Thank you, Dr. Thafer."

"I'm glad you came."

Thafer puts his head between his hands, feeling completely helpless on his first day of work at OAPEC and wondering what he is getting himself into. He is now suspected of being a spy for the CIA, with all its menacing implications for his people. Hardly an auspicious beginning, he thinks.

"They've all gone, sir," says Saeed, knocking softly on Thafer's door and opening it quietly. "I've cooled the limousine. Whenever you're ready, sir."

The wind outside is still blowing shrilly when Thafer and Saeed leave at 2:00. The heat is blistering, but the limousine is cool and quite comfortable.

"I told you about my brother this morning, Saeed."

"Yes, sir."

"He's an older man whom I call Uncle Muneer, but he's actually my brother."

"Yes, sir."

"Uncle Muneer has several children living here in Kuwait. One of them, Fuaad, has a women's clothing shop in Hawalli, but I don't know the street number. I only know the name of the shop."

"Did you say Hawalli, sir?"

"Is this how it's pronounced?"

"Yes, sir. It isn't too far from here, a mile or two. That's where the Palestinian ghetto is, sir!"

Thafer feels gooseflesh rising on his arms.

"What's the name of the shop, sir?'

"Eve's Clothing Shop."

"We'll find it, sir."

"When can you take me there, Saeed?"

"At 5:00 P.M. All the shops close between 1:00 P.M. and 5:00 because of the heat. They open again at 5:00. I'll come to get you at 5:00, sir."

"Thank you, Saeed."

Thafer returns to the hotel, physically and emotionally drained. He throws himself face down on the bed and sleeps instantly.

X

The traffic is heavy, the ride slow and leisurely. Thafer marvels at the modern buildings and admires the wide, paved streets. There are many pickup trucks and much horn blowing. He is wholly absorbed, as he was in Beirut, observing the people filling the streets.

They have driven a mile when, almost imperceptibly, the scene begins to change as they move slowly to the south. The streets become narrower and are unpaved. The buildings are older and have fallen into disrepair.

"We're now in Hawalli, sir," says the driver matter-of-factly.

The streets and places of business in Hawalli have the traditional names of Palestinian towns and cities—the Lydda Restaurant, the Nablus Sweet Shop, the Haifa Tailor Shop, and the Jerusalem School. The Palestinian women wear colorful traditional costumes. Thafer is touched by their beautifully embroidered long dresses because the design and color of the embroidery on each dress identifies the town or area of its origin. Silken red or blue cummerbunds add to their authenticity. Some of the older women have tattoos on their otherwise unblemished faces, and thin white mantillas lay on their partly covered heads. Some of the younger women wear Western dresses like those one might see in Europe or in the United States. Children play in the vacant parcels of land between the decaying old buildings. They seem unperturbed by the heat. Boys play soccer, and girls jump rope and chant Palestinian songs.

"The Kuwaitis refer to Hawalli as the West Bank, sir," says the driver.

"They do?" Thafer says.

"There are a lot of Palestinians in Hawalli, sir."

"Really?"

"More than three hundred thousand, sir."

"That many?"

"Even more. The Kuwaiti government doesn't admit the true number of Palestinians in Hawalli. They're afraid of the Palestinians."

"But why?"

"They're afraid that the Palestinians will take over Kuwait."

"Even if it were heaven, the Palestinians wouldn't want Kuwait. They want to return to Palestine, if only they could."

"I know that, sir."

"Let's stop right here, Saeed. Pull over to the side and park. We'll just mingle with the crowd, and I'll ask someone where the store is."

As they walk slowly, Saeed by Thafer's side, people stare at them, but Thafer is not concerned. He continues, moving closer and closer to a throng of Palestinians.

"Be careful, sir," cautions Saeed.

Observing the mosaic formed by the variously colored women's clothing, Thafer notices an older woman walking toward him. She wears a long white embroidered dress and a red silk cummerbund. A thin white mantilla covers part of her white hair. Her attire and her sad, wrinkled face place her squarely in the ancient heritage to which his people belong. He wants to touch her as she comes closer, to make sure she is real. He wants to hold her frail hand and kiss it as an expression of ultimate respect. He wants to embrace her, and by embracing her, he will embrace his heritage, his people, his family's farm, his town, and his native land. He wants to speak to her about his stepbrother and his family. He is sure she will know.

The elderly woman comes closer. It is still hot, and he is perspiring. He walks toward her, Saeed trailing him. As she looks at him, her tranquil eyes become disturbed.

"Mother, Mother," he entreats, using the customary expression to show respect for an elderly woman. "I'm looking for Eve's Clothing Shop. It's owned by my brother's older son, Fuaad Allam. I wonder if you know where it is."

Startled, the elderly woman looks around, then stares at him, her lovely old face bewildered. "Where did you come from?" she asks sharply. "Who are you?"

Her words and accent give him solace. "I'm a newcomer to Kuwait," he answers in the same Palestinian dialect. "I haven't seen my family in many years."

The elderly woman's face changes abruptly, her perturbed eyes regaining their serenity. She reaches for her mantilla, pulls it higher over her silver hair, and looks at him closely. She appears to be examining his suit, then pauses and looks at Saeed. "Do you know him?" she asks the young driver softly.

"Yes, Mother," replies Saeed in his unmistakable Yemenite accent. "I'm his driver."

The elderly woman hesitates, then looks at Thafer, her eyes moist. "Yes, I know where the shop is. It's not too far from here. I'll have my son show you."

Thafer and Saeed follow her a short distance until they come to a dilapidated old building.

"Wait until I get my son," she says. She goes into the building, then comes out with a moustachioed man, perhaps in his early forties.

"You want Fuaad Allam's clothing shop?" asks the man in white Arab dress.

"Yes, sir."

The elderly woman then disappears into the building.

"My mother is suspicious of strangers," apologizes the woman's son.

"I don't blame her," Thafer says.

"You've been away a long time?"

"About twenty years."

"That's long. Eve's Clothing Shop is just around the corner. Your relatives will be happy to see you. Do they know you're coming?"

"No, they don't."

The amiable man leads Thafer and Saeed a little way, then he points to a small store on the corner of a narrow street where a sign in Arabic reads, "Eve's Clothing Shop: Women and Children."

"I'm sure they'll be delighted to see you. They're honest, and they work hard."

"Thank you. I'm grateful, sir."

"I'm glad to help. Good luck. I hope we meet again, maybe in the homeland."

"Thank you again. I'm sure we will."

The tiny, dimly lit shop has a high, wide doorway, but no windows. A three-foot high counter extending from one side of the shop to the other, with a little space at each end, separates Thafer's nephew from his customers. About five feet from the back wall, it is cluttered with women's and children's clothing. Several women are in the small shop, looking at cheaply made dresses, underclothes, socks, skirts, shoes, and children's clothes. The women shout as they bargain good-naturedly with Fuaad Allam.

Standing at the entrance of the shop, Thafer anxiously waits for an appropriate moment to walk in and talk to his relatives. He last saw Fuaad almost twenty-three years ago. Fuaad was twenty-two, and Thafer fourteen. A superb soccer player, Fuaad was thin and wiry. Now he is quite heavy—his face full and his hair graying—but his features have not changed very much.

The old man, Uncle Muneer, is sitting quietly on the chair facing Fuaad. He can't see Thafer, but Thafer recognizes him even though he is in his seventies now and seems even older. His thinning hair is white, his drawn face solemn and wrinkled. He appears quite fragile.

Uncle Muneer's father, Ayoub Allam's older brother, died when Uncle Muneer was an infant. Ayoub Allam, Thafer's father, then married his brother's widow and brought up his nephew as his own son. So Uncle Muneer is Thafer's step-brother and first cousin, but Thafer and even his older brothers have always called him "Uncle Muneer." Thafer's father was "Father" to Uncle Muneer, and Fuaad always called him "Grandpa." Uncle Muneer and his wife, Mama Adla, and their children lived with Thafer's family on the family farm. Mama Adla used to help Thafer's mother care for Thafer when he was small and often bathed him. Thafer and Fuaad grew up together in the same house as though they were brothers. Thafer remembers being jealous when he heard Fuaad and his brothers and sisters call Thafer's father "Grandpa." Thafer, too, wanted to call him "Grandpa," but that only drew laughter from his family. Thafer did not understand then why his family laughed.

Thafer wants to go in, but is nervous and waits a little. Fuaad now sees him, but doesn't recognize him. Maybe I should go in now and kiss Uncle Muneer's hand, he thinks: then Fuaad will know who I am. But he waits for a moment because a lot of strangers are inside the shop. He is excited and afraid there will be a lot of emotion.

Fuaad glances at Thafer again, but still doesn't recognize him. He hasn't seen Thafer since Thafer was fourteen.

"Father," says Fuaad Allam turning to the old man, "there are two men near the door. I wonder if you could see what they want."

Before the old man moves from his chair, Thafer walks to him.

Fuaad looks again in Thafer's direction.

Thafer reaches for the old man's hand, wanting to kiss it as a gesture of ultimate respect in keeping with Palestinian tradition.

Fuaad seems puzzled. He drops the yardstick he holds in his hand and comes closer to look at Thafer.

"Kamal?" the old man then asks, thinking Thafer to be Thafer's older brother.

"No, Father!" exclaims Fuaad with astonishment and delight. "It's Thafer! It's Thafer!"

"Thafer's in America, Fuaad," says the old man in confusion.

"I was, Uncle Muneer." Thafer, feels the excitement. "I came back just last night."

Tears rolling down his cheeks, Fuaad jumps over the counter and extends both arms to Thafer. "I can't believe it, Thafer. I can't believe it, Thafer," he repeats, embracing him.

The two hug and kiss and cry like small children. The
women in the shop, unprepared for this emotional encounter,
are speechless and also begin to cry.

Thafer then walks back toward the old man, who also is
weeping. The old man kisses Thafer and hugs him, repeating
his name and not wanting to let go of him. Finally exhausted,
he walks slowly to his chair, his head down, and sits quietly.

"These are tears of joy," says one of the women in the
shop. "How long has he been away?" she asks Fuaad.

"More than twenty years."

"Your brother?"

"My father's kid brother."

"Why does he call his brother 'Uncle'?"

Fuaad does not answer.

"I'm glad for his safe return," she then says to the old man
and glances at Thafer in astonishment.

"Thank you," the old man replies, more composed now.

The other women walk to the old man, shake his hand,
and congratulate him on Thafer's safe return. Then Saeed also
shakes the old man's hand and congratulates him.

"Who's the young man, Thafer?" asks Uncle Muneer.

"Saeed and I work together, Uncle Muneer," Thafer says,
"and he was kind enough to bring me here."

"Thank you, Mr. Saeed," says the old man, "thank you
very much indeed."

"You're very welcome, Mr. Allam," says Saeed, who has
also been moved by the reunion.

All the women have now left. Thafer sits next to the old man.

"Let's go home early today," says Uncle Muneer. "Call your
brothers and sisters and tell them, Fuaad. Also call all our
cousins, all the relatives. Call our friends and tell them too."

"I will, Father."

"Where did you sleep last night, my boy?" asks the old
man.

"In the Hilton, Uncle Muneer."

"Why there, Thafer?"

"My new employer, Uncle Muneer, made a reservation for me there."

"Who's your new employer, my boy?"

"The Organization of Arab Petroleum Exporting Countries, Uncle Muneer."

"I've never heard of them. Have you, Fuaad?"

"Yes, Father, they're good."

"That's good. Now, Thafer, go with Fuaad and fetch your luggage from the hotel. You're going to stay at your uncle's house."

"I will directly, Uncle Muneer."

XI

O Yee, O Yee,
My fawn has now returned,

yodels his aunt, Mama Adla, as he enters her crowded second floor apartment in the Palestinian ghetto.

O Yee, O Yee,
When he left he was small and tender,
O Yee, O Yee,
He's now as solid as timber.
Lolo, lolo, lolwee.

There are tears in her eyes as she yodels. Thafer himself struggles to hold back tears. Uncle Muneer and his children, as well as other relatives, are waiting for him.

Thafer glances at his father's picture hanging on the wall. He can't look at it without his eyes stinging. He has never seen it before. It must have been taken when his father was a youth. His father was old the last time Thafer saw him—even older than Uncle Muneer is now. Mama Adla looks old now too—her hair gray and her happy face wrinkled. Her voice has become weaker with age. More than thirty people are in the tiny living room, but Thafer can recognize only two faces, Mama Adla and Cousin Wahby's. Cousin Wahby was a schoolteacher. His hair and moustache are now a distinguished gray.

Then a tall, handsome man with a thin moustache and graying temples walks toward Thafer and embraces him warmly. "Let's go to America with a mule and two jute bags, Uncle Thafer," the man says, grinning.

"Haitham!" says Thafer, shaking his head and smiling.

"For heaven's sake, Haitham! You still remember that?" exclaims the old man.

"Do you think we could survive that again?" asks Thafer.

"I don't even dare think about it."

Thafer remembers how during the first Arab-Israeli war, shortly after the Israeli army took control of the area where their farm was, he and his younger nephew "infiltrated" their farm one dark, moonless night at Thafer's instigation. Thafer was fourteen and his nephew a few months younger. They took the only mule the family had been able to rescue from the farm and two jute bags with them. Leaving their summer home in Tulkarm at about 8:00, they walked almost five miles in the pitch dark night. They reached the farm just about 10:00. It was deserted—no animals, no chickens, and no sign of habitation. Some of the trees were damaged. The door to the big barn was wide open, and no equipment had been left in it. The door to the farm house was broken. Most of the furniture had been removed and what remained was damaged. The house appeared to have been ransacked. Thafer tied the mule to a tree. Then they each took a jute bag and went into the fields. Thafer gathered cucumbers and onions, while his nephew picked tomatoes and squash. Then both picked oranges, lemons, and tangerines. They were about to load up the mule when a powerful beam of light flashed in their direction. It came from an Israeli patrol, either in a jeep or an army tank. The two threw themselves to the ground. Thafer remembers how they were shaking as they hid among the plants. They were petrified. "Don't breathe," he had whispered to his nephew. He was worried that the Israeli soldiers would spot the mule on the other side of the farm, but he had tied it behind a small barn. The light came closer, flashing relentlessly in their direction. They remained motionless, pressing their bodies to the earth. As the patrol came closer, Thafer could even hear men talking, but the Israelis never saw them. They must not have seen the mule. Finally, they turned around and at length disappeared in the distance. He and his nephew finished filling the two bags, loaded up the mule, and began their trip back. They stumbled in the dark, not saying a word to one another. The fields were empty, and the silence was frightening. They could hear only their own footsteps and the plodding hoofbeats of the mule. They got home after midnight. No one had had any idea of where they had gone or what they had done, but when Thafer's father found out, he was shocked.

If they had caught us, Thafer muses, neither one of us would have come back to tell what had happened.

"You're both survivors, my dear Thafer," the old man says.

"And Haitham will go with you anywhere, Thafer dear," says his elderly aunt.

The old man then relates what happened in Fuaad's shop earlier. He recalls how upset the Allam family was when they received Thafer's letter from Kuwait in early 1951, telling them that he wanted to go to America. "Going to America in those days," says the old man, "was like going to Mars."

"How do you find Kuwait, Thafer, after twenty years?" asks one of his relatives.

"I'm quite impressed with the change in Kuwait," Thafer says. "In the late forties and early fifties, Kuwait was a community of barely thirty thousand people living in very primitive conditions. Now it has a population of more than one million. Except for Hawalli, Kuwait looks like any modern Western city."

"The Kuwaitis resent us," his relative says. "They're afraid of us We've helped them develop their country. We've built hospitals and provided doctors. We've built schools and provided teachers. We've built roads and provided engineers. Yet they're suspicious and resentful of us. Our boys have built a police force and an army for them. Yet if the Kuwaiti government thinks it could get away with it, it would probably expel most of us. Where would we go? We have no place to go."

"Uncle Thafer," says Thafer's young nephew, Nizar, "May I show you the room we'll be sharing?"

"Of course."

Nizar leads Thafer to a small room. "Make yourself at home, Uncle Thafer. I'll be right back."

Thafer looks around. There are two single beds, a small table and a chair. His suitcase is on top of one of the beds, so he concludes that bed is his. The overhead light is dim. There is no table lamp. The window air conditioning unit is roaring.

At least the tiny space will be cool, he muses.

Then he notices a picture of the Virgin Mary holding the baby Christ hung on the wall next to a framed passage from the Holy Quran stating, "Almighty God, help me attain more learning."

"When do you have to be at the office, Uncle Thafer?" asks Nizar, returning to the tiny room.

"At 7:00, Nizar."

"Would getting up at 5:30 give you enough time?"

"More than enough."

"Did you enjoy the relatives, Uncle Thafer?"

"Very much. How many do we have in Kuwait?"

"Between close and distant relatives, there are about two hundred. You'll eventually meet most of them when they come to greet you. Most of them have educated their children, who have become doctors, engineers, and teachers. You're the only lawyer in the family. You're both a nuclear engineer and a lawyer. Is that right, Uncle Thafer?"

"That's right."

"They all think you're only a nuclear engineer."

"I'm sure the family doesn't need a lawyer."

"You never know."

"The family push to become educated is really impressive, Nizar."

"Our family is not the only one to do this; it's common practice among most Palestinians."

"So I understand."

"Two themes run through the lives of our countrymen, Uncle Thafer—a hunger for more education and a thirst to return to the homeland. It's hard work, but we never lose sight of our goals."

"I'm sure that education is a very good thing."

"I know it is, Uncle Thafer. It will eventually help us return home."

"What about life for Palestinians in Kuwait, Nizar? It was upsetting this evening to hear about the Kuwaitis' treatment of them."

"What you heard is true, Uncle Thafer. The Kuwaitis resent us. To them, we are intruders. We've come to their insecure country, educated our children, lived modest lives, and survived. They marvel at our resilience and envy it, but this envy then turns to resentment. Would you believe that Palestinian children born in Kuwait are forced to leave when their parents lose their work permits?"

"But there's discrimination against Palestinians in other parts of the Arab world, isn't there?"

"Yes, there is, but it's the worst here in Kuwait. It's an irony, but the pressure of discrimination in Kuwait and in some of the other Arab countries always reminds us that we must return to the homeland."

Thafer listens.

"Did you hear, Uncle Thafer, that the Kuwaitis are afraid the Palestinians might take over Kuwait?"

"Yes, I heard that."

"This is the furthest thing from our minds. We would never want Kuwait for our home, even if it were handed to us. This is ludicrous. First, Kuwait will never be an adequate substitute. No place in the entire world will be an adequate substitute. Even Lebanon and Jordan never can be. There are more than four million of our people living in and around the homeland hundreds of miles away from Kuwait, but, most important, we would consider it shameful to do to an Arab country what the Jews have done to us. The Kuwaitis don't seem to understand this."

"Why do you think the Kuwaitis feel this way then? Have the Palestinians ever done anything to justify the Kuwaitis' fear?"

"Never, never, Uncle Thafer. The Kuwaitis talk about it and spread rumors. Then they begin to believe their own rumors. They have great wealth from oil and have made some wise investments of their oil income. They've been blessed with some brilliant advisors, most of whom are Palestinians. But because of this very wealth they have not attached much importance to education, which keeps them unsophisticated and insecure. If they were to reach a higher level of education, I feel sure that they would become less suspicious and less fearful of us. I'm not talking about eradicating illiteracy; I mean real, solid higher education. They can afford it. As it is, they feel that as long as they have all this wealth, why do they need education?"

"What about the Kuwaiti government? Doesn't it encourage its citizens to continue their education?"

"The Kuwaiti government, Uncle Thafer, is corrupt. It's feudalistic. It's afraid of its own citizens. It throws money at the Kuwaitis in order to pacify them. It gives them money from the day they're born until the day they die. This is why the Kuwaitis are born insecure and die insecure. They're also irresponsible and have no respect for property. They can also be heartless."

"Do they ever work?"

"Very few do actual work. Class B Kuwaiti citizens, who are not entitled to vote, do actually work. Class A Kuwaiti citizens, who can vote, hardly ever work. Why should they? It's this class of Kuwaitis who tend to become heartless. They don't know what it means to be hungry, to be without a country, to have eight or nine children but not enough food or space for them. That's why I say the Kuwaitis can be very thoughtless."

"This ghetto is wretched, Nizar. Why are the Palestinians confined to it?"

"We are not actually physically confined to it. Some wealthy Palestinians live outside it, but very few. Palestinians cannot own real estate in Kuwait, Uncle Thafer, even if they were born here or have lived here for twenty or thirty years, or even for all their lives. My parents rent this apartment, and we're at the mercy of the Kuwaiti landlord. Seven of us live in the apartment, now eight. We're all at the mercy of our Kuwaiti landlord. He may come tomorrow, raise the rent, or threaten to evict us. We have no recourse. We work hard and pay high rent. The Kuwaiti government doesn't help us or care about us. It always supports the Kuwaiti landlords, whether they're right or wrong."

"Don't they have rent control laws here?"

"They do, Uncle Thafer, but the courts always rule in favor of the Kuwaiti landlords. The Palestinians don't have a chance. They don't even bother to go to court anymore."

"This is sad."

"I'm sorry, Uncle Thafer. I know I'm saddening you."

"It's all right. I need to know this."

XII

On the second day, Saeed picks up Thafer at his uncle's and aunt's apartment. The morning traffic is very heavy and wild. Saeed first takes Thafer to the house to which he will move in a few days, but he sees only its exterior. About two hundred yards from the sea in an expensive and exclusive area, the three-story house of white stone and marble is grand and palatial.

Only the receptionist, the office secretaries, and the janitors are on the job when Thafer arrives at OAPEC's offices. It is almost 7:00 A.M. when he enters his office. He sits at his desk, on which he sees a calendar, an attractive marble desk set with two shiny gold pens, and a gracefully ornamented small clock.

He has been at his desk only a minute when someone knocks softly at his door. "May we come in?" asks a woman's soft voice.

He is not expecting anyone that early. "Please come in," he says and springs to attention behind his immaculate, tidy desk. He looks at seven well-dressed women at the door. He moves toward the hesitating women and cordially invites them to come in. He recognizes the face of Lemya, the secretary to the secretary general. The frightened look on her thin face the day before, when the secretary general wanted his two assistants in his office, left an impression on Thafer. He also recognizes the pretty face of Reem, the woman with the Egyptian accent. She seems to be the leader and is the one to enter first.

"I'm Reem, Dr. Thafer, Mr. Hamdan's secretary. We met yesterday. I have some of my friends here at OAPEC. They would like to meet you. I understand that you've met Lemya."

"Right," says Thafer, "nice to see you again."

Lemya nods her head. "Nice to see you, Dr. Thafer."

Turning to a fastidiously dressed woman in her early thirties, Reem says, "And this is Nahida, Mr. Mukhtar's secretary."

"How do you do," Thafer says.

"How do you do, Dr. Thafer," she responds, looking at him playfully.

"And this is Salwa," Reem says, turning to a shy woman in her middle twenties, humbly attired in a long light blue dress and a matching mantilla, which covers her hair. She wears no makeup.

"I'm pleased to meet you," says the chaste-looking woman, her head lowered.

"I'm pleased to meet you," Thafer says, recognizing the woman's Palestinian accent.

"And this is Leila," says Reem, "Dr. Suhaila's secretary."

"Hello, Dr. Thafer," says the poised woman. She is older than the others and wears a long, straight cut dress that completely conceals her figure. She has a pleasant face.

"Hello," says Thafer, curious about the woman's accent.

"This is Selma," says Reem. "She works in the economics department and does work for Sheikh Mahmood and Mr. Zaher."

"Hello," says Thafer.

"I'm glad to meet you."

"And this is Suha, who works with Salwa in accounting."

"Hello," says Thafer.

"Hello, Dr. Thafer. I have a brother in the United States."

"You do? Where?"

"In Lubbock, Texas. He's at Texas A & M, studying civil engineering."

"How long has he been there?" Thafer asks.

"Three years. We just hope he comes back before he marries his American girlfriend."

Thafer is bewildered, then becomes embarrassed when he realizes that they have noticed his bewilderment. He feels heat going through him as he begins to sweat. "This is what happens to me when I'm surrounded by beautiful women," he says awkwardly.

The women burst into loud laughter as he leads them to a round table and maroon chairs, all gleaming from their early morning dusting.

"The senior people never come before nine," says Reem. "I'm sure they don't expect you before nine, Dr. Thafer."

"I'm an early riser. I don't mind coming early."

"Shall we all come and join you for coffee every morning?" asks Nahida playfully.

"I'll be happy to see all of you," he says awkwardly.

"Are you sure?" she persists.

The women burst into loud laughter again.

"How many children do you have, Dr. Thafer?" asks Leila.

"Four, two boys and two girls," he says.

"Is your wife American?" asks Suha.

"He's already answered that," says Nahida.

The women laugh again loudly.

"Now seriously," says Leila. "Why do our men do this? They go to America to get educated, so we rejoice. Then they fall in love with American women, marry them, have children, and never return. We lose them forever. What's wrong with our women?"

"It's partly our fault," says Reem. "The American woman is less demanding than we are. She's also more liberated. In a way I don't blame our men, but I agree that those who go to America to get educated have an obligation to return with their families."

"It isn't the Arab woman's fault," says Leila. "The Arab woman is a victim of our culture. She's been abused, exploited, ignored, and sometimes enslaved. Most Arab men don't treat their women kindly. Arab husbands can divorce their wives at the drop of a hat. We need our enlightened men to return, marry our women, and encourage their liberation. Even if they should decide to marry American women, they should return with their wives. Maybe their wives could help in emancipating us."

"What do you think, Dr. Thafer?" asks Reem.

Thafer looks at the seven women, their serious faces now all directed toward him. "In that day, seven women shall take hold of one man"—he remembers the verse in the Book of Isaiah. "I'll tell you what I think," he says. "I know that some Arab males have been unkind to their women, but Arab males are not the only ones. Some American males have been just as unkind to their women, sometimes even more so. It is true that the American female has made long strides, but only after years of struggle for equality. Arab women must emulate their American sisters. Arab males will not voluntarily relinquish the advantages they have, nor will they do for their women what they do for themselves. Why should they?"

"You're inciting us to revolution, Dr. Thafer," says Nahida.

The women laugh again.

"I agree," says Leila. "The Arab woman has to liberate herself. The Arab male won't do it for her. I have five children, four boys and one girl. I worship my daughter, but I wish they were all boys."

"But why?" asks Reem.

"Because this is a man's world," says Leila.

The women then stand up.

"We should be going," says Reem. "The bosses will be coming soon."

They walk to the door and say their good-byes.

"We'll be back tomorrow," says the good-natured Nahida as the seven women laugh.

"Marhaba, Dr. Thafer," says Suhaila Sa'adeh, rising and cheerfully extending her hand as Thafer enters the conference room of OAPEC.

The tall woman's animated greeting exhilarates him. "Marhaba, marhaba, Dr. Suhaila," he says, walking toward the

Palestinian woman and giving her a warm handshake.

"Please sit down, Dr. Thafer," she says inviting him to sit next to her.

"Have you been here long, Dr. Suhaila?" he asks.

"Not more than a minute." She pauses a little. "Won't you please call me Suhaila?"

"Of course. Please call me Thafer."

"They'll be here soon, I'm sure," she says.

They sit a chair or two from the head of the table, where a sign reads, "The Secretary General." She has taken a chair closer to the secretary general. Thafer takes the seat to her right.

Hamdan enters and greets them.

The secretary general enters, smiling broadly.

"Good morning, Brother Ziyad," they all say, rising from their chairs.

The secretary general walks toward Thafer and shakes his hand firmly. "I hope your suite at the Hilton is comfortable. I understand it won't be long now. Your house is being cleaned and decorated. You should be able to move in after a couple of days."

"Everything is just fine, Brother Ziyad."

"Please be seated," says the secretary general. "I thought we'd have a meeting this morning in order to acquaint Dr. Thafer with some of our pending projects. I also thought that we'd discuss our timetable. I want Dr. Thafer to get to know both of you. The more urgent projects are essentially economic and you need to clear all the legal problems with Dr. Thafer. So he needs to work closely with the two of you, especially with you, Dr. Suhaila." He pauses. "We have piles and piles of work, Dr. Thafer. The first thing you have to help us with is the Arab Shipping Company, centered in Bahrain and authorized by the Council of Arab Oil Ministers two years ago. Your predecessor prepared the articles of incorporation, which were approved and ratified by all the member states. They have also authorized and ratified a total capital investment of $450 million out of which the board of directors of the Arab Shipping Company has authorized the issuance of only ninety million dollars of stock as a beginning. As you know, OAPEC has eleven members now. It had only nine members when the issuance of ninety million dollars was authorized. Shortly before your arrival, Dr. Thafer, Egypt and Syria became OAPEC's newest members."

Thafer listens, taking notes as the secretary general speaks deliberately in Oxford English.

"We've already requested each of the nine member states to pay a share of $50,000,000," says Hamdan.

"Is that right, Dr. Suhaila?" asks the secretary general.

"I wasn't aware of that," she says.

"Oh yes, I made the computation," says Hamdan.

"I now remember signing the request for payment," says the secretary general. "The payments should be coming soon."

If the board of directors, Thafer asks himself, authorized the issuance of only ninety million dollars to be distributed among nine members, how could they request the payment of fifty million dollars from each member state? But he says nothing.

"When we're through here, Dr. Suhaila," says the secretary general, "please take Dr. Thafer to your office and review the pending projects with him."

"I'll be glad to do that."

"I know that you're anxious to make a trip to the West Bank, Dr. Thafer," says the secretary general. "So we won't overload you now. When do you have in mind leaving?"

"On April 25, and I'll be back in one week."

"We'll plan it that way then. Please take Dr. Thafer to your office, Dr. Suhaila. Show him the pending projects and work out a plan between the two of you. That's all I have now."

After the brief meeting with the secretary general, Suhaila and Thafer walk to her office. "Please come in," she says, opening her office door for him.

Feeling instant kinship with the Palestinian woman, he is completely at ease, instinctively trusting her. "The computation Hamdan made concerning what's due from each member state for the Arab Shipping Company's issued capital was wrong, Suhaila."

"I know," she says smiling. "Instead of dividing the ninety million dollars issued capital by nine and requesting only ten million dollars from each member state, he divided the entire $450 million authorized capital by nine and demanded a walloping fifty million dollars from each member state. That's Hamdan."

Thafer smiles. "It's actually not an uncommon error."

"I didn't realize they already made the request for payment. What a mess!"

"That can easily be corrected," Thafer says.

"I hope so."

"I just had a pleasant meeting with Mukhtar. What a gentleman! He helped me open a new account in the National Bank of Kuwait and ordered a month's salary in advance after paying me early for April."

"It sounds just like Mukhtar."

"I want to tell you about a conversation I had yesterday with Hamdan."

She looks at him with a faintly scornful smile. "I suggest that you be careful with him. I wouldn't pay attention to what he says about Mukhtar or about anyone. I'd just listen to him politely."

"Actually, I gathered that much, and that's what I'll do. But that's not really what's worrying me."

"Hamdan thrives on gossip. Unfortunately, his gossip has hurt many people, but he's known around the organization for his gossip, sadly, and people tend to take what he says with a grain of salt."

"Yesterday he came to my office. After lambasting practically everyone I had met, excluding you, he told me that the staff of OAPEC assume that I work for the American CIA."

Her hazel eyes narrow, and she frowns. "That Hamdan! He's sick! Ignore him! Ignore him completely! Don't let this trouble you in the least. Just go on with your work as though you haven't heard it."

There is a long pause.

"I understand that you had some visitors this morning," Suhaila says, smiling.

"Yes, how did you know?"

"Leila told me. The women of OAPEC are impressed."

"I hope they don't carry out their threat to come every morning."

"They won't. They just came to introduce themselves. I'll come to the office early, and that should discourage them."

XIII

Thafer's older brother, Rassem, who lives and works in Saudi Arabia, is expected to arrive in Kuwait that evening, but he shows up unexpectedly early in the morning. When Thafer goes to Uncle Muneer and Mama Adla's apartment in Hawalli for lunch he does not realize that his brother Rassem has arrived. His reunion with his brother is highly emotional. Afterward, the Allams sit for lunch.

"I want you to say grace, Muneer," Mama Adla says to her husband. "Let's thank the Almighty for Thafer's reunion with all of us. And I want Thafer to hear his family's grace. He hasn't heard it in many years."

All the Allams—men, women and children—bow their heads as they sit around the food spread on white sheets on the floor of the crowded living room. Thafer holds his brother's hand tightly.

The old man clears his throat: "Our Lord God, we thank you for all your mercies. We thank you for returning our child to us. We thank you for our being, for Your Providence, whether we are healthy or sick, wealthy or poor, and we thank you for our life in this land and for the times we lived in our own. You are All Wise and All Powerful. Make us always aware of our brethren who live far away and of our countrymen who still live in refugee camps. You know all. We know very little. Amen."

After lunch, Thafer and his brother Rassem retire to the room of their young nephew, Nizar. Thafer looks at his older brother's graying hair and deep-set dark brown eyes. He becomes fascinated by his brother's long eyelashes. It is as though a younger Ayoub Allam, their father, is now mysteriously before him. "I admire your resemblance to Ayoub Allam," Thafer tells his brother.

"That's a compliment! Many people have told me lately that I look a lot like Father. I'm not as tall though. As I get older, my face begins to look like his. Even I can see that when I look at myself in the mirror. It gives me a funny sensation."

"Father was a tall man!" says Thafer.

"About six foot four! I'm only five foot ten. Kamal is also five foot ten. Saleem, may the Lord's mercies be upon his resting soul, was six foot four. How tall are you, Thafer?"

"I'm six foot two inches."

"You and Kamal look very much like Mother. Saleem and I take after Father."

"I often wonder what Mother looks like now."

"She's aged, Thafer! She's aged!"

"When was the last time you saw her?"

"About six months ago."

"I'm going to the West Bank soon."

"When?"

"I've arranged to go on May 10. I'll go to Amman first to see Kamal and his family. Then I'll cross the bridge to the West Bank."

"You may know that Kamal can't go to the West Bank because of his involvement with the PLO."

"I know."

"Now that you're back, I hope you'll settle down. We need you here. We all do. You're a rare commodity here. We are all proud of you. All the Allam family is proud of your education and of your coming back. They all consider it an honor that you are an Allam, Thafer."

Thafer remains silent.

"I don't know what you're thinking, but what you can do to help our homeland no one else here can do, Thafer."

"I understand that we can't contact Mother by phone."

"Not by phone, but we can send a message to her with someone. You'll probably get there before the message, though."

"I think it's better that we don't send a message. God forbid, if anything happens and I am delayed, we don't want her to worry."

"I agree."

"I want to ask about Father, Rassem. Where did he get his military training?"

"In Turkey. Why do you ask?"

"When I was in Beirut a few days ago, Father's involvement in the 1936–39 Palestinian Uprising came up. Hani Amri spoke in glowing terms about Father's role in the uprising. I'm curious about that. What did Father actually do? How did he become a military tactician?"

"He played a very important role in the Uprising. He nearly drove the British out of Palestine and was a brilliant military tactician. Actually, he did not elect to be a military man. It was imposed on him when at age twenty-five he was forcibly inducted into the Ottoman armed forces during World War I. He began as a foot soldier. After two years, he became a junior officer. His superiors apparently discovered that he was a talented man, so they sent him to an elite military academy in

Adana, Turkey, where he received an extensive military education and in fact became a high-ranking instructor there."

"What was Father's role in the uprising?"

"He was the brains. You don't remember this because you
were too young, but the British put a price on Father's head.
They wanted him dead or alive. He had outsmarted and outmaneuvered the superior British forces with fewer than five
thousand poorly equipped, ill-fed, but dedicated rebels."

"What exactly did he do? How did he do it?"

"He controlled the hills. He and his forces hid during the
day and drove the British forces out of their minds at night.
Father knew every hill, every cave and every inch of the homeland. He also knew where the enemy was. He knew the value
of intelligence. In those days, no one utilized intelligence. Our
people were peasants. Their struggle was based on unorga-
nized hit or miss tactics, which got them nowhere. Father had
a plan—part of it to demoralize the enemy. His approach
included a great concern for the lives of his men. Early in
1937 his forces had control of more than 80 percent of the
homeland, with minimal losses. Then the British introduced
one hundred thousand troops with tanks, aircraft, and artillery
and committed one of the worst acts of barbarism against
men, women, and children civilians: they mercilessly pounded
the hills day and night from the air and with heavy artillery.
So in 1939 the uprising was crushed. Father was demoralized.
He lost most of his troops in battle. When he came home, he
was a broken man, Thafer, and the British pursued him, even
after the uprising was crushed, but they never caught him.
Then World War II broke out, and they had other and more
serious things on their minds. That's the tragic story of our
father. It's the tragic story of all of us. Sooner or later, history
will avenge Father's humiliation. I just hope that we'll live to
see it. Some of us, I'm sure, will play a role in that. I'm ten
years older than you, Thafer, so it may be too late for me, but

I hope that you'll be able to honor Father's memory by your contributions. I hope that our children will, too."

XIV

Having accepted the invitation, Thafer goes by himself to Hamdan's house two weeks after his arrival in Kuwait. He is received at the door by Hamdan and his gracious American wife. At first he doesn't recognize Hamdan. In his Western black suit and black bow tie, with his curly black hair and boyish face, Hamdan looks like a waiter. He looked more distinguished in the white Arab robe, and the checkered red and white headcloth somehow gave him more dignity.

Hamdan's wife wears a long, blue silk evening dress, which draws attention to her blue eyes. She is quite friendly to Thafer.

"Ahlan Wa Sahlan," she says, using the traditional Arabic greeting—"you are kin, and this is your home." "Tafaddal," she adds, "please come in."

"Shukrun, Shukrun, Mrs. Mishaan," Thafer replies, "thank you, thank you."

"Joan, please. Just Joan."

"I'm Thafer. No one ever calls me Dr. in the States."

"This is the land of titles," she continues as they stroll toward the spacious living room. "I understand that you've been living in New York for more than twenty years."

"Yes, we lived in Ithaca for nearly eight years, and we've been in Ashfield for about twelve years. Ashfield is a suburb of Osaga, which is a twin city of Syracuse."

"I've heard of Syracuse, but I don't believe I've heard of Osaga. I'm from New Haven, Connecticut. My parents still live there. My father is connected with the university. Please come in and make yourself comfortable. Our other guests will begin to come soon."

How on earth did this sweet, beautiful woman end up marrying him, Thafer wonders.

"We've invited the American ambassador and his wife," she says. "A few other couples from the American embassy are also coming tonight."

"That'll be nice. I look forward to meeting them. There must be many Americans in Kuwait."

"About a thousand American families. You may want to register your name with the embassy. It isn't required, but it's a precaution should there be an emergency."

"I think I will."

Other couples begin to arrive.

Hamdan's wife goes to the door to receive some guests.

"Alcoholic beverages are allowed only at embassies in Kuwait, Dr. Thafer," Hamdan says as Joan greets the guests and leads them toward Thafer. "We get ours through our friends in the embassies."

"I see."

Joan introduces Thafer to the American ambassador to Kuwait and his wife—Thomas and Helen Hatfield.

"Just Tom and Helen, Thafer," says the American ambassador.

"Hi," says Thafer.

"It's about time we met an Arab who speaks as we do," jokes Helen Hatfield. "Practically all of our educated Arab friends speak like the English, even though most of them have slight Arabic accents. It's refreshing to meet an Arab who speaks like an American."

"So, Thafer, how long have you lived in the States?" asks the ambassador.

"About twenty years, Tom."

"As long as I've lived in the Middle East. I was born in Egypt, where my father was a U.S. foreign service officer, but I grew up in the United States."

"You must speak Arabic."

"Yes, fluently. I speak like an Arab, but someone like you would immediately spot me as a foreigner. I still have a slight American accent. I can also read and write Arabic."

Joan brings another American couple, John and Sally Kazolas, to meet Thafer. John Kazolas is the embassy's economics officer. He is tall and has Eastern features.

"We're Greek Americans from Philadelphia," says the amiable Sally Kazolas. "Is your family coming?"

"They might," says Thafer hesitatingly.

"I'd like to come to talk to you in your office sometime before long if it's convenient," abruptly interjects her husband.

"Anytime," says Thafer, trying to conceal his surprise.

"I'll call you before I come," he says as he moves away.

The embassy's political officer and his wife, Charles and Nancy Cunningham are the next couple to be introduced to Thafer.

"Nice to see you," says the political officer, not looking at Thafer.

"Hello, sir."

"You just arrived two weeks ago?" his wife asks.

"That's right."

"Welcome to the inferno," she laughs and moves on.

Thafer looks at the Americans who have just come in. Then he walks around and converses with some of them.

On the whole, the conversation with the embassy people is pleasant enough, especially with some of the women. The men seem somehow distant. Only a few appear straightforward or relaxed, and he can find no kindred spirits among them. He likes Sally Kazolas, the pretty, petite wife of the economics officer. He thinks that Mary Pat would have liked her too, but he finds himself repulsed by some of the embassy wives' elaborate evening dresses and overpowering perfume. This bit of ostentation seems to him inappropriate and not in line with the modest and unpretentious America he would like to see represented.

He is also unhappy with the way this reception is going. He was invited to come for dinner at 8:00 P.M., presumably to meet his new colleagues and their families. The presence of the American embassy staff was supposed to be secondary. Now it is almost 9:15, and none of OAPEC's staff have arrived. That's a funny coincidence, he thinks. He wonders if he is being scrutinized. No, he decides; Joan, Hamdan's cultured wife, probably thinks it is nice for me to meet some Americans. Although he doesn't want to be paranoid, he continues to think that he is being scanned. He wonders why Charlie Cunningham, the political officer, ignores him. Because diplomats are sometimes arrogant, he decides. He remembers that Suhaila told him to forget what Hamdan said about the CIA.

At long last the Arab guests begin to arrive. He relaxes.

Ziyad, the secretary general, is greeted warmly by all the embassy staff. That's to be expected, Thafer muses. Ziyad is a very important man.

"Hello, Brother Thafer, hello," says the secretary general, smiling and embracing Thafer and shaking his hand.

"Hello, Brother Ziyad," says Thafer, happy to see his new boss.

"What are you drinking?"

"Champagne," says Thafer, feeling pretentious.

"That devil Hamdan, he's got champagne. I think that's what I'll take then."

"Are we the first ragheads to arrive?" jokes the secretary general.

"I guess we are," Thafer laughs.

"Did you recognize Hamdan when you came in?"

Thafer, laughing, couldn't contain himself.

"I keep telling him to stick to his white robe, but he insists on looking like a busboy."

Thafer laughs hard again.

"When I was in college in England in the early forties, some Arab students insisted on wearing the white robe, which was all right, but they looked quite comical when they wore an English derby with it."

"Thafer," says Hamdan's wife, Joan, coming up to Thafer and holding his arm, "I want you to meet Reem's husband, Professor Salah."

"Excuse me, Brother Ziyad," says Thafer. "I'll be right back."

"Go ahead," says the affable secretary general. "This is your evening."

The secretary general is warm and witty, a side of him Thafer hadn't seen. Thafer is also surprised to see Reem Makram because she is the only OAPEC secretary at the party. She is with her husband, and Joan is taking him to meet them. They must be good friends, he muses.

"Thafer," says Joan, "you already know Reem. This is her husband, Dr. Salah Makram. The Makrams are good friends of ours."

"It's an honor to meet you, Dr. Thafer," says the tall, dignified, athletic-looking man.

"I'm honored to meet you, sir. Good evening, Reem."

"I'm always uncomfortable in the company of so many diplomats," says Salah Makram uneasily.

"Probably as uncomfortable as I am."

"Reem said that you've lived in the United States all of your adult life, Dr. Thafer," says Makram, while his wife smiles nervously.

"That's true, Dr. Salah."

"When one lives in another country for so long," he says as he looks at Thafer, "one even begins to look like the people of that country. I know you're Palestinian because Reem told me you were, but if I had seen you on the street, I would never have guessed it. I would've thought you were an American. Looking at your face close range," he continues, "I can see the Palestinian in it. Yet, the minute you move or talk, even when you speak Arabic, I see the map of the United States all over you."

"I wouldn't know," says Thafer, feeling self-conscious, but liking the natural and unaffected way the man speaks. "We never know how others see us, but your observation is probably accurate."

Dr. Makram and Reem smile as they continue to look at Thafer with amusement.

"What brings you to Kuwait, Dr. Makram?" Thafer asks.

"Please call me Salah. I'm on loan as a science professor at Kuwait University. I understand that you are a nuclear engineer, Dr. Thafer."

"Just call me Thafer, please. Yes, I studied nuclear engineering, but I am basically a lawyer. Everything I studied about nuclear physics in the fifties is obsolete now."

"That's not necessarily so. I bet if you wanted to do something with it someday, you could."

"I think I'll stick to law."

Salah Makram and Thafer Allam are quiet for a while, watching the gathering crowd.

Suhaila arrives. She has an older woman with her. Both are wearing modest Palestinian dresses, long and embroidered, but without the colorful cummerbund. Suhaila does not wear the mantilla, but the older woman has a white one that covers her hair.

"Thafer," says Suhaila, "I want you to meet my mother."

"Hello, hello, a thousand hellos, Thafer," Suhaila's mother greets him, sending shivers down his spine.

"Hello, hello," he answers as he walks toward the slender, dignified older woman and extends both hands. He looks into her tender eyes and suddenly feels dizzy.

The older woman holds his hands, looks into his eyes, then releases him. She reaches to straighten her white mantilla, then walks toward the Egyptian couple.

"They know one another only too well although they have never met," Suhaila tells the puzzled Egyptian couple, perhaps responding to the astonishment in their eyes.

Thafer walks away dazed, hardly knowing what has happened to him. He hears a loudspeaker blaring in his ears. You must all leave at once. His dignified slender mother had reached to her head for her white mantilla, her gentle face anguished. Let's go to Tulkarm, my dear, she had entreated his father. Now, my dear, she had pleaded.

A Kuwaiti businessman's wife is introduced to Thafer as a Sudanese, but she has a fair complexion, light brown hair, and hazel eyes.

"How is it that you're so fair?" he jokes. "They don't make these in the Sudan, do they?"

"My parents came from Aleppo in North Syria," she replies, smiling. "There are many fair Syrians in Aleppo."

"Yes, I know," says Thafer. "Were you born in Aleppo?"

"I was born in the Sudan," she says, "and lived there with my parents most of my life until I was married."

The group grows to a motley mix of nationalities with clothing styles, accents, languages, and professions of all descriptions. Indian waiters serve drinks and pass trays of hors d'oeuvres. Thafer is hungry. He had not realized that the main course would not be offered until close to midnight.

Around 11:30 Mukhtar is the last to arrive with his wife and sister. "It's customary to serve dinner late at these receptions," he tells Thafer.

"I now know."

"Those who are not great socializers, like us," says Mukhtar smiling, "may come an hour or so before dinner."

Finally at midnight dinner is served. An enormous spread of Western and Eastern foods: soups, salads, egg dishes, fish, poultry, and meat dishes; Eastern dishes with chickpeas and lentils, the traditional foods of the poor; French, English, and American foods; Arab foods seasoned with spices, garlic, onions, and herbs; Western and Arab breads; assortments of rice and vegetables; various kinds of pickles; as well as puddings, cakes, sweets and fruits. It is truly a feast.

After dinner, they have coffee. Then guests begin to thank Hamdan and Joan, and leave.

"Would you stay a while, Thafer?" whispers Hamdan's gracious wife as good-byes are being said. "I've asked some couples to stay."

"Yes, I'll be happy to."

The spacious living room seems quiet. Those who stay gather in one corner as traditional rhythmic Arabic music plays in the background from a stereo in the now almost empty room.

The Sudanese woman and Joan join hands, dancing to the beat of the music. Reem Makram joins them, trying to match their natural perfection in a beautifully executed Eastern dance. Helen Hatfield, the ambassador's wife, joins as well.

Where did Joan learn this? Thafer asks himself. She's dancing the dabkah. She's leading.

Two Arab men start another circle and motion for him to join them.

He has not danced the dabkah since he was a boy growing up on his family farm. He doesn't know whether he can still dance it, but he decides to try. I hope I don't make a fool of myself, he thinks.

The music grows louder, louder, and still louder.

He lets himself go. He moves naturally. He is ecstatic, in a trance. He stamps his feet and jumps.

Joan leaves her group and takes his arm. She dances the dabkah with him. He follows her expressive, graceful movements, stamping his feet and jumping in unison with her.

"Dance, Thafer, dance," she says.

He feels the hypnotic music as they all cheer.

Dance, dance, dance, he tells himself. Where did she learn this? he asks himself again.

They dance and dance and dance until the rhythmic music slows and finally stops.

XV

"Thafer, my dear," says Mama Adla, as they approach his cousin Wahby's house in Fuaad's old red Saab, "there'll be a lot of friends and relatives at Wahby's house."

"Yes, I know, Mama Adla."

Uncle Muneer and Mama Adla sit in the back seat with Thafer. Thafer's brother, Rassem, sits in the front next to Fuaad. Thafer's cousin Wahby's house is in the same Hawalli ghetto. Cousin Wahby, the Arabic language administrator of Kuwait's Ministry of Education, has invited Thafer and his relatives for dinner that night.

"Rassem," Mama Adla resumes, reaching over the front seat to tap Rassem's shoulder. "They're all prepared for a big political discussion, and I don't like that. They're all ready to ask questions. Tell them your brother is tired. He's just had a very long journey. We want this to be just a social get-together. What do you think, Muneer?" she turns to her husband.

"I don't think we can do that, Adla," replies the old man. "If we tell them this, they'll all think he's afraid to talk. It won't look good. He can handle it."

"I don't think they want to be hostile, Mama Adla," says Rassem. "They're curious. They'll probably ask about his job, about life in the United States, and the like. I agree he can handle that."

"Anyway, Mother," says Fuaad, "wherever he goes in Kuwait, he'll run into Palestinians. The family might as well expose him to their questions and anxieties."

"You'll handle them, Thafer dear," says his aunt, her hand touching his shoulder gently, "I'm sure of it. You're a lawyer."

They get out of Fuaad's car and proceed to Wahby's house.

Several relatives, friends, and neighbors are already there when they arrive. The scene is similar to the one at Thafer's uncle and aunt's house two weeks before. Wahby's house is a little bigger, however, and its living room is more spacious. There are also several new faces, more people than were at his uncle and aunt's house. Some speak with an Egyptian accent and some with a Kuwaiti accent.

Thafer is touched by the mothers who bring their children to tell him how they are related to his children. First and second cousins, cousins once and twice removed, nephews and nieces from his half-sisters with their children—crowd the living room. More than fifty people all come to welcome him that night.

The women begin to yodel, as Mama Adla dabs at her eyes. Thafer has rested all afternoon, nearly four hours, and he is determined to be in complete control of his emotions.

A big Palestinian dinner is prepared in his honor, and it smells good. It is like many family gatherings in Jerusalem and on the family farm in the past. He watches as two whole, spit-roasted sheep are brought in—one placed on the table in the living room for the men, the other on the floor of the adjacent room for the women. The men and the women begin to separate.

It is a festive evening. Fuaad and Wahby begin to dismember the sheep with their bare hands.

Pick up a plate and eat like everyone else, Thafer tells himself. You can't be squeamish. You've got to use your bare hands like everyone else.

He tries not to look surprised and doesn't want to watch the way they eat.

I should just eat like they do, he muses, but he can't help looking around. Oh boy! he exclaims to himself.

Yet these are his people, who love him. He wants to eat with them and be one of them. He doesn't want to make any mistakes or appear as though he has forgotten his heritage and his upbringing.

His brother Rassem looks worried. He walks toward Thafer and wants to help him, but Thafer confidently reaches for a plate, fills it himself with his bare hands, moves to a chair in a corner, and sits. He hopes that his two brothers will come and sit with him, and they do.

"When was the last time you saw an entire sheep on a plank like this, Thafer?" Rassem asks.

"Not since the days on the farm."

"Those were the days," Uncle Muneer sighs.

"Yes, those were the days," Rassem says.

Thafer is quiet.

"You don't have to eat with your bare hands, my boy, if you don't want to," says Uncle Muneer. "Use a fork or a spoon, whatever makes you comfortable."

"Let him eat with his bare hands, Uncle Muneer," says Rassem. "It's good for his soul."

"I'm sure it is," Thafer says.

"Whatever you feel like doing, my boy," says Uncle Muneer. "You'll see some eating with their hands and some using forks and knives or spoons. Whatever makes you comfortable, Thafer."

"I think I'm going to eat with my bare hands. I haven't done this in a long time."

"Good for you, Thafer," says Rassem.

What would Mary Pat think if she saw me eating like this? Thafer asks himself.

The commotion subsides. Thafer washes his hands and comes back to his seat.

The men and the women gather in the living room again. Everyone is looking at him. His relatives and their friends are sipping their coffee and tea. The living room and the hallway are quiet. Except for a little clattering of dishes, the entire apartment is unnaturally, even ominously still, as Uncle Muneer sits on Thafer's right and Rassem on his left.

Rassem reaches for Thafer's hand and presses it, and Uncle Muneer moves his chair a little closer to Thafer's.

"Brother Thafer," comes a voice from across the room, "we're hoping that you can share some of your experiences in the United States with us."

Thafer looks in the direction of the voice and sees a moustachioed man wearing a light gray flannel Western suit and a checkered black and white Arab head cloth.

"Can we ask you some questions that are on our minds, Brother Thafer?" the man continues, his dark brown eyes fixed directly on Thafer. Worry beads occupy his restless fingers.

"I'll be glad to answer any questions," says Thafer, confused by the man's accent and struck by his attire. "I want to say," he continues, a slight tremor in his voice, "that even though I spent many years in the United States, I'm no expert on it."

"We're all your kin and family, Brother Thafer, " the man resumes, no doubt taking note of Thafer's nervousness. "Our questions are not intended to rattle you. We rarely have a chance to discuss these matters with someone like yourself who is both one of us and, so to speak, one of them."

Thafer looks at the man again, still not sure of his accent, but liking his forthright approach. He relaxes a little.

"We're a bitter people, Thafer," the man says, "and bitterness tends to blind us. Were I to guess, I'd say that your vision is better than ours."

Thafer listens intently.

"The American foreign minister," the man continues, "is coming to Kuwait in a few days. As you know, the U.S.

government, without warning, devalued the dollar by 10 percent six months ago, then by 10 percent more a few days ago. The oil-producing countries of the world, most of whom are Arab, sell their crude oil for about two dollars per barrel. The producing countries have been struggling with the more advanced industrial consuming countries for several months to raise the price of crude oil by fifteen cents per barrel. Finally, they reached an agreement to raise the price ten cents a barrel, which is a modest increase considering the enormous profits the buyers make. Mind you, they buy the Arab crude for about two dollars a barrel; spend less than two dollars for transportation, insurance, refining, and other expenses before they make it available to the consumers; then sell it to Americans and other consumers for about forty-eight dollars per barrel. You can see, Thafer, the unconscionably high profits that are being made at the expense not only of the Arab producers, but of the consumers. After long and difficult negotiations that lasted months, the Arab and other oil-producing states agreed with the Western buyers to raise the price of crude oil by this meager ten cents per barrel, only to find themselves thirty cents per barrel poorer thanks to the 20 percent devaluation of the dollar. Is Mr. Rogers, Thafer, coming to the Middle East this month in order to sugarcoat the pill of devaluation? What can the weak oil-producing countries do? How long do we have to endure this double-dealing?"

The man is really upset, Thafer notices.

"Can we benefit from your knowledge, Thafer? You're a product of both cultures. Do you think we're justified in feeling the way we do? How can we communicate to the American foreign minister, without inviting a military invasion, that we deserve an equitable part of this enormous profit that derives from our oil? Don't our people also deserve schools, hospitals, housing and good highways?" Still composed, he asks, "Do you feel like addressing these concerns?"

Thafer isn't prepared for this. He thinks the discussion
will center on the Palestinian-Israeli conflict, but the man's
question really impresses him. It is an honest question, and he
is determined to give an honest answer. He does not want to
repeat his timid conduct of a few days ago in the Amris' car,
but wants to be careful. This man, he guesses, like many of
the relatives and friends gathered here, is highly educated. He
thinks about what his young nephew Nizar told him about
the educated Palestinians, and he remembers what Professor
Salah Makram said—that although he could see the Palestinian in Thafer's face, he could also see the American in his
movements and demeanor. So Thafer wants to avoid saying
anything arrogant or cocky. He wants to speak as calmly as
the intelligent man spoke and say something helpful, without
being condescending.

His relatives and their friends are all looking at him ex-
pectantly. We're all your kin and family, he remembers the
man saying to him. Uncle Muneer's loving hand presses his,
reminding him that his two brothers also sit next to him.

"Your question is well taken, sir," Thafer starts cautiously.

"Safi, Thafer," the man interrupts. "I'm your cousin."

"Safi," continues Thafer, "of course our people deserve a
higher standard of living. Of course they deserve schools and
hospitals and housing and good highways. But first and foremost they deserve to be rid of the tyranny of corruption and
the madness of fear. The devaluation of the U.S. dollar by the
government of the United States, in my opinion, is a despicable, underhanded trick, harmful not only to the oil-producing
countries but to the United States and to its people. The
people of the United States are sometimes as much victims of
the misguided acts of their government as are the others affected by these acts. The devaluation of the dollar, which harms
the Arab people, is no exception and is bound to bring as
much harm to the people of the United States as it has to the

people of the oil-producing countries and to others. The devaluation reduces the purchasing power of the oil-producing
countries by 20 percent. From where do these countries pur-
chase their automobiles and refrigerators and television sets?
To whom do they look to design and build their schools and
hospitals and highways? To the industrial countries of the
world—the United States, Western Europe, and Japan, of
course. But if the oil-producing countries' purchasing power
is reduced by 20 percent, then the industrial countries' ability
to market their products is likewise reduced. If the developing
countries are unable to buy, who will? The industrial countries' factories would be forced to manufacture less, which
would result in higher unemployment and eventual recession.
The tragedy is that the perpetrators of this foolhardy act do
not seem to understand the consequences. In my opinion, the
coming years, or even months will be difficult for the people
of the industrial countries, including the people of the United
States, as a result of this reckless move."

Thafer speaks with conviction, making a determined effort
to control the tone of his voice. They are all listening attentively and waiting for more.

"I read that the American foreign minister is coming to
the Middle East and is visiting Kuwait," Thafer continues. He
pauses a little. "In the United States, Safi," he explains, "they
refer to their minister of foreign affairs as the secretary of
state. If I were to give advice to the minister of foreign affairs
in Kuwait as to what he should tell Mr. Rogers during his
visit here," he continues, "I would advise him to tell the
American secretary of state that the oil-producing countries,
including Kuwait, will increase the price of crude oil by thirty
more cents, and if the U.S. government wishes to continue to
devalue its dollar, then the Arab oil-producing countries will
continue to raise their prices until the U.S. dollar becomes
worthless. In the meantime, all the Arab oil-producing coun-

tries should convert their reserves to Swiss francs, Deutsch marks, and Japanese yen."

They all look at Thafer with surprise.

"You expressed concern, Safi," he continues, "that in talking to the U.S. secretary of state, the Arab people should be concerned about inviting a possible American invasion. I am saddened by this concern, but I can understand it. I am saddened that the United States has become a source of violence and a symbol of peril rather than of peace and security. In my opinion, however, it is in no position to undertake such a move, which might bring about a direct confrontation between it and the Soviet Union. The Middle East, after all, borders the Soviet Union. I doubt that the Soviets would remain quiet were the United States to undertake such a dangerous step. But this fear saddens me, and the Arab governments must conquer it. Unless they do, they will have difficulty improving the living standard of their people. They will not easily build schools and hospitals and housing and good highways."

"Thafer," says Cousin Wahby, "if the United States does not see that the devaluation of their dollar is harmful to the American people, as you've just explained, then we must conclude that they don't recognize the economic and political significance of our part of the world to them."

"The American people haven't the slightest idea of the potential significance of this part of the world to the world economy or even to their own economy."

"Why is that, Thafer? It seems strange."

Thafer looks at his cousin and appears flustered.

"Is it that the Jews of the United States and their lobbies, about which we hear so much, are partly responsible?" asks Wahby. "Do the American Jews still portray us as camel herders and pearl fishermen?"

Thafer continues to look flustered. "I don't think," he hesitates, "I don't think, Cousin Wahby, that we can blame all

Jews or only Jews for negative portrayals of the Arabs." Thafer pauses. There is complete silence in the room. He becomes nervous, afraid to repeat the clumsiness of remarks he made in Beirut when he told the Amri brothers that Israel was smarter than the Palestinians. They are all looking at him. "Yes, there are special influence groups in the United States, Cousin Wahby," Thafer says cautiously. "And it's true that one of the most powerful of these is the American-Israeli Political Action Committee, AIPAC, sometimes referred to as the Jewish or the Israeli lobby. This group is supported by an organized American Jewish community, but not by the entire American Jewish community."

"This is the first time I've heard about anything called the organized American Jewish community, Thafer," says Wahby. "What's the difference between them and American Jews?"

"In my early years in the United States, Cousin Wahby," says Thafer, now feeling a little more confident, "I used to think that all Jews in the United States were actually Zionists, organized in some corporate community, which, as the Palestine problem grew in world importance, was solidly and uncritically supportive of Israel. But as I became more acquainted with Americans, I found, even when I was a university student, this was not accurate. I met many Jews who expressed serious reservations about Zionism and about Israel. I discovered that there is a difference between the Jewish community in general in the United States and the organized Jewish community. There's no recognized process in the United States for electing spokesmen or leaders to represent all American Jews. What does exist is a structure of Jewish leaders, representing various Jewish organizations that are established for religious, political, social, and educational purposes. It's this structure that I refer to as the organized Jewish community. The organized Jews and the Israeli or Jewish influence groups have made Israel the focal point of their activities."

"I'm distressed, Thafer," says Wahby, "to hear you say that the American people don't have the slightest idea of the economic and political significance of our part of the world on their economy and on the world economy. That so-called organized Jewish community surely must consider these issues. Are Americans also uninformed about the Palestinian-Israeli and the Arab-Israeli conflicts? Or is there debate about this conflict as a serious problem affecting the national interest of the United States?"

"The complexities of the Palestinian-Israeli and the Arab-Israeli conflicts are rarely fully and intelligently debated as major questions affecting the national interest of the United States. In my casual contacts with Americans, especially American Jews, when it somehow becomes known that I am a Palestinian, the Palestinian-Israeli and the Arab-Israeli conflicts may then creep into the conversation. With Jews, I never initiate discussions of the conflicts, but they may ask. And when I'm given an opportunity to explain even a little of the history of the conflict, or something of our family's experiences or my own experiences, they're very often surprised. Only occasionally do I get a rebuttal delivered with anger or malice. Most Americans, including Jews, with whom I have had discussions about the conflict have no idea what the American Israeli Political Action Committee is. Most know nothing at all of the rights of our people. Some don't even know who the Palestinians are or what their grievances and their struggle are all about. Most of them, particularly the Jews, are under the impression that the Palestinians left Palestine voluntarily, at the urging of the Arab states, which had teased them with the illusion that they could return after an Arab military victory in which the Israelis would be driven out and the Palestinians would reclaim their lands. Actually, these myths were deliberately created and spread by Israel and its supporters through a public relations campaign unmatched in history and are spread even to this day. Scholars in the United States and in England are only now beginning to provide evidence of the untruthfulness of these myths. But very few Americans, even American Jews, know of the terrorist raids of Begin or Shamir and of their Irgun and Stern terrorist organizations, which drove our people from their homes and lands."

"Doesn't the American government know what's going on, Dr. Thafer?" a man with an Egyptian accent asks.

"I'm sure it does, sir."

"What about these so-called Arab-American alliances, then?" the Egyptian continues. "Doesn't the American government care about them?"

"Through the media, sir, and through its own well-financed public relations undertakings, the organized Jewish community and its lobbies have succeeded in portraying the Arab people as unreliable nomadic barbarians living in remote desert sheikhdoms, as Cousin Wahby has said. They've also skillfully equated Israeli interests with the U.S. national interest and have used the hostility between the Arabs and Israel to undermine Arab-American alliances."

"Are you saying, Dr. Thafer," asks the Egyptian, "that these alliances are worthless?"

"The organized American Jewish community, sir, nurtures the so-called U.S. alliance with Israel. In reality, there is no such legal alliance. But they work hard at preventing American alliances with those states they consider hostile to Israel, including the Arab states, or if such alliances are formed, they work to prevent them from succeeding. They have a great deal of influence on the U.S. Congress. They target any part of the world they consider hostile to Israel and try to prevent it from having close relations with the United States. They are capable of that. Even Soviet-American relations can be affected by what the organized American Jewish community and its lobbies want. If the U.S. government enters into negotiations with the Soviet Union regarding disarmament or bilateral trade, the organized American Jewish community might institute a public relations campaign accusing the Soviet Union of human rights violations against Russian Jews. Then it would solicit the signatures of senators who are beholden to it in a letter urging the president not to negotiate with the Soviet Union until thousands of Russian Jews are allowed to emigrate to Israel."

"What about the American people, Dr. Thafer?" asks the Egyptian. "Do they realize that their Congress is in the palm of these Jewish organizations?"

"I don't believe that they do. Unfortunately, democracy can't guarantee the availability of honest information. These Jewish organizations have also devised an effective weapon: they accuse anyone who criticizes Israel or the activities of the organized Jewish community of being anti-Semitic."

"Thafer," says Uncle Muneer. "Do you think these Jewish organizations had anything to do with the devaluation of the U.S. dollar?"

"I doubt it, Uncle Muneer," says Thafer, surprised by his uncle's question.

"But if they are very strong and organized," says, Thafer's brother Rassem, "and have so much influence, why wouldn't they? This way, they would weaken the Arab states and worsen relations between the Arabs and the Americans."

"I just don't know. I doubt it."

XVI

"I want you to take it easy at the border when you cross the bridge, Thafer," says Mama Adla. "Don't let the Israelis provoke you. Whatever they ask you, answer them calmly. Uncle Muneer will give you Kamal's address. I'm sure the taxi driver will know how to find it."

"That's right, my boy," says Uncle Muneer. "And go to the U.S. embassy and to the Jordanian Ministry of the Interior by yourself. Kamal doesn't need to go with you."

Thafer listens attentively to his aunt and uncle.

"Let's eat first," Mama Adla says. "You have a lot of time. The flight to Amman is at 5:30 this evening. I'm sure you'll get there before dark."

"You spend the night with Kamal, my boy," says the old man, "and get a special passport from the U.S. embassy the next day. After that you go to the Jordanian Ministry of the Interior for the exit visa. Then take a taxi to the border. Once you cross the border, take another taxi to Tulkarm."

Thafer's heart beats hard when Uncle Muneer says "take another taxi to Tulkarm."

"And tell Jihan we all miss her and love her." Mama Adla wipes away a tear. "Remember, dear, don't let the Israelis provoke you. Answer their questions calmly."

"They won't give him any trouble," says Uncle Muneer. He's an American citizen."

"Just the same, dear, take it easy, and don't let them ruffle you."

"I won't, Mama Adla."

"Excuse me," says a man in his fifties wearing a Western suit, "my wife and I have the middle and window seats."

"Certainly." Thafer stands and allows the middle-aged couple to take their seats. The woman is conservatively dressed. Thafer sits down, fastens his seat belt, and waits for the Jordanian airliner to take off.

The woman holds her husband's hand tightly and closes her eyes as the plane races down the runway and takes off.

Thafer remembers the elderly woman whose hand he held in New York. The nightmares of nineteen centuries of homelessness, of countless pogroms, ghettos, and ultimately the Holocaust can burn themselves into a Jewish soul and make the creation of a secure homeland for the Jewish people a psychological and spiritual necessity.

He looks down at the city of Kuwait and remembers July of 1951, when he left Kuwait on his way to the United States. Kuwait had looked desolate from the air. There were no tall buildings and no high minarets or towers with modern design. There were only tiny shacks, which looked like toy blocks scattered over the sand. The tents resembled white umbrellas. There was only one small airstrip that was referred to as the airport. He remembers the small two-engine plane that took him to Damascus in 1951. It left Kuwait at 10:00 in the morning, defying a sandstorm. He reached Damascus at 2:00 in the afternoon. A pleasant breeze greeted him as he stepped out of the plane. He stayed overnight there because he could not cross the border between Syria and Transjordan owing to the assassination of King Abdullah of Transjordan that hot July day. He remembers how he aimlessly roamed the ancient streets of Damascus as he waited for the borders to reopen.

"Is the brother Arab American?" asks the man next to him.

"That's right."

"Syrian American?"

"Palestinian American."

"Same thing." The man reaches for his pocket, gets out a card, and hands it to Thafer. "I am Mustafa Shahwan. We are importers of all kinds of agricultural supplies and equipment. And this is my wife, Ghada."

"Hello. I'm sorry I don't have a card, but my name is Thafer Allam. I work for OAPEC, in Kuwait."

"What was the family name?"

"Allam."

"Are you going to Damascus?"

"To Amman."

"Are you a petroleum engineer?"

"I'm a lawyer."

"You're the lawyer for OPEC?"

"OAPEC."

"We buy a lot of urea from Kuwait."

"Do you?"

"Do you have any contacts with the oil companies?"

"I'm actually new here."

"I thought you were. You speak Arabic very carefully. You speak it like we do, but I can tell you're careful not to make mistakes." He smiles.

"Your Arabic, Mr. Allam," says the man's wife, "is beautiful. It is very impressive."

"Thank you, Mrs. Shahwan."

"You should visit Syria," she says. "Don't believe what they say about us in America."

"I don't believe everything they say in America."

"Mr. Allam is like us," Mustafa Shahwan says. "He knows what's going on."

"I'm sure he does," she says. "Mr. Allam, why does America hate Syria?"

"It doesn't hate Syria. It is just uninformed."

"Whenever do you think it will become informed?" she asks.

God only knows. "It takes time, Mrs. Shahwan."

"I hope it becomes informed before they blow us up. Are you related to General Ayoub Allam?"

"He's my father."

"I knew it," she says. "I just felt it."

XVII

As the flight leaves Damascus for Amman, Thafer sits by himself, taking the window seat and remembering how black flags were hoisted on governmental buildings and on shops and houses that July day of 1951. He had wanted to leave

Amman as soon as he arrived, but an official-looking man dressed in civilian clothes stopped him for identification. He showed the man his Jordanian travel documents.

Where have you been?

In Kuwait.

What were you doing in Kuwait?

Working.

What were you doing in Damascus?

The Kuwait Oil Company plane dropped me in Damascus, but I couldn't enter the Hashemite Kingdom of Transjordan yesterday because the border was closed.

Where are you going now?

To Tulkarm.

What's in Tulkarm?

My family lives in Tulkarm.

Come.

They walked to a nearby government building, where Thafer was made to sit for hours on a chair in an empty, small room. He was then taken to another room where a smartly dressed, high-ranking police officer sat behind a desk.

Is your name Thafer Ayoub Allam?

Yes, sir.

Ayoub Allam's son?

Right.

Who is Saleem Allam?

He's my deceased brother, sir.

With steely eyes searching him relentlessly, the police officer handed Thafer the travel documents and let him go.

Why the United States, Thafer? his aging father asked.

An American priest I met in Kuwait told me it's the only country in the world where I can work my way through college, Father.

But that's too far away, Thafer dear, his anguished mother said.

How long will you be gone, my boy? his father asked.

Five years, Father.

It's too long, Thafer. Your father is not a young man.

I'll write you a letter every day, Mother.

We don't know anyone there.

Education is a good thing, his father said. We'll wait.

Thafer is troubled. Then he remembers how, with the conniv-
ance of Great Britain, King Abdullah and the Zionist leaders,
met in Amman, dispersed the Palestinian people, and prevented the establishment of a Palestinian state. Although all
the Arab leaders knew of King Abdullah's treachery, they
appointed him general commander, stupidly hoping that this
would make it difficult for him to continue his course. Because of his position, however, they had to reveal to him the
size, composition, and strategic plans of their armies, which
he dutifully conveyed to the Israelis. He invited Golda Meir
to come to Amman disguised as an Arab woman. Shortly after
that, his forces abandoned the Palestinian towns of Lydda and
Ramla, causing more than sixty thousand Palestinians to flee
their homes and lands. King Abdullah then conspired with
the Israeli forces; he allowed them to launch an offensive against
the Egyptian forces in the Negev and told the Israelis that he
wished to see the Egyptian forces crushed. He also told them
that he wanted to prevent the Egyptians and the Syrians from
taking hold of any Palestinian areas. King Abdullah's collu-
sion with Israel became common knowledge in March of 1949,
when Israeli troops moved south to conquer Eilat, along the
Araba Valley. King Abdullah's troops had been stationed there
to block the way to Eilat, but he withdrew his forces and gave
them strict orders not to engage the advancing Israeli forces.

King Abdullah's cooperation with Israel made its victory
in the 1948 war inevitable. Israel had encouraged Abdullah's
ambitions and made promises to him about Greater Syria,
promises it had no intention of keeping.

Finally, Abdullah declared to a Western member of the Palestine Conciliation Commission, "I know that my time is limited . . . and that my own people distrust me . . . because they suspect [me] of wanting to make peace without any concessions from Israel. . . . without any concessions, I am defeated before I even start."

Less than a month after he made that statement, in July of 1951, when Thafer was traveling from Kuwait to Damascus aboard that small twin-engine Kuwait Oil Company plane, defying a sandstorm, King Abdullah of Transjordan was assassinated by a Palestinian in Al-Aqsa Mosque in Jerusalem.

The modern sleepy city of Amman is waiting to welcome me, Thafer thinks to himself. It's going to look innocently peaceful. The officials in its small airport are going to be courteous. The streets will be clean. The weather will be delightful. The contrast between the Amman I saw in 1951, a town of about seventy thousand, and the Amman I'll soon see, a city of about a million, will be striking. Yet beneath the surface is a lot of anger and fear. The present monarch of Jordan, King Hussein, is an absolute ruler. Jordan is not a democracy. So I have to watch my step.

There's something else I should remember, he thinks. This kingdom of about three million, two-thirds of whom are my own Palestinian people, is maintained and protected by none other than that greatest superpower and democracy of all, whose political and educational institutions I've been taught to revere—my adopted homeland, the United States of America. So I shouldn't try to be a hero. I should just attend to my own business as though I don't know any of this. And when I go to the embassy of my adopted homeland, the American flag will be flying comfortably in the breeze, as though the kingdom of Jordan is one of the freest democracies on earth. And the seal of the United States, with the eagle, will be impressed on the door, like in Kuwait's U.S. embassy, as though to warn anyone who might dare to think of challenging the tyranny of this little kingdom that the mighty air force of that great democracy, the United States of America, will not tolerate such a challenge.

XVIII

"I wish Father was still with us to see that you're back at last, Thafer," says Thafer's brother, Kamal. "Thank God, you're back."

Thafer is overwhelmed.

"Now, tell me about your children. Did you bring pictures?"

"Yes, I brought pictures." Thafer reaches for his handbag and gets out a few pictures. "I have more, but we can begin with these."

"Which one is this?"

"This is Colleen, my stepdaughter. She's twenty-two."

"She's beautiful! Look at those beautiful blue eyes and the blond hair."

"And this is Kathleen. She's seventeen."

"That's Thafer's daughter all right. Mother will be delighted with these pictures, but they won't be a substitute for the real thing, Thafer."

"God willing, the children will join me in Kuwait after school is out. I plan to bring them to Jordan, then go with them to the West Bank to see Mother."

"I wish Ayoub Allam could've seen your children!"

"And this is Andrew. He's nineteen. He's six foot six inches."

"He takes after his grandfather. What a handsome young man."

"And this is the youngest, Sean. He's fifteen."

"What a beautiful family, Thafer!"

"I'm quite excited about going to see Mother, Kamal."

"I know you are, but you've got to be prepared for a hard time getting there. The enemy is heartless and hateful. I don't think they'll abuse you the way they abuse other Palestinians. They'll think twice before they do that, but they may try to provoke you, and when they see your name, they'll ask you many questions. They'll ask about Father."

"Do you think they will?"

"I'm sure they will, Thafer."

"I want to ask a few questions about Father. Where did Father get his height, Kamal?"

"Many of the Allams are tall people. Father's older brother, Uncle Muneer's own father, was a tall man, almost as tall as Father was. Height isn't too common among Palestinians, Thafer. To undermine him among his people, the British used to spread propaganda about Father because of his height— that he wasn't really a Palestinian, that he was a Turk. Father only received his military education in Turkey. We all know he was a Palestinian through and through."

"I know."

"You're going to be very busy tomorrow trying to get your trip to the West Bank organized, and we may not get another chance to talk."

"We have a lot of time tonight," Thafer says.

"There's a matter I'd like to discuss with you, Thafer."

"What is it?" Thafer asks with some apprehension.

"We're trying to build a nuclear bomb. We're not only looking for the necessary materials, but more importantly, we're looking for the human resources, the brains. I want you to become involved with us."

Thafer is speechless. He looks at his older brother in complete astonishment, not knowing what to say.

"I don't want you to feel pressured, Thafer. I want you to think about it. I won't let anyone force you or make you uncomfortable. I promise you that. I know this is a sensitive matter, and you'll want to think about it very carefully. If you decide you can and want to become involved, your family and your homeland will be eternally indebted to you. Ayoub Allam will also be proud of you."

Thafer pauses, distressed and puzzled. My brother doesn't beat around the bush. "I know nothing about building nuclear bombs, Kamal," he finally says.

"But you're a nuclear engineer."

"Everything I learned about it is obsolete, outmoded. I've been practicing law for the most part. My involvement in nuclear engineering has been minimal. It has to do with the contractual aspects of buying and selling nuclear plants. That's all."

"Your contacts and knowledge will be priceless. Why don't you think about it? I'm not asking you to make a commitment. All I want you to do is consider it."

"I will do that, but introducing the nuclear factor into this conflict is crazy."

"We're not the ones who've introduced it. Israel has, with American help."

"But if they are stupid, does that mean that we should be also?"

"Thafer, this is not an issue of stupidity or of morality; it's an issue of survival. As long as Israel has the bomb, we must strive to get it, and we will. It's as simple as that."

"Where will it all lead?"

"To peace."

"How?"

"The only language Israel understands is the language of force. And as long as they have the upper hand militarily, they'll never budge an inch or negotiate seriously. And why should they?"

"But how does going nuclear lead to peace? If the Israelis have nuclear weapons and we acquire nuclear weapons, then neither will dare use them, and we are back to square one."

"If they have nuclear weapons and we don't, they may be tempted to use them against Egypt or Iraq, which are far from Israel. This would not affect the Israeli population centers.

They might also be tempted to use tactical nuclear weapons against Syria or Jordan."

"Using nuclear bombs against Iraq will affect Iran, which is an ally of the United States and a neighbor of the Soviet Union. Neither the United States nor the Soviet Union would ever tolerate that. Using nuclear bombs against Egypt will also affect Europe. Again, neither the United States nor the Soviet Union would tolerate that."

"The Israelis could still use tactical nuclear weapons. If they have that option, we should also have it."

"This is all insane."

"We are not the ones who have introduced the insanity. All we want is to go home."

"But do we have to have nuclear weapons to go home?"

"Look, I'm not asking you to commit for anything now, Thafer. All I'm asking you to do is to give it some thought. I'll respect your decision, whatever it is. Go see Mother, and when you come back, we'll discuss it again."

XIX

"What's your nationality?" asks the officer at the Jordanian border. He notices Thafer standing in a long line.

"I'm a U.S. citizen."

"May I see your documents?"

"Yes, of course." Why do you suppose he has singled me out? Thafer asks himself. Because I stick out like a sore thumb in this crowd of Palestinians, Thafer decides, as he looks at the men carrying their luggage and the women with their babies. He watches the young children in the crowd holding tight to their mothers' long skirts. They are only a few yards from the Allenby Bridge which separates Jordan from the West Bank.

The officer takes Thafer's passport and exit permit into a crude, makeshift office. Thafer knows he is going to give him priority.

What if I answered the officer in Arabic, using my Palestinian peasant accent? Thafer asks himself.

"You're all set, sir," says the Jordanian officer, handing Thafer's documents back to him.

"Thank you very much indeed."

"That way, sir." The officer points to the bridge.

Now Thafer is on his way. He feels a little uneasy. He looks around, then starts toward the bridge with his suitcase and handbag. An armed Israeli soldier carrying an automatic weapon stands at the entrance to the bridge. Thafer walks toward him.

"Can I see your passport?" asks the Israeli soldier, speaking like a native American with a New York accent.

"Yes, of course." Taking comfort from the soldier's accent, Thafer hands him the passport.

"You were born in Jerusalem?"

"I was."

"Are you Jewish?"

"No, I am not."

The soldier looks at Thafer, hands him back his passport and points to a line of Palestinians. "This way."

"Thank you," Thafer says, smiling. Well, he thinks, that grouchy Israeli from New York wasn't so friendly. Why didn't he direct me to the shorter line of Europeans and Americans on the other side?

After waiting nearly an hour in line and observing that all the Europeans and Americans in the other line have already entered, Thafer realizes the significance of being directed to this long line of Palestinians waiting to cross the border at the bridge. He knows he is going to be grilled. Not only that, he is going to be humiliated, and like all his anxious countrymen, he is going to be delayed for hours.

"Can I see your passport?" says the Israeli customs agent when it is finally Thafer's turn.

"Yes, sir." Thafer hands over his American passport.

The customs agent opens the passport, looks at Thafer's picture, and looks at Thafer. "You're Thafer Ayoub Allam, born in Jerusalem on December 15, 1934?"

"That's right, sir."

"That room over there," says the customs agent, pointing to a crude enclosure. "You'll get your passport there."

"Thank you."

Without looking right or left, Thafer carries his suitcase to a makeshift hut.

"Ahlain, Ahlain. Ya meet marhaba, Thafer! Ya meet marhaba!" says the Israeli, speaking in flawless Palestinian Arabic, when Thafer enters the unpleasant dark room.

"Ahlain feek ya seedi. Ya meet marhaba feek, ya seedi," says Thafer. But he wonders if the "Ahlain" is a genuine double welcome, and the "meet marhaba" is a sincere hundred hellos. Suspecting that the Israeli is taunting him, Thafer wonders if calling the Israeli "ya seedi"—"my sir"—and being polite to him will make him worse. He wonders if he should speak English and behave like an American. He is, after all, a citizen of the United States. He shouldn't act like a downtrodden submissive weakling. He decides to remain humble. He wants to see his mother.

"May I hang your jacket?"

"It's all right, sir," Thafer says, not knowing the procedure. "I'll keep it on."

"You have to give me your jacket, Thafer."

"All right, sir." Thafer takes his jacket off and hands it over to the Israeli, feeling actual fright for the first time since crossing the bridge.

"Sit down. Sit down, Thafer." The Israeli points to a stool and takes Thafer's jacket to an adjacent windowless room.

Thafer walks to the stool, sits and waits, and waits. He begins to wonder what is taking the Israeli so long. Now the Israeli has my passport, my money, and my ticket back to Kuwait, Thafer thinks. Everything I have is in my jacket. I guess there is nothing I can do about it. He remains calm and tries not to appear frightened, although he is both frightened and angry. He wonders with exasperation about the delay.

"Well, well, well!" says the Israeli when he comes back at last. He gives Thafer a searching look. "Thafer Ayoub Allam!" The Israeli's Arabic rendition of Thafer's full name is flawless.

"Yes, sir."

Carrying a yellow pad and now obviously recognizing who Thafer is, the Israeli appears uneasy. "We want you to take off your shoes."

"Excuse me, sir?"

"Take off your shoes and no questions," the Israeli snaps.

"Yes, sir." Why is he angry? Why does he want me to take off my shoes?

"Carry your shoes to the door, leave them there, and come right back," screams the Israeli at Thafer in a frenzy.

"I will, sir." Thafer carries his shoes as instructed. He is shaken. What a bastard! Why is he screaming? What does he want to do with my shoes?

"How old were you when Ayoub Allam died the first time?"

"My father died in 1959, sir."

"How old were you in 1939?"

"Four or five, sir."

"In 1948?"

"Thirteen or fourteen."

"Were you living with Ayoub Allam in 1947?"

"Yes, I was."

"He wasn't dead then?"

"No, sir."

"Did you know that Ayoub Allam was a terrorist?"

"My father was a soldier."

The Israeli stares at Thafer. "What countries have you been to during the last twenty years?"

"I've lived in the United States since 1951. I went to Saudi Arabia in 1959. I went to Canada with my family in 1965. I left New York for London about twenty days ago. I didn't get off the plane in London. From London I flew to Beirut. I stayed one night in Beirut. The next day I flew to Kuwait. Two days ago, I flew to Amman and then came here."

"Why Kuwait?"

"I work there, sir."

"Where?"

"I work for the Organization of Arab Petroleum-Exporting Countries, OAPEC, sir."

"What do you do?"

"I'm their legal advisor, sir."

"Are you a lawyer?"

"Right, sir."

"Who do you work with in OAPEC?"

"I'm new there. My boss is Mr. Ziyad Ghassan, sir."

"Is he a lawyer?"

"I don't think so, sir."

"How long have you known Taleb Hasseeb?"

Thafer is jolted. "I only met him in Amman, sir." How on earth does he know I was with the Amman taxi driver?

"And who is Mustafa Shahwan?"

Thafer now realizes with amusement that the Israeli has been searching his pockets and takes time to answer. "Mr. Shahwan is a businessman I sat next to on the flight from Kuwait to Damascus on the way to Amman, sir," Thafer answers calmly. "He gave me his business card. The taxi driver also gave me his card, sir. I put both cards in my pocket, sir."

"How long were you in Damascus?"

"Twenty-five minutes, sir."

"Before traveling to Kuwait, you said you stayed in Beirut?"

"Yes, one night."

"Where in Beirut?"

"At the home of friends of my family, sir."

"Their name?"

"Amri, sir."

"OK. Go into the next room and take off your clothes."

"I beg your pardon, sir?" Thafer asks in astonishment.

"You heard!"

Thafer is startled.

"You heard what I said!!" the Israeli shouts, his face and voice strained. "Go in the next room, *and take off all your clothes.* Clear?"

Terrified, Thafer feels his pulse racing. What is this? he asks himself. I am not going to take off all my clothes.

But you won't see your mother then, he tells himself. You have endured up to this point. Let the sons of bitches strip-search you, what of it? If you don't let them, they won't let you in.

They are not going to let me go see her anyway, he tells himself. They are just giving me a rough time before they tell me I can't go see her.

You can't be sure, he admonishes himself. Take it easy; chalk this whole thing up to experience, cooperate, and don't lose your sense of humor.

He sits on the low stool, sweat soaking his shirt, and suddenly begins to laugh hysterically. He is very frustrated. He walks barefoot into the adjacent windowless room. He loosens his necktie, takes it off, and throws it on the dirty floor. He takes off his white shirt and places it on the lone chair in the middle of the dark room. He takes off his trousers and his underclothes and stands by the chair waiting. Look at me, he says to himself. Naked came I out of my mother's womb.

At long last, the Israeli returns with a flashlight. "Turn around," says the angry voice.

Thafer turns around nervously.

The Israeli points the light at Thafer's private parts for what seems an eternity.

Why is he doing this? When is he going to let up?

"You can put your clothes back on," says the Israeli.

Thafer puts his clothes back on and returns to where he was interrogated. He waits and waits, pacing the floor and not knowing what to do with himself.

Finally, a high-ranking Israeli officer in uniform comes. "You may go get your shoes, Mr. Allam. I'll wait for you here."

"Thank you, sir." Thafer is demoralized. He walks to a pile of shoes, looks for his, puts them on, and returns.

"We're not going to admit you, Mr. Allam."

"May I know why, sir?" asks Thafer, "I need to see my mother. She's an elderly woman, and I haven't seen her since 1959."

"I can't tell you why, Mr. Allam," says the unperturbed Israeli officer. "These are security matters, but you told our investigator you haven't been back since 1951."

"I haven't been back in Palestine, or in the West Bank I should say, since 1951," shouts Thafer, "but I last saw my mother in 1959 in Saudi Arabia shortly before the death of my father."

"We're not going to admit you, Mr. Allam," repeats the unmoved Israeli officer, now frowning. "Please pick up your luggage and go back to the bridge. One of our officers will accompany you and give you your passport at the exit."

"But why?" screams Thafer. "Why? I'm a U.S. citizen. All I want to do is see my mother for a few days. She's an elderly woman."

"Mr. Allam," says the Israeli firmly, "I told you I can't tell you why. These are security matters. Please pick up your luggage and move."

"What security matters?" shouts Thafer scornfully. He is seething with rage. "I've never been involved in any military activity in my entire life. I've never even carried or touched a weapon. I want to see our ambassador." He is outraged.

"See your ambassador in Amman."

"See your ambassador in Amman," mutters Thafer, picking up his luggage and looking contemptuously at the Israeli officer. "All the aid your government gets from the U.S. government is taxpayers' money. It's my and other taxpayers' money. You won't get away with this very long, I promise you. I promise you you won't get away with it." Thafer is furious. Don't say more, he admonishes himself. I know who I'll speak to, you rotten bastards! He carries his luggage, an armed Israeli officer accompanying him, and returns to the bridge.

"Here's your passport, Mr. Allam," says the armed Israeli officer.

Thafer takes his passport, puts it in his pocket, and walks toward the Jordanian border station. There are no Palestinians left at the station. There are no men carrying their luggage or women carrying their babies. There are no young children holding tight to their mother's long skirts. They've all gone back to live under occupation.

They'll never get away with this, Thafer repeats to himself.

"I need to reenter Jordan, sir," says Thafer, addressing a Jordanian officer at the border station and handing the officer his passport.

"Welcome, sir," says the friendly officer.

"Do you think I can get a taxi to Amman?" asks Thafer.

"Yes, sir," says the officer. "We'll make sure you get one." He stamps Thafer's passport, hands it back, and walks with him to an army jeep, where a Jordanian soldier is sitting behind the wheel. "Take this American to town. He wants a taxi to Amman."

"Yes, sir," says the Jordanian soldier, jumping out of his jeep and reaching for Thafer's suitcase.

"Thank you, officer," says Thafer. "This is very kind."

I should report this to the embassy in Amman, Thafer first thinks, but he decides that this is bigger than the embassy, much bigger than the embassy. All he wants now is to go back to Amman, see his brother briefly, then return to Kuwait.

He thinks of his mother and talks to her. Hold on there, Mother. The cowards won't let me come home. They are scared of my name. Father's ghost still hovers over the homeland.

He sees his youthful mother wearing a bright red scarf, drawing her dark brown hair into a bun. He sees her raking leaves and picking up dead branches from his family's farm and feeding them to the fire of the old-fashioned oven to bake bread.

I hoped to make it, Mother. I did, but the cowards wouldn't let me enter. I'm sure you'll understand. I came as close as the Allenby Bridge, but I just didn't make it.

Thoughts of his young mother keep coming.

I have a special story to tell you, she said, motioning for him to sit beside her on the mattress near the brazier in the middle of the living room in their home in Jerusalem. It was a dark and cold night. He had pressed closer to her.

I'm a grown man now, Mother. But the child in me yearns to put his head in your soft lap. I want to listen to your loving voice. I want to feel your soft hand on my brow. I want to be with you. But the cowards won't let me come home. Hold on there! Hold on there, Mother! This can't go on much longer. Your grandchildren adore you, even though they've never seen you. It won't be long! I'm sure it won't be long!

Then he remembers his mother's prayer: "Our Lord God, give us the strength to defend ourselves against the evil of those who are intent upon hurting us and the fortitude to love and forgive them."

XX

"What happened?" Kamal asks.

"They wouldn't let me in."

"The bastards! Did they tell you why?"

"Security."

"What security? You're a U.S. citizen, accountable to your government and should be supported by it. Didn't you tell them that?"

"I did, but it's more complicated than that. The U.S. government is not master of its own house when it comes to Israel. I'm a little upset now, and I don't feel like explaining. Maybe when we are both calmer we can discuss it. Is there any chance that Mother may come to Amman in the near future?"

"Every time she comes out or goes back in, the sons of bitches give her a rough time. That's why her visits are few and far between. But I'm sure if she knew you were in Amman, she'd come to see you."

"I want to go back to Kuwait either tonight or tomorrow. I'll probably come back in two or three months. Maybe I'll bring the children with me then. Can we send word to her to prepare for that, so I can begin to arrange with OAPEC for another trip? The reason I want to go back now is so that I don't lose more time on this trip. Then OAPEC may let me take off for another week or so in a couple of months."

"There's a flight to Kuwait tonight. I'm sure we can get you on it if you want to go back tonight."

"I would like that."

"I've made the reservation for tonight, Thafer," says Kamal.

"Very good, I think it's better that I go back tonight."

"I agree. Shortly after the Russian Revolution many American Jews used to engage in activities in the United States that were hostile to the policies of the Soviet Union. The Soviet Union began to prevent American Jews from visiting their relatives in the Soviet Union. The U.S. government strongly protested the Soviet policies, and demanded that all Americans be treated equally, regardless of their faith or ethnic origin. Now, the United States should apply that same principle to Israel and tell it that it cannot give American Jews preferential treatment over American Palestinians, nor should the U.S. government tolerate Israel's mistreatment of American Palestinians, because of their ethnic or national origin. What do you think?"

"These are good thoughts. Unfortunately, you're assuming that the U.S. government will act in this fair fashion. I regret to tell you that the Congress is corrupted by Israel's supporters in the United States and that the State Department itself is infiltrated by such supporters. Even if it weren't so infiltrated, I doubt that the State Department would take on the rotten Congress on account of a lone Palestinian American who was abused at the border and prevented from visiting his aging mother."

"Everything that happens to us is for a reason," says Kamal. "Maybe some good may still come out of this. I knew you were apprehensive this morning, but I never thought they would deny you entry. I just thought your being American would make them think twice before turning you back. Try not to let it upset you. I know you're disappointed, but we have to pick ourselves up and go on with our lives. The struggle will go on, my dear Thafer, until justice is attained. Go take your coat off, wash your face, and take a little nap. That'll calm your nerves. I hate to see you like this. You'll get a chance to see Mother soon, and your children will too. What can I do to cheer you up?"

"You've done a lot, Kamal. I just have to get it out of my system. I think that I'll take a nap."

"I will too. The cab will be here at 4:30."

The two brothers are quiet for a moment.

"Before we rest, Kamal, I want to discuss the nuclear matter. I promised that I would tell you how I feel about it after coming back from the West Bank."

"I don't want you to make your decision today, Thafer. You're under a lot of emotional strain today."

"I didn't make the decision today, and today's events haven't changed my mind. I can't participate in the nuclear program, Kamal. I hope you will not be mad at me, but I can't bring myself to do it. The mere thought of taking part in something so potentially devastating gives me the shivers. I just can't do it. Please forgive me. And I promise on Ayoub Allam's grave that I'll always do my best to help our people return to the homeland. I'll always be a Palestinian, proud of my roots and of my heritage, but I don't want to be involved in violence. I want to think of alternatives to violence and destruction and war. Today's experience convinced me, more than ever before, that Israel is much weaker than we all think. It's a petrified country. All the armament and military superiority it has attained will not bring it security or peace. It won't do it any good. And if the Palestinians obtain nuclear weapons, Kamal, the situation will be worse and more dangerous. Accidents often take place as a result of irrational fear. Why add to the insecurity of an already very insecure people?"

Kamal does not respond.

Thafer paces the floor and wonders what he will tell Ziyad.

"Can you believe, Kamal, that they strip-searched me today? And when I was naked, a soldier carrying a machine gun on his shoulder and a flashlight in his hand entered and screamed, 'Turn around!' Even as he screamed, believe me, he was scared, and I could sense that he was. Then when he pointed his flashlight at my penis, I could see his hand shake. These are scared people, my dear Kamal. There has to be another way. Nuclear weapons will not be the answer. They'll only make things worse for us and for them, and maybe for all humanity."

"I'm moved, Thafer," says Kamal. "I'm moved. I didn't think that my kid brother could do that. But I have another point of view. You've heard it said, I'm sure, that if power corrupts, then absolute power corrupts absolutely. Israel is the absolute power in this neighborhood. Hence its conduct. I believe that its conduct is driven not by fear, but by arrogance. Only balancing the equation, as I said yesterday, will bring an end to this arrogance. Israel is building settlements in the occupied territories in a way that no one is able to challenge. That is not the conduct of frightened people, Thafer. It's the conduct of brazen people who don't care, who believe that might makes right, who will do what they think they can get away with."

Thafer continues to pace the floor.

Kamal himself now begins to pace the floor. "You're a refined man, Thafer, who has been lucky enough to live among decent people who have been kind to you. Their kindness is reflected in your thinking and in your conduct. If you had stayed here and experienced Israel's tyranny the way we have, you would be a different man. Frankly, I thought that today's experience would change you. It's to your credit that it hasn't. Yet I will tell you that I respect your decision, and as I promised you, I will not bring up the subject again. Your Palestinian brothers will not pressure you, I assure you of that."

"I don't want you to think that today's experience hasn't changed me. It has. Believe me, it has, and the change scares me. Yet I still want to believe that the answer is not violence. There has to be another way."

"If a way could be found that would allow us to go home without violence, I'd be the first to advocate it. Realistically, I'm not convinced that there is a way. I hope I'm wrong, my dear Thafer, and I pray that you're right."

| PART TWO |

I

"In the Name of God, the All Merciful, the All Compassionate," says Bahrain's oil minister, presiding over and officially opening the sixth session of the Conference of Oil Ministers of the Organization of Arab Petroleum-Exporting Countries. Wearing a western suit, he stands erect as he looks out at the eleven delegations of oil ministers who represent OAPEC sitting in front of him in the Conference Hall of the Kuwait Sheraton. The secretary general of OAPEC, Ziyad Ghassan, and his senior staff comprise the secretariat delegation and sit to the right of the presiding minister. The secretary general's two assistants sit next to him, Hamdan to his right and Mukhtar to his left. Suhaila Sa'adeh and Thafer Allam sit behind him.

The presiding minister strikes the table with a small gavel. "Peace be on you, my brothers," he says, clutching the gavel. "I beg the Almighty God to reward our efforts with success. May He lead us to a fruitful session that we may so serve Him. May He protect our governments and guide them in their efforts to advance the lot of our peoples." Still holding the gavel, he looks at a paper in front of him. "Excellencies," he says, "we have three old items on our agenda and one new item. I propose that we start with the old items first, dispose of them, then proceed to discuss the new item—the devaluation of the U.S. dollar. If there are no objections, we will begin."

"A point of order, Excellency," cries a man in western clothes who is sitting at the head of the Iraqi delegation. "Mr. President, in view of the importance of the matter of the

143

devaluation and its economic implications for all of us, may I ask Your Excellency, in your discretion as president, to move item four to the top of the agenda, if this is acceptable to the honorable members?"

"I have no objection," says the presiding minister, looking to see if there is an objection.

There is silence.

The presiding minister is ready to announce that the session will begin with the issue of devaluation.

"Mr. President," a voice cries.

Thafer looks in the direction of the voice, which is clearly the voice of the head of the Saudi delegation. Suhaila very gently pinches the skin on Thafer's hand as if to alert him to something exciting about to happen.

"The issue of devaluation," says the Saudi minister, "is an item more appropriate for the agenda of the Organization of Petroleum-Exporting Countries, OPEC, than of this organization, OAPEC. OAPEC was established to engage in the creation and development of joint industrial projects. It was not established to engage in political decisions, such as how we should respond to the devaluation of the U.S. dollar. We can discuss some economic effects of the devaluation on our various projects, but moving the devaluation issue to the head of the agenda seems unnecessary unless we will be discussing the problem from a political point of view. We should refrain from that. Thank you, Mr. President."

"May I respond, Mr. President?" the Iraqi oil minister asks, raising his hand.

"Please."

"The Council of Arab Oil Ministers can discuss and act on any relevant matter that affects the industrial projects undertaken or contemplated to be undertaken by the organization. It is clear to us that the devaluation of the U.S. dollar is a relevant matter. Under the charter, we are not precluded from discussing and acting on this item, if we choose to do so, in all its aspects, economic and political. It seems to us that our Organization should encourage rather than discourage open debate on matters of this importance. May we verify this by calling on the legal advisor of the organization? Thank you, Mr. President."

Thafer looks at Suhaila, hoping for encouragement and advice from her.

She points to a text of the provision of the charter and places it directly in front of him. She has underlined the pertinent part.

"Esteemed legal advisor?" asks the presiding minister.

Thafer rises and looks at all the faces trained on him. "Mr. President, Excellencies," he starts nervously. "According to the charter of OAPEC, at your discretion you may discuss and act on any relevant matter that may be brought before you. My interpretation is that a majority of the delegates may decide to discuss this item if it is deemed vital from an economic angle, whatever that is, or from a political angle, whatever that is. I hope, Mr. President, I have answered the question." He sits down.

"Are there further questions?" asks the presiding oil minister.

No one raises his hand or speaks.

"Mr. President," says the Iraqi oil minister. "Let me then move that item four of the agenda be placed at the top of the agenda, and that the matter of the U.S. dollar devaluation be discussed and acted upon in all of its aspects—economic, political, social, and historical—without limiting our discussion or action to those aspects."

"Mr. President," says the Algerian oil minister, "I second the motion."

"Are there any amendments or points for discussion?"

"Yes, Mr. President," says the Egyptian oil minister, rising to his feet. "I see no harm in discussing item four in all its aspects. The subject is of vital importance to all of us. Thank you, Mr. President."

"Mr. President," says the United Arab Emirates oil minister. "The United Arab Emirates has no objection to having item four of the agenda moved to the top, if our discussion of it is confined to its economic and financial implications. We would like, therefore, to amend the motion before this honorable body and confine our discussion of item four solely to economics and finance. Thank you, Mr. President."

"I second the amendment motion, Mr. President," says the oil minister of Qatar.

"Are there any further points, amendments, or motions?" asks the Bahraini oil minister.

The hall is hushed.

"There being no further discussion, amendments, or motions," he says in a low voice, "I will call for a vote first on the amendment. Those in favor of the amendment, please raise your hands."

Five delegates raise their hands: Saudi Arabia, the United Arab Emirates, Qatar, Dubai, and Bahrain.

"Those against the amendment, please raise your hands."

Six delegates raise their hands: Iraq, Egypt, Algeria, Syria, Libya, and Kuwait.

"The amendment is rejected. I will now call for a vote on the original motion. Those in favor of the motion, please raise your hands."

Six delegates, the same ones who had voted to defeat the amendment, raise their hands.

"Those against the motion, please raise your hands."

The five delegates who voted for the amendment raise their hands.

"The motion is carried," says the presiding minister. "It is now five minutes before noon. We shall recess for lunch and return at 1:30 this afternoon."

"Any surprises, Thafer?" Suhaila asks as the two leave their seats and walk out of the Conference Hall.

"The whole thing is a surprise."

"In what way?"

"I am surprised by the civilized manner in which they conduct themselves."

At first she looks down and blushes. "Do you realize what you've just said?" she then asks softly, shaking her head and looking at him with obvious disappointment.

"I'm sorry. I shouldn't have expressed it the way I did."

"It's all right."

He pauses a minute, trying to be careful, but still wanting to explain why he is surprised. "You see, I've been living in the United States all my adult life. I'm brainwashed. On television, in the movies, in their literature, in their newspapers, and even in their schools and colleges the people of the United States are taught to see Arabs as either camel herders and pearl fishermen or high-living billionaire sheikhs. To them, Qatar, Kuwait, Bahrain, Abu Dhabi, Dubai, and even Saudi Arabia are remote and backward lands. But I don't mean to be offensive, I assure you."

"I know you don't. Don't worry about it."

"It's the way many Americans feel about Arabs."

"That's certainly the way they felt when I was in the United States in the fifties. We're now in the seventies. Arabs have changed."

"Maybe Arabs have, but Americans haven't."

"That's too bad. I don't understand it. And you'd think that the American people would by now know more about the economic and political significance of the Middle East."

"They haven't the slightest idea of the potential significance of those desert sheikhdoms for their economy or for the world economy. They have their own illusions."

"The Israeli and Zionist propaganda must still play a significant role in discrediting Arabs, but you'd think that Americans would have become too smart for that by now."

"They haven't."

"But why?"

"Arabs must bear part of the blame. They need to speak to the American people."

"How can they? The Zionists have used the persecution of Jews throughout history, particularly during the Nazi era, as a perennial issue that can be made to justify supporting Israel. They are an organized, committed, and well-financed community, Thafer."

"Arabs should emulate them."

"They don't have what it takes to do that."

"They have the monies and the numbers."

"But they don't have the organization. The organized Jews have worked very hard at portraying them, like you say, as barbarians. The Arabs wouldn't be able to do that to the Jews, even if they wanted to," says Suhaila.

"It's true that through the media and their educational institutions the Zionists and the organized Jews have contributed to the barbaric image of the Arabs, but the oil sheikhs have made things worse. They certainly haven't helped their own image or the image of Arabs in general. And I'm not advocating that the Arabs should portray Jews as barbarians. I'm just saying that they should develop a sound public relations program."

"They view public relations as a tool of falsification, Thafer."

"If the entire Middle East conflict is presented in an honest way, not only to the American people but to the whole world, through a sophisticated public relations program, no one can accuse the Arabs of falsifying."

"Even when I was in the United States, when the problems of the Middle East were presented by objective American scholars, the Zionists used to challenge anyone who'd say anything, true or false, that was unfavorable to Israel."

"The problems of the Middle East, Suhaila, are rarely fully and honestly presented to the people of the United States as major issues that affect their own national interest. That's the approach the Arabs should take. Even I, a Palestinian native who should know better, am influenced by the repeated portrayal of the Arabs as either backward shepherds and fishermen or billionaire sheikhs. I must tell you that I am moved by what I saw this morning."

"Doesn't the U.S. government know what's going on?"

"Sometimes I wonder. Even if it does know what is going on, democracy is a fragile institution. It does not guarantee the enlightenment of its citizens. The Arab states need to educate the people of the United States about the Middle East and its importance to the American people."

"They will never do that. If the U.S. government wants to act irresponsibly, its actions will one day come back to haunt it. It's hard for me to believe that there aren't responsible people in the government who know that their national interest would be served best if they acted fairly and justly in the Middle East. Someone should know what's going on."

"There may be some who do know, but they are weak, and they lack influence. It is the American people, apathetic in any event, who don't know the whole story and who should be informed. These are the people to whom the Arab states should be talking. They are the people who count." Thafer pauses. "Almost every member of the U.S. Congress has a connection with a Jewish organization that expects him to speak out in defense of Israel, whether Israel is right or wrong, and to vote for the enormous economic and military aid that the U.S. government annually gives to Israel, Suhaila. These members of Congress receive substantial campaign contributions from the organized Jewish community in the United States on a regular basis, in order to do exactly that."

"Isn't that a form of bribery?"

"It's legalized bribery. Of course it is. And the organized Jewish community distributes to American Jews records of how members of Congress vote on matters affecting Israel. Stories about the community's influence tell of its ability to secure more than seventy senators' signatures on letters endorsing the absurd amount of annual aid Israel receives from the Treasury Department of the United States and on letters opposing the sale of arms to friendly Arab states, such as Saudi Arabia and Jordan. It is fearful that a reassessment of U.S. foreign policy in the Middle East might lead to an improvement in relations with the Arab states. It has been able to secure a letter signed by more than sixty senators opposing any attempt by the U.S. Department of State to examine its policy in the Middle East."

The two sit at a table in the cafeteria, which is open only to participants in the conference. She puts her elbows on the table, her head between her hands.

"It's frightening. It's frightening, Thafer. These so-called Arab-American alliances are a farce. The Arab masses know that. I've always suspected that Israel has the Congress of the United States in its pocket."

"Of course it's frightening. The tragedy is that the people of the United States don't realize the extent of Israel's influence on their lives. Israel and its supporters have not only the Congress in their pockets, but practically the Departments of State and Defense as well. They've also infiltrated U.S. Intelligence."

"And the American people don't really know what's going on?"

"Very few know."

"Can Arab Americans do anything about this?"

"Arab Americans are splintered, Suhaila. They're not organized. They're not politically conscious. They are in no position to counter the well-financed, well-organized, politically conscious, and fanatically committed supporters of Israel in the United States."

"Why don't they organize? They are the ones who should work on improving their own image and the image of Arabs in the Middle East. They are in a much better position to do this than the Arab states, Thafer. They're the ones who can expose Israel for what it is."

"It just doesn't seem fair to put the whole burden on Arab Americans. And it's a big burden. The American people themselves, it seems to me, should also bear some responsibility. The damage that Israel and its supporters are doing doesn't just affect Palestinians and Arabs, it's bound to affect the United States and its relations with other parts of the world in the long run."

"It's been my experience, Thafer, that if the American people are convinced of the worthiness of a cause, they'll rally behind it."

"The trick is to convince them."

"They don't like to be lied to or to be manipulated, Thafer. If they are convinced that Israel and its supporters have bought their Congress, they'll be angry."

"I agree. Sooner or later, I'm sure they'll find out."

"What else surprised you?"

"Kuwait's vote."

She smiles. "That's what I was looking for when I first asked you if there were any surprises. Kuwait is afraid of Iraq. You'll see more of the way Kuwait votes in the afternoon session."

"What about Saudi Arabia?"

"Saudi Arabia itself avoids confronting Iraq unless it is sure of U.S. support. And the Saudis understand Kuwait's predicament. They never press Kuwait on an issue that is not of vital importance to Saudi Arabia."

"This debate, Suhaila, over whether the devaluation of the U.S. dollar should be discussed at an OAPEC Conference or an OPEC Conference remains a mystery to me. What difference does it make? Why does Saudi Arabia make such a big issue of it?"

"Saudi Arabia is an American ally, Thafer. Those who voted with Saudi Arabia are all American allies. Iran, which is a member of OPEC but not of OAPEC, is also an American ally. Iran is a force to be reckoned with in OPEC. Both Iraq and

Saudi Arabia know this. Iraq prefers to go to OPEC's conference armed with a resolution on this issue, preferably unanimously approved by OAPEC, in order to offset Iran's weight.
Saudi Arabia prefers to let the matter be settled at OPEC's
conference, where Iran and Saudi Arabia would take a united
stand against Iraq and its supporters. This is what the United
States prefers. There's more to it than first meets the eye,
Thafer."

"I can see that."

"Do you think Israel benefits from the devaluation Thafer?"

Her question catches him by surprise.

"You seem confused about that."

"What do you think?"

"Well, it benefits Israel because it slashes Israel's debts to
the United States by 20 percent. It decreases the price of
everything Israel buys from the United States by 20 percent.
It also devalues the Arab oil-producing states' reserves by 20
percent. As you've already seen, this is bound to strain relations between the Arab states and the United States, so actually both are losers. The Israelis benefit the most. I bet that
Israel's supporters had a hand in the devaluation."

"Isn't this a little far-fetched?"

"Why? They would encourage the devaluation in a way
that would seem clever and anticommunist, you know. They
would present it as a measure to compete against Japanese and
German international trade. The Americans wouldn't know
what hit them. It affects not only the Arabs but the Japanese,
the Germans, and others as well. It's a dirty game that's being
played. This devaluation will one day come back to haunt the
U.S. economy."

They walk out of the restaurant to a throng of journalists,
television interviewers, and others who want to know what
has happened during the morning session. Famous journalists
and their crews from around the world and from the Middle

East have gathered around the oil ministers. They want to know about the Arab Shipping Company. They ask if any decision has been made concerning the status of its British contractor, which has been accused in the Arab press of having built six submarines for Israel.

"We have another forty-five minutes," Suhaila says. "Let's go up to the top floor. There's a quiet suite reserved for the staff of OAPEC."

II

They sit across from each other, quietly, by themselves—reflecting and looking at the calm waters of the bay of Kuwait below.

Thafer wonders how long the silence will last. He looks at Suhaila, and their eyes meet.

"I'm sorry you couldn't see your mother," she finally says.

"How did you know?" he asks in a low voice.

She comes to sit next to him. "We'll share my mother for now," she says, her voice barely whispering. She places her hand on his forehead. "My friend Thafer."

He puts his arm around her, then puts his head on her bosom.

She presses it.

He raises his head to kiss her. A feeling of comfort settles in him as he rests his head on the softness of her bosom.

She caresses his brow, and they kiss tenderly again.

"Oh, Thafer, I feel dizzy."

"Suhaila!" He kisses her passionately.

She looks at him, then quickly turns away, and begins to arrange her hair. "I think we should get ready to go down."

"Yes," he says, rising.

"I'll be right back." She rushes to the women's room.

Where's this going to lead? he asks himself. I'll never be the same man again. This woman will change me. In many ways she's like me. She feels my pain. She instantly reads my anguish. She instinctively senses my insecurity. She'll truly comfort me.

Then he remembers a dream he had the night before. Mary Pat was angry with him. Thafer, she said, you were married to me all those years, but you never told me you could dance that beautiful Palestinian dance, let alone teach me how to dance it.

He sits on the sofa and remembers the summer of 1952. He remembers a Thursday night in August of that summer. He was sorting cards in the library stacks. It was quiet, and the stacks were nearly deserted. Mrs. Connally walked toward him, and as she approached, he began to blush. She bent over his shoulder. "How's Thafer tonight," she asked softly. A flash of electricity went through his body. "You shouldn't work too hard," she whispered. "I know," he said, rising in awkwardness. She held his head in her hands and kissed him, then left hurriedly.

At 10:00 P.M. that evening, the Cornell Main Library bell rang. Thafer was ready to walk home. Mrs. Connally offered him a ride. He knew what was going to happen. She parked near where they lived, turned off the lights and the ignition, and put her hand on his brow. I'm tired, Mrs. Connally, he said, putting his head in her lap, her warm hand still on his brow. Mary Pat, she had said. Just Mary Pat, Thafer. We better go in; otherwise, my grandmother will wonder where I am. He sat and watched her hurry in. Then he ran into the dark street and up the steps of his rooming house.

"Thanks for waiting," Suhaila says.

He takes her hand and squeezes it. "We still have a lot of time to get there."

"The afternoon session will be quite interesting."

"I'm sure."

"You'll now hear the Arabic language at its best. These are eloquent people," she says.

"So I'm learning, all over again."

"There'll be a lot of anger, though."

"I'm sure."

"This devaluation has hit a lot of sensitive nerves, you know."

"I can well imagine."

"Serves some of them right."

"Why?"

"Some are more American than the Americans."

"How's that?"

"The feudalistic monarchs and sheikhs could never survive without U.S. support. They are willing to do anything to ensure that support. I mean anything, even if it is against their national interest. You'll see for yourself what they'll say this afternoon. Of course, they receive instructions from Washington, which they follow faithfully and obligingly."

"What do you think is going to happen this afternoon?"

"You've noticed that there are two blocs in OAPEC. One is going to condemn the devaluation, and the second is going to play it down. Then they'll have a resolution expressing their frustrations, which will eventually pass. Then they'll go home, and the United States will do as it pleases anyway."

"The whole thing is a tragedy," he says.

"It just shows how the strong always take advantage of the weak," she says. "It also shows that the United States of America is either heartless or stupid."

"I think it is just stupid."

"Whatever it is, Thafer, it has dealt the budding economies of these weak states a severe blow. One day it will pay an economic price for this, a heavy one."

The doors to the Conference Hall at the Kuwait Sheraton are closed. It is a little after 2:00 in the afternoon. The oil ministers and their staffs have taken their seats. As members of OAPEC's delegation, Thafer and Suhaila sit behind the secretary general and his two assistants.

"Brothers," says the Bahraini Oil minister, "I hereby declare open the second part of the sixth session of the Conference of oil ministers of the Organization of Arab Petroleum-Exporting Countries. The former item four of the agenda, has, with the approval of this body, now become item one. The floor is open for discussion and action on item one in all its aspects." He pauses, then recognizes the Algerian oil minister.

"Mr. President," says the Algerian minister. "During this morning's session, we had a healthy debate on the item before us. We did that not unmindful of the concerns expressed by some of the brothers, concerns that we should take into consideration in our discussions and in the action we ultimately decide to take. The government of the United States, Mr. President, has devalued the U.S. dollar twice during the past six months, 10 percent each time. Needless to say, this devaluation affects every phase of our economic lives. It decreases the purchasing power of our reserves, most of which are in U.S. dollars, by 20 percent. It decreases the value of our oil reserves by 20 percent. It decreases the value of our own currencies, most of which are tied to the U.S. dollar, by 20 percent. In effect, the U.S. government by a stroke of its pen has decided overnight to raid our treasuries and our resources. This may not be the end of the story, Mr. President. There may be more of the same to come, in one form or another. If we do not take joint action to counter the devaluation measures, we will not be serving our peoples and future generations well. In all candor, Mr. President, Algeria does not know what is the proper course of action. Algeria wants to listen to the counsel of its sister states. Algeria feels, however, that we should be united in whatever action we take. There is no other way for us during this critical period in our national lives. Thank you, Mr. President."

"Bahrain agrees with sisterly Algeria," says the presiding minister. "We should be united. We cannot afford to be divided. Whatever united action we take will surely influence

OPEC's final stand." He pauses, then recognizes the Syrian oil minister.

"Mr. President, your sister state, Syria, one of the three states bordering Israel and continuously confronted by it, is grateful to sisterly Iraq for making this discussion possible so that we might review the devaluation of the U.S. dollar and its effects. The act taken by the government of the United States in devaluing the dollar, my brothers, is Zionist inspired. Make no mistake about it. The Zionists, who control the financial institutions of the United States, aim to destroy us economically. But we too have a trump card that we should have the courage to play now. We must decide to accept only a currency other than the U.S. dollar for the sale of our oil. We must not continue to tie our currencies to the U.S. dollar. We must not keep any reserves in U.S. currency. First and foremost, we must never buy anything from the United States, which finances and sharpens the Zionist dagger aimed at the heart of our Arab nation. Thank you, Mr. President."

Thafer and Suhaila exchange looks.

"The chair recognizes His Excellency the oil minister of sisterly Qatar."

"Mr. President, brothers," says the soft-spoken Qatari minister. "Qatar realizes that our organization faces one of the most serious problems it has faced since its establishment and that the consequences of any action we take are bound to affect our governments and our people for years and perhaps generations to come. Therefore, we must reflect thoughtfully upon all our actions and study all possible repercussions. We agree with sisterly Syria that the devaluation of the U.S. dollar is treacherous and that it may very well be Zionist inspired. Yet, my dear brothers, we should have the wisdom and the integrity to know the difference between what we would like to do and what we can do. Mr. President, in all honesty, can we retaliate against the United States of America? If we were to retaliate, would we not be inviting the United States to strike back? Where would it all end? Are we in a position to provoke a powerful nation, albeit unjust and exploitative, to take devastating economic or military action against us? We are all small and weak states. Some of us have only recently attained our freedom from the yoke of colonialism. Can we afford to give to the heartless colonialists a pretext to invade our defenseless countries? The realistic answers to these questions, Mr. President, should determine our course of action. Thank you, Mr. President."

The sober speech by the Qatari minister leaves the hall hushed.

"Thank you, Excellency. The chair recognizes His Excellency the Libyan oil minister.

"Mr. President, if there is one single enemy of which we all have to beware, as much as we have to beware the imperialists and the Zionists," says the Libyan minister, "it is fear. Our adversaries would like nothing more than to see us paralyzed by self-inflicted fear, for which our peoples would never forgive us. The era of gun diplomacy, my brothers, has ended. Mr. President, Libya agrees with sisterly Syria that we should take firm measures to protect our interests. What is there to prevent us from insisting on being paid for our oil in whatever currency we desire? Why can't we invest our assets in whatever financial institutions we may choose? What should prevent us from trading with whatever nation we wish? But if we allow ourselves to be intimidated, then we do not deserve to lead our peoples in the glorious march of progress and prosperity. Thank you, Mr. President."

There is a moment of silence. The Kuwaiti minister has risen to his feet. "I intend to say only a few words, Mr. President. We have heard eloquent representations of two different approaches—one advocating that certain measures to be taken in response to the devaluation of the U.S. dollar and the other counseling caution. Kuwait is inclined to favor caution, but it is undecided about what measures we should all take. We

wonder if it is time for us to discuss specific proposals that
could be put in the form of a motion so that this body can
debate it. Thank you, Mr. President."

"I met that man years ago," Thafer whispers to Suhaila.

"You did? Where?"

"Here in Kuwait. I'll tell you about it later."

"Is there a motion? The chair recognizes His Excellency
the oil minister of sisterly Egypt."

"Mr. President," says the Egyptian minister, "I will make
a motion. But first I would like to say that Egypt understands
the anger of its sister states—Algeria, Syria, and Libya. Egypt
also understands and commends to this body the caution of
sisterly Qatar. As our Syrian brother has reminded us, Egypt
is one of the three states bordering the Zionist enemy and is
continuously confronted by it. My brothers, when in 1956
Egypt exercised its sovereign right and nationalized the Suez
Canal Company in accordance with international law, it was
subjected to a cowardly surprise attack by air, sea, and land,
launched on October 29, 1956, by Israel, Britain, and France.
That vicious attack against Egypt is now history. It is referred
to in the history books as the Tripartite Aggression of 1956.
Need I remind any of you what the imperialists are capable of
doing? Need I remind any of you how Israel can be used
against us? Need I remind any of you that Sinai, the Golan
Heights, and all of our beloved holy land are still occupied by
Israel? Need I remind you that Israel derives its strength,
indeed its very existence, from the United States? Brothers,
we must be cautious, but we must also be intelligent. Caution, my dear brothers, is not cowardice. It is prudence. It is
true that we have a trump card. The time has not come for us
to play it, however. We must wait, be vigilant, and remain
united. Above all, we must be patient. We cannot afford to be
rash." The elderly Egyptian minister pauses and looks at the
oil ministers. "Mr. President, I have said enough. I am ready
to make a motion."

The attention of all the oil ministers is focused on the Egyptian minister. The crackling of crisp paper fills the room as he unfolds the document he has prepared. "Mr. President, I move that the members of the Organization of Arab Petroleum-Exporting Countries, OAPEC, as a block present the following program to OPEC, the Organization of Petroleum Exporting Countries, at OPEC's next meeting of oil ministers:

1. OPEC condemns as a provocative act the devaluation of the U.S. dollar by the government of the United States.

2. OPEC puts the government of the United States on notice that in view of the great losses sustained by the member states of OPEC as a result of this reckless economic act, OPEC's members shall be free to take whatever steps may be appropriate individually and jointly to protect their assets and other interests.

3. In the interest of international economic harmony and in order to avoid economic retaliation, which would be harmful to the stability of the world economy, the member states of OPEC call on the government of the United States to make voluntary and adequate adjustments in order to compensate OPEC's members for the enormous losses they have sustained.

4. OPEC invites the government of the United States to discuss the above points with a delegation of OPEC's members.

Thank you, Mr. President."

"Thank you, Excellency. The chair recognizes His Excellency, the Kuwaiti oil minister."

"I second the motion, Mr. President. I also wish to address this honorable body, Mr. President."

"Very well," says the presiding minister. "We will first take a brief recess. The chair will arrange to have copies of the motion distributed after a twenty-minute recess."

"Mr. President,"the Kuwaiti minister resumes, "whether we like it or not, my brothers, the U.S. dollar is supreme. There is nothing we can do to challenge its supremacy. Were we to challenge it, we would hurt only ourselves. The United States has the world's largest and freest economy. Non-Americans can invest in practically anything in the United States if they hold U.S. dollars. Investors of all nationalities have always considered it a safe place to make investments of all kinds. Over the years, the United States has had a low inflation rate. Its money market is considered to be the best in the world. Mr. President, the whole world has decided to use the U.S. dollar as international currency to conduct its international business. Who are we, my brothers, to tell the world to select another currency? I respectfully submit that we are in no position to do so. Were we to try, the world would mock us. Suppose, Mr. President, that we make a decision today, unanimously, to challenge the U.S. dollar. Suppose all of us, eleven OAPEC members, decide to convert all of our U.S. dollar assets to something else—say, German marks or Swiss francs. Suppose we all decide to refuse to accept U.S. dollars as payment for our oil. My brothers, were we to implement such a plan, all our oil fields would close down for lack of international orders. Most countries of the world, whose reserves are in U.S. dollars, would not be able to buy our oil. This would ruin our economies. We would face major problems with the rest of the world. We would be accused of bad faith by friend and foe. Above all, my dear brothers, we would have internal problems of our own. Our people would be out of work and out of bread. What would we say to our own people? Must we not pause before we embark on a course that could ruin our economies and bring suffering to our people? That is all I have to say, Mr. President. Thank you." The Kuwaiti minister sits.

The Conference Hall is quiet.

Now the Saudi minister of oil raises his hand.

"The chair recognizes His Excellency, the oil minister of sisterly Saudi Arabia."

"Mr. President, the action of the United States, thoughtless and harmful to us and to many others as it may be, is beyond our control. We may protest it, condemn it, explain its effects on our young economies, and fret over it, but we must avoid a course that could jeopardize our economies even further. Mr. President, the devaluation of the U.S. dollar, in our opinion, is bound to bring more harm in the long run to the economy of the United States than to ours. The days, months, and years ahead will show that a stable world economy is beneficial not only to us, but to them and to all countries. The devaluation of the U.S. dollar has shaken world confidence in it. No matter how strong its economy is, the United States cannot afford to sacrifice the world's confidence to misguided domestic greed. We are a patient and glorious people, my brothers, with a distinguished heritage. We will not always be weak. The world needs our oil just as much as it needs the U.S. dollar. If we remain prudent and united, we may still play a role in the world economy, but we must restrain our passions and must use our God-given talents wisely. May He lead us along the straight path. Thank you, Mr. President."

"The chair recognizes His Excellency, the oil minister of sisterly Iraq."

"Mr. President, Iraq has listened with keenest interest to our brothers who have spoken this afternoon. We wish to say, Mr. President, that we are in favor of the motion made by His Excellency, the oil minister of our sister Egypt, who has reminded us of the aftermath of the nationalization of the Suez Canal Company and of how Israel, Britain, and France conspired in the criminal invasion of Egypt. Yet, in fairness to history, we must recall with appreciation the role that the United States played under President Eisenhower in preventing the aggressors from reaping any benefit from their aggression. That was a different era, however, Mr. President. Iraq has now nationalized the Iraqi Petroleum Company in an effort to be master of its own oil and resources. This is the only way for all of us. We must control our own oil and our other resources. Until we do, the imperialists will continue to exploit us. Mr. President, Britain is attempting to isolate Iraq economically because Iraq dared to nationalize its oil industry, but Iraq will face this challenge. It is determined to control and defend its wealth and resources. Mr. President, we agree with our Algerian brother that the government of the United States has raided our treasuries by its devaluation of the dollar and that unless we are vigilant, it is liable to repeat its action. We are also inclined to agree, Mr. President, with our Syrian brother that the U.S. action is Zionist inspired and that we too have a trump card. But this is not the time, in our opinion, to play our trump card. We cannot and we should not even attempt to sell our oil in a currency other than the U.S. dollar at this time. In this respect, we agree with and support the wise counsel of our Kuwaiti brother. In this respect also, we agree with our Qatari brother, that we cannot delude ourselves about what we can do. Mr. President, it is our firm conviction that the U.S. government's misguided action was motivated by greed and selfishness. The United States is determined to maintain its high standard of living at the expense of poor countries like ours and at the expense of the rest of the world. It is acting unwisely, as our Saudi brother has told us. We do not believe that the United States would be in a position to undertake military action against us were we to take measures to protect our interests. We agree with our Libyan brother that the era of gun diplomacy has passed. We also agree that the United States would think twice before undertaking military action against us because we are on the southern borders of the Soviet Union. Although we must always recognize the honorable stand taken by President Eisenhower during the Tripartite Aggression, we must never forget that the Soviet Union played an important role in bringing an end to that aggression. Yet we should refrain from provoking either of the two superpowers. That would not be in our interest or in the interest of the world. We must never become involved in the rivalry between them. We must remain nonallied. We believe that the motion of our Egyptian brother is balanced. And we agree with our Saudi brother that the world needs our oil just as much as it needs the U.S. dollar, which is why we should strive to control our own wealth and resources. In the long run, this is the safest path to economic security and prosperity. Thank you, Mr. President."

"Thank you, Excellency," says the presiding minister. "The chair recognizes the oil minister of the United Arab Emirates."

"Mr. President, we wish to offer a few amendments to our Egyptian brother's motion, as follows:

"Delete paragraph number one of the motion, which 'condemns' the devaluation of the U.S. dollar 'as a provocative act,' and replace it with, 'OPEC regrets the devaluation of the U.S. dollar by the government of the United States.'

"Delete paragraph number two, which we believe is a threatening paragraph, and replace it with, 'OPEC's members call on the United States to reconsider its action.'

"Delete paragraph number three of the motion.

"Thank you, Mr. President."

"I second the motion to amend, Mr. President," says the oil minister of Dubai.

"Any further amendments or points of discussion?" asks the Bahraini minister.

No hands are raised.

"I call the question," says the Libyan oil minister.

"We will vote on the amendment first," says the Bahraini minister. "Those in favor of the amendment made by His Excellency the oil minister of the United Arab Emirates, please raise your hands."

The ministers of Qatar, Saudi Arabia, the United Arab Emirates, and Dubai raise their hands.

"Those against?"

Six hands are raised: those of Egypt, Syria, Iraq, Libya, Kuwait, and Algeria.

Bahrain does not vote.

"The amendment is defeated. We vote now on the motion. Those in favor, please raise your hands."

Eleven hands are raised.

"The motion is carried unanimously. We recess until 10:00 A.M. tomorrow."

III

"What did you think?" Suhaila asks Thafer after the session as the two walk to her car in the parking lot of the Kuwait Sheraton. It is a clear evening and stars fill the sky.

"It is an education."

"Who impressed you the most?"

"The Kuwaiti minister for his wisdom and economic knowledge, and the Iraqi minister for his pragmatism and strength, but they all impressed me. What did you think?"

"They were all good. I didn't agree with the Kuwaiti minister that our oil fields would shut down if we were to insist on selling our oil in a currency other than the U.S. dollar. I think that the Saudi minister is right. The world needs our oil just as much as it needs the U.S. dollar."

"I still question the wisdom of trying to sell oil in other than U.S. currency."

"Such a move would rock the world economy, Thafer, but it's inevitable. As long as the United States pulls stunts like this, the Arab states and others will have to try to think of ways to protect their interests."

"It's not likely to happen soon, anyway."

"I doubt that it will happen in the foreseeable future. The Arab states are still intimidated."

"They still talk about 1956."

"They will for a long time. That's why some Arab states want to become nuclear. But it's too bad that some of them believe that the United States might use force."

"That'll never happen, Suhaila."

"Never say never, Thafer. You don't know what warmonger may occupy your White House. Anyway, the United States is capable of resorting to means other than direct military intervention, although I wouldn't put it past them to do that."

"You really believe that, Suhaila? What about the Soviet Union?"

"The Soviet Union has been less prone to undertaking ventures than the United States. If the Soviet Union itself is threatened, or any of the Eastern block countries, it would move. But if the United States were to invade one of the Arab countries, I doubt that the Soviet Union would rush to the rescue. It might try to balance the equation by invading another part of the world it considers vital, as it did in 1956 when they invaded Hungary during the Suez Canal crisis."

"Direct American intervention in the Middle East now, Suhaila, seems unlikely. We have our hands full in Vietnam. The American people would never support another venture now."

"They can still instigate the shah of Iran or Israel to move."

"Even if this were to happen, it would still be reckless. It would destabilize the region, which is vital to the United States, Western Europe, and Japan. They all need Middle East oil. As the saying goes, it's easier to start a fire than to put it out."

"What did you think of the Saudi minister?"

"He was impressive. I agree with what you said earlier about his statement asserting the importance of oil, but I still believe that in a confrontation between oil and the U.S. dollar, oil will come up second."

"I wouldn't bet on that. The U.S. dollar could be the mightiest currency that ever was, but if oil is needed, it's those who need it who have to pay for it in the currency that the supplier dictates. I don't care what the Kuwaiti minister says. Those who have the gold make the 'Golden Rule.'"

"You may be right, but doesn't it depend on who actually has power over the gold?"

"I guess," she says.

"What did you think of the Iraqi minister?"

"I thought he was quite good. I was surprised to hear him speak kindly of the Americans under Eisenhower."

"I was too."

"The Arab people have long memories, Thafer. They never forget. They remember the good and the bad for a long time."

"And how about the Iraqi minister agreeing with everyone?"

"That was kind of funny. He agreed with the Algerian minister that OAPEC should take a united stand. He agreed with Syria that the devaluation of the U.S. dollar was Zionist inspired. He agreed with Qatar that the United States should not be provoked. He agreed with Libya that the era of gun diplomacy has passed. He endorsed Egypt's motion. He even praised the Kuwaiti minister. And he agreed with the Saudi minister that the world needs Arab oil just as much as it needs the U.S. dollar."

"But he didn't agree with Syria on all the retaliatory measures she wanted to take. Maybe the Syrians didn't mean it."

"I'm sure the Syrians meant it, Thafer. I think the Iraqi minister was sincere. What he did was to agree with a part of each minister's statement because he wanted a united and unanimous approval of the motion."

"Eventually he got that."

"I want to tell you something, Thafer. I'm surprised at the American brain trusts. How could they let something like this go through?"

"They were probably not consulted."

"That's hard to believe, but even these so-called brain trusts are most likely infiltrated by Israel's supporters. Their advice is bound to be colored by their prejudices. Obviously, with all its scholarly institutions and think tanks, the United States knows that in devaluing the U.S. dollar, other countries would sustain enormous monetary losses."

"Responsible people in these groups know, Suhaila. They understand the significance of what was done, I'm sure. But they are not the decision makers. I would venture to guess that Nixon and his secretary of state, William Rogers, did not know the havoc this devaluation would raise with the economies of developing countries such as OAPEC members."

"This is hard to believe. You don't have much regard for the intellect of the president of your country, the most powerful country in the world. You may be right, though."

"It's not hard to believe, Suhaila, if you've lived in the United States as long as I have. You'd then believe anything."

"Well, maybe. Anyway, Thafer, do you want me to pick you up at 9:00 this evening?"

"I'm supposed to be there at 8:30. Ziyad wants me to be in the receiving line so that he can introduce me to the oil ministers. Is this reception going to be an elaborate affair?"

"There'll probably be a lot of people. All the oil ministers and their staff members will be there, plus about twenty members of OAPEC's staff; maybe fifteen from the staff of Kuwait's Oil Ministry; ambassadors and staff members of the various Arab states, particularly the oil-producing ones; as well as some non-Arab ambassadors and members of their staffs. All in all, about two to three hundred guests."

"That's a lot."

"This kind of affair will be riddled with intelligence people from all over the world, Thafer. Most of them will be gathering information. Often, much of OAPEC's so-called confidential information is picked up at receptions like this."

"Is that right?"

"In fact, much of the Arab states' secret information is casually divulged in just such parties. Even the Israelis will be represented there tonight. Anyway, will you be coming with Saeed?"

"I think so," he says.

IV

"That's the Kuwaiti oil minister," whispers the secretary general, pointing to a man serenely making his evening prayer on the floor in a distant corner of the spacious empty hall of the Kuwait Sheraton. The Kuwaiti is wearing the traditional white robe and a white head-cloth. Having fallen off when he knelt, the black rope that usually rests on top of the headcloth is on the floor in front of him. The secretary general, his two assistants, and Thafer wait for him to complete his prayer and join them in the reception line.

Rubbing his face with both palms after having murmured his concluding prayers, the Kuwaiti minister reaches for the prayer carpet he has placed on the floor in front of him, folds it up, places it under his arm, and rises. He walks toward the four OAPEC men. When he comes close, the secretary general motions for Thafer to join him in greeting the minister.

Memories of Thafer's first arrival in Kuwait in 1949 flash through his mind again.

He had applied for a menial job at the labor department of the Kuwait Oil Company. A tall thin man with a thick dark moustache, probably in his late twenties or early thirties, looked at him with glittering dark brown eyes. How old are you? the man asked.

Eighteen, he lied.

You're not more than thirteen.

He was scared. I'm fifteen, sir.

We can give you a job as a messenger at the Magwa Hospital.

Thank you, sir, very, very much. I'll take it.

You are a Palestinian?

Right, sir.

Yes, yes, I know. Would you like to attend night school?

I'll be grateful for that.

We'll arrange that for you.

The Magwa Hospital was fifteen miles south of the town of Kuwait. It was an army barracks in the middle of the desert with white tents around it for the employees. There were no houses, no trees, and no roads. The staff of the hospital, mainly British, was referred to then as senior staff. The non-British hospital staff was referred to as junior staff, and the laborers, such as Thafer, were referred to as artisans.

Now, the secretary general introduces Thafer to the man who gave him that job in 1949.

The Kuwaiti minister extends his hand. "Ahlan Wa Sahlan," he greets Thafer with the traditional Arab greeting—"you are our kin, and this is your home."

"Feekum," says Thafer, gripping the minister's hand and noting his kindly, mature face. Behind the minister's horn-rimmed glasses there is tenderness in his gentle dark brown eyes. His moustache is gray, his face full.

"We've met before, Excellency," Thafer tells the unassuming soft-spoken minister. There are no wrinkles in his face, no remarkable change in his fine features.

"We have?" He looks at Thafer with surprise. He obviously does not remember him.

"You wouldn't remember, Excellency," Thafer hastens to say, feeling awkward about having made the minister uncomfortable. "I was a very young boy, but you gave me my very first job at the Magwa Hospital when you were the head of the labor department."

"Oh," says the Kuwaiti minister, obviously relieved, "that was a very long time ago."

Thafer tries to remind him of their encounter in 1949.

"I'm touched," says the minister.

"And I'm still grateful."

"My father used to say, 'Do a good deed and drop it into the sea. It'll come back to you.'" He searches Thafer's face, then shakes his hand warmly. "Ahlan, Ahlan," he repeats and moves to stand next to the secretary general in the reception line.

Thafer is sure the minister does not remember him.

The first guest to arrive is the Iraqi oil minister, a short, thin man in his middle forties. His pleasant face is serious but friendly. The Kuwaiti oil minister is the first to greet him; then the secretary general embraces him warmly and introduces Thafer to him.

The next to arrive is the Algerian oil minister, a man with a sad thin face and glittering eyes. He first greets the Kuwaiti oil minister, then the secretary general and his two assistants, and finally, Thafer is introduced.

"It is a pleasure to meet you, Dr. Allam," says the Algerian in classical Arabic.

"I am honored and happy to meet you, Excellency."

The Syrian minister of oil comes and is introduced to Thafer. The youthful, hazel-eyed Syrian sports a light brown moustache. His complexion is fair.

Then the Saudi oil minister arrives, accompanied by the ministers of Egypt, Libya, Bahrain, Qatar, Dubai, and the United Arab Emirates. They are greeted by the Kuwaiti oil minister and by the secretary general, then introduced to Thafer.

V

Holding a nearly empty glass of tasteless orange juice and trying to avoid jostling anyone as he moves, Thafer finds himself face to face with a tall, fair man standing by himself. "This place is packed," Thafer says, trying to walk slowly by the blond man.

"Yes, it is," says the man.

The man's accent arouses Thafer's curiosity. He stops and looks at his clean-cut, youthful face. I'll bet he's German, he thinks, standing directly in front of him.

"I'm the Soviet ambassador to Kuwait," the man says, extending his hand.

"Oh," Thafer says, "I'm honored to meet you, Excellency. I am OAPEC's new legal advisor."

"You speak like an American," the Soviet ambassador says.

"I am an American."

"You're an American, and you speak like an American," says the Soviet ambassador, "but you're courteous. Americans are not usually honored to meet Soviet ambassadors."

"Why not? The United States and the Soviet Union were allies in World War II. I'm sure many Americans have a lot of respect for the sacrifices your country made." Thafer pauses. "I am of Palestinian origin, Excellency. I respect the Soviet Union's fair stand concerning the Palestinian people."

"You're a Palestinian American! Yes! Time is on the Palestinians' side. Come and visit us."

"Thank you, Excellency." Thafer moves away.

I bet His Excellency thinks he has found an easy recruit. He sure gripped my arm tightly.

Thafer has seen Suhaila talking to two men. The way to her corner is still crowded. There's a man with an unlit pipe who's just broken away from a group. He is looking for someone to talk to. Thafer, only a few steps away, moves toward him.

"How do you do." The man nervously thumps his empty pipe against his open palm; his British accent is unmistakable. "I'm the British consul in Kuwait."

"How do you do, sir," says Thafer. "I'm OAPEC's new legal advisor."

"Oh," says the Englishman, "I knew your predecessor."

I have seen this man before, Thafer says to himself.

The Englishman reaches for the tobacco case in the pocket of the light green, checked jacket he wears, dips his pipe into it, and fills it without looking at Thafer. "Have you been here long?" he casually asks Thafer.

"About three weeks. And you?"

"Eighteen months. I have six months to go, then I retire."

"Oh."

The Englishman pauses.

Thafer looks at his face as he bites his packed pipe. I have seen this face before, Thafer repeats to himself. I know I have. He begins to feel uneasy.

The Englishman draws on his pipe. "You're a Palestinian," he finally says, "and you must've attended English schools before going to the United States. I can still hear some British notes in your speech. At first I thought you might've lived in New England, but some of your pronunciation is still distinctly British."

Thafer is fascinated.

"The Palestinians resent us," the Englishman continues. "In all honesty I can't say I blame them. We, more than any other country in the world, are responsible for the tragedy of the Palestinians. I'm approaching my sixty-fifth birthday, and if there's anything I regret in my life, it's the role I played in Palestine during the British Mandate there. I was in the Palestine police troopers of the British Mandate. I was in Jerusalem, in Bethlehem, in Haifa, in Jaffa, in Nablus, and in Tulkarm. I know all of Palestine. I know its countryside, its villages and towns. I know its hills and its valleys. I know its people, its farmers, and its intellectuals. What we the British did was unforgivable. We killed more than five thousand Palestinians during the 1936—39 uprising led by that fox, Ayoub Allam, and maimed more than twenty thousand."

Thafer has goose flesh all over him.

"We blew up their houses. We tortured their fighters, who were battling us for their very existence. We jailed them

without trial and for no justifiable reason. We crushed them.
Many of us in the troopers force resented what we were doing,
but we did all that. We carried out our superiors' orders. I was
a young man, but if I had it to do over again, I would never
go through with it. And what did the Jews do? They turned
against us. They began to use terror against us."

Thafer listens, his head down.

The Englishman is of medium build. His thinning gray
hair is straight, his dark blue eyes constantly watery, but he
sheds no tears. He speaks matter-of-factly, as if in a confes-
sional. He pulls up his left pant leg and shows his wooden leg
to Thafer. "This is what I got from the Jews." He pauses and
stands erect, as if to defy the leg. "Don't you have anything
to say?" he asks Thafer.

"We've met before."

"Are you sure?"

"Quite sure."

"Could it be anyone else?"

"No."

The Englishman, perhaps sensing Thafer's unease, looks
uneasy himself.

"Excuse me, sir. I know we have met before."

"Where?"

Thafer does not answer.

"You don't know where?"

Thafer looks down at the floor. He remembers the English
troopers who had petrified him and his mother in 1938 when
they were looking for his father and searching their home for
weapons. He remembers the English trooper who tucked the
black toy pistol under his belt. He is sure it is the man standing in front of him.

"Excuse me," the Englishman says and he limps away.

"I've been trying to find you," says Suhaila. "Where have you
been? Is something the matter? You look upset."

"Nothing. It's just the crowd. I've been trying to join you, but the place is packed."

"Yes, I saw you trying to plow through."

Thafer nods his head, still thinking about the Englishman he was talking to.

"Is something the matter, Thafer?" she repeats.

"No, it's just the noise and the smoke. Let's get out of here."

"Let's go down. There's a quiet restaurant on the first floor."

"Who were those men you were speaking to?" Thafer asks Suhaila as the two sit by themselves in a secluded booth in the restaurant.

"One is the head of the PLO office in Kuwait," she whispers. "They're all curious about you. They know you're a physicist, and they want you to become involved."

"How do they know?"

"From your family."

"I could never feel comfortable with those people."

"You have been away for more than twenty years. I can't believe that we've become so close in such a short time."

He looks at her, feeling the warmth and sweetness of her presence. "I know," he says softly.

"Twenty years is a long time. The land of our birth always attracts us."

Fear, love, passion, and nostalgia come together to overwhelm him. He looks into her hazel eyes and feels that he wants to melt with her. "I love you, Suhaila," he whispers, his voice confident.

"I love you too, Thafer." She looks into his eyes. "And I feel comforted and at peace when I am with you."

"Suhaila," he murmurs, "you have no idea how much comfort and peace I too felt when I put my head on your breast. I could even hear your heart beat softly. Suhaila, I need to utter the sound of your name."

She lifts her eyes.

"And I want to be with you always."

"I do too, Thafer."

"But I'm scared of something."

"What is it?"

"The PLO and its men."

"Why?" she asks in astonishment. "You shouldn't be. They're all like us, Palestinians who want to liberate the homeland."

"I'm uneasy about this nuclear stuff."

She pauses. "I know you are."

"What am I going to do?"

"You do whatever your mind and heart tell you, Thafer."

"That's just it. They keep sending me mixed signals. I'm frustrated."

"That's natural."

"I want to give of myself to the homeland, but I don't want to be involved in violence. Yet something happened to me at the bridge. I keep thinking of that. It frightens me when I think about it. It isn't what happened that frightens me; it's my thoughts about it all—I can't be free of it. Maybe the homeland needs more science than law at this time, I find myself saying now. I never used to say that, and it troubles me. It makes me uneasy. I'm also annoyed with myself for the discomfort I'm feeling. That's why when I meet people from the PLO, I feel uneasy. That's why I'm uncomfortable with the PLO. Even my brother makes me uneasy."

"I know how you feel. I know how uncomfortable you've been."

"Do you think they know?"

"Probably, but don't worry about it. They all understand. Just like I did when I first saw you."

"How is that?"

"The anguish of the land of our birth unites us. We all feel it. I read it on your face the minute you walked into my office when you first arrived. I even sensed it in the way you moved."

"I too, read it on your face and somehow felt it in your presence."

"After my husband's death, I was sure that I couldn't become interested in a man again. But when you walked in my office, I felt something exhilarating happening. Maybe it was those unspoken messages we both sensed. Maybe also it was your name because I knew who you were and who your father was. And that's another thing. Everyone, rightly or wrongly, expects something of you because of your father. They feel that because of your father's history, you belong to the homeland—that you're its property and that the homeland has a right to claim you. You're therefore expected to respond to its call."

Thafer's heart pounds.

"Of course, the way you respond is a matter between yourself and your conscience, Thafer. I know how difficult it has been for you. I want to support you in whatever way I can."

"Thank you."

"Is Saeed going to take you home?"

"I think I better go with him."

"Yes, I have to go find Joan. She's invited me to their home."

"I better get going then."

"Take it easy, Thafer, and I'll see you in the morning."

VI

"Would you like a cup of tea this morning, Dr. Thafer?" asks the young Yemenite who arrives at OAPEC's headquarters early as usual, about the same time as Thafer.

"Yes, I would. Thank you, Khaled. Are we the first here?"

"I think I hear Dr. Suhaila and some of the secretaries arriving."

Thafer wonders why he always gets there early, knowing by now that only the janitors and the secretaries come at this hour. Something in him compels him to be at his desk by 7:00 A.M.

The first day of the conference was a surprise to him. He expected neither the discipline nor the sophistication with which it was conducted. It was also a dramatic introduction to the contradictions of the Middle East. He's now seen and heard firsthand its logic, its passion, its anger, its fear, its calculations, and its miscalculations. He can't help bowing his head in awe and respect as he ponders what may happen next.

He opens his briefcase and looks at his voluminous notes. He reads some of them and turns to the words of the Kuwaiti minister. He imagines a world economically and politically united, where all governments cooperate in an unprecedented effort to do away with all of humanity's miseries—ignorance, disease, greed, and its crimes against its own kind. He imagines nations destroying their weapons, releasing their political prisoners, and agreeing to one world government, and opening their borders to all, regardless of race, religion or status. He imagines a world with one nationality, the human nationality, and scholars from all over the world then gather to create a new language to be taught to all peoples.

As he looks across his spacious office at the globe on the other side, he can't help feeling how unrealistic his dream is. He feels very much alone. He moves to the small table on the other side of his freshly dusted office. His friend will be coming to join him soon. It won't be very long, he assures himself. He can't wait to see her. He's always comforted when she's near him. He looks at the furniture and the windows. Despite the dusting and the glass cleaner that has been rubbed on the window panes and on the glass top of his elegant desk, there is still a peculiar smell in his office, the smell that comes with sandstorms.

The handle of his door is turning. There is a gentle knock, and the squeaky door opens. He knows it is Suhaila, his countrywoman, to whose every word and every move he is alert.

"May I come in, Thafer?"

"Yes, Suhaila." He stands and watches her face as she looks toward the empty chair behind his desk. "I'm here," he says, hearing the excitement in his own voice. "Come in."

"I didn't see you at first."

He remains standing, watching as she leans against the door she has just shut. "Are we ready to go?" he asks.

"It's too early, and we need to talk a little."

"What's on your mind?"

"The memo that the secretariat sent to the OAPEC members who want to participate in the Arab Shipping Company, the one requesting the payment of fifty million dollars before the end of September."

"What about it?"

"As you know, the request is incorrect."

"Yes, we discussed that."

"The Iraqi minister is going to raise some questions about it. He asked me if the fifty million dollars could be paid in installments, and he's going to bring the matter up this morning. A correction has to be made, but I don't know how."

"This isn't an uncommon error," says Thafer. "It shouldn't be difficult."

"People around here are not willing to admit mistakes. They're afraid to admit mistakes. I should be the one to draw the mistake to Hamdan's attention. I think I can handle it."

"Yes, you're in a good position to tell him. This is a mathematical slip that could easily be corrected by the economics division."

"As soon as the conference is over, I'll talk to Hamdan
about it. It'll be corrected, I'm sure."

"Good. Shall we go now?"

"I think we better."

VII

During the last session of the conference, the secretary general
gives a brief report. He tells the ministers that he or members
of the secretariat delegation will be glad to answer questions.

The Iraqi minister of oil rises. "I wish to ask a question.
In your letter addressed to the members of OAPEC, Mr. Secretary General, you request the payment of fifty million U.S.
dollars in cash from each member state before the end of
September. You have advised us that this is the amount due
from each member state for the Arab Shipping Company. My
question is whether we may pay this amount in installments
and whether we may pay part of the amounts due in kind,
instead of in cash."

Suhaila and Thafer look at each other.

"Mr. President," says the secretary general, "the secretariat
will address the questions of His Excellency and forward copies of its findings to all the members."

"You were right," whispers Thafer.

"I'll speak to Hamdan as soon as the conference adjourns,"
she whispers back.

"Any further questions or comments?" asks the secretary
general.

The Conference Hall remains quiet.

"My brothers," the presiding Bahraini oil minister says,
"we are about to conclude our conference. I want to thank you
one and all for your magnificent cooperation. You have all
been splendid. It has been an honor and a privilege to preside
over this historic conference. May the Almighty God crown

our efforts with success. May He protect our countries and our peoples from those who wish us harm. May He guide us to the straight path." Smiling broadly, he strikes the table with his gavel. "We are adjourned."

The Conference of oil ministers has given Thafer much to think about. It has forced him to wrestle with a controversial economic decision made by the most powerful economic and military power on earth, his adopted country, the United States of America.

He's gotten used to decisions and actions taken by his government supposedly in the national interest, although their full effect on the lives of other nations has not been taken into account. Unfortunately, the American people complacently accept even far-reaching actions by their government that affect their own destinies.

One day, he thinks, a startled American public may discover the folly of its government's foolish actions, which have had and will have disastrous consequences not only for others, but to the American people themselves. He is sure that history will show one day that the devaluation of the U.S. dollar was one such action.

He wants America to hear Safi's complaints, to see the misery in Beirut and in Hawalli, and to become interested and curious about the Middle East. Perhaps one day they might. When they do, neither fear nor domestic politics will deter them from ferreting out the story of the Middle East. The trick is to make them curious.

Someone knocks at his door.

"Come in," he said.

"Excuse me, Dr. Thafer," says Lemya, the secretary general's secretary, "there'll be an extraordinary meeting at Mr. Ziyad's office in a half hour. Mr. Ziyad wants you to attend. Mr. Hamdan, Mr. Mukhtar, and Dr. Suhaila will also attend."

"Thank you, Lemya. Do you know what will be discussed?"

"The question the Iraqi oil minister raised at the end of the conference."

"I am aware of the problem."

VIII

"I apologize for calling this meeting so late and on such short notice," Ziyad says, "but I need to respond promptly to the question raised by Iraq. As it turns out, Egypt and Syria are in the same predicament. They too would like a prompt reply. Do you have any ideas how we should respond to Iraq's question, Dr. Thafer?" the secretary general asks.

"I noticed a mathematical error that will affect the way we deal with this. The legal aspects may become moot."

"What is that?" asks the secretary general.

"The Arab Shipping Company, Brother Ziyad, has $450 million worth of authorized capital stock, but it has issued only ninety million dollars worth of stock for distribution. What is due from the member states of OAPEC is each member state's share of the ninety million dollars of stock issued for distribution, not of the total $450 million worth of authorized capital stock. It was therefore incorrect to request the member states to pay their share of the total authorized capital stock. They should have been requested to pay only their share of the ninety million dollars worth of stock issued for distribution. At the time the letter was sent, Brother Ziyad, OAPEC had only nine members. These nine member states should have been asked to pay ten million each, not fifty million dollars each." Thafer stops, looks at the secretary general, and waits for his response.

"You're right. Whose bright idea was it that we request them to pay $50 million?" The secretary general looks through his file with annoyance until he finds a letter, signed by him, requesting payment of fifty million U.S. dollars by each of the nine OAPEC member states. Egypt and Syria were not asked because neither was a member of OAPEC at that time. Then he flips the pages attached to his letter and examines a hand-written memorandum signed by Hamdan showing the computation that resulted in the fifty million dollar obligation for each member and proposing the form of the letter to be sent. "What a mess!" the secretary general says with obvious irritation. "How do you propose we correct this, Brother Hamdan?"

There is silence.

"Brother Hamdan?" repeats the secretary general.

"This can be easily corrected, Brother Ziyad," says Hamdan, his voice irascible. "We should send a letter stating that because Egypt and Syria have become new members, it has become necessary to redivide the total amount due by eleven members instead of by nine members. We'll tell them that the amount now due is only eight or so million dollars. We needn't mention the fifty million dollars, or say we made a mistake. They'll never notice it anyway."

Ziyad stares.

Mukhtar and Suhaila become restless.

"I can't believe they won't wonder about the drastic reduction from fifty million dollars to eight million, Brother Hamdan," Mukhtar says.

"I wonder about that," says Ziyad.

"I don't think they'll notice the difference," says Hamdan.

"Dr. Suhaila?" Ziyad asks.

"Someone might question it, Brother Ziyad," she says in a very low voice. "We should think of a better way."

"What do you think, Brother Thafer?" asks the secretary general.

"I think, Brother Ziyad, that we should send a letter promptly advising all the members of OAPEC that an inadvertent error was made in the original letter, that the correct amount due is ten million U.S. dollars, not fifty million. We should tell them that in view of the fact that Egypt and Syria have become new members of OAPEC, what is expected of each member state of OAPEC now is about eight million. We should be forthright about the error and avoid complicating it. We should make the correction promptly without confusing them. I'll be happy to write you a memorandum on this and a proposed letter to send."

"I don't want us to say that we made a mistake, Dr. Thafer," the secretary general says emphatically. "Go ahead, write a memorandum on the whole matter and what we should do. I'll wait."

His Excellency doesn't "goof," Thafer muses. He's uptight. "I'll work on that right away, Brother Ziyad."

"I'll appreciate it, Dr. Thafer. I'll wait."

Thafer returns to his office and begins to draft a memorandum. He repeats in writing what he explained orally to the secretary general: he writes that according to the articles of incorporation of the Arab Shipping Company, installment payments are not permitted when the amount due is less than ten million U.S. dollars, and that payments in kind are specifically excluded. He also recommends that a letter be circulated to the member states of OAPEC, stating that a mathematical error was made in the earlier communication, which the secretariat regrets, and that what is actually due is about only eight million U.S. dollars.

It is close to 3:00 P.M. when Thafer takes his legal memorandum to the secretary general. It is most unusual for the secretary general and for OAPEC's senior staff to be in their offices much beyond 1:00 P.M. But they are all waiting. A sense of crisis prevails in the offices of OAPEC as the secretary general meets with his senior staff again to review Thafer's legal memorandum.

"I'm not going to say we made a mistake, Dr. Thafer," says the secretary general firmly. There is tension and uneasiness in his voice. "We will send a letter along the lines proposed by

Brother Hamdan and see what happens." He pauses. Then he turns to Hamdan. "Brother Hamdan, would you prepare a letter advising the members of OAPEC that because Egypt and Syria have joined OAPEC, a new division has to be made and the new amount is about eight million. Also advise Iraq, Egypt, and Syria that installment payments and payments in kind will not be allowed. When they see the reduced figure, Brother Thafer, they will decide that installment payments are not necessary, and there will be no problem." The secretary general pauses again, his face grim. "I'm going to Beirut tomorrow," he says. "Brother Hamdan will take my place, and he will send the letters as I have requested."

What if the member states of OAPEC write back asking for an explanation? Thafer asks himself. He looks at the secretary general's strained face. Maybe he's unhappy with me because I mentioned the error, he wonders. Maybe he wants me to resign. Maybe I should resign anyway. No, I can't do that. At the very least I should wait and see where this will lead.

"Thank you, Brother Thafer," says the secretary general, standing and looking very unhappy as he walks from behind his desk. He shakes hands with Hamdan and Mukhtar. "I'm sorry I kept you this late, Dr. Suhaila," he says shaking her hand also. "Thank you again, Dr. Thafer," he says, extending his hand.

Standing, Thafer walks clumsily and extends his hand to the secretary general. What should I do now? he asks himself. Nothing. He isn't going to change his mind.

"I'll be back in a few days," says the secretary general as he walks out of his office.

IX

After the meeting, Thafer sits in his office, feeling uneasy. His phone rings.

"Thafer?" Suhaila says.

"Yes, Suhaila."

"Do you want me to come to your office, or do you want to come to mine?"

"I'll come to your office."

"I feel badly about the whole thing, Suhaila," Thafer starts. "What do you think?"

"I don't know what to think. Ziyad is very sensitive about admitting a mistake."

"I can see that."

"He was shocked. He panicked and agreed with Hamdan. We have to see what will happen."

"Oh boy, life is too complicated."

"Yes it is," she smiles. "You know the Arabic adage, 'It's easier to deal with reasonable enemies than to deal with unreasonable friends.' "

"I haven't heard it in a long time. I need to remember that one."

"I'm disappointed in Ziyad. My concern now is how he'll react if the ministers don't buy his explanation."

"What will Mukhtar do?"

"Mukhtar probably won't get involved. He might say something if things get out of hand, but we'll see."

"The whole thing sounds comical, Suhaila."

"In many ways it is, but these comical things can turn tragic."

"It's the kind of thing Westerners ridicule. That's why some of them think of the Arabs as medieval, proud tribesmen who have just stepped into the twentieth century."

"But these weaknesses are not peculiar to the Arabs, Thafer," she answers sharply. "Those who think this way forget that in the seventh and eighth centuries the Arabs gave the world a sophisticated culture that has deeply influenced modern times. The Ziyads and the Hamdans of the Arab world should not distract you or others from the positive side shown by those eloquent and thoughtful ministers."

Thafer winces. Be careful, he says to himself. As much as this lovely woman cares about you, she's also a proud nationalist who cares deeply about our heritage. Don't say anything that might offend her.

"I agree, Suhaila. I'm sorry. I shouldn't have said that."

"I'm sorry too, Thafer. Today Ziyad and Hamdan ride high. Tomorrow, they may be nothing. You know that famous Arabic verse:

> Carouse, ye sovereign lords!
> The wheel will roll,
> Forever to confound and console:
> Who sips today the golden cup,
> Will drink may hap tomorrow in a wooden bowl

"I like that."

"So, Thafer, 'Let all receive thy pity, none thy hate.' "

"They'll have all my sympathy, Suhaila. I will hate no one."

"I'm sure you won't, Thafer."

After their discussion in her office, Thafer invites Suhaila for lunch at his house, which OAPEC provided for him. It is a luxurious three-story house, four spacious bedrooms, and two full baths on one side of the third floor, and a very large master bedroom with a private bath and a lounge on the other side. The living room, the dining room, a private study, another full bath, and the kitchen are on the second floor. The living room is larger than the entire first floor of Thafer's house in Ashfield and can easily accommodate a hundred guests. It is extravagantly decorated, but Thafer had nothing to do with that. The dining room is very spacious and lavishly furnished, the large kitchen fully equipped with new appliances. The study, about the size of the living room in Thafer's house in Ashfield, is on the side of the house facing the sea. From the picture window, when it isn't windy, Thafer can see the Bay of Kuwait only a couple of hundred yards away. Suhaila is awed by the imposing house.

"Look at this priceless rug!" she says as they both walk into Thafer's study.

"Yes, I know." Thafer thinks of the night he spent at the home of the Amri brothers on the edge of the refugee camp in Beirut and the few nights he spent at Uncle Muneer and Mama Adla's apartment in the Palestinian ghetto.

"Lunch is ready, sir," says the tall, elderly Pakistani cook, standing at the door of Thafer's study.

"All right," says Thafer, "we'll be right with you."

As Suhaila and he walk out of the study into the hallway, he can hear the reverberation of their footsteps on the hard marble floor.

"What a magnificent dining room," Suhaila says, admiring the English bone china and the soft luster of the sterling flatware.

The Pakistani cook, in an immaculate long white shirt over ballooning white pants that taper to his ankles, is standing smartly behind a chair immediately to the right of the head chair. "Right here, ma'am," he says.

"Thank you, sir."

He gently pulls back the heavy chair, making it easier for Suhaila to seat herself, moves to the head of the long dining table to seat Thafer, and leaves the room.

"I wonder how old he is," Suhaila whispers.

"He's probably in his seventies. That high white chef's hat makes him seem taller than he is."

"He looks at us so respectfully," says Suhaila.

"He probably thinks we are aristocrats."

"Little does he know that we belong to peasantry, hardworking people probably like his, some of whom now live in the Palestinian ghetto in Hawalli and who would doubtless identify with the poor among his people."

"I'm always humbled and embarrassed whenever he seats me in this stately chair. I feel uncomfortable whenever he leans over to serve me the food he prepares and I notice the wrinkles on his face."

"The poor soul," she says.

Thafer rises to pick up a dish filled with broiled chicken and leans over to serve Suhaila.

"Thank you, Thafer. This is absurd. This fork is heavy."

"The cook is outside. He'll be insulted if we don't eat a lot."

She smiles. "It's delicious, but I'm a slow eater."

"And we have to leave some room. He's made a special dessert."

"What is it?"

"A big dish of caramelized, glazed nut clusters."

"Oh, my!"

"I hope you like the dessert, sir," says the cook, at last reaching for the empty plates.

"I'm sure we will," says Thafer.

"And would you like coffee or tea, ma'am?"

"I'll take tea, please."

"And you, sir?"

"Tea, please."

"I hear a little British in the cook's accent," Suhaila says.

"His entire demeanor is British. He's been around English people."

"Why does he retreat to the kitchen?"

"That's part of his training. He's mindful of his place, lest he intrude."

The cook places a big dish of caramelized, glazed nut clusters on the table in front of Suhaila.

"Oh, my!" Suhaila exclaims again. "He's putting the whole thing in front of me! Look at this big dish of luscious dessert, Thafer! Do you remember the young Palestinian vendors in the streets of Jerusalem? They would carry big round metal trays of these things, balancing them on their heads over coiled pieces of soft cloth, and weave skillfully through the streets on their bicycles chanting, 'Taza! Taza! Fresh! Fresh!' "

"Yes," says Thafer in a distant voice, now hearing the echoes of other vendors ringing in his ears. "Qumsan! Tawaqui! Bashakeer! Shirts! Hats! Towels!"

Resting his head on her breast, Thafer holds Suhaila close to him.

"Let's go to sleep a little," she whispers, kissing him and looking into his eyes with devotion, "then I have to go home."

"I wish you could stay all night!"

"I wish I could too, but I need to go back. My mother will worry about me if I stay too long."

"Let's just rest a little."

"All right," she whispers. "I love you."

"I love you too."

He can't go to sleep. It is as though he is embracing his homeland. Hearing her breathe, he feels comforted and protected by her presence. Her breasts remind him of the gentle hills of his homeland, her smooth soft skin of its plains, and her long, light brown hair of the rays of its sun. He wants to tell her that he loves her eyes and her lips, that he loves to hear her whisper softly in his ear, that he's comforted when she is with him, that he loves every word she says in defense of their heritage, that he regrets being insensitive to her feelings, and that he understands her passions. He wants to tell her that he loves her because she understands his emotions and feels his pain. Do I dare tell her, he asks himself, that I want to go back to the United States? That I can't continue working with idiots like Ziyad and Hamdan? That I don't want to become involved in the nuclear madness of the Middle East? That I want her to go with me to the United States?

She'll never go. She is more committed to the homeland than I am. She accepts the Middle East, with all its weaknesses, for what it is. She will give me up before she will give up the Middle East or the cause. That scares me. I will break her heart if I abruptly return to the United States—a fragile heart that has already been broken once by fate and that she has entrusted to me.

He is sure he can never leave her behind.

Why shouldn't I be involved in the nuclear madness of the Middle East? he asks himself. Am I not the son of that soldier whose legendary deeds have rendered me more inescapably a part of my homeland? Didn't this lovely woman whose every word and action I trust, tell me that? Didn't that experience I had at the bridge change me forever?

"What time is it, Thafer?" she asks, waking up.

"Seven in the evening. Did you rest?"

"I did, but I kept dreaming that you went back to the United States; then I woke up and you were holding me in your arms and I went back to sleep feeling secure. Then I dreamt that you decided to become involved in the nuclear program, and I woke up scared, but you were still holding me in your arms and I felt safe again."

"Do you think I should become involved in that nuclear insanity?"

"If I had your training, I would. Unfortunately, I don't know anything about it. That's a matter between you and your conscience, Thafer, isn't it?"

"It's getting late, I need to go home, Thafer."

"And I need to go to Hawalli. I'll follow you."

"Why?"

"I'd like to go see my family."

"You have a family in Hawalli!?"

"Yes, I go there every day."

"You never told me that. Tell me more about your family, Thafer. I want to know."

"My stepbrother and his family live in Hawalli. He's actually my first cousin."

"I read one time that Ayoub Allam's first wife was the widow of his older brother, but I didn't want to ask you about that."

"I want you and your mother to come and meet my family sometime."

"I would like that. My mother would too."

"No one in OAPEC knows that I have relatives here, Suhaila, except Saeed. And I would like to keep it that way."

"I won't tell anyone, Thafer, but I'm touched. So you know what it's like in Hawalli."

"I know exactly what it's like in Hawalli."

She pauses. "Thafer, everyone is talking about going nuclear, as though going nuclear is a breeze. I'm just wondering whether you think it's feasible. I mean, is it possible for our people and for the PLO to build nuclear weapons?"

"Everything is possible, but it isn't a breeze, as you put it. It's a very involved and complicated process, also very dangerous and above all very expensive. Only governments with extensive resources can afford it."

"Nuclear plants are expensive, I know."

"Suhaila, it isn't just nuclear plants that are expensive; the entire dangerous and complicated process of building nuclear weapons is prohibitively expensive. People around here talk about going nuclear as if it were like going to a grocery store to buy a loaf of bread."

"Just tell me a little about it so that I'll have an idea of what's actually involved."

"The location of any nuclear reprocessing plant, if it's to remain undetected, has to be underground. Nuclear reprocessing plants by their very nature are extremely sophisticated because they are very hot and have a very high level of radioactivity. You need hundreds and probably thousands of highly skilled, trained people who can be trusted to maintain the confidential nature of their work. It is hard for me to believe that such a plant wouldn't be easily detected, especially in the Middle East. A cluster of plants very deep underground would pose tremendous engineering problems, Suhaila, that would demand immensely sophisticated planning and intelligence, which I doubt the PLO is capable of."

"Maybe the PLO wouldn't be able to do it, but I'm sure some Arab governments would."

"I doubt it. A project of this magnitude is suited for a superpower with huge financial resources, one that is culturally equipped to cope with the project's problems and snags. It is not suited to a nearly penniless liberation movement or to governments, some of whom still live in the fourth and fifth centuries, Suhaila."

"I'm sure that in many respects some Arab states are still living in the fourth and fifth centuries, but then you'll be surprised how advanced some have become. Someone like me hears about the so-called clean bomb. What does it take to construct a clean bomb?"

"Oh, Suhaila! The so-called clean bomb is the dirtiest invention of man. It is a vicious and barbaric killer."

"I'm sorry. I just want to know what's involved."

"What I've described will cost tens of billions of dollars. For what? To destroy human life. Only sick people do that."

"I agree that only sick people do that, but the Americans, the Russians, the British, the French, the Chinese, and now the Israelis are doing it. If the Israelis are doing it, we have to do it, for our own survival."

"Truthfully, I don't believe that either the Arab governments or the PLO has what it takes to carry on such a project. I'm sorry, but I'm being frank."

"It won't be easy, but you underestimate the Middle East. If the Israelis have been able to do this, I'm sure Iraq, Egypt, Algeria, Syria, Libya, and even the PLO will be able to."

"It'll be the height of insanity. I have difficulty convincing myself that our people should become involved in this madness."

"Maybe it is the height of insanity, but as long as Israel has nuclear weapons, other countries of the Middle East should have them as well, and they will. That's the sad reality," she insists.

X

Almost a month has now passed since Thafer submitted his legal memorandum to the secretary general concerning the error in the distribution of the issued stock of the Arab Shipping Company. The secretary general is still in Beirut. In the meantime, something curious happens to Thafer because of that incident. He now understands the secretary general's childlike and stubborn resistance to admitting the error. How could he admit a mistake? Thafer begins to ask himself. After all, those who make mistakes in the Middle East are punished, ridiculed, beaten, tortured, imprisoned, dismissed from their jobs, and sometimes even executed. The secretary general can't expose himself to any of that. As he finds himself rationalizing the secretary general's human weakness, he finds himself resenting Hamdan's pompous arrogance. That's because he knows the mistake originated with him. There is also something about Hamdan's attitude that Thafer resents: if one makes a mistake, one does anything to cover it up. One just doesn't care whether one lies, cheats, pulls the wool over others' eyes, or even hurts others in the process. He finds this total disregard for the truth, and for the consequences of obscuring it, indigestible. It's different from anything he has seen among the staff of

OAPEC. Thafer has an irresistible urge to expose it. He knows that he can get hurt in the process, but he doesn't care.

Having been summoned by Hamdan's secretary, Thafer walks to Hamdan's office. Maybe I can reason with him, he thinks, but I don't want to fight with him. He knows that Suhaila is at Hamdan's office. Maybe she is still with him. Maybe she will soften him. He enters Hamdan's office.

"Hello, Dr. Thafer," says Reem Makram, standing and walking to Hamdan's door. "I'll tell him you're here. Dr. Suhaila is with him."

Thafer goes in and greets both Hamdan and Suhaila.

"Please have a chair, Dr. Thafer," Hamdan says, pointing in front of him to an empty chair next to Suhaila's. He looks perturbed. "Ziyad is still in Beirut. We expected him back three weeks ago." He looks at a letter he holds in his hand, then at Thafer. "Have you discussed the matter of the distribution of the Arab Shipping Company's stock with anyone, Dr. Thafer?"

"Not since I discussed it with the secretary general just before he left for Beirut," says Thafer icily.

"Not within OAPEC or outside it?"

Thafer's eyes narrow as he looks at Hamdan again. He is about to explode, but struggles to contain his agitation. "Not within OAPEC or outside it," he says intensely.

"We've received this from the Kuwaiti Ministry of Oil, Dr. Thafer." Hamdan hands Thafer a letter addressed to the secretary general and signed by the legal advisor of the Kuwaiti Ministry of Oil.

The letter is to the point. It asks for an explanation of the drastic reduction in the amount requested as payment for the distribution of stock of the Arab Shipping Company—from fifty million U.S. dollars requested on March 15, 1972, to eight million dollars requested on June 17.

Thafer reads the letter, places it in front of him on Hamdan's desk, and looks at Hamdan, giving no sign of emotion. What am I to tell him? he asks himself. Nothing! But I feel like telling the idiot that I hope it will get worse and worse! He observes Hamdan's distress. Well, maybe he's as much a victim as the secretary general is, he thinks; maybe I've got to be understanding. Besides, Hamdan is the key to correcting the error if I can reason with him. Thafer looks at Hamdan's worried baby face. He's like a frightened kid who's using childish methods to escape punishment. If I don't help him, he'll hurt not only himself, but also others who are innocent. Maybe he'll even hurt the woman I love, who's sitting next to me, wondering what I am going to say. But how can I help him without making things worse? Since Hamdan is the one who made the error, maybe I should find a way to let him save face. He's asked me to come to his office because he needs my help. But the fool started by accusing me of discussing this outside OAPEC, which only betrayed his inability to confront his problem. Thafer again looks at Hamdan's confused and anxious face.

"I guess we have a problem, Brother Hamdan."

"I guess we do," says Hamdan in a low voice.

There is a brief pause. Hamdan seems subdued.

"By the way, and before we get into this, I want to tell you that I thought His Excellency the Saudi oil minister was quite eloquent during the conference."

"Did you like him?" asks Hamdan instantly.

"I thought he was superb," says Thafer, exaggerating.

"He was disappointed in the outcome of the conference."

Thafer remains silent.

"OAPEC is an economic organization, Dr. Thafer. Many of us feel that if OAPEC becomes politicized, it will soon be dead. That's why the Saudi oil minister tried very hard to avoid discussing the devaluation of the U.S. dollar. I was frankly disappointed in your interpretation of that provision of the charter. I believe that you were in error."

"Yes, Brother Hamdan," says Thafer, keeping a straight face, "I may have goofed that one. These interpretations are

not easy to make. I tell you I was pretty keyed up. I looked
at all those strange faces, not knowing any of them and not
knowing at first how to start. Then I decided to make the
interpretation I made, hoping it would satisfy all of them. I
wouldn't have minded if they had appointed a committee to
review what I told them. In fact, it would've made me feel
better about it. We're all susceptible to error. We all make
mistakes. If we didn't, we wouldn't be human."

Hamdan looks somewhat surprised.

I've got to be careful, Thafer muses. I wonder if I've been
too transparent.

"That's right," says Hamdan. "We're all human. You Americans always say that. But if it's a big mistake, you have a way
of blaming your mistake on someone else. We make mistakes
here too. God knows I've been guilty of that many times. I
just hope I never get caught. If I am"—he makes a slashing
gesture across his throat.

"That doesn't apply to an inadvertent, trivial mistake,
Brother Hamdan, does it?"

"It depends. If some bastard is out there to get you, he can
make life difficult."

"I can see that. On the other hand, if it's a small human
error, isn't it better to correct it while it's still small—to
prevent some bastard from hurting us if it gets big?"

Hamdan, examining Thafer closely, seems less worried as
he tries to answer. "I know what you're driving at, Dr. Thafer,
but you still don't understand."

"I'm trying to," says Thafer calmly, looking at Hamdan
intently.

"We don't live in Europe or in the United States, Dr.
Thafer. You're proposing an American solution to an Arab
problem. It won't work."

"I beg to differ with you, Brother Hamdan," says Thafer.
"I'm proposing a human solution to a human problem. Errors
and mistakes are not peculiar to the Arabs or to the Americans.

Everyone is susceptible, whether he's Arab, American, or Chinese. What makes people angry, I think, is having to suspect that someone is trying to pull the wool over their eyes. Frankly, if I were in the oil minister's shoes I would be very angry to think that someone is trying to do that to me, which is why I thought from the beginning that the sooner we admit the error and correct it, the better it will be for everyone." Thafer is forceful.

"I respect your frankness, Dr. Thafer, but I don't agree with you. I still think that you're providing an American solution to an Arab problem." Hamdan rotates his chair away from Thafer and looks at the large portrait of the king of Saudi Arabia hanging on the wall of his office. He stares at the ceiling, his head resting on his clasped hands. Appearing tranquil, he is in deep thought.

Thafer sneaks a look at Suhaila, who has sat quietly through the discussion. Thafer now decides that Hamdan is frightened and feels sorry for him. The letter from the legal advisor of Kuwait's Ministry of Oil and Finance has shaken him up and shattered his confidence in his solution.

"How can I be of help, Brother Hamdan?"

"I don't know, Dr. Thafer," Hamdan says, the worry returning to his face. "I know and Ziyad knows what you want us to do. I was sure Ziyad didn't want to do that. I thought I had a solution, but my solution isn't working, and it's only making things worse and more complicated. Maybe in retrospect we should've listened to you. My problem is that Ziyad's not here, and I can't do anything until he comes back. But I'm going to recommend to him that we do what you're suggesting. It'll be up to him, Dr. Thafer."

Thafer is flabbergasted.

Hamdan rotates his chair and looks at the king's portrait again, the same portrait that was hanging in Thafer's office his first day of work, the king appearing to have smelled something terrible. "I think that on the basis of the letter we have just received from Kuwait, we can assume the explanation we gave was unsatisfactory, but I'm not going to respond to Kuwait's letter until Ziyad returns. If he doesn't accept your advice, he has to figure a way of getting out of this." He grins childishly as if he has made a great discovery, the anxiety disappearing completely from his youthful face.

XI

It is a very hot July day. Thafer sits in his office wondering about the secretary general and OAPEC. The secretary general returned to Kuwait five weeks later than originally expected. He is in a good mood, rested, and relaxed, as though a big load has been lifted from his back.

His relaxed mood puzzles Thafer. There is no sense of urgency or crisis at OAPEC now. Suhaila is giving Thafer emotional support and valuable advice, and he is thoroughly engrossed in his legal work. He is drafting an important constitution and rules for the proposed Arab Court of Justice and is enjoying it, but he misses his children and continues to wonder if he has done the right thing in coming to Kuwait. The heat is unbearable, worse than he remembers it being in Kuwait in 1950 and 1951 when he was a young boy living in the desert. His children are going to visit him in early September, when the weather will be more bearable. They will stay with him a couple of weeks. Remembering their visit cheers him up, but before then he has to make OAPEC-related trips to Baghdad, Cairo, and Damascus. He is uneasy about these trips.

"There is a meeting at Mr. Ziyad's office at 11:30 this morning, Dr. Thafer," says Lemya, speaking to Thafer on the phone.

"Thank you, Lemya."

Why a meeting so soon after the secretary general's return from Beirut?

He walks to the secretary general's office.

"Where's everybody, Dr. Thafer?" asks the secretary general cheerfully. "Come right in and pull up a chair. This is going to be informal."

"Thanks. I'm sure they'll all be here soon."

"Dr. Thafer, I want you to know that I valued your advice concerning the error in the distribution of the Arab Shipping Company's stock. I know it is the correct advice, but I can't follow it. I'm not going to tell anyone we made a mistake. Hamdan has informed me about the conversation you had with him a few days ago. He's recommended that we write another letter admitting our mistake. Something within me keeps telling me this is not the way to go. We've already put all of them on notice that what's due is about eight million U.S. dollars. That's done. We've also responded to Iraq's questions. So that's also out of the way. The rest—the error, who made it, why, and how it was made—I'm not even going to address. I'm not going to respond to Kuwait's letter. They want me to come out and say I've made a mistake. I'm not going to do it. If someone wants a pound of flesh, so be it."

The secretary general speaks calmly and emphatically, almost convincingly. There is no hesitation in what he says; he is determined. He looks at Thafer as if hoping that he will agree.

Do I have to say something? Thafer asks himself as the secretary general stares at him, waiting for a response. "I understand, Brother Ziyad."

"I'm sorry, but this is the way I feel."

The two assistant secretaries general walk into the office. They are followed by Suhaila.

"Let's all sit around the table on the other side of the office," says the secretary general, leading his senior staff to a round table near a picture window overlooking the bay of Kuwait.

The four senior staff members of OAPEC sit at the table, their eyes trained on Ziyad as if they are expecting him to say something important.

"I have an announcement to make," Ziyad says. "I have submitted my resignation to the Council of Arab Oil Ministers, but they've asked me to stay on for another six months, in order to give OAPEC time to nominate a replacement. I have agreed. I want you to know that my reasons for resigning are strictly personal. I want to share this with you lest you hear rumors and become concerned. Please keep my resignation confidential until a formal announcement is made, which should be in a couple of months. In the meantime, our work will go on."

"We're all going to miss your thoughtful leadership, Brother Ziyad," says Mukhtar.

"I'm going to miss all of you," says the secretary general, smiling broadly, "but I look forward to going back to a quieter life with my wife and children. The constant traveling has been too much."

"We all wish you the best," says Suhaila.

"Thank you, Dr. Suhaila. I have nothing else to discuss this morning. We can always meet again whenever something comes up."

They all stand.

The secretary general moves from behind his desk, comes around to Thafer, and extends his hand. "I'm sorry we won't have more time to work together, Dr. Thafer."

"I'm sorry too, Brother Ziyad. I wish you the very best."

"When will you make your trips, Dr. Thafer?"

"Soon. I'll be leaving in two days."

"Who's going with Dr. Thafer, Brother Mukhtar?"

"Ali from public relations will go with him to Baghdad. They'll meet Dr. Suhaila in Cairo. Dr. Thafer and Ali proceed to Damascus from Cairo, and Dr. Suhaila returns to Kuwait."

"I'll be here when you come back, I'm sure, Dr. Thafer," says the secretary general. Moving toward his assistants, he embraces and kisses them. Then he turns to Suhaila. "You've been wonderful, Dr. Suhaila. Give Dr. Thafer all the help you can."

"I will. Thank you for your special kindness to me, Brother Ziyad."

The next day, Suhaila comes to Thafer's office. She has not been in to see him since their meeting at the secretary general's office the day before.

"Come right in," Thafer says.

She walks in and stands dejectedly in front of him, her eyes down.

"Won't you please sit down?"

"I'll be seeing you a little later, won't I?"

"Yes, of course. What's the matter?"

"I'm having a problem with Hamdan."

"What's the trouble?"

"Hamdan now says that the error in calculating the distribution of the stock of the Arab Shipping Company originated with me. I think he wants to blame the whole thing on me."

"He can't do that!" says Thafer, every nerve in his body aroused. "He won't get away with it."

"Don't get upset, Thafer. I know how to handle him."

"How're you going to handle the crazy fool?"

"Don't worry about me. You need to prepare for your trip to Baghdad tonight. I'll be able to take care of the problem. I know how."

"How are you going to take care of it, Suhaila? The guy is demented. He might become vicious."

"Don't worry about it, Thafer. I know how to handle him."

XII

"Dr. Thafer," the Iraqi minister of oil says after Thafer has been greeted in the minister's modest office, "Iraq is in the process of developing nuclear energy for civilian purposes as part of its industrial program. This alternative form of energy is strictly for peaceful purposes. It is nonmilitary in nature. We have been relying on the French to assist us in developing our program. Yet we're not unaware of the great strides that the Americans have made in nuclear technology. We would like you to help us seek this advanced American technology. We want to do this properly and legally, through the appropriate U.S. governmental channels. We're willing to submit our plants to periodic inspections. We're also willing to have what we produce in any nuclear plant we acquire from the United States or from any other country inspected on a periodic and regular basis. We understand that you've assisted other developing countries with similar projects."

"Yes, Excellency, I have."

"Do you think you can help us?"

"Indeed, I can, Excellency, as long as it is for civilian and nonmilitary purposes and as long as Iraq is willing to allow regular periodic inspections."

"How do we go about it, Dr. Thafer?"

"I'll contact my senior law partner in the United States, and I'll present to him Your Excellency's wishes."

"We don't want to do it by telephone. The confidentiality of what we are trying to do is of utmost importance to its success. I needn't tell you that."

"Yes, Excellency, I understand. As long as the nuclear plant is for peaceful purposes, it's perfectly legal, but I respect your approach in wanting it to be cleared through the proper governmental channels. Exporting nuclear plants, Excellency, requires a validated export license that has to be issued by the U.S. Department of Commerce. Our law firm in the United States can handle all the details when the time comes, but I need to ask some questions, if I may, Excellency."

"I'll answer what I can, and what I can't, I'll get answers for from those who know."

"Thank you, Excellency. Where is this plant going to be installed?"

"Most likely in the northern part of Iraq, which can produce nuclear energy cheaply and efficiently because of the deposits of uranium there."

"How will the plant be paid for, Excellency?"

"Through an irrevocable, confirmed letter of credit issued by our government."

"When does Iraq wish to have the plant, Excellency?"

"As soon as possible, but we're aware that a complicated transaction of this nature takes time."

"Excellency, would you or a team from Your Excellency's ministry be willing to make a trip to the United States to discuss this matter with my senior partner in New York, if I can arrange such a meeting?"

"Without a doubt. I will go myself, and I will take a team of engineers, scientists, and lawyers with me. When can you arrange this, Dr. Thafer?"

"I can arrange the meeting with my senior partner almost immediately, but I suspect he would want to clear the project with one or two manufacturers, as well as advise the Department of Commerce."

"As an initial step, Dr. Thafer, do you think your senior partner would be willing to come to Iraq?"

"If need be, he would."

"Good, I will have him meet one of our very high officials."

"I'm sure I can arrange that, Excellency."

"Will you be able to make the arrangements for your senior partner to visit Iraq before you leave Baghdad?"

"Certainly."

"When he comes, can you return to help in the negotiations?"

"I'll be happy to return."

"And when you return, we'll arrange for my trip to the United States with my team. You'll be welcome to accompany us."

"I don't think it'll be necessary for me to accompany you to the United States. After I put Your Excellency in touch with my senior partner, who I'm sure will be happy to come to Baghdad, he'll arrange everything for you. I'm certain of that. If it becomes necessary that I go to the United States, I'll be happy to."

"I know you have a lot of work at OAPEC, and you need to attend to that. OAPEC may become interested in a nuclear plant."

"Yes, but it's easier to undertake a project like this with one party because it doesn't require the approval of eleven states."

"We will do whatever is necessary to proceed."

"I'll do what I can to help, Excellency."

"Let me now tell you about the program we have for you during your visit. We'll have lunch at a restaurant in the old section of Baghdad that overlooks the Tigris. Senior members of our ministry will join us. After lunch we'll give you a tour of this old section. Tomorrow we will visit ancient Babylon, and the day after tomorrow we will take you to the northern part of Iraq. I understand that the next day you'll depart for Syria and that your trip to Egypt has been postponed."

"Yes. I need to return to Kuwait after a brief visit to Damascus. The program sounds exciting. I look forward to seeing Baghdad and ancient Babylon. I'm eager to see northern Iraq because I've always heard about its beauty."

Salah Eddeen, where Thafer spends a day with the Iraqi minister of oil, is nestled in the magnificent mountains of northern Iraq. It is a Kurdish village that overlooks vast prairies several thousand feet below. Thafer is not prepared for the breathtaking view of grasslands and meadows below.

"I didn't realize northern Iraq was this beautiful, Excellency."

"Do you see that range of mountains in the distance, Dr. Thafer?" The Iraqi minister points to a location northeast of them.

"Yes, Excellency?"

"Our troops are in constant combat with the Kurdish tribes on those mountains over there. Iran arms and organizes the mountain Kurds in an effort to drain our economy and weaken Iraq. The shah of Iran is one of the worst despots of our region and very unpopular within his own country. One day there'll be a revolution in Iran. Those who have been supporting the shah will not be forgiven by the people of Iran, but the present regime there poses a great threat to Iraq. Iraq needs to be strong to face both Iran's threat from the east and Israel's threat from the west."

"Is that range of mountains in the distance in Iran?" Thafer asks.

"No, it is in Iraq. It is rich in minerals, including copper and uranium."

"The whole area is strikingly beautiful."

"Iraq wants to develop the area for tourism, but before we can do that, we need to stabilize the region and put an end to Kurdish uprisings. That'll be difficult as long as Iran supports the Kurds."

"Is there a way Iraq can negotiate with Iran on that issue, Excellency?"

"We've tried, but Iran wants control over half of our Shatt al-Arab waterway, the 120-mile confluence of the Tigris and Euphrates rivers that flows into the Persian Gulf."

"I always thought that Shatt al-Arab was Iraqi territory. I've never understood how the dispute with Iran over it started."

"Yes, Shatt al-Arab is Iraqi territory, but Iraq has had a long history of struggle trying to maintain its control over this vital waterway. In 1847, when Iraq was under Ottoman rule, the treaty of Erzerum between the Ottomans and Iran settled the issue, confirming that Shatt al-Arab is an integral part of Iraq. That treaty was reaffirmed in 1911 by the Teheran Protocol. In 1913, when we were still occupied by the Ottomans, the Constantinople Delimitation Protocol adjusted the frontier line of Shatt al-Arab to give to Iran a three-mile place of anchorage in what is now the Iranian port of Abadan. Abadan is historically part of Iraq, and its population is Iraqi Arab. 1913, Dr. Thafer, was a bad year for Iraq. In 1913, under pressure from Britain and without Iraq's consent, the Ottomans also allowed the creation of the sheikhdom of Kuwait, carving Kuwait out of the Iraqi province of Basra."

"I know about Kuwait, but I didn't know about Shatt al-Arab dispute."

"The two problems are interrelated. They have to do with Iraq's access to navigable outlets to the sea. Kuwait is our natural outlet, but it was stolen from us during the Ottoman rule by Great Britain. When Iraq gained its independence in 1932, it immediately laid claim to Kuwait and to Shatt al-Arab. Iran continued to claim parts of Shatt al-Arab until 1937, when we entered into an agreement with them in which we retained control over the Shatt except for the small area near the ports of Abadan and Khorramshahr. Iran continued to violate its treaty obligations throughout the 1950s and the 1960s. Then in 1969 it unilaterally abrogated the 1937 treaty with us, demanding the division of the river along the middle of its main channel. To force us to accept its demand, it incited the Kurds, who were living on those mountains you can see to the northeast of here, to rebellion against Iraq. And that's where we are with respect to Shatt al-Arab and the Kurdish uprising."

"Waterways and outlets to the sea are always important."

"Kuwait was always part of the province of Basra until 1899, when Great Britain signed a secret agreement with a Bedouin who murdered his two brothers to become chieftain.

Great Britain paid him fifteen thousand Indian rupees to sign the secret agreement that created the sheikhdom of Kuwait and deprived Iraq of its natural access to the sea. When the Ottoman governor of Baghdad ordered the new chieftain arrested and tried to bring him to Baghdad for trial, the cheiftan sought British protection. The British refused his request. He turned for assistance to Britain's archrivals, the Russians and offered them a coal-loading station in Kuwait. Fearing that a Russian foothold in the Persian Gulf might jeopardize their access to India, the British were alarmed. So in 1899 they signed their secret agreement with this Bedouin chieftain to ensure that no territories would be leased, sold, or given to any other power without British consent and to guarantee to the chieftain and his heirs and successors British protection from the Ottomans, plus payment of fifteen thousand rupees. That chieftain's heirs and successors learned their ancestor's lesson well. They have been playing one power against another since then to maintain their feudalistic rule over Kuwait. That won't go on forever, I assure you, Dr. Thafer. Kuwait is Iraqi territory and will one day be returned to Iraq."

"These matters take time."

"They do," says the Iraqi minister as he fixes his gaze on the mountain range in the distance.

XIII

"Syria," says the Syrian minister, "is not interested in building nuclear weapons, Dr. Thafer, nor is it in a position financially and technologically to do so. Syria would like to see the Middle East free of all weapons of mass destruction. We believe that the very idea of stocking them is the height of lunacy, but Israel has embarked on a relentless program of building these weapons on a large scale, and the government of the United States has closed an eye to this insanity. If Syria sits and watches, it will be courting disaster. How can we obtain nuclear weapons without having to acquire a nuclear plant or building them ourselves?"

Thafer looks with surprise at the Syrian minister. "I don't have any access to nuclear weapons, Excellency. This is outside my field. Nuclear weapons, Excellency, aren't available on the market. They aren't like other weapons."

"You'll be surprised, Dr. Thafer. If the price is right, one can acquire almost anything. All countries of the Middle East will acquire nuclear weapons sooner or later. As long as Israel has nuclear weapons, others will. Otherwise, what will prevent Israel from blackmailing the rest of us?"

"Those who have nuclear weapons manufacture them, I suppose."

"The logistics are impossible. We've studied such a project very carefully. We believe it to be beyond our capability as a developing nation. It's also an expensive undertaking, and our budget won't allow it."

"These matters are a constant reminder that the world is crazy," says Thafer.

"That's right. Why should we be concerned about building nuclear weapons when some of our people are still barefoot and hungry? Why should the two superpowers lead the world in that direction? But we have to worry about Israel, which the United States has planted in our midst in order to divert our attention from building up our economies and raising our standard of living. The weapons merchants—including, of course, the United States—would like us to buy armaments produced by them and live in constant fear and insecurity. Those responsible for this mockery don't belong in the family of civilized nations. I regret to say that the United States is the leader of this scheme, although it's portrayed as the model of democracy and the guardian of justice and peace. Ask the Latin American countries what they think of the guardian of justice and peace. Ask the Blacks and the Hispanics and the downtrodden in the United States what they think of the angel of charity and brotherhood. Ask your own Palestinian people what they think. Who is helping Israel to oppress our sons and daughters in Palestine? Who is helping it to deprive our fathers and mothers of their livelihood? Who arms Israel to drive our grandfathers and grandmothers from their homes and land? You must know who's mainly responsible. The greedy unprincipled imperialists divided Syria, as you undoubtedly know, after World War I. That great deception of the imperialists is the darkest episode of their history and will bring them infamy and disgrace as long as they live, but infamy and disgrace are not enough because the imperialists are shameless. We must be strong to protect ourselves against their evil deeds. We must be strong. We must have enough weapons to deter our enemies from making reckless ventures against us. We must acquire nuclear weapons. Only when we acquire nuclear weapons will we be safe. Only when we acquire nuclear weapons will we be in a position to demand justice for our people. Only then will there be peace in our region."

XIV

"May I come in?" asks Sheikh Mahmood, tapping gently on Thafer's office door. It is early morning. Thafer returned to Kuwait the night before from his trips to Baghdad and Damascus.

"Please do, Sheikh Mahmood." Thafer, remembers the first time he met the bearded Egyptian. He has not seen or talked to him since.

"Do you remember me?"

"Of course I do. You're Dr. Suhaila's senior assistant."

"Right, and I have a message for you from her."

"What is it?" he asks in a panic.

"I'm sorry," Mahmood says, no doubt noticing Thafer's anxiety. "Dr. Suhaila has resigned."

"Where is she?" Thafer, clears his throat.

"In Egypt."

"Do you know why she resigned?"

"She had a disagreement with Mr. Hamdan. She'll probably go back to her former position in the Ministry of Oil in Egypt."

"Do you really think so?"

"The Egyptian oil minister feels that some injustice has been done to Dr. Suhaila here."

"How do you know that?"

"She told me. The Egyptian oil minister asked her to go to Cairo for consultation. She asked me to tell you that she'll be here in a few days to take her mother back to Egypt. They may move back there."

Thafer stares out his window at the rolling waves in the bay below.

"The general atmosphere is not reassuring, Dr. Thafer. There's tension in OAPEC. Mr. Ziyad is leaving. Although his departure is not unexpected, the timing and the circumstances surrounding it have created anxiety among the staff here. Something must've happened at the Conference of Oil Ministers that has produced a sense of crisis in OAPEC. This has never happened before, not since I've been with the organization. I have asked Dr. Suhaila about it many times, but she doesn't tell me anything."

He pauses.

"Have you heard that Kuwait has requested a special meeting of the Council of Arab oil ministers?"

"No I haven't. I've been away. I came back last night. Who advised you of the special meeting?"

"Mr. Mukhtar."

"Did Mr. Mukhtar say why Kuwait has requested a special meeting?"

"No, he didn't."

Thafer notices one or two gray hairs in Mahmood's otherwise black beard, but no gray in the dark short hair of his head. He wonders how old he is. He can't be much older than me, he thinks, but the man's beard and dark clothing make him look older. "A lot of strange things are happening," Thafer says, finally relaxing a little.

"True."

"Do you have any idea when the special meeting will take place, Sheikh Mahmood?"

"In a week or two," he says, standing and preparing to leave. "If I hear anything important, Dr. Thafer, I'll let you know."

"I'll do the same." Thafer, stands and gives him a warm handshake. "Thanks for coming. I'll talk to you soon."

"Thank you, Dr. Thafer."

"Thafer, just Thafer."

"And I am Mahmood, Thafer."

Suhaila is back in Egypt! Thafer says to himself. Hamdan has decided to blame her for his mistake. That's why our people lose wars; that's why their lands are still occupied; that's why they're not ready for the nuclear age. As he puts his head down, he remembers the conversations he had with the Iraqi and Syrian ministers in Baghdad and in Damascus and begins to debate with himself.

Are you sure, he asks himself, that Iraq wants a nuclear plant for civilian, nonmilitary purposes?

I have no idea and I won't ask.

Why don't you want to ask? You've already arranged for Jim Tucker to go to Iraq. You know he's going to put Iraq in touch with one or two manufacturers of nuclear plants and other sophisticated equipment that could be used to build nuclear weapons. Shouldn't you warn your elderly partner about all this?

Jim Tucker knows his business. He wasn't born yesterday.

But he has no idea that Iraq may be thinking about nuclear weapons.

Neither do I.

Aren't you putting your head in the blessed sand again?

I have no right to assume anything. This is a civilian transaction, and I'm going to let it go at that. If the transaction becomes serious, it has to be presented to the Department of Commerce. Let them do their investigation.

What if Jim Tucker decides to introduce Iraq to a manufacturer outside the United States?

Jim knows his business. I'm not going to interfere with his judgment on these matters.

You're not as straight as you pretend to be. What about all the talk about pacifism and nonviolence? Are you sure you don't want to see Iraq become a nuclear power? Have you changed?

No, I haven't changed.

Yes, you have! What happened at the bridge changed you, and you know it. You've become like Ayoub Allam, the warrior. It all began in Beirut, at the refugee camp. That impassioned young officer of the PLO, Adnan Amri, touched you with his anger. The ghetto in Hawalli tore your heart. Your brother Kamal and what he said about Ayoub Allam fueled the smoldering fire within you. Then those encounters with Suhaila, your countrywoman, awakened that slumbering passion hidden within you. But it was the humiliation at the bridge and your inability to see your mother that changed you forever.

XV

"I thought I'd walk with you to the meeting, Thafer," says Mahmood as he enters Thafer's office at about 10:15 the next morning. He appears comfortable, ready to go.

"Come in, Mahmood."

"I haven't been to a senior staff meeting before."

"They are informal," says Thafer as they walk together to
Ziyad's office.

"Good morning, gentlemen," the secretary general says. The
senior staff of OAPEC rise as he walks to his chair at the head
of the table. He seems anxious and preoccupied. "Welcome
back, Dr. Thafer. I'm sorry we interrupted your trip. Please be
seated, gentlemen. We have only one item to discuss. Kuwait
has requested a special meeting of the Council of Arab Oil
Ministers to review and discuss the distribution of the stock
of the Arab Shipping Company. That's the only item on the
agenda so far. I doubt that there'll be any other. Because we
are all involved, I thought we should discuss the matter be-
forehand. Brother Hamdan, do you have any thoughts?"

"I don't," says Hamdan curtly. The question takes him by
surprise. He did not expect to be singled out. He appears
worried, and the direct question seems to have angered him.

"How about you, Brother Mukhtar?"

"Yes, I do have a suggestion, Brother Ziyad. We're allow-
ing this to get out of hand. I think that the secretariat should
respond to Kuwait's letter of inquiry about the distribution of
the stock immediately. I think that we should tell the legal
advisor of Kuwait's Ministry of Oil that indeed there was a
mistake in the original distribution of the stock, that we regret the mistake, and that a correction has been made. Failing
to respond is bound to compound the problem. We don't need
that, Brother Ziyad. We should also respond in the same way
to Iraq's inquiry. Ignoring these letters won't make them go
away. It's only going to aggravate an already tense situation,
and things will get worse. God knows we don't need that now,
Brother Ziyad."

"We've already corrected everything, Brother Mukhtar."

"No, Brother Ziyad, we haven't. Otherwise, we wouldn't
be getting these inquiries."

"Why do we have to dwell on this?" the secretary general asks angrily, his voice becoming shrill. "I am simply not going to stand there and tell everybody, 'We are fools, we made a stupid mistake.' That's not my way of doing things. It isn't my style. I simply won't do it. Period."

"Brother Ziyad," says Mukhtar, lowering his voice, "do you honestly think that Kuwait and Iraq don't know that a mistake has been made?"

"I know they do," shouts the secretary general, visibly irritated. "That's exactly the situation. That's exactly what's going on. Someone in their legal department is trying to rub our nose in it. I won't let them do that to us. I won't allow it."

"Brother Ziyad," Mukhtar repeats calmly, "the legal department of any ministry does what the minister instructs it to do. This is true of Kuwait, and it's also true of Iraq. I think that we'll all look more foolish trying to justify our original mistake. Attributing drastic reduction of the amount due to a modest increase in the number of OAPEC members makes no sense to anyone who can add two and two. We should simply say we made a mathematical error. I just don't understand why this is so bad."

"It's because they know we made a mistake," screams the secretary general, "and they are trying to have us come down on our knees and beg their forgiveness. That's uncalled for, and I won't do it, whatever the consequences." The secretary general's face is flushed with anger.

"You can do what you wish, Brother Ziyad," says Mukhtar in frustration. "You asked for my opinion. Now you know what I think." Then he turns to Hamdan. "That's what bad advice does, Brother Hamdan."

"My position is not based on Hamdan's advice," the secretary general shouts angrily. "Please withdraw your comment. This is how I feel about the situation. This is how I felt about it from day one. Hamdan has been trying to persuade me to change my mind. Dr. Thafer knows that. This is my own position, and I am going to stick to it."

"I'm sorry, Brother Hamdan. Do what you wish, Brother Ziyad. I'm sorry I said anything."

There is silence.

Thafer looks at Mahmood, who appears confused and doesn't seem to know what prompted the angry exchange.

"Do you wish to say anything, Brother Hamdan?" the secretary general asks.

"I support your position, Brother Ziyad."

"Dr. Thafer?"

"When will the special meeting be held, Brother Ziyad?"

"On September 15, at the Kuwait Sheraton. Those present at this meeting shall comprise the secretariat delegation. Do you have any new thoughts on the matter, Dr. Thafer?"

Thafer pauses. "I really don't, Brother Ziyad. I wish there were a way a correction could be made without embarrassing or hurting anyone."

"I wish there were too. I thought Hamdan's idea of correcting the error without making it appear that we made a stupid mistake was clever, frankly. But it hasn't worked. I'll stand by my position. Perhaps I'll regret this later." He turns to Mahmood. "Do you have any new ideas, Sheikh Mahmood?"

"Frankly, I don't understood what the problem is about, Brother Ziyad."

"Well," Ziyad says, "I don't either."

"I'm sorry, Brother Mukhtar," the secretary general finally says. "I respect your views, and I respect Dr. Thafer's views too. Please forgive my emotional responses. I think that we may be blowing this out of proportion to its deserved importance. That's all for now. I'll see all of you a day or two before the special meeting."

XVI

Thafer and Mahmood sit in the living room of Thafer's house after lunch later that afternoon. They discuss the morning meeting with the secretary general.

"What you've told me puzzles me," says Mahmood, "but if Hamdan tries to put the blame for the mistake on Suhaila, I'm sure Egypt will not stand for it."

"What if Ziyad backs Hamdan?"

"I doubt that Ziyad will do that, but one never knows. Ziyad is acting funny on this. He certainly was angry this morning."

"I've never seen him so out of control. We'll wait until Suhaila comes back from Egypt. I'm anxious to know what happened between her and Hamdan after I left for Baghdad."

"I heard her scream at Hamdan. She called him a liar and a coward. I didn't know the background of the problem, but I can see now why she was furious."

Good for Suhaila!

"Then she went to Ziyad's office and submitted her resignation."

"Do you think he will accept it?"

"I don't know, but I don't think she wants to come back and work with Hamdan. 'Why should I work for an unprincipled coward?' she told me."

Suhaila, my love, you will be a scapegoat, like the rest of our wretched people, scapegoats for the Middle East's ugliness. "Did she say she wanted to go back to Egypt?"

"She did, and that surprised me."

"Why, Mahmood? Wouldn't she get a good position there?"

"She might, but Egypt isn't different from other Middle East countries. Egypt has its Hamdans too, Thafer. It has a lot of problems, believe me. As a Palestinian woman, Suhaila will be respected in Egypt, but Egypt—oh, dear Egypt!—Egypt has become the laughing stock of the Middle East."

Thafer listens with anticipation, scrutinizing the bearded man's anguished face.

"Egypt claims to be the leader and protector of the Arab world, but it can hardly lead its own people. It can hardly protect its own territory. The Sinai is still under Israeli occupation. Our government wants Saudi Arabia, Kuwait, and other Arab oil-producing countries to use oil as a weapon. Yet it has shown itself unable to use its own weapon. Each day that goes by brings more humiliation for our people because of the incompetence and corruption of our government. Your friend Suhaila is going to be just as disappointed in Egypt, Thafer."

"I'm sorry to hear you say that."

"But she will be better off in Egypt, in spite of all the problems we have there. She knows Egypt well, and her children are there. Her late husband was a respected officer in the Egyptian army."

"Was he?" asks Thafer, blushing. "We'll find out what happened between her and Hamdan when she comes back," he says, trying to conceal his emotions.

The two men are silent.

"Suhaila is a lovely woman," says Mahmood.

"I'm going to miss her."

"She wanted me to tell you that she'll be back. She didn't want anyone else to know that she was conveying a message to you through me."

"I'm grateful," says Thafer, extending his hand to Mahmood. "I'll always remember this. Thank you very much."

"You can count on my friendship, Brother Thafer."

"I know I can."

XVII

"You're still at it?" asks Zaher, the young, nonchalant economist, looking at his watch.

"I guess so." Thafer feels a little irritated by his unannounced entry and looks at him with some surprise.

"We met when you first arrived."

"I remember that," says Thafer.

"It's almost 1:00."

"I know," says Thafer, remembering when Hamdan took
him to meet Zaher at his untidy office.

"You seem pensive," smiles the happily uninhibited young
man.

"Do I?"

"Yes," he says, reaching for a cigarette and lighting it.

He sure entered my office in a cavalier way, not even
knocking. But Thafer doesn't mind the young economist's
visit because he has seen him only once before, nor somehow
does he resent the man's arrogant air and the rudeness of his
unexpected appearance.

"Do you mind if I call you Victor?" the young economist
asks Thafer.

"I'm not used to that," says Thafer, noticing the amused
economist's unsteady eyes. "Thafer will do."

"Victor is nice," Zaher smiles childishly.

"I'm not used to being called Victor. No one ever calls me
Victor."

"But it's the English equivalent of Thafer," he says, still
smiling mischievously. "It's a nice name."

"But it's not my name. I'm not used to it."

"My brother-in-law is coming for lunch at our home today. Would you like to join us? I'm sure you'd like him."

"I'm sure I'd like him too," says Thafer, trying in vain
to read something in the young man's face, "but I can't
today. Thank you very much. I appreciate your thinking of
me."

Zaher looks at Thafer with amusement.

What does he want from me? Thafer asks himself. Nothing, he's just curious. And he's probably amused by my stiff

demeanor and unfriendly disposition which I can't help. Maybe not, but it's probably obvious to the young man.

Zaher's eyes become steadier. His smile fades. "I don't know if you remember my first name."

"I do. You're Zaher, an economist."

"I guess I'm a half-ass economist."

"How long have you been working for OAPEC, Zaher?"

"About a year. Actually, I'm an employee of the Ministry of Finance, but I'm assigned to this position. Most of OAPEC's employees are assigned to their positions by their governments. Usually after two years we return to our original positions, although some get reassigned if they make themselves useful. I don't expect that to happen to me," he laughs. "Even those who make themselves useful are not secure in their jobs, but I'm not one of those. I don't like it here anyway. I'm going to go into business for myself sooner or later."

"Good for you,"

"I studied in the United States," he says proudly.

"You did? Where?"

"Brigham Young in Utah, Mormon country."

"A great university."

"The best," he says, his face serious. "They're very kind people. Where did you study?"

"I went to Cornell University in New York State."

"Ivy League," he says. "We have a chalet on the southern tip of the Gulf, about seventy miles from here. Saeed knows where it is. We're having a party there this weekend. I've invited Ziyad and Hamdan and Mukhtar. I've also invited Mahmood. They probably won't all come, but maybe you would like to come if you can. It'll be a relaxing affair. We eat, drink, and swim." His nervous eyes calmer and his persistent smile somewhat subdued, the young man's appearance is now pitiful.

"May I let you know later?" asks Thafer guardedly, beginning to feel Zaher's warmth and friendliness.

"Sure," he smiles.

Maybe I'll ask my young nephew Nizar to go with me, Thafer thinks.

"I'll check with you tomorrow."

"Please do."

"Victor," yells Zaher, "we have Egypt, Kuwait, Lebanon, Bahrain, Morocco, Iraq, and Tunisia represented. From Europe, we have representatives of Germany, France, Italy, England, and Holland. Unfortunately for you, neither the United States nor Palestine is represented." He laughs, holding his drink, then staggers away.

Serves me right, muses Thafer. I knew I shouldn't have come. Ziyad, Hamdan, and Mukhtar aren't here because they know better. Saeed and I are the only OAPEC employees here. Yet it's strange. There are many distinguished people here— men and women, Kuwaitis, Egyptians, Lebanese, and other Arabs. There are also American, French, English, and Italian guests, some of them embassies' staff and others from the private sector, but the representatives Zaher referred to are not these distinguished people. He was pointing to the prostitutes at the party.

Thafer moves around to make the best of it. He feels out of place. He thinks he might take Nizar and Saeed with him and go swimming, as some guests are doing, but he stays and watches the unfolding scene.

Some guests eat, drink and chat, some play pingpong, some play pool, and some sit on the floor and play chess. Still others sit in a corner and play cards.

Now Egyptian, Lebanese, Moroccan and Iraqi women appear in transparent cellophane bathing suits. They move seductively among the screaming Arab men. Then similarly attired German, Dutch, French and Italian women appear. Thafer watches as the Arab men go wild, screaming and making obscene gestures. The prostitutes move about inviting attention and making themselves available. Kissing and openly making advances, they sit in the Arab men's laps. Thafer looks at his young nephew and at Saeed. He stays in a quiet corner and sees a young Arab unzip his pants and scream. A European prostitute puts her hand inside his pants.

Thafer now notices a young American family with a three-year-old child. They have been swimming in the hot water of the Gulf. They come and sit next to him.

What on earth are they doing here? he asks himself. He turns around and looks at the pretty young mother and her clean-cut husband. They are American he decides. He moves toward them. "What brings you to this glorious place?" he asks the young American couple.

"We were invited and we came," says the young husband, as his attractive wife turns away smiling. "How about you?"

"I was invited and I came."

The young couple laugh.

It is an enormous feast, comparable in quantity to what was served at Hamdan's house a few weeks ago. This food is uniquely Eastern, though: lamb and chicken; vegetables such as beans, okra, peas, eggplant, potatoes, stuffed cabbage, stuffed zucchini, and carrots; rice, lentils, chickpeas, herbs, olives, figs, grapes, raisins, dates, almonds, and other nuts. The foods are cooked in Bedouin and peasant dishes.

Everyone sits on the floor of the main room in the spacious chalet. Thafer motions for Nizar and Saeed to sit next to him. Men, women, guests, servants, and prostitutes sit together on the floor. All join in the feast of Arab food.

"It's like the Arabian Nights, Uncle Thafer," whispers Nizar.

"Wait until we leave, Nizar, please."

"I'll bet there are more than a hundred people," says Nizar.

"I'll bet there are two hundred," adds Saeed. "There are twelve whole lambs on spits, and I'll bet more than two hundred chickens."

"It's enormous, I know," says Thafer. "What do they do with the leftovers?"

"They give them away to the poor, sir," says Saeed. "Here comes Zaher, sir."

"Welcome, welcome, my friends," smiling, Zaher greets the crowd.

"He's about to say grace, Uncle Thafer," says Nizar.

"That too?"

"In the name of God the All Merciful, the All Compassionate," Zaher bows his head. "Please feel at home, all of you."

"Like the Arabian nights!" exclaims Nizar on the way back to Kuwait.

"I'll bet they didn't have tall blue-eyed blondes with nylon legs in the Arabian nights," quips Saeed.

The two young men, sitting in the front seat of the limousine burst out laughing.

Thafer sits by himself in the back seat. He has closed the glass separating the front from the back of the limousine and is trying to sleep, but he can hear the young men's conversation.

"They didn't have transparent cellophane bathing suits in the Arabian nights," says Nizar.

"They didn't need them," cracks Saeed.

The two laugh again.

"They didn't have condoms in the Arabian nights," continues Saeed.

"Columbus hadn't discovered America," Nizar retorts. More laughter.

"Do you think they know how to use a condom?" asks Saeed.

"The European prostitutes will teach them."

"That'll be part of the bargain."

The two laugh again.

"I felt sorry for the Arab girls," says Nizar.

"Why?" asks Saeed.

"They were ignored."

"They were lucky," Saeed hurls back.

The two can hardly contain themselves.

"Did you hear Zaher bless the food?" asks Nizar.

"Yes, and all the whores bowed their heads."

"They were being blessed too."

The laughter continues.

Thafer sits up and peeks through the glass. The limousine is going ninety miles an hour. "Not more than seventy miles an hour, please, Saeed," Thafer says to the happy driver.

"All right, sir."

The traffic is light and the highway reasonably good. Kuwait has no enforceable speed limit.

There is silence for a few moments. Thafer is quietly amused and wants to laugh as hard as the two young men do. He knew about his nephew's sense of humor, but he never suspected the polite, reserved Saeed of being so witty.

The two new friends continue to joke, reviewing the orgy and making reference to the lusty reactions of the Arab men to the Western prostitutes, and commenting again on the Arab prostitutes' being left out. They mimic the various accents of the screaming and squealing Arab men. They recall how one took his pants off when one of the European prostitutes touched his penis.

Finally, they quiet down.

What are they thinking about now? Thafer wonders. They're probably imagining themselves in the arms of beautiful, blonde, blue-eyed women. He thinks of the wealthy, irresponsible Arabs and their preoccupation with sex—their vulnerability in political, economic, and military affairs because of this weakness. He thinks of how the Arabs' wealth is squandered, their resources wasted, and their ambitions misguided. He thinks of the very poor among them, the hungry, the homeless, and the deprived. He thinks of the refugee camp in Beirut, of the ghetto in Hawalli, and of the millions in the Middle East who are illiterate. He thinks of the scarcity of schools and hospitals, of the filthy streets and inadequate housing, of the contaminated water supplies, of the shortage of healthful foods, and of the lack of medical supplies. Yet there is no shortage of money.

All of a sudden he begins to think of his four children, whom he left in the United States.

Colleen, his twenty-two-year-old stepdaughter. Tonight he is more concerned about her than ever before. He wants to protect her and give her strength and security. Andrew, his nineteen-year-old son. He sees him in his young nephew, Nizar, in his young driver, Saeed, and in the boundless enthusiasm and passion of Adnan Amri. Kathleen, his seventeen year old. He wants to hold her and protect her, too. He sees her among the young Palestinian girls who chant songs about the homeland, and in the beautiful faces of his young nieces, whom she resembles in a way he never thought was possible. And Sean, his fifteen-year-old son. He sees him everywhere he goes in Hawalli, in the cramped homes of the Palestinians, in the dusty school buses of Kuwait, and among the marching Palestinian youth who dream of liberating the homeland. He saw him in the refugee camp in Beirut, among the Palestinian youth crossing the Allenby Bridge and returning to the homeland, and in the youthful picture of Ayoub Allam.

Yet he doesn't want his children to be warriors. He wants them to be messengers of peace, but to carry the torch, nonetheless, to bring justice and equality to their people, who still live under occupation and in refugee camps. Their grandfather carried it on a sword and a shield, but he wants them to carry it on a wreath of olive branches.

Tonight, my dear children, he imagines himself saying to them, you are all on my mind, and I want to speak to you from the very depth of my heart. Tonight, the Middle East is also on my mind. Its frustration, its instability, its social upheaval, its anger, its political turmoil, its destructiveness, and its lack of purpose. Its masses are destitute and hungry. They have no way of changing this place where they live. The very wealthy are corrupt and cruel, and the very poor are helpless. Our government has sided with the strong against the weak. That frightens me, my dear children. It frightens me because the Middle East is primed for madness.

XVIII

"When will your children be in Kuwait, Dr. Thafer?" asks Reem Makram. She comes to Thafer's office as he is about to leave.

"About September 15. I can't wait for them to arrive."

"I am very happy for you. Dr. Thafer, you met my husband only once when you first arrived. He has been urging me to invite you for dinner. I keep telling him that our apartment is terrible. Would you mind a humble apartment near Hawalli, where all the poor people live?"

"Of course not," he says.

"Would you like to come to our home for dinner this Thursday, Dr. Thafer? There'll be only my husband Salah and me."

"I'd like that very much."

"Salah can come to pick you up. That'll be very nice, Dr. Thafer."

"Thank you. I look forward to it."

"We'll see you on Thursday, then," she says smiling happily and hurrying toward the door.

On the day of the visit to the Makrams, Reem's husband, Professor Salah Makram, picks up Thafer. Professor Makram's white car is immaculately clean. A tiny Holy Quran swings on a chain hung from the rearview mirror as the professor drives to his home near Hawalli. He drives fast, but skillfully.

"Have you been to Hawalli before, Dr. Thafer?" asks the professor.

"Yes, I have. Please call me Thafer."

"And I am Salah. You know, there are hundreds of thousands of Palestinians in Hawalli. The Kuwaiti government barely provides their minimum needs."

"So I understand," says Thafer.

"Arab governments are as guilty as Israel, Thafer. They're heartless; they have no compassion. All of them, including our own government. Did you know that there's an Arab League resolution that forbids any of its members who are host to Palestinians to resettle the Palestinians permanently?"

"Why would the Arab League have such a resolution?"

"Arab governments, as a matter of policy, want to keep the Palestinians in shacks and in refugee camps; they claim to believe that if the Palestinians become too comfortable they might give up their struggle to return to their homeland."

"Oh?"

"The Arab states have been telling the Arab masses that the liberation of Palestine is just around the corner, giving them unwarranted hope, although the liberation of Palestine is the farthest thing from these governments' thoughts. Our corrupt and cruel governments have kept the people of Palestine in subhuman conditions and have rationalized that giving them a comfortable life would make them forget their homeland. That's only an excuse to relieve them of having to spend some of their wealth in helping the miserable Palestinians. This is particularly true of the wealthy Gulf states, which the Palestinians understandably have come to resent. It won't go on like this forever, I'm sure, Thafer."

"I'm sure it won't."

"Well, here we are," says the professor, pulling his car up to a four-story, white concrete building just outside Hawalli. "Our building belongs to the University of Kuwait, and it's within walking distance of the small campus of the university.

I'm sorry, but the building doesn't have an elevator. We live on the third floor."

"I don't mind climbing the stairs," says Thafer, ignoring the hot, humid air. "It's good exercise."

"I guess so." The professor leads Thafer into the building.

They climb two flights of stairs without saying a word to one another. The professor leads Thafer to the door upon which is affixed a brass Arabic number seven.

"We're here, Reem," says the professor.

She is wearing a sleeveless, light cotton dress, and her dark brown hair is pulled into a bun. She wears no makeup. "I'm glad you could come, Dr. Thafer," she says, extending her hand and smiling.

"Thank you both for inviting me," says Thafer, observing their tiny, tastefully decorated living room.

"I'm sorry about our cramped apartment," says Professor Salah. "College professors don't do better than this."

"But your apartment is beautiful. Actually, I've always wanted to be a university professor."

"I understand that you used to teach in the United States."

"Only as an adjunct."

"It's a poor life, believe me, Thafer. Yet it's also rich. I'm on loan from Cairo University. I teach biology, and we're trying to help our Kuwaiti friends in the sciences. This is a long, arduous process. They're even talking about a medical college, but these things take time. I'm sure that eventually we'll get there."

"That's an ambitious goal."

"It is, but the Kuwaitis want it, and they have the money for it. What they don't have is organization and technical know-how. They know enough to look for these two requisites elsewhere."

"Good for them."

"Won't you sit here, Thafer," says the professor, leading him to a leather armchair, apparently reserved for guests, and seating himself on a smaller chair across from him where there are three other chairs but no sofa.

"Would you like something to drink, Thafer?" Reem asks. "We have only soft drinks."

"I'll have whatever is available."

"We've been looking forward to this, Thafer, believe me," says the professor, his hands clasped. "We have many things we would like to discuss, and we also want to be helpful."

"Wait for me, Salah," cries Reem from the kitchen.

"We're just warming up. We'll wait for you."

"I'm coming," she says, walking in and carrying a tray with two glasses of lemonade. She offers Thafer one and gives the other to her husband. Then she hurries back to bring her own.

"Here's to a long friendship," says the Egyptian professor, "and welcome to our modest home, Thafer. I hope we can toast in Jerusalem before long."

The three stand briefly for the toast.

"When President Nixon was elected in 1968," says the Egyptian professor abruptly, "our president sent him a telegram of congratulations." He looks apologetic about the sudden shift in topic. "I mention this because our president, Gamal Abdul-Nasser, met President Nixon in 1963, when Nixon was out of office. Nixon came to Egypt carrying a letter of introduction from the late John F. Kennedy. At that time, President Nasser gave instructions that Mr. Nixon should be given the royal treatment. 'We should never forget,' he told the people of Egypt, 'that Mr. Nixon was President Eisenhower's vice president in 1956' when Israel, Britain and France conspired against Egypt and invaded Suez. President Eisenhower took a firm and honorable stand against the aggressors. Egypt will always remember that, Dr. Thafer. Mr. Nixon was flown to Aswan in President Nasser's own special plane to inspect the high dam. When Mr. Nixon came back, he told a press conference that the U.S. withdrawal from the financing of the

Aswan Dam was one of the gravest blunders of the Eisenhower administration. Mr. Nixon blamed Secretary of State John Foster Dulles for that mistake."

"Yes, that was a tragedy," says Thafer.

"Perhaps I haven't told you anything you don't already know," says the professor.

"It's encouraging to be reminded that in spite of mistakes, the United States could still have a potential friend in Egypt," says Thafer.

The Makram's small dining room is an extension of their tiny kitchen. The white metal dining table with three white metal chairs around it and placed against the counter separating the kitchen from the dining room reminds Thafer of the student apartment he and Mary Pat had when they were newly married.

"I've cooked musakhan, " Reem says.

"Smells good," Thafer says, wondering how she knew about this food that he grew up with, a traditional Palestinian dish of the countryside.

"Please take that chair, Thafer, and Salah, you sit there," she says, pointing to the chair facing Thafer. She takes the chair facing the kitchen.

"Each says his own grace," says the professor.

The Egyptian professor and his wife bow their heads in silence, as does Thafer.

"Please help yourself," Reem says.

"I will. Thank you very much."

"Although the food is Eastern, we'll eat like Westerners. Please feel at home."

"Feeling at home is really Eastern, isn't it?" says the professor. "Your children will be joining you soon, I understand, Thafer."

"In four weeks."

"You'll be very happy, I'm sure." You're Palestinian, Dr. Thafer, and you married an American woman. I think that intermarriages are good for humanity. They might save the species. My wife and I are both Egyptians, but she's a Coptic Christian, and I'm a Sunni Muslim. We met in college, I presume the same way you met your late wife. If Greeks and Turks, Indians and Pakistanis, Arabs and Jews, Americans and Russians, Irish Catholics and Irish Protestants, South African Whites and South African Blacks were to intermarry, if there were intermarriage around the world on a large scale, the disputes between these various groups might decrease and eventually die out. What do you think? Here's to love as the solution to all international conflict!"

"That's fine," says Reem, smiling with amusement, "but if marriages fail, and some do, the bitterness between these various groups might get much worse."

"We were playing bridge with Hamdan and Joan one evening," says the professor. "She did something he didn't like. You should've heard him shriek at her. It was as though she had committed treason. He called her names, made reference to American arrogance, and almost threatened to shut off the supply of oil to the United States."

The three of them laugh.

"He always yells at her," says Reem. "I don't understand how or why she takes it. She never says a word to him. I'll bet one day she'll just take off."

"Families always fight. We do. Don't we, Reem?"

"Never!" She laughs. "We put up a good front in public, don't we?" She continues laughing.

"I think that she understands him," says the professor. "She knows his temper and probably realizes that he doesn't mean it most of the time."

"I really doubt it. His public outbursts are very embarrassing to Joan. She's complained to Suhaila and me about it many times. She's very unhappy about it."

"I can understand that," says the professor, "but I think they'll be all right."

"The other day in the office he had a fit. The Iraqi Ministry of Oil has now written the secretary general with an inquiry similar to the one made by Kuwait about the distribution of stock. The Iraqis are making veiled accusations of bad faith. Hamdan had a temper tantrum because Ziyad referred the letter to him to answer."

"I've heard about the mistake in the distribution of stock, Thafer," says the professor. "I have a special interest in this. My interest is not related to OAPEC, but to my own country and to the Arab states. I'm of course concerned about a serious flaw that is prevalent among us. That flaw is our refusal to face reality. This flaw, this inability to face reality, is responsible for our dismal defeat in 1967. This is why I feel strongly that the conduct of people like the secretary general and Hamdan is tantamount to treason. These are the people who bring disaster to the Arabs. They bring humiliation and suffering to all of us. They should never be given positions of responsibility. There are thousands like them, Thafer. That type caused the unforgivable disaster to our air force and to our army in 1967. These people must be exposed. We must get rid of them. I feel very strongly about that."

"How do you expose them, Salah?" asks Reem. "How do you get rid of them? They're entrenched. Someone will cover up their misdeeds, or they'll blame their misdeeds on innocent people like Suhaila. The whole system is corrupt, my dear. I see this every day."

"We all do." The professor turns to Thafer. "The most tragic chapter in Egypt's history, Thafer, began after the June War of 1967."

"That wasn't a tragic chapter for Egypt only," says Thafer. "It was tragic for all Arabs."

"That's right," says the professor. "Egypt and all Arabs sustained an enormous defeat that shocked everybody."

"Everybody was stunned and confused," says Thafer. "The Arab people were left defenseless in the midst of the wreckage. That's when Nasser resigned."

"Yet instead of celebrating his resignation, our people— not only in Egypt but all over the Arab world—went out to the streets and implored him to stay on," says the professor.

"That always amazed me," says Thafer, "because it was apparently spontaneous and genuine."

"Yes, it was spontaneous and genuine because our people didn't know any better. That to me was a sad chapter in the modern history of the Arabs. Gamal Abdul-Nasser and his whole administration should have been tried for criminal negligence, which, of course, would not compensate for the disastrous military defeat, but it would have established the basic principle that corruption and negligence involving the very life of our nation cannot be tolerated. But Nasser, despite his humiliating defeat, was given another mandate."

Thafer looks at the professor's visibly disturbed face.

"He was given the mandate, Thafer, despite his proven incompetence. The people of Egypt should've asked for his head. That's our tragedy. Our people don't know what's best for them."

"Yes, it is a tragedy," says Thafer.

"A national leader," says the Egyptian professor, still showing high emotion, "who has proven to the whole world that his leadership is a failure, is asked by the very victims of his failure and incompetence to continue that same leadership. And Nasser did continue his old methods and didn't seem to learn from his mistakes. He didn't even want to admit that he made mistakes. Who would have even dared to suggest that he made mistakes? He continued to appeal to the emotions of the Arab masses in his usual demagogic way. He continued to rely on the Russians."

"Of course, immediately after the war," says Thafer, "the Soviet Union probably wanted to know what actually happened."

"They did, and they were as shocked by our defeat as all of us were. Soviet President Podgorny came to Egypt bringing with him the chief of staff of the Soviet army to see what went wrong. Do you think our leaders leveled with the Soviets?"

"I don't know," says Thafer.

"The Soviet Union wanted to know the truth. They regarded Egypt's defeat as their defeat because their equipment and weapons were involved. But our president lied to the Soviet Union and blamed the defeat on everyone except himself and his clique."

"And he continued in his old ways," says Reem.

"He continued his unimaginative methods," says the Egyptian professor, "based on purely defensive tactics; he told us that the United States was using Israel as an instrument to impose a new order in the Middle East."

"The truth of the matter," says Thafer, "is that it's Israel who's using the United States to advance its own program through the powerful Zionist organizations there."

"I don't doubt it," says the professor. "Our president continued encouraging the Soviet Union to become more involved in the Middle East in order to offset American superiority in the region. I agree with you, Thafer. I think that Nasser's basic assumptions were totally wrong. The United States wasn't using Israel, Israel was using the United States."

"Israel, Salah," says Thafer, "wants Egypt and the entire Arab world to become more involved with the Soviet Union. In this way, it can effectively persuade the United States that she's its only friend and ally in the Middle East worthy of huge financial and military assistance."

"That's why Israel was delighted to see Nasser continue his bankrupt policy of courting the Soviet Union to get them more and more involved in our region. That's the policy that brought humiliation and suffering to the Egyptian people and to all Arabs."

"Exactly."

"Besides, the Soviet Union isn't stupid. They're too smart to allow themselves to be used or manipulated," says the professor. "That's why President Podgorny's visit to Egypt immediately after the war failed. In his simplicity, Nasser wanted to make the Russians feel that the Americans had defeated them in June of 1967."

"Oh boy."

"The Russians, of course, resented that implication. Not only that, they were very angry because most of their sophisticated equipment and weapons were captured by the Israelis and handed over to the Americans."

"They lost faith in the Egyptian armed forces," says Reem.

"They began to distrust the capability of our armed forces and hesitated to give us still more sophisticated armament, but our leaders were stupid. They were insensitive to the concerns of the Russians, concerns that I think were legitimate. We continued to brazenly demand more fancy weaponry. Our demands were excessive."

"Wasn't there a way to make Nasser see that he was hurting his own country?" asks Thafer.

"How?"The Egyptian professor is visibly frustrated. "Our leaders never make mistakes. No one dares discuss anything with them. The pros and cons of any issue are never debated in our countries. Once one of our leaders reaches the top, he remains there until he dies or until someone assassinates him. Now we have a new president. He's just as bad as the one before him when it comes to debating the pros and cons of an issue, although he is more foxy. I bet he'll be president for life. He'll either die in office or be removed by violent means."

"Let's move back to the living room," the professor suggests after their dinner.

"I could offer coffee or tea," Reem says.

"I'll have tea. Thank you, Reem," says Thafer. "What time is it?"

"It's 10:30," she says.

"I should be going."

"The night is young, Dr. Thafer," she says. Then a peculiar knock at their outer door is heard. The knock upsets Reem. She looks at her husband in confusion. "Salah," she says, worried, "let's take Thafer inside."

"We'll do nothing of the sort." His face betrays his annoyance. "Calm down, my dear," he says gently. He stands up. "What brings them here tonight?" he mutters, going toward the door.

Reem rushes out of the room.

The professor looks at Thafer, smiling. "That's Hamdan and Joan. That is Joan's special way of knocking." He shakes his head and opens the door. "Come right in," he says, offering his cheek to the American woman.

Joan is wearing slacks and appears relaxed.

Hamdan wears a white robe and nothing on his head. He turns, noticing Thafer, and seems surprised. His smile fades.

"Hello, Salah," Joan greets the professor, her lips barely touching his cheek as her eyes meet Thafer's. "Hello there, Thafer, hello," she says in excitement, leaving the professor abruptly and moving impulsively toward Thafer. "It's so good to see you!" she says, embracing him warmly.

"Hello, hello," says Thafer, embarrassed by the encounter.

"I haven't seen you in ages," she says. "I keep asking Hamdan to invite you for dinner. When are your children coming?"

"In four weeks," he says, still recovering from the surprise.

"I want to meet them," she says. "You'll have to bring them over."

"I will," says Thafer. "Hello, Brother Hamdan," he then says, shaking his hand.

"Hello," says Hamdan coolly.

"Where's Reem?" asks Joan. "Your phone's been giving a busy signal for the last four hours."

"Have you been shopping?" asks the Egyptian professor.

"Yes, and the traffic is just impossible tonight. We thought we'd drop in until the traffic eases a little, but we should get back soon. We left Jaafar with our cook."

"The traffic is always bad on Thursdays," says the professor.

"What a nice surprise seeing you, Thafer," she says, turning to Thafer again.

"It's good to see you, Joan," Thafer agrees, flustered.

"Are you doing anything tomorrow, Joan?" asks the professor. "Why don't both of you come over tomorrow?"

"We can't tomorrow. We're having dinner with Helen and Tom Hatfield at the embassy."

"Do you always do your shopping on Thursdays, Brother Hamdan?" asks Thafer.

"Not always," Hamdan says.

"I think we should get going, Salah," says Joan, standing. "Tell Reem I'll call her."

Thafer stands up.

Hamdan, who has scarcely said a word, walks toward the door.

"I'm glad you both stopped in," the professor says. "I'll have Reem call you, Joan."

"Yes, have her call me."

"There's a lesson to be learned from every experience," says the professor as he drives Thafer back to his home. "Reem had taken our telephone off the hook. That's why our phone was giving a busy signal. I feel certain that Joan wouldn't have come without calling us first. She always does. The irony in all of this is that Reem had planned everything, at my request, so that we could be private. I really wanted to have a private visit with you. Reem and I were touched by your encounter with Suhaila's mother at Hamdan's home when you first came. You had never seen one another, but the sad fate you share united you instantly. On your face was a loving look for the older woman for the world to see, Thafer. I could see it as you extended your hands to her. She knew it, and it brought tears to her eyes. Then she walked away. When we came home late that night, Reem and I reviewed what had happened. There was an undertone of your people's despair even as you and Joan danced that beautiful Palestinian dance. We all commented on it after you left that night. Joan herself was taken by it. She cried after you left. Did you know that Joan's father is Palestinian?"

"Is he really?" asks Thafer with surprise.

"Yes," says the professor. "Even the American ambassador's wife was touched by the dance. I've been urging Reem to invite you to our home since that night. She's been hesitant about it, afraid that Hamdan would get wind of it and question her loyalty to him, particularly after the Conference of Oil Ministers and what happened there. The lesson, Thafer, is that no matter how careful we are in what we plan, if one little thing goes wrong, the whole plan is spoiled. I want you to know, anyway, that Reem and I consider it an honor and a privilege to have you in our home."

"Thank you, Salah."

"So that you won't be surprised, I should tell you that Reem has decided not to continue her work at OAPEC."

"But why?"

"She can't, Thafer. She knows that, and we have already discussed it. She has no respect for her boss, Hamdan, and feels no loyalty to him after what happened to Suhaila."

"But she's been transferred to Sheikh Mahmood's office, Salah."

"Hamdan is still in charge of the whole division, and just as he got after Suhaila, he's going to get after Reem. She won't be able to take that. Suhaila is a very strong person, but even she couldn't take it. Reem doesn't have Suhaila's strength. Besides, it would be unfair to herself to continue working for him. Maybe fate is telling us something."

"What about Joan?" asks Thafer impulsively. "I couldn't help noticing her distress as they left."

"I saw it too. After seeing it, I now doubt that the relationship will last."

"That's too bad. They have a beautiful child."

"Yes," says the professor, pulling up to Thafer's house. "Jaafar is almost six now."

"I just want to thank you for everything, Salah. Please give Reem my thanks too."

"We're both glad you could come. When Suhaila comes back from Egypt, we'll all get together again."

"That'll be great."

XIX

Thafer has been in Kuwait more than four months, and he is enjoying his work. He has become more acquainted with Kuwait and has been driving around in a small, used sedan he bought in order to avoid the cumbersome and ostentatious OAPEC limousine. His aunt, Mama Adla, always feels uncomfortable when the OAPEC limousine parks near her home in Hawalli. He has also bought Arab clothing and has occasionally ventured by himself into the old Souk (market) wearing Arab attire. There, he has mixed unnoticed with people of many nationalities, bargained, and bought fruits and vegetables. He has been feeling like part of the new old world he has missed for more than two decades.

One Friday afternoon, he is feeling lonely for Suhaila. She hasn't returned from Egypt, and he wonders why. He has just come back from Uncle Muneer's and Mama Adla's tiny apartment, and is feeling depressed. He is counting the days until his children visit Kuwait.

Feeling restless, Thafer puts on his white robe and white headcloth, and decides to go to Hawalli. He keeps asking himself why Suhaila hasn't come back.

Driving through the narrow dusty streets of Hawalli, he impetuously decides that he would like to see the elderly woman who led him to her dilapidated house and had her son show him Fuaad's shop.

I'll never find her, he tells himself. It'll be like looking for a needle in a haystack. I'll try anyway. Maybe that'll get my mind off all the things I've been worrying about.

He drives slowly through the deserted, dirty streets. The traffic is light on Friday afternoon, but it isn't like Sunday afternoon in the immaculately clean streets of Ashfield. In late August, Hawalli is very hot and humid even at sunset. He thinks it must be about 125 degrees Fahrenheit with 100 percent humidity.

When he spoke to his children a little earlier, they told him it was a beautiful summer day in Ashfield, seventy-eight degrees with low humidity.

He drives slowly until he approaches the place where his driver Saeed parked OAPEC's limousine so that they could inquire about Fuaad's shop when he first arrived in Kuwait.

"I think I'll park near there," he mutters. Almost instinctively, he walks toward the dilapidated house of the elderly woman he and Saeed encountered as they looked for his relatives. He wants to see her again. He wants to find her. He walks by her house. Several men are squatting in front of the house. He goes a little distance, then comes back. The men look at him, as though wondering if he is looking for someone. He walks by them again. Maybe they'll talk to me or ask me if I need help, he tells himself.

"Are you looking for someone?" asks one of the men as Thafer walks by them a second time.

"I was here about three months ago looking for my relatives' shop, and I asked an elderly woman for assistance. She brought me to this house." He points to the crumbling building. "Her son then walked me to my relatives' place. In my excitement I didn't get his name. I'd like to see him."

"I heard about that," says one of the men. "I know the man who walked with you."

"Do you?"

"Yes. Do you want me to go get him?"

"I'll be grateful." Thafer, now begins to wonder why he is doing this.

"I'll be glad to," the man says, walking toward the house.

"Do you live in Kuwait?" another man asks Thafer while they wait.

"I do."

"Who do you work for?"

"The Organization of Arab Petroleum Exporting Countries, OAPEC. I work in their legal department. I've been in Kuwait only about four months."

"Where were you before?"

"In the United States."

"How long?" the man asks, now eying Thafer.

"About twenty years." Thafer feels the pressure of the man's questions.

"He'll be right here," says the other man, as he comes out of the old house. "He remembers. He knows who you are."

"Thank you, sir." What on earth am I doing? Thafer asks himself.

"Hello, hello, Dr. Thafer, a thousand hellos, Dr. Thafer," says the man who walked with him to Fuaad's shop says. He walks hurriedly out of the dilapidated house toward Thafer and extends both hands, as though he and Thafer have been lifelong friends. "Hello, hello, a thousand hellos, Dr. Thafer," repeats the thrilled man, now embracing Thafer warmly.

"Hello, sir, hello," Thafer says, feeling embarrassed but moved by the man's reception. "A thousand hellos to you, sir."

"Please come in, Dr. Thafer." The excited man holds Thafer's arm and walks with him toward the old house. "I want all of you to come in," he says, turning to the astonished men. "Please come in, all of you."

The elderly Palestinian woman is at the entrance of the old house waiting. She starts to yodel:

> O Yee, O Yee, Ayoub Allam's son is here,
> O Yee, O Yee, We'll all soon return home,
> O Yee, O Yee, God willing our liberation is near,
> O Yee, O Yee, And we'll surely visit the Dome.
> Looloo looloo loowee, Looloo Looloo loowee.

There are tears in Thafer's eyes as the yodel catches him off guard.

"Welcome, welcome." The elderly woman extends both hands to him and embraces him, her beautifully lined face glowing.

"Thank you, thank you, Mother," he says, wiping away a tear. He bends, reaches for her hand, and kisses it. He lifts his head, holds the elderly woman's hands, and looks into her watery eyes. There is a hand-hammered silver bracelet on her thin wrist, and she wears a red amber necklace made of the sap of the date palm trees of their homeland. Her dress is white linen with embroidered seams. Various geometric figures are embroidered on the front with red, green, and black silk, and she wears a chest piece typically worn by married women.

"We saw you on television," says the elderly woman, a smile spreading over her kindly face. "I called for my son. 'Tayseer, Tayseer,' I said. 'Come see General Ayoub's son, who was looking for his relatives.' And he came running."

Thafer looks at the elderly woman, sweat running down his cheeks.

"I forgot who you were with. They were important people, I know."

"Let's all go into the living room," says her son, leading him and the other men to a small, simply decorated adjacent room.

A handwoven white shawl hangs on the wall facing them as they enter. A cross-shaped design is stitched on it in colored silk, like some his mother has made. He looks at the worn out floor cushions and the reclining pillows placed on the floor along the four walls of the small room. The cushion covers of handwoven silk are elaborately decorated with intricate cross-stitching of silk thread in many bright colors.

"Please sit and make yourselves comfortable," says the son to the other men, as he leads Thafer to one of the cushions at the center.

"Thank you very much," says Thafer as the son sits down next to him.

Thafer notices a pine wedding box, carved and inlaid with mother-of-pearl, placed near the door in front of him. On the wall behind the wedding box there is a straw mat covered with a colored cotton cloth that is decorated with silk tassels and beads, and with a cluster of sequinlike tiny mirrors attached to it. A multicolor woven straw egg basket, with fringe and mirror decorations, sits on top of the wedding box.

Thafer remembers his mother's wedding box in its place in their home in Jerusalem. A mirror of Syrian design was hung on the wall behind it, and a set of chairs was placed around it. Every woman, from north to south, owned one of these boxes to store her dowry.

"Welcome, welcome," says the elderly woman again. "What a pleasant surprise!"

"I've been wanting to do this for several weeks, Mother," says Thafer, "but I didn't have the courage to come. I'm glad I finally did."

"We're your kin and family," says the elderly woman as she stands by the wedding box. "Our home is your home.

General Ayoub was from Jerusalem. We're from Hebron. We're neighbors."

"I used to go to Hebron with my father when I was a small boy," Thafer says. "I remember the factory there for handblown glass that my father took me to see once."

Thafer remembers the finely tanned leather, the thrown and hand-decorated ceramic, the handwoven woolen articles, and the distinctive embroidery he used to see in Hebron. "Hebronites are a hardworking and creative people, Mother," he says.

"You're very generous," she says.

A young woman enters the room carrying a tray with small cups and a brass coffee pot.

"This is my daughter," says the elderly woman, moving toward the young woman to help her.

"Hello, brothers," says the daughter, "a thousand hellos."

"Hello, sister," the men all say, standing.

She is an attractive woman in her late thirties or early forties. She wears a fishnet hat, crocheted of blue cotton thread with small glass beads sewn in various flower, star, and geometric shapes. Her embroidered dress is made of handwoven blue linen.

"Welcome, welcome, brothers," says the young woman, passing the coffee and looking down at the tray she carries. "Welcome, welcome to our home, Brother Thafer," she says, bowing and offering him the tray with the small coffee cups.

"Thank you, sister," Thafer says, standing.

The mother and daughter leave the room, and the men sit quietly sipping their black coffee.

When the elderly Palestinian woman comes back with a dish of sweets, she is wearing a different dress. It is a Jerusalem dress of purple velvet embroidered with silver and gold in a floral design. She wears a thin white mantilla on her shoulders, leaving her silver hair exposed.

"Your dress is beautiful, Mother." Thafer is taken by surprise.

"This is my wedding dress. I haven't worn it in years. It was made in 1920, and I'm wearing it just for you."

He bows his head and remembers his mother's wedding dress, which consisted of a jacket and a skirt of the same purple velvet, embroidered with gold and silver thread in floral and branch designs. His mother had a shawl with her dress, made of silk with small silver pieces sewn on it. "Do they wear the Jerusalem dress in Hebron, Mother?" Thafer asks.

"Not usually. My husband came from Jerusalem. We lived there until he was martyred in 1937. He is buried in Hebron."

"Hebron is the ancient sacred city of holy men, like Bethlehem and Jerusalem, Mother. Abraham, Jacob, Isaac, Joseph, and their wives are all buried in Hebron. Your husband is in good company."

"You're a beautiful man." She is visibly moved by his recognition of Hebron.

"I'm just curious, Dr. Thafer," one of the men asks. "What do you think? Is there any hope for us? Do you think we'll one day go back to our homes and lands, or is this a conspiracy against us, with the conspirators stronger and more resourceful than we are? Could you give us the benefit of your opinion?"

"I'll be glad to," says Thafer, mulling over the man's question.

"I heard the question," says the elderly woman, rushing back into the tiny room. "General Ayoub's son is a guest in our house. You're all as acquainted with the problem as he is. Instead of his telling you what you already know, why don't you all speak? Don't put him on the spot. He's been away a long time, you know."

"I didn't mean to put Dr. Thafer on the spot. I thought he might be able to tell us something new from his own experiences. We need to hear that. That's all. But I'll speak. I don't mind. I'm sorry, Dr. Thafer."

"Never mind, I'd like to hear your views, sir."

"Our problem is not the problem of one individual or one group, as we've just heard," the man says. "It's a problem for us all. Before I say more, I want to say that I'm not associated with any group, political or otherwise. I'm a schoolteacher whose life has been taken up with children. In my opinion, there are five fundamental matters at the core of the problem. The first is that Palestine is a small geographic area that is not divisible. It's the only homeland we have. The second is that Israel is a racist country, created and maintained in our homeland by certain international powers who may feel guilty about the holocaust, but whose aim is to impede progress in the Arab world. The third is that ever since the creation of Israel, the United States has been openly hostile toward the Arab people and their ambitions, and hostile to the hopes and aspirations of the Palestinian people for freedom and independence. The fourth is that some Arab governments have strong relations with certain nations whose goal it is to exploit and waste the resources of the Arabs. These Arab governments are in effect agents for those imperialists. And fifth, history tells us that at the end of the day a people's struggle for justice, freedom, and independence will prevail in spite of the hardships. That's truly what I think."

"I agree with what you say," says another man. "This is why our people have refused compensation and resettlement. This is why our people have sacrificed many of their sons. We've paid dearly, in lives and materials, in order to liberate our soil. Yet we still face many problems. Most of these problems are not of our making, but some are. We all know of the obstacles to liberation placed in our path by some Arab states. We all know of the oppression, political suppression, and torture suffered by our people, brought on by some Arab governments. Yet we must admit that our people have received the same treatment from our own leadership. While Israel is united and works diligently to accomplish its goals as a Zionist state in our homeland, our leadership remains divided. We seem to repeat the pattern that existed in the early twenties when our families and clans fought one another, while our enemy ran well-organized, well-financed institutions that were created and operated in accordance with sound principles. Our institutions and our organizations, I regret to say, still suffer from the same defects and weaknesses that plagued us when we were fighting the cruel British Mandate. Since 1965, when our revolution started in earnest, we have endured one setback after another. We've been splintered and divided. Every splinter group has associated itself with a corrupt Arab state that itself might be beholden to an imperialist power. Some of our leaders are linked with Arab states that are in turn beholden to the United States, but the government of the United States and its institutions are themselves corrupt, controlled, and manipulated by powerful Zionist organizations. Some of these splinter groups have engaged in acts of terror that have hurt the very cause they claim to defend. I dare say that these terrorist acts have helped our enemy, who has exploited them effectively. Our people still suffer from his cruel occupation."

"I'm a bank teller. I know very little about these matters," says a third man. "The thing that saddens me is that our people know all this, but they're caught. They're helpless. They keep hoping that our leaders will one day reform themselves."

"I'm a journalist," says a fourth man, "and I can tell you from my own knowledge that strong voices within the Palestinian leadership are urging reform, and reform is imperative if we are to regain our homeland and our rights. What is needed now is a common goal that we can reach by democratic means. This is the best path to victory. It is bound to unify the various splinter groups. Unity will then prevent exploitation by the various Arab states that have used us and our problem for their own selfish purposes."

"I have a question," says a fifth man. "Someone just said that Israel is a racist society. I firmly believe it, because all of

Israel's institutions are discriminatory. I happen to be a lawyer.
I can tell you from my own research and study that four of
Israel's fundamental laws promote discrimination on the basis
of religion, race, and descent. The first is the law of return,
which provides that any person born to a Jewish mother or
any person who converts to the Jewish faith may return to
Israel. All of us in this room were born in the homeland, but
we cannot return to our towns and villages because we were
not born to Jewish mothers. If we convert to the Jewish faith,
we can return. Now, Jews who can prove that they were born
to Jewish mothers or those who convert to the Jewish faith
will be automatically granted Israeli citizenship upon their
arrival in Israel under the Israeli law of citizenship. None of
us in this room, natives of Palestine, or of what is now called
Israel, could ever attain Israeli citizenship. Not even Dr. Thafer,
even though he is a United States citizen, and some of his tax
money is used to maintain the Israeli system. By the way,
under the legal system that exists in Israel, there is no such
thing as an Israeli nationality. There's only an Israeli citizenship. But under the Israeli registration law there are two types
of nationality in Israel, one Jewish and the other Arab. Under
the Israeli status law, Israeli citizens with Jewish nationality
are entitled to certain rights and privileges—such as the use
and ownership of land—not available to Israeli citizens of
Arab nationality. There are about a million Israeli citizens of
Arab ancestry in Israel who are classified as Israeli citizens
with Arab nationality. My question to you, Dr. Thafer, is this:
How can the United States of America—which has been preach-
ing to the world about democracy, justice, freedom and equality—support and finance a state like Israel?"

The question impresses Thafer.

The elderly woman enters to hear him.

"It's a fair question. I want to assure all of you that I won't
try to defend indefensible conduct by the government of the
United States. I can only tell you why it does things the way

it does. I'll try to be as forthright as you all have been. I want
to say at the outset that I make a distinction between American politicians and the American people. American politicians
support Israel's racial policies either out of ignorance or out of
greed. Despite their phenomenal endurance, the economic and
political systems in the United States are vulnerable. I'm sorry
to say that the American government, which is run by politicians, has fallen prey to well-financed and highly organized
lobbies. The American-Israeli Political Action Committee,
which is the Zionist lobby in the United States, is one of the
most powerful lobbies in the history of the United States, if
not the most powerful. American politicians compete shamelessly in making promises to this lobby group. In return, they
receive contributions of hundreds of thousands of dollars intended to ensure that pro-Israeli policies and programs are
carried out. In this respect, there is no difference between the
two major political parties in the United States. Democrats
and Republicans alike are guilty of this behavior. As for the
American people, although they know the nature of their
politicians, I believe that they are unaware of the grip that the
Zionists have on these same politicians and therefore on their
society. Unfortunately, the American government, because of
the lack of moral fiber among those who run it, often supports
the strong against the weak, the rich against the poor, and the
oppressor against the oppressed. Politicians in the United States
often ignore the lessons of past oppression and simply per-
petuate the same injustices. The people of the United States
are also often as much the victims of the greed of their politicians as are our oppressed people living in refugee camps
under occupation."

"The Arab states themselves compete shamelessly in serving the interests of the American government," says the elderly woman. "Why should American politicians and the
American government change their attitudes toward us if the
Arab states don't reform themselves?"

XX

Thafer takes a nap after he comes back from Hawalli that evening, and he has a dream. It is frightening. He dreams that he sees an Israeli Jew laying wreaths on the graves of his father, his brother, his brother's wife, and their two children. He walks to the Israeli and tells him that these are Palestinian graves, that he knows for sure they are the graves of his father, his brother, and his brother's family.

Yes, I know, the Israeli replies, but we stole their home and farm.

Why did you do that? he asks the Israeli Jew.

I don't know why. It was a terrible thing we did, but as sure as the day follows the night, they'll get it back.

But my father, my brother, and his family are dead, he tells the Israeli Jew.

It doesn't matter. They'll get their home in Jerusalem back, and they'll get the farm near Tulkarm back too. Believe me, they will.

But Ayoub Allam is dead, Thafer repeats, and my brother Saleem and his family are dead too.

Your brother and his family were murdered by us, says the Israeli Jew, but Ayoub Allam isn't dead.

Are you sure he isn't? Thafer asks.

I'm very sure.

Where is he?

He's right here in your house. Go to your living room, and you'll find him sitting right there.

Thafer walks to the living room, and there is his father wearing his military uniform and holding a white robe and a white headcloth. Thafer, my son, he says, I'm going to retire and take off this uniform and wear this white robe and headcloth in its place. I'm going to give you the uniform to wear. His father takes off his uniform and hands it over to Thafer. Wear it, Thafer, he says, wear it. Do it now! Right now.

At first Thafer hesitates, then he puts his father's uniform on while his father watches him.

His father puts the white robe and headcloth on and, like an angel, ascends to heaven.

Thafer goes to look at himself in the mirror and finds that he looks just like his father. He has his father's white bushy eyebrows, his long eyelashes, and his piercing dark eyes.

The Israeli Jew tells Thafer, now you'll get your home in Jerusalem and your farm near Tulkarm.

Thafer hears a voice coming from the heavens that sounds just like his father's. Thafer, my dearest, Thafer. You've gone to the United States, and you promised to write us, but you haven't written as much as you promised. You said your education would take you five years, but it has taken you more than twenty years. We have waited long enough. And the homeland has waited long enough. We have all been waiting for your return. We're all counting on you, Thafer. The people of the homeland are counting on you, and I am counting on you, Thafer. Open the gate to Jerusalem, Thafer, open it. Millions of our people are behind you waiting to enter. Open the gate, Thafer, open it.

Thafer tries to open the gate, but the key won't turn.

Break the lock, his father's voice shouts. Break it. Break it. You have to break it, Thafer; that's the only way.

He tries to break the lock, but he can't.

Explode it, Thafer, explode it, the voice from heaven then says.

Thafer becomes frightened and doesn't know what to do.

The bomb is in your pocket, Thafer. Take it out. It's the only way.

Thafer takes a tiny bomb out of his pocket and ties it to the lock of the gate.

This will do it. Tie it firmly, and move back. Move back, Thafer. Run to the hills, Thafer, run to the hills.

Thafer runs and finds himself in Deir Yasseen. He watches the lock explode. The gate to Jerusalem is destroyed, and the whole city is on fire. Then it begins to rain and rain and rain until the fire is out. The meadows become green, and the Israeli Jews begin to leave in airplanes.

Didn't I tell you? the Israeli Jew says to Thafer. Now you can go back to your home in Jerusalem, and you can go back to the farm near Tulkarm.

Thafer begins to look for their home in Jerusalem. When he finds it, it looks just as it did the last time he saw it.

The elderly Palestinian woman he met in Hawalli, her son, and all the Palestinians who were there, all meet Thafer near his home in Jerusalem. We're all going to look for our homes, Thafer. Thank you, Thafer, the elderly woman says to him.

XXI

Reem Makram does not return to work at the OAPEC offices, and there is no news from Suhaila. The women of the OAPEC staff seem in conflict over the turn of events and are keeping their distance from Thafer. They appear to be taking care not to be seen near his office or in conversation with him, and he doesn't know what to make of it all. His main concern, though, is that he hasn't heard from Suhaila. He is hoping that Mahmood will know something, but even Mahmood is not coming to his office very often these days. Demoralized and feeling lonely and isolated, Thafer doesn't know how secure he is in the crazy place. And his children are due to arrive in two weeks. He wonders if he should let them come. Of course I should, he scolds himself, even if I were to be fired from my job before they come. After all, Uncle Muneer and Mama Adla and all his relatives are dying to see them. His brother Rassem is going to bring his wife and children to Kuwait to meet them, and his brother Kamal is doing everything in his power to persuade his mother to come to Amman so that he can take the children to see her there. He is determined that the children should come to Kuwait no matter what.

His poor mother doesn't know what happened to him at the bridge, and she is still insisting that he should take the children to see her in Tulkarm. But he isn't going to try that again.

He wonders how to contact Suhaila's mother. Maybe I shouldn't, he tells himself. I'll bet Suhaila's mother is as worried about her daughter as I am, even more. I should leave the poor soul alone.

Someone knocks at his door.

"May I come in, Thafer?" Mahmood's somber voice belies his smiling face.

"Please do, Mahmood," Thafer says cheerfully, "I'm delighted to see you."

"I have news about your friend, Dr. Suhaila."

"What is it, Mahmood?"

"She won't be coming back to Kuwait. OAPEC has canceled her work visa."

"Why did they do that?" Thafer asks, feeling distressed.

"I don't know, Thafer. This is getting ugly, I'm afraid."

"Who in OAPEC canceled her work visa?" Thafer asks irately.

"Who else? It has to be the secretary general."

"Really?" Thafer asks in astonishment. "I didn't think he would do that."

"What can I say, Thafer?"

"What about her mother? How's she going to manage?"

"Dr. Suhaila wondered if you could accompany her mother to Egypt, after the Special Conference of Oil Ministers."

"Of course. I'll be glad to take her mother to Egypt." He reflects. What about my children? I can manage to go and come back before they come. "Where in Egypt, Sheikh Mahmood?"

"Alexandria."

"In the meantime, do you know if Suhaila's mother has enough to live on?"

"I've advanced her some money," says Mahmood. "Dr. Suhaila said that she'll return the money to you when you go to Alexandria, but that's not important really, Dr. Thafer."

"Do you know where Suhaila's mother lives, Sheikh Mahmood?"

"She lives in Hawalli. I can take you there if you wish to go."

"When can we go?"

"After work."

The two men pause. Thafer clasps his hands behind his head, leans back in his swivel chair, and stares at the ceiling. Mahmood folds his arms and looks down.

"Do you know, Brother Thafer, that Reem Makram has suddenly quit?"

"Yes, I do."

"That has surprised many people in OAPEC. Reem and Salah Makram have been very good friends of Hamdan and his American wife. Reem's abrupt departure was a bombshell. The women of OAPEC are still shaken up over it. No one knows what's behind it. Hamdan himself is brooding over it, but he doesn't discuss it. I know for a fact that it has nothing to do with her transfer to our department."

"I know it doesn't. I know a little about why Reem Makram left."

"Do you?"

Thafer pauses. Tell him, he urges himself. Tell him. "Reem and Salah Makram made the mistake of inviting me to their home, Mahmood. I had met Reem's husband at Hamdan's house at the party they had for me when I first arrived here. I liked the man. He is a professor at the University of Kuwait, and we kind of hit it off. Apparently, he's been asking his wife to invite me to their home ever since, and she's been hesitating, perhaps afraid that Hamdan would get wind of it. Why that should be a concern I never quite understood."

"I'll tell you why after you finish," says the bearded man, smiling, "but go ahead, finish. I want to hear this."

"Tell me now, Mahmood."

"Hamdan is a very insecure man. Just because Reem works for him, he thinks that he owns her. There's nothing more to it than that, I'm sure. That's our reality in the Middle East, Thafer, I regret to say. The Americans would call us male chauvinist pigs. Maybe we are."

"It's hard for me to believe that that's all there is to it, Mahmood."

"There's nothing more to it than that, Thafer. I'm sure there isn't."

XXII

The Special Conference of Oil Ministers of OAPEC is held in the Conference Room of the Kuwait Sheraton. The Egyptian oil minister presides over the conference.

"Brothers," says the Egyptian oil minister, "this meeting will come to order. Our sister state, Kuwait, has requested this special meeting. I would like to call on our brother, the oil and finance minister of sisterly Kuwait."

"Thank you, Mr. President," says the tall, bespectacled Kuwaiti. "I want, first of all, to welcome all of you to Kuwait. Last March, Mr. President, the secretariat advised all of us that fifty million dollars was due from each member state to qualify it for participation in the Arab Shipping Company of OAPEC. Kuwait, after obtaining authority from its emir and parliament to pay its share, was about to forward its payment to the Arab Shipping Company. We then received, as all of you have, another communication from the secretariat advising us that in view of the recent admission of sisterly Egypt and sisterly Syria to the membership of OAPEC, the distribution of stock had to be recalculated. The admission of two new members would not justify a drastic reduction from fifty million to eight million dollars. I requested the legal advisor of the Ministry of Oil of Kuwait to write to the secretariat of OAPEC for an explanation; all of you have copies of this letter. As of this date, neither Kuwait nor any of you has received a response. Kuwait, Mr. President, is a good neighbor of sisterly Iraq and had nothing to do with the inflated request for fifty million dollars. Kuwait, Mr. President, would not condone excluding Iraq from participation in this project. It is as much in the dark as all of you about the drastic reduction in the payment requested for the Arab Shipping Company. I call on the secretariat to explain to all of us the reasons behind the drastic reduction. Perhaps, Mr. President, the legal advisor of OAPEC would tell us why he has not responded to the inquiry made by the legal advisor of our ministry. Thank you, Mr. President."

How do you like that? Thafer asks himself. What a mess! I'll just tell them why I couldn't respond. I have been criticized. I know I have, and I am a little peeved.

Mahmood, who sits next to Thafer, at first seemed amused by all this, but now he is looking at Thafer with concern.

"Before we call on the legal advisor of OAPEC," says the presiding Egyptian oil minister, "the chair recognizes His Excellency the minister of transportation of sisterly Iraq, who's acting on behalf of His Excellency the Iraqi minister of oil."

"Mr. President," says Iraq's minister of transportation, rising to his feet. "Give me just half a minute." He sits and confers with a member of his delegation who sits next to him.

Earlier that morning, Thafer noticed the very tall Iraqi limping into the Conference Hall. The minister is probably six feet four inches tall and carries a cane. His gray hair and dark eyes add to his distinguished appearance, but he seems angry. Thafer is relieved that he has a chance to collect his thoughts while the Iraqi minister speaks. Then he remembers Salah Makram, whose wife Reem quit because Hamdan saw Thafer in their home. The Egyptian professor spoke about the defeat of the Egyptian armed forces in the War of 1967 and about Gamal Abdul-Nasser, who was rewarded for his blunders. The professor commented that those who blundered had blamed others and had refused to accept responsibility, thus causing many innocent people to suffer. Thafer remembers the Egyptian professor saying that those who blunder and cover up their blunders are guilty of treason. The word treason rings in Thafer's ears. He looks at the Kuwaiti oil minister, his head resting in his hands and looking unhappy. He's probably petrified, wondering what the Iraqi minister is about to say. Should I speak up? Thafer asks himself nervously. You bet you should, he answers himself. Without a doubt you should.

Mahmood gently taps Thafer's hand, reminding him of Uncle Muneer's reassuring touch when Thafer was about to be interrogated by his relatives and their friends at the home of his Cousin Wahby, soon after he arrived in Kuwait.

"Mr. President," resumes the Iraqi minister, "I am also grateful for His Excellency's disavowal of any connection with the treacherous attempt to exclude Iraq from active involvement in the economic life of our region. This dangerous action was designed to pit our struggling countries one against another, thereby weakening our Arab nation. Those who have participated in this action are stooges of the imperialists. They are traitors who should be exposed and punished. My brothers, Iraq is one of you. Its strength is your strength, and its weakness is your weakness. There are those who wish to isolate Iraq, not only in order to weaken and destroy it, but also in order to weaken and destroy our Arab nation. I implore each and every one of you to beware the conspirators. For its part, Iraq does not wish ill to any of its sisterly Arab states. It has no designs on any of its sisterly neighbors. Iraq firmly believes that we must be united, that we must help one another, and that we must never allow the imperialists to divide us. Thank you, Mr. President."

Not too bad, Thafer muses. Maybe I shouldn't speak in the way I originally thought I should. I shouldn't add fuel to the fire of Iraq's anger.

The secretary general turns around to speak to Thafer. "Dr. Thafer," he whispers, "I want to say a few words before you speak."

"Sure," Thafer whispers back, nodding his head approvingly and hoping the secretary general will admit the error in the distribution of the stock.

"Mr. President," says the secretary general, raising his right hand, his voice trembling. "Mr. President, I would like to say a few words before the legal advisor speaks."

"Please do, Excellency," says the presiding Egyptian minister.

"Mr. President," says the secretary general, the unsteadiness of his voice embarrassingly obvious, "I want to assure our brother, His Excellency the Iraqi minister, that the secretariat of OAPEC has no information or knowledge of any attempt on the part of any member of OAPEC to isolate, exclude, or weaken sisterly Iraq or to remove it from its leading and natural role in the economic life of OAPEC and, indeed, of our region. The secretariat of OAPEC always acts in the interest of all its members in good faith. The feeling that some states are engaged in a conspiracy to isolate, exclude, or weaken sisterly Iraq is without foundation and is unwarranted. We regret it deeply. Thank you, Mr. President."

"Why then, pray tell," asks the Iraqi minister, springing to his feet angrily, leaning on his cane, and directly addressing the secretary general, "did the secretariat, knowing of Iraq's economic difficulties, request us to pay fifty million dollars, when in fact only ten million dollars was due?"

"We did not know that what was due was only ten million dollars," says the secretary general indignantly. "I did not make the calculation. I only signed the letter that went out with a figure based on the calculation made by our former senior economist. I asked for her resignation because of her grave mistake. The mistake has now been corrected. We have informed all of you that what is due is not fifty million dollars but only about eight million dollars. We did that as soon as we found out about the mistake. I do not see any reason for the accusation of bad faith or for the anger."

The Conference Hall is hushed.

"Mr. President," says the Kuwaiti minister, rising to his feet."May I ask a question?"

"Please, Excellency."

"My question is addressed to OAPEC's legal advisor, Mr. President. Why has OAPEC's legal advisor ignored the inquiry made by our ministry's legal advisor concerning this matter? If he had not, we would all have known that there had been an error in computation and would have acted accordingly. There would have been no reason for suspicion or for thinking that some of us were acting in bad faith. I would like OAPEC's legal advisor to address my question."

"I will be glad to, Excellency." Thafer is calm and confident. "The letter from the legal advisor of Your Excellency's ministry was not addressed to me; it was addressed to His Excellency, the secretary general of OAPEC. In his absence, the assistant secretary general for economics, however, discussed it with me at length. Before that, I had drawn to the attention of OAPEC's secretary general the mistake in the amount due from each member. I did that on the day when the last Conference of Oil Ministers was concluded, after the Iraqi minister of oil asked whether installment payments and payments in kind would be acceptable. When the secretary general asked my opinion about the question, I drew to his attention that there was a mistake in computation. It was an innocent mistake made by the assistant secretary general for economics. When I drew the mistake to the attention of the secretary general, he decided not to advise you of it. Instead, he elected to accept the recommendation of the assistant secretary general for economics to attribute the reduction in the amount due to the increase in the membership of OAPEC. The assistant secretary general for economics felt that the significant change would not be noticed. When Your Excellency's legal advisor sent his letter, I was consulted again, this time by the assistant secretary general for economics because the secretary general was in Beirut. I again urged that the mistake be forthrightly admitted to all members of OAPEC and that the correction be explained. I warned that failure to do so would tend to confuse the member states and might even cause some to think that the secretariat was acting in bad faith. The assistant secretary general for economics agreed to talk to the secretary general again and to try to convince him to accept my recommendation, but the secretary general decided not to respond to your ministry's inquiry or to that of Iraq, despite the by now strong urgings of the assistant secretary general for administration."

Thafer pauses, then turns to all the ministers. "Excellencies, I cannot in good conscience let something told to this honorable body go uncorrected. You have been told by the secretary general that the error in computation was made by Dr. Suhaila Sa'adeh and that she was asked to resign because of that. Dr. Suhaila Sa'adeh is not here to defend herself. It is therefore my solemn duty to advise you that the mistake was not made by her, but by the assistant secretary general for economics. I know that for a fact. The secretary general knows that too. On the day that the issue arose, Dr. Suhaila Sa'adeh tried to explain the error in computation to the assistant secretary general for economics, but he insisted that his computation was correct. Dr. Suhaila Sa'adeh, however, was unjustly blamed for a mistake she did not make. Your Excellencies, an injustice has been committed against Dr. Suhaila Sa'adeh. She was unjustly dismissed and sent back to Egypt. Her work permit in Kuwait has been canceled. Her elderly mother is now by herself in Kuwait and penniless. Thank you, Mr. President."

"Mr. President," cries the Iraqi minister, rising to his feet and pointing to the secretary general with his cane, his face flushed with anger. "Mr. President, the secretary general is a liar. He is dishonest and unfit to be the secretary general of this esteemed body. Iraq demands that he be dismissed."

XXIII

"I have never attended a Conference of Oil Ministers before," says Mahmood as he and Thafer leave the Conference Hall after the meeting is adjourned. "Are they all like this?"

"The only other one I attended wasn't like this at all. This one was crazy."

"I had no idea all this was going on. Suhaila never told me what was disturbing her. But I admire your courage. What you did was the only right thing to do. They're not used to this, I know. But it's the only way. It's the only way."

"Why do you suppose Ziyad and Hamdan blamed it all on Suhaila?" Thafer asks, seating himself in Mahmood's old car. "Did they think they would get away with it?"

"I'll bet the two of them were stunned," Mahmood says, squinting. "They misread you. Your mild demeanor is deceptive, Thafer. Even I misread it. But your performance at the conference was that of a determined man, unafraid to tell the truth. You were superb."

The two men are quiet as they ride in Mahmood's car. The heat is unbearable, even with the windows open. Thafer looks at Mahmood's dark eyes. They squint constantly as though in contempt of Kuwait's unrelenting heat. "What do you think will happen now?"

"Who knows? Ziyad is not a strong man, as you've already discovered. I bet he'll run off to Beirut. This time he'll never come back."

"And Hamdan?"

"He's more thick-skinned and callous. He'll never leave on his own. He has to be told. And who's going to tell him? The oil minister always comes to rescue him whenever he gets himself in hot water. I'm sure this'll happen again here."

"I was kind of surprised to hear the Iraqi minister call Ziyad a liar so quickly. I would've thought the conference might conduct an investigation of the whole mess."

"But it was obvious that you were telling what had happened. All Ziyad had to do was to stand up and deny it, but he didn't. I kept looking at him, expecting him to respond, but he didn't. All the ministers were looking at him too, waiting to see what he would say. His silence was what angered them, I'm sure. And that's why they all concurred with the Iraqi minister's pronouncement. The whole thing was sad. It was unmanly to pick on a poor Palestinian woman, whom they knew had no one to protect her rights, and blame her for their own foolish mistake. That really angered me too."

"Well, Mahmood," Thafer says as the car pulls up in front of his house, "I think I'll take Suhaila's mother to Egypt this weekend. My children will be coming the following Thursday. If we leave this Wednesday afternoon, I'll be back in Kuwait Friday night. I'll have ample time to prepare for my children's arrival."

"You can do that, Thafer, and I'll take you to the airport."

"Good. We also need to contact Suhaila to let her know I'm coming."

"She doesn't have a phone where she's staying, but I know how to contact someone who can reach her and give her the message. I'll take care of it," Mahmood offers.

"I also need her or someone to meet us at the airport in Alexandria. I don't know my way around Alexandria."

"I'll make sure that someone other than Suhaila meets you to help you clear customs. That's no problem. I'll make reservations for you for two nights at the Alexandria Hilton."

"Good, Mahmood. I'm excited."

XXIV

It is late Thursday afternoon. Thafer and Suhaila have returned to the Alexandria Hilton. As they sit on a sofa in their suite overlooking the Mediterranean, he tells her that he intends to return to the United States when his contract with

OAPEC is concluded. He asks her to marry him. She says she will marry him, but cannot go to live in the United States. They discuss the matter at length, sometimes emotionally, but can reach no conclusion.

"How am I going to endure," she says. "I feel doomed."

"Think of the time we've had together these past two days," he says. "We must find a way. Maybe you can think again about coming back to Kuwait at least."

"After all that had happened at OAPEC, nothing will bring me back except your being there. We both know how long that will last. I have to take a hard look at the offer from the University of Alexandria. It does appeal to me. If I accept it, I'll also be with my children. Neither of us can be sure of what OAPEC will be like after the special conference. I could never be comfortable living in the United States. I am committed to staying here to serve the cause of our homeland. This is where I belong."

"I understand." He examines the floor pensively.

"I cannot abandon the homeland. I need to stay here, where I can look at the Mediterranean and know I am not too far."

"Do we have to be near the homeland to serve it?"

"Maybe you don't, but I know I must remain close. Maybe with your talents and experience you can serve best by being in another part of the world. I just can't."

"And the permanent relationship we've been hoping for, Suhaila? Can't we find a way?"

"Oh, Thafer, I can't live in the United States."

"It'll be an impossible adjustment for my children to live here."

"You know how much I love you and love to be with you," she cries. "Sometimes I think that I won't be able to cope. Maybe something will change; maybe the conflict between us and Israel will change; maybe the world will change."

"Nothing is going to change, I just saw a high-ranking Syrian army officer in civilian clothing in the lobby of the hotel. I'm sure he's the Syrian chief of staff. I met him when I went to Damascus, but I don't think he recognized me. He's probably on vacation and is having a good time in Alexandria while part of his country is under Israeli occupation. If we wait for things to change, we'll wait forever."

"I don't think we have to wait forever, but we both know that a changed world and a changed conflict are not likely soon, no matter what our hopes are. It's not that I don't want marriage. I do, very, very much, but I don't see how we can be married without sacrificing something neither one of us can sacrifice."

He looks down.

"I don't want you to be sad or disappointed," she says, now choking back tears. "I've never loved anyone the way I love you."

He continues to look down.

"Say something," she says, crying. "Don't look so grim and sad. I wish you would say something."

He reaches for her hand and holds it. "I wish I could say something that would be comforting to both of us. I'm so deeply moved by your commitment to staying close to the homeland. How can I argue with that? I feel guilty about my own feelings."

"You shouldn't," she says, still weeping. "I know that the kind of service you can give is unique, and because of that you should live wherever you think best. Even though I can't be near you, my mind and my heart will always be with you. The way you stood up for me as a Palestinian and a woman has made me very proud." She pauses. "I want to see your children, Thafer." Her eyes tear again. "I'm very emotional today, and I was determined not to be. I thought I was stronger than that. Give me a little of your strength."

"You're not weak, Suhaila." He hugs her and wipes away her tears. "You yourself have given me a lot of strength. We can't let this get the best of us. We have to get a hold of ourselves."

"I know we do," she says, crying, "but how do I do it? How do I do it?"

"You're a very strong person. I know you are."

"Not any more," she sobs. ".How did I come to this?"

He holds her tightly.

"I shouldn't be like this," she says. "I love you, and I'm glad I love you, but I don't know what's happening to me tonight. I guess it's because I now know that we can't have each other, and I feel sad."

He gently kisses her eyes.

"I'm sorry," she says, trying to regain her composure. "I'm sorry, my friend, my countryman, my love. I admire your strength so much. I do want to marry you." She pauses again, this time longer. "Maybe we are already married. Our marriage is different. It's a marriage that death does not part. Our marriage cannot be broken by separation. And when our homeland is liberated, and our people come home, we'll have a wedding, and your mother and mine will yodel, the way your relatives in Hawalli yodeled when you first arrived in Kuwait, the way the old Palestinian woman yodeled for you when you went to visit her. And we don't have to be sad."

He searches the face of his beloved, his countrywoman.

"We are already married," she repeats in a soft voice, "even if the wedding has to await the liberation of our homeland."

Thafer presses her head to his chest.

"I don't feel as badly as I did," she says. "I'm convinced that we'll have a wedding and a celebration, that justice for our people will come, and that our homeland will be liberated. So you go ahead; do what you have to do, and I will wait for you here. Each will do his task. One day, before long, you and I will walk freely through the streets of our homeland, arm in arm, as though all of this has been a bad dream. Our children and their children will remember it and tell it to future generations to remind them that they must be vigilant."

He presses her hand, then kisses it.

"Look at the blue Mediterranean, Thafer," she says, pointing to the sea. "Doesn't it make you feel hopeful? Don't the waves tell us something? The power that moves the waves and delivers them safely to the shore will one day deliver us safely to our homeland. I know it will."

Thafer continues looking at his countrywoman. Her eyes are now dry and determined.

"I think that we better get ready," she says, looking at the sea. "Your flight is at 9:00."

"I know."

"I'll take you to the airport. Thank you for bringing my mother to Alexandria. Next time, we'll both take her home. The keys to the gates of Jerusalem are in your pocket."

Stunned by her words, he cannot speak.

"Next time, we'll both take her home, to Jerusalem, and she and your mother will both yodel," she repeats. "There in Jerusalem our people will dance and celebrate in the streets. I'm so sure of that, I'm not sad any more, and I won't be lonesome. I'll wait for you. Will you wait for me?"

"Of course I will." He embraces and kisses her.

XXV

Thafer's children step out of the plane and into Kuwait's furnacelike wind. The heat is merciless. It stops them for a moment.

"Dad," cries Kathleen, rushing to her father. Ignoring the officials and the intolerable heat, she jumps to embrace him. "You've lost a lot of weight. What happened? Haven't you been eating well?"

"Kathleen, sweetheart!" He embraces his daughter. He turns to Colleen and kisses her. "Colleen, darling, Colleen!"

"Dad," Colleen says. "You're tanned! You must've lost more than twenty pounds! Have you been sick?"

"I've been all right, as a matter of fact. Where are Andrew and Sean?"

"They're looking for the luggage," says Kathleen. "We snuck in here hoping to see you.

"I see Andrew and Sean." Thafer waves to his two sons as they enter pushing two carts loaded with luggage.

"Hi, Dad," says Sean, embracing his father. "Your hair is longer."

"Oh, Sean!" Thafer says, embracing his fifteen-year-old son. "Andrew!" He walks toward his nineteen-year-old son and warmly shakes his hand.

"What happened, Dad?" Andrew asks. "Have you been doing your morning exercises in the sun or what? You look ten years younger! You even look taller. You lost a lot of weight. That's great."

"I know I lost weight because my pants are loose; otherwise, I wouldn't have noticed. I eat well, more than usual, as a matter of fact. These past five months have seemed like forever without you."

Thafer introduces Uncle Muneer to his four children, who have been quietly looking in awe at Thafer's older brother.

"I'll go and tell the family they are here safe," says Uncle Muneer. "You go ahead, Thafer. Take them to your house, and we'll all see you there."

"The limousine is cool now, sir," Saeed says, lifting a suitcase. "I'll bring it to the door."

"Good," Thafer says. "Thank you, Saeed."

"Is this the young driver you've been writing us about, Dad?" asks Kathleen.

"Right. I'll introduce you to him once we get to the house."

"How can you stand the heat, Dad?" asks Sean.

"I rarely stay out."

"We should've helped the driver," says Andrew.

"You're not acclimated to the heat. Saeed is. We'll go to the house and meet the family."

"Who, Dad?" asks Colleen.

"There'll be a lot of relatives."

"Are we expected to greet them in a special way?" asks Andrew.

"The Arab people are a very warm people, Andrew. Men kiss and embrace one another as a sign of affection and respect. Just as Uncle Muneer kissed both you and Sean on both cheeks and embraced you, so will most of the relatives."

"Should we also kiss them?" asks Sean.

"If you like."

"How about us, Dad?" asks Kathleen.

"The same thing, darling."

"Will both men and women kiss us?" asks Colleen.

"The young men will shake hands with you and Kathleen, sweetheart, but the older men may kiss and embrace you. The women will kiss you on both cheeks and embrace you. Just be yourselves and try not to be nervous."

"I'm already nervous," says Kathleen.

"So am I," says Colleen.

"They are very kind people, believe me. They haven't come out of curiosity; they've come to pay their respects to you as my children and as the grandchildren of my father."

"Was your father someone special?" Kathleen asks.

"He was a respected man in the family. I'll tell you more about him a little later."

"I'm dying to see the inside of your house," says Kathleen.

"Me too," says Sean. "Will Mama Adla come?" Sean asks.

"She will, Sean."

"Do they all speak English?" Kathleen asks.

"Most of the young people speak English, but you have to speak slowly and avoid slang. The older folks, like Uncle Muneer and Mama Adla, don't speak English. I'll be your interpreter as I was at the airport when Uncle Muneer greeted you."

"When are we going to see Grandma?" asks Sean.

"We'll talk about that tonight."

"Will we see your brothers?" asks Kathleen.

"My brother Rassem and his wife and children are coming to Kuwait tomorrow. They'll stay with us."

"Great," says Sean.

"Do they speak English?" asks Kathleen.

"My brother and his children do. My brother's wife doesn't."

"What about your other brother?" asks Colleen.

"We'll go to Amman to meet him and his family. I'm hoping that Grandma will come to Amman from the occupied territories too so that she'll see all of you."

"That's great!" says Andrew.

"I can't wait to hear about home. How did you all do in school?"

"Not bad," says Colleen."

"Now, tell me about your flight. How was it, Sean?"

"I was scared all the time. I kept thinking of what happened a few days ago at Olympic Village in Munich."

"Did you hear about that?" asks Kathleen.

"I did, but the reports here glorified the incident. How was it reported in the States?"

"A few days ago, early morning on September 5, to be exact," says Andrew, "eight Palestinians climbed over a fence at Olympic Village in Munich and forced their way into dormitories of the Israeli team. They killed two athletes and took nine others as hostages. The Palestinians demanded the release of two hundred Palestinian prisoners who they said were held in Israeli jails unjustly. They also demanded an airplane to take them to an unspecified Arab capital. Israel refused to negotiate with the Palestinians. High German authorities tried to negotiate with them, even offered to pay unlimited ransom or substitute four Germans for the Israeli hostages."

"Did the Germans really offer to do that, Andrew?" asks Thafer. "That wasn't reported here."

"That's what was reported at home, Dad," says Andrew. "After a lot of give and take between the Germans and the Palestinians, and several extensions of the deadline for the ultimatum given by the Palestinian group, the Palestinian attackers and their Israeli hostages were flown fifteen miles by helicopter from Olympic Village to a NATO airport. There was apparently a deal with the Palestinian group that they would be allowed to board a Lufthansa jet for an Arab airport, but that never happened. Something went wrong: I don't exactly know what. Someone opened fire, and the Israelis were killed."

"There were five German sharpshooters," says Colleen. "They were backed up by police and were supposed to be waiting to confront the armed Palestinians. When two of the Palestinian guerrillas left the helicopter to inspect the Boeing 727, the one they were supposed to fly to Tunisia in, I think the Germans started shooting at them. One of the three helicopters was set on fire by an exploding grenade thrown by one of the Palestinians as he jumped out."

"I guess that's right," says Andrew. "Three hours after that happened, the Olympics Committee announced that all the Israeli hostages were killed."

"I knew that all the Israelis were killed," says Thafer.

"I don't have to tell you, Dad," says Andrew, "that incident didn't help the cause of the Palestinians in the United States."

"I'm sure it didn't."

"Why did the Palestinians do that?" asks Sean.

Thafer Allam hesitates, his face flushed and pained. "I don't know why, Sean. It was a terrible thing to do. It was a tragedy."

The children are quiet.

"Why didn't the Israelis let you visit Grandma?" asks Kathleen, changing the subject. "That was mean."

"Well, we'll talk about that later, sweetheart."

"I told my social studies teacher about that," says Kathleen. "She's Jewish and always tells us that Israel is the only democracy in the Middle East. 'There's a reason why they didn't let your father in, Kathleen,' " Kathleen says, mimicking the way her teacher spoke. " 'There must be a reason. Israel is a democracy.' I got so mad, Dad, I almost told her off, but I didn't."

Andrew and Sean laugh.

"I'm glad you didn't. I'm proud of you."

"Can you believe her telling me that, Dad?"

XXVI

The dress of family members at Thafer's house is full of contrasts. Thafer's two daughters wear simple, attractive cotton dresses, which they bought at Sears. They wear no jewelry and nothing on their heads. His two sons wear short-sleeved shirts, no neckties, and cotton tan pants, but no jackets. They have long hair. There is a beautiful simplicity in the four children's appearance.

Mama Adla and Thafer's female relatives wear characteristically Palestinian dresses. Some have inexpensive jewelry designed to wear with Palestinian garments. They remind Thafer of his youth in his native Palestine. Some of the Palestinian male relatives wear western clothes, and others wear the traditional long white robes and white headcloths.

"Here, take Thafer's daughters and dress them like young Palestinian women," says Mama Adla, smiling, to one of Thafer's female nieces. "Did you bring the little suitcase from Fuaad's car?"

"Yes, I did."

Amused, Colleen and Kathleen do not take the suggestion seriously.

But Mama Adla persists.

The two daughters are hesitant at first.

Thafer's two sons look at their father, wondering whether they also will be asked to wear something different.

Thafer shakes his head, indicating that they are safe.

When the two daughters return wearing two identical handwoven white linen Palestinian dresses embroidered with red and pink silk, the change is extraordinary. Colleen wears a necklace made of a chain with six more chains suspended from it. Kathleen wears a white mantilla over her head. On her wrists she wears handmade silver Palestinian bracelets. Each has a white cotton purse with wooden handles and embroidered in silk on both sides with branch and floral motifs. Thafer's relatives applaud.

"Look how beautiful you are in your Palestinian dresses," says Mama Adla.

"Are you Americans or Palestinians?" the elderly Uncle Muneer asks the two daughters in jest.

"Both," Kathleen says, without hesitation. Colleen remains reserved.

"Can't be," says Uncle Muneer smiling. "You're now Palestinians, pure and simple. Just see how beautiful you are in your Palestinian dresses."

Thafer's two daughters are uneasy, unsure how to respond. They walk slowly and sit next to their father, looking tentatively toward Uncle Muneer and Mama Adla, who return loving smiles.

It is a most unusual afternoon. Thafer's cook has prepared a quick meal for all the relatives. Men, women, and children sit on the floor around blankets on which the food is placed. Plates are distributed so that the relatives can help themselves. The two daughters seem apprehensive, but Andrew and Sean mix easily with the newly discovered young relatives. Colleen remains quietly reserved.

After dinner, the relatives are more relaxed, but Thafer is uneasy. This is the time my relatives ask their political questions, he says to himself. I hope they don't direct their questions to Kathleen. I should've alerted the kids that they might be asked questions. My relatives are gentle people, he assures himself. I am sure they won't embarrass me or my children.

Without warning the question comes. It is Uncle Muneer's youngest daughter, Hala, a beautiful teacher at a women's teachers' college. She looks at Colleen, who sits next to her sister Kathleen. There is a striking resemblance between Kathleen in her Palestinian attire and the attractive young Hala. "Cousin Colleen," Hala asks in perfect English, "what did you think of what our Palestinian heroes did a few days ago at the Olympic games in Munich?"

Thafer is horrified. He looks at his stepdaughter and can see the anxiety on her flushed, fair face.

Colleen hesitates. She turns to her father.

"Tell them what you think, Colleen."

"My two brothers," she stammers, a slight tremor in her voice, "are athletes. Sean is fifteen. He's almost sixteen. Andrew is almost twenty. Neither of them has much understanding of the U.S. bombing of Vietnam. I couldn't help thinking of them when I heard about what happened in Munich. My brothers are completely innocent of the acts committed by our government against the people of Vietnam. I would be inconsolable, devastated, if someone harmed my brothers in retaliation for the misguided deeds of our government." She pauses. "Could you blame me?" she asks her father's young niece.

"No, Cousin Colleen." The young college teacher is visibly moved. "I really wasn't thinking about it that way. I'm sorry I asked. I hope I didn't upset you."

"You didn't."

"I didn't like what happened in Munich," Mama Adla says in Arabic as Thafer translates. She turns to Thafer's children. "When you go back, my dear children, please tell Mr. Nixon about what happened to us. Tell him how the Jews took our homeland, how they stole our homes and farms. We never did the Americans any harm. Why does Mr. Nixon support the Jews against us? I don't understand that. Your dad's father was a great man. He fought to save the homeland, but the conspiracy was bigger than him, much bigger. All of you, remember your grandfather when you go back to America. Tell all your friends what happened to your family in Palestine. Won't you?"

The children remain silent.

Thafer looks at his children. He can see and feel the anxiety and frustration in their faces.

"I don't understand why Mr. Nixon supports the Jews against us," repeats Mama Adla.

"I don't understand why either, Mama Adla," Colleen tells her.

XXVII

"Well, how did you like our relatives?" Thafer asks his children after the relatives leave.

"They are very sweet," says Colleen.

"I loved them," says Kathleen.

"I felt sorry for them," says Andrew.

"I liked them very much, Dad," says Sean. "I wish Uncle Muneer and Mama Adla could speak English, though."

"Do you think they liked us?" asks Kathleen.

"I'm sure they loved you."

"I just felt bad answering your pretty niece's question the way I did," Colleen says. "They were quiet after I spoke, and it made me feel terrible. I still feel terrible about the whole thing."

"Your answer was very good, Colleen. The whole thing is an awful tragedy."

"Their silence made me feel horrible, though. I don't think that I can ever know how these poor people feel. I should've said something else to them. I should've said that I feel for them, because I do. I'm upset by our government's indifference to what happened to them, and I don't like its materialism and militarism. I understand Palestinian anger and even Palestinian violence, but I just don't feel it's right to kill innocent civilians."

"I think they understand that's how we feel," says Kathleen.

"Do they, Dad?" asks Colleen.

"I'm sure they do."

"I hope so."

"Kathleen really looked like a Palestinian woman in that Palestinian dress," says Sean.

"They gave it to me and they gave Colleen the dress she wore."

"I was afraid they'd ask me something," says Sean.

"Aren't you glad they didn't?" says Kathleen.

"We didn't tell you, Dad," says Andrew. "Kathleen and Sean were really afraid in the plane. Especially Kathleen."

"Yes, we were," says Kathleen. "We keep hearing about Palestinian commandos and hijackers who are called terrorists at home. I'm scared of them. I was terrified riding the plane. I was afraid that some Palestinian would hijack us or throw a bomb at us."

Isn't it ironic? Thafer thinks. The Palestinian heroes to whom my niece Hala and hundreds of thousands of Palestinians like her look for their salvation are the same Palestinians my children fear.

"If Palestinian commandos would attack only the Israeli army and Israeli military," says Andrew, "not innocent civilians, there wouldn't be this great vehement outcry about Palestinian terrorism."

"How can I disagree?" Thafer says. "The Palestinian fighters have attacked the Israeli army and its military roads and installations, but Israel has always suppressed news of the effectiveness of these Palestinian attacks against the military. It's these senseless and vicious attacks against civilians that capture the headlines. The slaughter of Israeli children in a school or the killing of innocent Israeli athletes is as despicable as any crime committed by Israel against innocent Palestinian civilians."

"Who's Dr. George Habash?" asks Colleen. "It's hard to understand how a physician who's trained to do humanitarian deeds could become so heartless."

"Dr. George Habash is the leader of a small fringe group called the Popular Front for the Liberation of Palestine, the PFLP. In 1948, Colleen, Dr. Habash was caught up in a tragic drama near two small Palestinian towns, Lydda and Ramla, which transformed him. I have a book about him that a colleague of mine at OAPEC gave me to read a few months ago. Maybe I'll read you something he once wrote." Thafer goes to his study and brings the book about Habash's life.

"Why didn't you want to tell us about all this when we were growing up?" asks Kathleen. "Why didn't you tell us about the Palestinian problem, about your father, and about your family?"

Thafer pauses. Tell her the truth, he admonishes himself. Tell her about your feelings of guilt, about your desire to be Americanized, about your sense of shame for your own people, and about the confusion you had about the person you wanted to be. "I just didn't want to burden you with all this tragic history, Kathleen. I was sure you would hear about it either in high school or in college."

His children don't seem convinced.

That was an empty answer, he rebukes himself. Look at their faces. They are starved for a better response, one that is worthy of a loving father.

"We're finding out on our own now, Dad," says Kathleen. "What they say about it at school is biased. We should've heard more about it from you."

"Why didn't you tell us something about it, Dad?" asks Sean.

"When I arrived in the United States, Sean, I was a young man, barely a year older than you are now. I had no relatives or friends in the United States. I was confused about the kind of person I wanted to be. I was ashamed of my own people, who were defeated badly by the Israelis, who were outnumbered fifty to one. Then I met your mother and fell in love with her. I was barely eighteen when I married your mother, who was twenty-five. I began to have a burning desire to be an American. Even as I had all these feelings I've described, Sean, I also continued to feel guilty about having them."

"That's sad," says Kathleen.

"This is what Habash once wrote: 'Then it was [1948] and [the Israelis] came to Lydda . . . I don't know how to explain this . . . what this still means for us, not to have a home, not to have a nation, or anyone who cares. . . . [The Israelis] forced us to flee. It is a picture that haunts me and that I'll never be able to forget. Thirty thousand human beings walking, weeping . . . screaming in terror, . . . women with babies in their arms and children tugging at their skirts . . . and the Israeli soldiers pushing them on with their guns. Some people fell by the wayside, some never got up again. It was terrible. One thinks: this isn't life, this isn't human. Once you have seen this, your heart and your brain are transformed.' "

"Maybe what Habash says isn't true," says Kathleen.

"What do you mean maybe it isn't true?" cries Andrew. "First you ask Dad to tell us what he knows, then you begin to question what he says."

"I'm not questioning what Dad says. I'm just wondering if what Habash is saying is true. That's all."

"You have to believe me, my dear Kathleen," Thafer says. "I saw the same tragic scene Habash describes."

"Were you among those people, Dad?" asks Sean.

"I wasn't, Sean. I was in Tulkarm when the people of Lydda and Ramla arrived there on foot. Women were weeping and screaming. They were searching for their loved ones. Old men were terrorized, with no place to go. Husbands looked for their wives. Children cried for their mothers. It was a scene I'll never forget."

"How old were you when that happened?" asks Colleen.

"Thirteen. Your mother and I decided not to burden you with these things when you were growing up. We felt that you shouldn't carry your dad's scars with you through life."

"How can we help it?" asks Andrew. "We are your children. Your scars are also our scars."

"Sooner or later," says Kathleen, "we're bound to know. It's better that we find out from you. Even when I was quite young, maybe at four or five, I had a feeling that you had some sad secret that you didn't want us to know about. No one ever told me. I just had that feeling."

"Me too," says Sean. "And no one ever told me, but I just knew there was something sad that happened to you when you were very young."

"Kathleen once asked Mom about it, out of the blue," says Colleen. "Mom wanted to know if anyone had told Kathleen something, but Kathleen swore that no one had, that she just felt it."

"Mom told Colleen and me what happened to your family," says Kathleen.

"Okay, Dad," says Colleen. "Let's talk about your work and your Palestinian friend. Are we going to meet her?"

"Are we going to go to Egypt?" asks Sean.

"I expect that we will make a trip to Egypt. I want you to meet my friend, Dr. Suhaila Sa'adeh, who has left OAPEC. She is a professor at the University of Alexandria now."

"What does she teach?" asks Andrew.

"Economics."

"If they taught it in English," says Andrew, "I would love to spend a year studying in Egypt."

"You can do that at the American University of Cairo. If you're serious, we can look into that."

"I want something different," says Andrew. "I bet the American University of Cairo is just another American University. I was thinking that a year at an entirely different place might be interesting. I am not sure I want to spend a year in the Middle East, though."

"I want to stay here with you, Dad," says Sean.

"Can we all stay here with you until June, Dad?" asks Kathleen. "We all talked about that before we came."

"I would love it."

"Can I enroll at the University of Kuwait?" asks Kathleen.

"I'm sure it can be arranged. Some of their science courses are taught in English."

"That'll be great!"

"We can enroll Sean at the American School of Kuwait."

"I can take some graduate courses at the University of Kuwait, too," says Colleen, "but if Andrew decides he wants to go back, I'll go back with him."

"I'm going to stay with Dad," says Kathleen.

"I am too," says Sean.

"I'm glad to see you, Thafer." Mahmood greets Thafer warmly in the hallway. "Have your children arrived?"

"Yes, they have, Mahmood, and they're sleeping late this morning."

"Congratulations. I would like to bring my family to meet them."

"They will like that very much."

"We'll wait until they are rested, and whenever you're ready, we'll come."

"It'll be very soon, Mahmood."

"How was your trip to Egypt with Dr. Suhaila's mother?"

"It went well."

"OAPEC now has new leadership. Ziyad is gone, and he won't be back. Hamdan has been recalled, and he won't be back."

"For sure?"

"Yes, Mukhtar is now acting secretary general. Reem Makram is coming back. Mukhtar says that if Dr. Suhaila wants to come back, she can. He sent word to her, and he's waiting to hear from her."

"She's interested in a professorship she's been offered at the University of Alexandria."

"That may complicate things, unless you can persuade her."

"Well, she wants to be close to her children."

I proposed marriage, Thafer muses, but she's wed to something bigger than me. She's fed up with Kuwait. She wants to look at the Mediterranean and breathe the winds that may blow from the homeland. She wants to look at the sea and hope that its waves will one day carry her back to the homeland, Mahmood.

"As long as you're here, she'll come. If you leave us, she'll never come back."

She'll never come back to Kuwait whether I'm here or not. There's something bigger than me that occupies her mind and heart.

"Don't look sad, Thafer. Your children are here now. Ziyad and Hamdan have gone, OAPEC is a much more pleasant place to work, thanks to your courage. And Suhaila? What can I say? Let's hope she'll come back."

XXVIII

"How are the children, Dr. Thafer?" asks Mukhtar, who has invited Thafer to his office.

"They are doing well, Brother Mukhtar. At first, as you know, they hesitated about staying. But Kathleen, my younger daughter, has done very well in her first year at the University of Kuwait. She has made many friends and likes it here. The younger one, Sean, will be a senior at the American School of Kuwait next year. He has also done well. He is on the track team, plays baseball and basketball, and has been elected outstanding athlete of the year. My older daughter, Colleen, has been unhappy. She has taken a few courses at the University of Kuwait, but she doesn't find that challenging. In February she started working for an American company in Kuwait and bought herself a car. She's still unhappy here and feels confined. I don't know how long she'll last. The older fellow, Andrew, is also unhappy here. He wants to go back to the States for his last year in college."

"Are they learning Arabic?"

"They've all been studying it."

"Good. Have they been able to see their grandmother?"

"Not yet. We're going to try this summer. We sent word to my mother that I wasn't able to enter the West Bank when I tried. We're hoping she'll come to Amman to meet us early in July."

"I'm glad they'll at last be able to see her. It's outrageous that the Israelis would deny you entry to see your mother. I don't understand how the government of the United States can close an eye to that."

Thafer notices Mukhtar's face changing.

"Brother Thafer, I have bad news for you."

"What is it, Brother Mukhtar?"

The acting secretary general is reluctant to talk. His eyes are glued to his desk. "A month ago, Dr. Thafer," he finally says, "OAPEC received a letter, copies of which were mailed to all the oil ministers of OAPEC. I will show you the letter in a minute." He leafs through the pages of a letter in his hand.

Will I be accused of being a CIA agent, planted to disrupt the noble purposes of OAPEC? Thafer wonders.

"The main point in the letter, Brother Thafer, is that the position of chief legal advisor is, according to OAPEC's charter, a senior position and, quote, 'shall be reserved to the nationals of the member states,' end of quote. The letter argues that it is dangerous to allow this very sensitive and important position to be occupied by a citizen of the United States. I have discussed this point with our minister. Although he understands the concerns of the letter, he says that OAPEC deliberately made an exception when it appointed you to the position. I have sent copies of your application form and copies of all the correspondence relating to your employment to all the ministers. There's no doubt in anyone's mind that you disclosed your U.S. citizenship in your application. Because we needed a legal advisor badly at that time, we waived the citizenship requirement in consultation with a committee of oil ministers. Whatever action is taken by OAPEC now has to take this fact into consideration." Mukhtar hands Thafer a lengthy letter, the heading and signature of which are deleted.

"This communication," the letter starts, "is in reference to the status of OAPEC's able and conscientious chief legal advisor, Dr. Thafer Ayoub Allam. Although we have recognized his outstanding capabilities and keen intellect from the inception of his term in this sensitive position, we nonetheless feel constrained to bring to the attention of the members of the Organization of Arab Petroleum-Exporting Countries, OAPEC, the fact that Article 3 of OAPEC's charter reserves this senior position to nationals of OAPEC's member states. OAPEC's charter provides: 'All appointments as head of department and all other senior positions shall be reserved to the nationals of the member states of this organization.' "

After listing the various heads of departments and senior positions that under the charter are considered subject to this provision, including the position of chief legal advisor, the letter concludes: "In view of the above, we believe that engaging a citizen of a state that is not a member of the Organiza-, tion of Arab Petroleum Exporting Countries as chief legal advisor to the Organization of Arab Petroleum Exporting Countries is a serious violation of the charter. It should be rectified immediately."

"Thank you for letting me see this, Brother Mukhtar. I understand completely."

"You should know, Dr. Thafer, that I have discussed this with our minister, who has discussed it with other oil ministers. The quoted provision notwithstanding, the Council of Arab Oil Ministers wishes you to stay on until the end of this year. They would like also to make a fair settlement with you for the balance of your contract with OAPEC. You have offers from two member states to receive their citizenship if you wish to stay on and meet the technical requirement of OAPEC's charter."

"If I decide to leave immediately, can we also conclude a fair settlement of the contract I have with OAPEC?"

"I'm sure we can, but, if I may give you my personal and friendly advice, realizing that the final decision must be yours, I wouldn't ask for that because it will weaken your bargaining position. OAPEC needs you for these six months, even though the letter says that the error should be rectified immediately. I am sure that if you stay the six months, you'll be able to name your ticket. If, on the other hand, you leave in a huff, OAPEC will be off the hook. I can understand your disappointment, but you mustn't allow that to prejudice your decision. I haven't told you everything. You have the respect and the support of most of OAPEC's members. Most, if not all, would like to be helpful. The gesture made by two member states in offering you their citizenship is an indication of what's going on in the minds of many members. I understand your reluctance to accept their offers, but I wouldn't dismiss them out of hand. The letter has touched a sensitive nerve in many of us. After all, you are really an Arab, a Palestinian Arab."

"I am also an American. Except for these past few months, I've spent all my adult life in the United States. My children are all native Americans. Because of my national origin, I may be unhappy about the policies of the United States in the Middle East, but I am a U.S. citizen. I took an oath to uphold the laws and Constitution of the United States of America, which I have no intention of breaking. I am grateful for the generous offer made by these two states, but I cannot accept it. I would not want to pledge allegiance to a flag other than the U.S. flag now. Perhaps one day I'll be allowed to hold dual citizenship. That other allegiance will have to be to the land of my ancestors, my native Palestine."

"I certainly understand and respect that. I won't press you any further."

"You have no idea how grateful I am. I am honored and heartened by the gesture of the two states, but I shouldn't put myself in a situation that will create conflicts of allegiance for me. I am, of course, proud of my Arab heritage. I will always be emotionally attached to it. Yet I feel that I must be careful."

"I understand, Dr. Thafer. Don't let this get you down." Mukhtar walks with Thafer to the door. "These unhappy things have a way of coming to happy endings."

"Thank you for these comforting words." Thafer shakes Mukhtar's hand and feels both relief and sadness.

XXIX

The five Allams have just returned to their suite at the Alexandria Hilton after having dinner with Suhaila, her mother and Suhaila's two sons. "How did you like Dr. Suhaila and her family?" Thafer asks his children.

"They're very nice people," says Colleen. "Dr. Suhaila is a very intelligent woman."

"She loves you," says Kathleen. "I can tell."

"Kathleen!" exclaims Andrew. "Why don't you keep that to yourself, stupid?"

"Andrew!" Thafer silences his older son.

"I liked Dr. Suhaila," says Sean. "She's very nice. I also liked her kids."

"I loved her sons' accent," says Kathleen. "The older one must be about Sean's age."

"He is," says Sean. "That's Imad. He wants to go to college in the States."

"She's very pretty," says Kathleen. "She's also nice. I liked her very much."

"Yes, she's very pretty," says Colleen. "I liked her too."

"I didn't mean to silence you, Andrew, but this constant picking on Kathleen! Can we be a little more civilized when we talk to one another?"

"She gets on my nerves."

"Good," says Kathleen.

"How did you like Dr. Suhaila, Andrew?" asks Colleen.

"I liked her very much. She's a very educated woman and speaks perfect English. I loved her mother."

"I'll bet her outfit is like Grandma's," says Kathleen.

"Do you think that you might be interested in a deanship at the law school at the University of Alexandria?" asks Andrew.

"I don't know that I could even be offered such a position."

"Dr. Suhaila thinks you might be," says Sean.

"She is just speculating."

"Why doesn't she come to the United States?" asks Sean.

"She'd never do that," says Kathleen. "The way she talks about Dad's homeland is really something."

"I don't think that she likes the United States," says Colleen.

"Where did she go to college?" asks Andrew.

"She has a bachelor's degree in economics from the American University of Beirut, a master's in economics from the University of Virginia, and a Ph.D. from Stanford University."

"Wow!" says Kathleen.

"I'll bet she can name her ticket at any American university," says Andrew.

"She'll never go," says Kathleen. "Not her."

"How can you be so sure, smarty pants?" asks Andrew.

"You want to bet?"

"Would she ever come to upstate New York, Dad?" asks Colleen.

Thafer Allam pauses. Tell them, he tells himself. Tell them what you know, Dad. "Dr. Suhaila is committed to living in the Middle East."

"I'll bet," says Andrew, "that if she and her mother and the two boys come to visit us in Ashfield, she will like it. Why don't we invite them to come and visit us when you're through at OAPEC?"

"Yes, why don't we?" says Colleen.

Thafer looks down. Tell them. Tell them. Don't keep them in the dark, a voice within him says. "I've discussed this with her at length," Thafer finally says, feeling miserable and helpless. "She truly is committed to living in the Middle East."

The four children are quiet.

"Well, we have to get ready to go back to Kuwait tomorrow and get on with our lives."

"Do you think you'll be home by Christmas?" asks Colleen.

"If all goes well, that's my plan."

"I don't mean to say anything that would anger you, Dad," says Andrew, "but without realizing it, whoever wrote that letter has done you and your family a great favor."

"Yes," says Colleen. "I'm sure the experience of coming back to the Middle East and working with OAPEC has been worth it though."

"Yes, it has," Thafer says.

"If you had your way, Dad," asks Kathleen, "would you have preferred working longer in the Middle East?"

Thafer looks at his younger daughter. I don't know what I would've preferred, my love. I'm still as confused today as I was when I embarked on this venture. "Maybe, Kathleen."

"I was afraid of that," she says.

"You're coming home for sure," says Sean. "I mean, when you finish your work with OAPEC, you'll come back to Ashfield."

"That's my plan, Sean. I don't want you to worry about that. I'll never let you down."

"I know."

"Dad," says Andrew, "Colleen and I have been wondering if the two of us can go home as soon as we return to Kuwait. Kathleen and Sean want to stay in Kuwait a little longer."

"Whatever you'd like to do is okay with me. I hate to see you leave, but if that's what you'd like to do, of course it's all right."

"I want to stay with you until you come home," says Sean.

"Me too," says Kathleen, "but I may change my mind and go back if Colleen goes back with Andrew. I'm not sure. I don't know what I want to do. I'll decide when we go back to Kuwait."

"That's all right. We don't have to decide on anything now."

"Do you wish that Dr. Suhaila would come to Ashfield, Dad?" Kathleen asks.

"Kathleen!" cries Andrew, "Cut it out! Don't you have any sense? God Almighty!"

"Yes, Kathleen, I wish she would, but I also understand how she feels about going to the United States. I respect her feelings very much. I even identify with them. As far as I am concerned, you all come first. I wouldn't have come back to the Middle East if all of you, or even one of you, had strong feelings against my coming, especially after Mom's death."

"But we shouldn't come first," says Andrew. "We are grown ups now, or on our way. You have to live your life too. I certainly don't want you to put me ahead of yourself."

"That's right," says Colleen. "We don't want to be a drag on everything you want to do."

"I don't feel that you're a drag, sweetheart." He is visibly shaken. "Where on earth did you get that idea? You're my children, and I love all of you. I would give my life for you."

"We know that," says Andrew. "Colleen doesn't doubt that. None of us doubt that, but we want you to feel free to make the choices that will make you comfortable. You shouldn't worry about us. We'll be all right."

"That's right," says Colleen. "That's what I meant to say. It just didn't come out right."

"If you and Dr. Suhaila love each other," says Kathleen, "and that means you have to stay in the Middle East, you should, Dad."

"If you do that, can I still stay with you?" asks Sean.

"Of course, Sean, without a doubt, but I'm not sure this is going to happen. I'm undecided about what I want to do. We're just having a discussion, Sean. The whole thing is premature."

"If you decide to stay in the Middle East," says Kathleen, "I would like to stay with you too."

"We're ahead of ourselves. It isn't that easy. It's a little more complicated. There's more to it. I'm not sure of myself. I'm not sure what I want. I'm not sure I want to live in the Middle East, so let's not assume anything."

"Is Dr. Suhaila coming with us to the airport tomorrow?" asks Kathleen.

"I'm sure she is."

"She said she would go with us," says Colleen.

"I'd like to see her again," says Kathleen.

"Kathleen wants to give her another look, Colleen," says Andrew, smiling.

Sean laughs.

"We've exhausted the subject now. Why don't we get packed? We have to leave the hotel at 7:00 in the morning, and we have to be at the airport two hours before our flight takes off."

"Who's that man you spoke to when we came back to the hotel this evening?" asks Sean.

"He's a Syrian army officer. He's actually the chief of staff of the Syrian armed forces."

"You'd never guess he's a military man with those civilian clothes," says Andrew.

"I didn't recognize him when I first saw him here a few months ago. He was in civilian clothes then too. Either he didn't see me or didn't recognize me at that time. This time he did."

"How did you get to know him?" asks Andrew.

"I don't really know him. I met him at a luncheon a few months ago when I visited the Ministry of Electricity and Energy in Damascus. The last time I was here in Alexandria, shortly after the Special Conference of Oil Ministers I told you about, I ran into him in this hotel. I didn't talk to him at that time. As I said, I wasn't sure he recognized me. This time he did."

"Maybe he likes Alexandria," says Sean.

"Maybe he's on an extended vacation," says Andrew, smiling. "These military people like vacations. Even our military like extended vacations."

Maybe the Syrians are cooking up something, but what would it be?

"He had a lot of people with him," says Kathleen. "Did you know any of the other people, Dad?"

"I didn't."

"I wonder if they're planning something," she says.

"What would they be planning?" asks Andrew.

"I don't know. I'm scared of the Middle East. That's why I want to go home, but I want Dad to come home with us."

"That's the way she was when we flew from London to Kuwait," says Andrew. "She was petrified and got all of us scared."

"I couldn't help it," says Kathleen.

"I know you couldn't," Thafer says. "The Middle East is a little unstable, but it's quiet now. It's going to be all right, Kathleen. You shouldn't be unduly worried."

"And we're like everyone else," says Colleen.

"That's right," Thafer says.

"It isn't safer at home," says Andrew. "What if something goes wrong between us and the Soviet Union?"

"We and the Russians are not as mad at each other," says Kathleen. "The Israelis and the Arabs are furious with each other. That's what scares me all the time."

"We can't live in constant fear though, my dear Kathleen."

"I'm not always afraid, Dad," she says. "Only when there's a discussion about war or when I'm flying. When you're with us, I'm not afraid. I wasn't afraid when we flew from Kuwait to Alexandria. I'm not afraid even now, when we're discussing the Russians and us."

"It's quiet now, Kathleen. Nothing is likely to happen soon."

XXX | September 1973

"I'm sorry you'll be leaving us soon," Mahmood says to Thafer. "Those who did this to you are the losers."

"When something like this happens, we're all losers."

"Yes, but it isn't right. What Ziyad and Hamdan did was wrong. They put you on the spot, and you did what an honest man should do—tell the truth. Your reward is to lose your job. Frankly, I expected something might happen, but not this. The author of the letter raised a legitimate point for an illegitimate purpose. A true Muslim doesn't do this."

Thafer feels uncomfortable and changes the direction of the conversation. "The last time we talked, I wasn't sure what I wanted to do. I've now agreed to stay on with OAPEC until the end of December. OAPEC and I also agreed on a settlement of six months' salary, and a one-way ticket to the United States for me and for the two younger children, Kathleen and Sean. The older ones, Colleen and Andrew, went back last week."

"Mukhtar is a decent man, a true Muslim."

"He went out of his way to be fair and accommodating. The entire episode was distasteful to him."

"I'm sure you know where I stand. I wish there was something I could do."

"You've been very supportive, Mahmood."

"The Holy Quran teaches us not to despair over happenings in our lives that seem bad. They may be good in the long run."

"Before leaving for New York, my son Andrew told me that the author of the letter doesn't realize that he's doing me and my family a favor."

"The intent is to hurt, which is not proper Islamic conduct. Well, the holy month of Ramadan, the month of fasting and forgiving and praying, is approaching. May it bring blessings to you and your family. May it realize for you the return to your blessed homeland. May it bring peace and good health to all of us."

"May it bring blessings to you and your family, Mahmood," Thafer says, moved by his friend's words. "I always lose track of these things. Please forgive me. When does Ramadan begin?"

"Tomorrow."

"Really?!"

"Islam, Brother Thafer, recognizes Christianity and Judaism. Regrettably, neither Christianity nor Judaism recognizes Islam."

Thafer looks at Mahmood. What do I know about Islam or Judaism or Christianity? he asks himself. This is a topic for scholars.

"Did you mind what I said?"

"Not at all, but I'm frank to say that I'm ignorant about religion. I'm ashamed of myself."

"You shouldn't be. Westerners, Americans, and even many Arabs know very little about Islam. It's commonly recognized now that when Islam is mentioned in Europe or in the United States, it evokes an almost sinister image."

"True."

"Yet the Quran commands us:

> Say: We believe in God, and what has been revealed to us, and in what was revealed to Abraham and Ishmael and Isaac and Jacob and the tribes, and in what was given to Moses and Jesus and to the prophets from their Lord. We do not make any distinction between any of them.

"Your chanting is moving, Mahmood."

"This command is the core of Islam. It is the faith, the mention of which makes some Europeans and Americans cringe. It's the faith of people living in a vast region extending from Morocco through North and East Africa, across Central and Southwest Asia and on southward to the Java Sea. It's the faith of peoples of many nationalities, cultures, and languages. There are about one billion Muslims in the world today. Tens of millions of Muslims live in Europe, and more than four million in the United States. Yet writers in the Western world have ridiculed Islam and have made unfair attacks on the prophet Muhammad."

Thafer observes Mahmood's deep emotion and is moved. He wants to say something respectful to assure his friend of his own reverence for Islam, but he is fearful that the discussion might degenerate into the pitting of one religion against another. "Aren't these unfair attacks against Islam derived more from political conflicts than from religious differences, Mahmood?"

"That's true, but there's no reason for hostility to continue between the followers of three great religions, Thafer."

"I agree."

"Anyone who nourishes this hostility is not a good Muslim or a good Christian or a good Jew."

"Unfortunately, biased writers have often fanned the fires of hatred."

"That's only part of it. During the nineteenth and twentieth centuries, industrialization and the growth of military strength in Western Europe allowed the Europeans to control most of the Islamic countries, whose people have been victimized and dehumanized. Europeans have degraded and suppressed Islam. They have denigrated or ignored Islam's contributions to Western civilization. Then, in the latter part of the nineteenth century, Zionism came with designs on Palestine, thus adding fuel to the fire. Zionism has done more harm to relations between Islam and Christianity than is generally recognized, Thafer. It has also alienated Islam from Judaism, which Islam reveres."

"I am certainly aware of the extent of the Muslim world's resentment of Western support of Zionism."

"Western support of Zionism has been one of the most unifying factors for Muslims around the world. Muslims have had their differences, just as Christians have, and although many have resented the West's treatment of Islam, most unanimously decry the West's support of Zionism."

"I know that."

"I'm a member of the Muslim Brotherhood, a movement directed against injustice and oppression, Thafer. We say that if Jews can create a unifying movement based on religion, why can't Muslims?"

Looking at Mahmood, Thafer feels the strength of his conviction.

"Do you see what I mean, Thafer?"

"I do, but I am a believer in the separation of religion and state."

"They call that separation of church and state in America."

"That's right, they do. Mahmood, if the creation of any state is based on one religion, that state is not likely to do justice to those citizens who may be followers of a different religion. This is why I am against Zionism."

Mahmood, appears surprised. "You may be right, Thafer."

"You've also said, Mahmood, that Islam is the closest religion to Christianity. Of course I've always known about this closeness, although very few Westerners know about it. Considering the present conflicts, I find the reverence you've expressed—not only for Christianity, but particularly for Judaism—especially moving. The politics of Zionism aside, there's also a theological kinship between Christianity and Judaism, particularly in the United States. Having spent practically all my adult life there, I've grown to respect this kinship."

"There's nothing wrong with that, Thafer, but the kinship between Judaism and Christianity in the United States is actually more political than theological."

"Christians and Jews share so much that's essential to both their faiths."

"Perhaps, but there are actually more solid theological grounds for a closer kinship between Christianity and Islam. Islam recognizes and reveres the central figure of Christianity, Jesus of Nazareth, with almost the same intensity as Christianity does. Judaism neither recognizes nor reveres Jesus."

"Yet many elements of Christianity have their origin in the Jewish worship of the One God, the God of Israel," says Thafer. "In fact, Christianity's very knowledge of God comes from Judaism."

"Islam's knowledge of God, Thafer, comes through the prophet Muhammad with full recognition of both Christianity and Judaism. It does not challenge the same and One God, which Jews and Christians worship. You might say that much of Islam is a recognition of Christianity, which itself is a recognition of Judaism."

"I'm no theologian, Mahmood, but I've always been under the impression that despite the difficulties created by Zionism, Judaism and Islam are closer to each other than either is to Christianity. Both Judaism and Islam are religions of law. Both are centered in the purity of the monotheistic divinity. Both stress learning and reason in understanding God. Christianity, on the other hand, stresses faith as the basis for belief in God."

"Islam also stresses faith as the basis for belief in God, Thafer. It also recognizes both Christianity and Judaism, and reveres both."

"But Jesus, Mary, and the apostles were all Jews. The only Bible that the early Christian church knew was the Jewish Bible, the Tanach. The prayers that Jesus and the apostles prayed were those of the Jewish synagogue."

"All of this is true, Thafer, but the basic fact remains that Judaism does not recognize the central figure of Christianity, Jesus of Nazareth, nor does Judaism recognize the virgin birth of Jesus. Islam recognizes both. This is why Islam is the religion closest to Christianity."

"I want to talk to you about another serious matter, Thafer," Mahmood says. "I want to tell you something confidential," he continues as sweat now begins to form on his forehead, "but it must remain confidential."

"It will."

"I have reliable information that something very serious will take place soon, perhaps in a month. I'm not at liberty to share the details with you, but you have to take my word that it's authentic and truly serious."

Thafer feels his pulse racing.

"About a month ago, there was a meeting in Alexandria of Egyptian and Syrian generals and war ministers at the headquarters of the Egyptian naval command. The Syrian generals arrived in Egypt in civilian clothes. Our minister of war, General Ahmad Ismael, headed the Egyptian team. The Syrian minister of defense, General Mustafa Tlas, headed his own senior officers. The chiefs of staff, the directors of operations, the directors of intelligence, as well as the commanders of the navy, air force, and air defense of both countries were present. These men have been appointed as the military pinnacle of a joint Egyptian-Syrian command. They have now agreed on a plan for a simultaneous attack on the Israeli forces in the Egyptian Sinai and the Syrian Golan Heights. The attack will be in about four weeks. They have been planning this for a long time."

Thafer is overwhelmed. *Even if what he's telling me is true, he shouldn't be telling me.*

"The most stringent precautions have been taken to ensure that no hint of what's being planned will leak out."

Leak out! Thafer exclaims to himself, but he continues to listen with fascination.

"The exact timing, the day and the hour, have not been decided."

That's why the Syrian chief of staff was in Alexandria when I ran into him twice at the Alexandria Hilton, but how could Egypt participate in an all-out war against Israel if it can't count on the Soviet Union? Egypt's relations with the Soviet Union are strained. Only a few months ago Sadat ex-

pelled twenty-one thousand Soviet military advisors from Egypt. No leader in his right mind will dare launch an attack against Israel under these circumstances. "Thanks for the information, Mahmood," says Thafer, looking in stunned disbelief at the bearded man.

"I'll keep you informed, Thafer."

XXXI | October 6, 1973

"War has broken out, Dad," cries Kathleen, rushing into the house and looking terrified. She and Sean have just arrived from school.

As usual, Saeed has picked them up and brought them home. Both children are panicked.

"Saeed says to turn on your radio, Dad," says Sean. "He wants to talk to you."

"Ask him to come in."

"Did you know this was going to happen, Dad?" asks Kathleen. "You don't seem too upset or too surprised."

"I am surprised, Kathleen, although I have had an inkling something like this might happen sooner or later. I wasn't sure when. But I certainly didn't expect a war now."

"What's the news, Saeed?" Thafer asks his driver.

"War, sir." War has broken out. Egypt and Syria are at war with Israel. It's all-out war. Turn your radio on, sir."

"What station?"

"Any station, but try Radio Cairo."

"Who started it?"

"I don't know, sir."

Thafer, shaking his head, turns on his shortwave radio, as his two children and his driver Saeed stand in front of him in his study.

"Can you get an English station?" asks Kathleen.

"Yes," says Sean. "Get an English station."

"I'll try any station. If I get an Arabic station, I'll tell you what it says."

"In the Name of God, the All Merciful, the All Compassionate," says an Egyptian announcer. "At 14:05 on Saturday, 6 October 1973, falling on the tenth day of Ramadan, the anniversary of the glorious Battle of Badr, when the victorious forces of the prophet Muhammad defeated the much larger evil forces of the infidels and gave Islam the magnificent stature it has enjoyed ever since, Operation Badr with God's help has commenced. Victory, God willing, will be ours. Our guns, rocket launchers, and mortars opened against Israeli fortifications along the Suez Canal in the Egyptian Sinai. Our artillery barrage was supported by strikes from our aircraft. Fifteen minutes later, our troops crossed the Suez Canal in rubber boats. Elements of our Second Army captured the first fortress on the Bar-lev Line at 15:00 hours. Many others fell soon afterward. Our engineers with their water cannons succeeded in breaking down the sand rampart on the eastern bank of the canal and breached it in several places. The peace, the mercy, and the blessings of God be on you."

"That's all-out war all right," says Thafer.

"Try Radio Damascus, sir," says Saeed. "It repeats the first Syrian bulletin every fifteen minutes."

"I'm scared, Dad," says Kathleen.

"I am too," says Sean.

"The fighting is hundreds of miles from here," Thafer assures his children. "We're perfectly safe here."

"This is Damascus," says the Syrian announcer. "Our first bulletin. At 14:05 hours on Saturday, 6 October 1973, our guns, rocket launchers, and mortars opened fire against Israeli troops in the Syrian Golan Heights. This artillery barrage was supported by strikes from our aircraft. Fifteen minutes later, our troops crossed the truce lines. Several Israeli fortifications in their path were captured or destroyed. At 16:00 hours, our troops crossed the Syrian Golan Heights into Northern Israel, where they engaged Israeli forces in heavy fighting. Our forces successfully negotiated the Israeli antitank ditch and advanced at considerable speed. Several Israeli strong points fell to our advancing forces. The Israeli observation post at Jebel al-Sheikh with its complex electronic equipment was captured intact by our troops. Its contents were transported to Damascus."

"The news is astonishing," says Thafer. "I can hardly believe it."

"Do you think our government will come to the aid of Israel, Dad?" asks Kathleen.

"I have no idea, sweetheart."

"I hope not," said Sean.

"If we do come to Israel's aid," says Kathleen, "I'll bet the Arabs will get very mad at us."

"Will they, Dad?" asks Sean.

"They might. Could you answer the phone, Kathleen dear?"

"I'll bet it's Colleen," says Kathleen. "Hello. Colleen? We're all right, Colleen. Yes, here's Dad. We're all listening to the news. Here's Dad."

"Colleen."

"Are you coming home, Dad?"

"There's no danger here, Colleen. The war is hundreds of miles away from us."

XXXII | October 7, 1973

"This is it, Thafer," the Egyptian says, his face beaming with excitement. He walks toward Thafer and embraces him as the two men meet in OAPEC's hallway in the early morning of the second day of the war. They walk to Thafer's office.

"I can't believe what's happening," says Thafer.

"This is going to erase all the previous shame. Justice will be done, Brother Thafer. God willing, you'll go back to Jerusalem before the end of Ramadan. Just as the prophet defeated the infidels in the Battle of Badr, the Israelis, God willing, will be defeated in Operation Badr."

"Frankly, Sheikh Mahmood," Thafer says carefully, observing Mahmood's face flushed with joy and confidence, "I didn't take seriously what you said the other day."

"I was off by three weeks." Mahmood smiles.

"You certainly were right."

"Before dawn today, the Israeli Sinai command ordered all Israeli troops manning the Bar-lev Line fortress to choose between surrender and retreat eastward. Early this morning, our tanks were in complete control of the entire area."

"I can tell that you were up all night."

"I was, but somehow I'm not tired. I feel energized."

"I stayed up most of the night myself. Even the children were up."

"Let's see how it'll turn out. Let's hope that the United States keeps out of it."

"Let's." Thafer has an uneasy feeling that it won't, though.

"The Israelis are concentrating all their strength on the Syrian front today."

"They seem to have slowed the momentum of the two main Syrian thrusts."

"Israel is making a strong counterattack against the advancing Syrian forces. They must've decided to concentrate their main air and ground efforts on the Syrian front, to knock Syria out of the battle in order to turn their forces against our positions in Sinai."

"It's clear that the Egyptian and Syrian attacks have caught the Israelis by surprise. The Syrians are holding their ground so far."

"The Israelis received information that the attack was coming only a few hours before it took place."

"There was not enough time for them to mobilize or alert all their forces."

"Right. Now there remains the danger from the United States. If the United States intervenes or begins an air lift or supplies Israel with what it has lost or sends its sophisticated equipment and manpower, God knows what might happen."

"I doubt that the United States will do that."

"Why?"

"That will anger the Arab allies of the United States."

"What Arab allies? They're not allies; they're servants. They're stooges, but it will enrage the Arab masses."

"This is a very highly emotional struggle, Mahmood, and the United States knows it."

"It may know it, but it doesn't care."

"I've been attending OAPEC's ministerial conferences, Mahmood. If the United States intervenes on Israel's side, it will prompt immediate retaliation with an oil embargo this time. I'll bet on it."

"We've been hearing threats about that lately, but I doubt that OAPEC members will dare impose an oil embargo. Some members may ask for it, but Saudi Arabia will never go along with it."

"We never know."

"Why would the United States come to Israel's aid? All we're trying to do is liberate our land."

Seeing the grim face of his bearded friend, Thafer remains quiet, afraid to say anything that would inflame him.

"Wouldn't the American people object if the U.S. government were to ship massive supplies of sophisticated equipment to Israel now? Don't they know we are trying to liberate our lands?"

"A lot of what the American people believe is based on misinformation. Unfortunately, they are being told that it's in their national interest to support Israel militarily in order to prevent a communist takeover of the Middle East."

"There isn't a trace of truth in that. Islam, not Israel, is the greatest bulwark against communism. These empty claims of Israel's capacity, let alone willingness, to be a true strategic ally of the United States in the Middle East are grossly exaggerated."

"Believe me, Mahmood, I know."

"These claims are fraudulent. They're designed to deceive the American people. They're made in order to justify the enormous military and economic aid Israel receives from the United States. Israel is a small state that cannot survive without U.S. assistance. It lacks the personnel and the capability to be of any strategic significance to the United States. It can hardly defend itself within its own borders without U.S. assistance. Look at what's happening now. How could it possibly help the United States against the Soviet Union? Egypt could. With their vast resources, population, and strategic position, the Arab states could. But Israel couldn't, Thafer. Is this why the Congress of the United States supports Israel?"

"No, the Congress is corrupted."

"Doesn't the American public realize that Israel doesn't consider it her business to engage Soviet forces in case of a Soviet-American confrontation, Thafer?"

"I'm afraid it doesn't."

"How about all of those educated, avid readers in the United States? Aren't they slowly uncovering the facts?"

"That's the irony, Mahmood. They're probably the most misinformed. If you only knew what they read!"

"I better go back to my office now, but we'll be talking. As the Blacks of America say, 'We shall overcome.' "

XXXIII | October 15, 1973

"Sheikh Mahmood wants to see you, Dad," says Sean. "I invited him to the living room."

"I'll be right down."

"Can I come down, Dad?" asks Kathleen.

"Sheikh Mahmood is a very sensitive man, and I'm sure he's quite broken up now."

"I'll be careful. I promise."

"Can I come down too?" asks Sean. "I'll just listen."

"You can both come down."

"I'm glad you came, Mahmood."

"I'm sorry to interrupt your evening, Thafer," says the demoralized man. "Mr. Kosygin arrived in Cairo. I'm sure he's now meeting with President Sadat."

"I heard it on Radio Cairo," says Thafer, feeling his friend's frustration.

"The Russians are pressing for a cease fire. I'm sure they've been in close touch with the Americans about this."

"I don't doubt it."

"On the seventeenth, while the Council of Arab Oil Ministers meets here, foreign ministers of Saudi Arabia, Kuwait, Morocco, and Algeria will meet your president in Washington."

"The action will be here in Kuwait."

"I never expected the Arab states to be united," says Mahmood, "but believe me they are. Thank God they are. History will be made here in Kuwait."

"Are we going to be asked to attend the session on the seventeenth?"

"Both of us will attend with Mukhtar. I just picked up the notice. The three of us will represent the secretariat."

"What do you think went wrong, Mahmood?" Thafer asks, sensing his associate's fear of defeat.

"The Egyptian command blundered. It's as simple as that. It may be that what happened during the War of 1967 inhibited our military command from taking vital, bold steps in the early stages of the war."

"Are you talking about missing the opportunity to press toward the passes in the center of Sinai early?"

"Exactly, Thafer. I'm convinced that had our forces contin-ued their advance toward the passes after they penetrated Is-raeli defenses during the first two days of the war, instead of pausing as they did, they would've reached and occupied them without much resistance. They would also have liberated all of Sinai. You can well imagine what would've followed. As it happened, the pause of our forces allowed the Israelis to con-centrate their relentless counterattacks against the Syrians on the ground and in the air. The plan was for our forces to continue their advance so that the Syrian forces could reach the Jordan River and Lake Tiberias. That didn't happen. By the eighth, the Israeli northern command had transferred two fresh tank brigades to the Syrian front, which I'm sure they would've transferred to our front had we continued our advance. The Syrian command was furious. They appealed to us to con-tinue our advance in accordance with the plan agreed on earlier by the Joint Chiefs of Staff of Egypt and Syria in Alexandria. They pleaded with us to take quick action to relieve the pres-sure on them. But our president ignored the Syrian appeals."

"The Israelis were surprised by the stubborn resistance of the Syrians," says Thafer.

"They were frustrated by the gallant resistance of the Syrian troops. They were also stunned by the scale of their own losses."

"That's when they appealed to the United States for mas-sive military supplies."

"That's right. By the tenth, the Israelis had started bomb-ing civilian targets in Damascus and in Hums. It was an attempt to demoralize the Syrian civilian population. By the eleventh, the Syrian command was forced to commit its crack Third Tank Division to the battle, the division that was sta-tioned near Damascus as a strategic reserve. The Syrian presi-dent appealed to Anwar Sadat to resume fighting in Sinai and to retaliate against the Israeli bombing of civilian targets in Damascus and in Hums. Sadat did not respond. Syria then appealed to Iraq for help."

Thafer's children listen quietly.

"I share your anguish and frustration, Mahmood."

"I know you do. Thank God Iraq came to Syria's aid. Were it not for that, the Israelis would've marched to Damascus."

"I'm sure."

"Forgive me, but the United States is the real enemy. Last Thursday, the eleventh, when the Syrians were trying to stop the Israeli advance on Damascus, the U.S. government delivered more supplies to the Israelis right on the battlefield at the Syrian front. That's when the Syrians began to lose ground as the Israeli attacks got stronger, and that's how the Israelis were able to penetrate Syrian lines along the Kuneitra-Damascus road. Thank God Iraq came to Syria's aid. Iraq put several squadrons of its aircraft at Syria's disposal. It made its forward air bases in Iraq available for use by the Syrian and Jordanian air forces."

"Jordan was reluctant to join in the fighting," says Thafer.

"Jordan wouldn't even allow Palestinian commando units to enter the Aghwar area to cross into Israel and help alleviate some of the pressure on the Syrians."

"They too were probably afraid of a repetition of what happened to them in 1967."

"The gallant Syrians contained the Israeli attacks. The U.S. effort to help Israel knock Syria out of the battle failed. Thank God it failed. Henry Kissinger declared that within forty-eight hours of the start of hostilities, the Israelis would deliver a devastating blow to the Egyptian and Syrian forces. We're now well into the fifteenth, Dr. Thafer. Had it not been for the military pause by our forces in Sinai, we would've won the war by now. Our forces in Sinai paused too long. When the Egyptian command finally unleashed our forces in a drive toward the passes on the fourteenth, the Israelis were fully mobilized and waiting. The element of surprise was gone."

"I understand that there were serious differences of opinion in the ranks of the Egyptian military command about the offensive after that pause," says Thafer.

"Sure, there were. Some thought that it would be better to concentrate on defensive positions on the east bank of the canal. Others felt that although the ideal time may have been missed, there was no alternative to honoring the commitments to the Syrians and going forward, but as soon as the Egyptian troops left the cover of the air defenses and started their forward movement on the fourteenth, they exposed themselves to Israeli air strikes. The Egyptian tank commanders and crews fought bravely against the antitank missiles that the Americans helped the Israelis deploy on the battlefields. The Americans continued airlifting tanks and artillery for the Israelis directly to the battle area. Accurate fire from these new American antitank missiles stopped our advance twelve to fifteen kilometers from its starting point. We took heavy losses. Our forces were then ordered to withdraw to their starting line."

"There's a touch of irony in all this," says Thafer. "The Syrians, who pleaded with your forces to help ease the pressure on them, were actually standing their ground against the Israelis. The Syrians' stubborn resistance now helped your forces."

"Very true. That's why our lengthy pause came back to haunt us. It was our concern for Syria that prompted our ill-conceived offensive of the fourteenth."

"Ahhh, Mahmood. This is the tragedy of war. No one can predict what will happen. And we may never know why the Egyptian command paused as long as it did."

"Sheer cowardice, Thafer. It's pure cowardice. Thank God the Israeli drive toward Damascus was blunted. A crack Jordanian tank brigade, though belatedly, joined in southeast of the Iraqi tank brigade. Moroccan and Kuwaiti troops were already helping the Syrians. A unified Arab command was in action against Israel, Brother Thafer. If I didn't understand the mentality of our command on the Egyptian front, I would've said that the pause was an act of treason. I would've accused our command of collaboration with the Israelis."

"Well, Mahmood, you and I are helpless observers. What can we do?"

"If Ayoub Allam had had our weaponry and our forces, Thafer, he would've stopped only after taking Jerusalem."

Watching his children's faces, Thafer is overwhelmed by a feeling of sadness.

"I said the other day, Brother Thafer, that God willing, you'll go back to Jerusalem before the end of Ramadan. God does not will it under Egyptian command. Perhaps He wills it only under Palestinian command. Perhaps He's preparing another Ayoub Allam for the march to Jerusalem. Yet I'm confident of His willing it someday. Egyptians, Syrians, Iraqis, Jordanians, Moroccans, Kuwaitis, Saudis, and other Arabs, with Palestinians in the forefront, will one day liberate your homeland and march to Jerusalem. I have no doubt they will."

XXXIV

"That was scary," says Kathleen shortly after Mahmood leaves. "He's very upset."

"He's real mad," says Sean.

"I couldn't understand this business about the pause and the passes," says Kathleen. "Why are the Syrians mad at the Egyptians?"

"After the Egyptian's successful crossing of the Suez Canal, Kathleen," says Thafer, pointing to the Suez Canal on a map of the Middle East hanging on a wall in his study, "and the destruction of the Israeli Bar-lev Line by the Egyptian armed forces, the Egyptian military command ordered its troops not to advance any further for several days. Mahmood refers to this decision as the operational pause."

"Maybe they got tired," says Kathleen. "I'll bet it isn't easy to cross the Suez Canal and continue advancing forward."

"It wasn't easy crossing. The Egyptians had to fight while they were crossing, and the Israelis were fortified."

"So why were the Syrians complaining?" asks Sean.

"The Syrians complained that this operational pause was in violation of the Egyptian commitment that they would not pause, Sean. Before the war started, the military leaders of Egypt and Syria met in Alexandria to coordinate their military plans. The Syrians say that Egypt had pledged that its armed forces would pause only after they had reached the strategic passes here in the center of Sinai." Thafer shows his children the position of the passes on the map.

"Could they have continued on, Dad?" asks Sean.

"Those of us who're not involved in the actual fighting, tend to expect too much. I don't know whether the Egyptian forces could've continued sooner than they did or not. It does seem that the pause was too long, though. We'll probably know more later about why they paused for so long."

"That Syrian man in civilian clothes," asks Sean, "the guy who greeted you in the lobby of the Alexandria Hilton, was he actually a military man?"

"He was the Syrian chief of staff," says Kathleen. "I'll bet they were cooking up this whole thing when we were there in Alexandria. What do you think, Dad?"

"They probably were."

"That's neat," says Sean.

"So it was the delay or the pause that was responsible for Syria's troubles," says Kathleen. "It wasn't American aid to Israel. I hate to think that it was all our fault."

"What do you think, Dad?" asks Sean.

"What are you thinking about?" asks Kathleen. "For a minute you looked as angry as Mahmood."

"Did I? I'm sorry. I'm trying to think. The delay, along with the massive air supply effort by our government, allowed Israel to mass the bulk of its forces against the advancing Syrian forces. Without our government's supply campaign, I doubt that the Israelis would've been able to cut short the Syrians' attempt to reach the Jordan River and Lake Tiberias as originally planned by the joint Egyptian-Syrian military command."

"I can see how the Syrians would get mad at Egypt and at us," says Sean. "They should be madder at Egypt though."

"They should be madder at us," says Kathleen. "Why do we have to get involved in this fight? The Syrians are trying to liberate their lands. We shouldn't help Israel occupy someone else's lands. Right?"

"Right, but it's a little more complicated."

"It's because the Russians were helping the Egyptians and the Syrians," says Sean. "Right?"

"That's a major part of the equation. Those who accept military assistance from the Russians many times automatically become our enemies. Then we begin to help their enemies. And it's true that from the tenth on, the Soviet Union began to supply both Egypt and Syria with arms and munitions, almost in parallel with our government's giving supplies to Israel. These two competing supply efforts intensified."

"We're better at it than the Russians," says Kathleen. "Egypt and Syria should've tried to be our allies."

"Yes," says Sean. "Why did they choose the Russians?"

"They didn't actually choose the Russians. Israel has very powerful political support in the United States that has made it difficult for Egypt and Syria and, as a matter of fact, for several other Arab states, to receive economic or military support from the United States. So Egypt and Syria, as well as other Arab states have found themselves forced to rely on Soviet economic and military support."

"What do you think will happen now?" asks Sean.

"These last few days have turned the tide in favor of Israel, Sean."

"This is why Mahmood is angry," says Kathleen.

"All the Arabs are angry," says Sean. "Right?"

"Right. They're angry and embittered."

"And you?" asks Sean.

"I'm disappointed, Sean."

"I really thought the Arabs were winning for once," says Kathleen. "But after the first few days, when our government began to supply Israel, things turned sour for the Arabs."

"Did we have to fly all this stuff all the way from the United States?" asks Sean.

"Most of this sophisticated equipment came from NATO's storage facilities, Sean, sometimes even depleting NATO's own supplies."

"That's crazy," says Kathleen. "What if the Russians attack us in Europe?"

"The Egyptians and the Syrians just couldn't follow up on their first attacks," says Sean.

"Is it true that if your father were the commander, he would've continued on?" asks Sean.

"It would depend on the situation in the field. Sheikh Mahmood was being nice to your dad."

"I really feel proud when your father is mentioned, Dad," says Sean. "He must've been quite a guy."

"Me too, Dad," says Kathleen. "The Palestinian kids at the University of Kuwait refer to me as the granddaughter of Ayoub Allam, and that makes me feel like someone special. It makes me very proud."

"It makes me want to be like him," says Sean. I've actually been thinking about joining the PLO. That might be the only way to liberate Dad's homeland. Then we'll all go see Grandma!"

"I understand now why Suhaila doesn't like the United States," says Kathleen. "These past few days have made me dislike my own country."

"You shouldn't feel that way, Kathleen," says Thafer, "but you have plenty of reason to disagree with Middle East policy."

"It's actually more than that," she says. "After seeing you go through the June War of 1967 and now this, I'm ashamed of what my country is doing. Getting to know your family has been a special experience. Who would want to hurt poor people like them? This trip has opened my eyes to a lot of things. I wouldn't mind staying here longer. We're a cruel country. See what we're doing in Vietnam. What is it that makes our leaders monstrous killers? Why does our country help the oppressor against the oppressed?"

XXXV

"Dear Colleen and Andrew," Thafer writes to his older children. "It won't be long now. Kathleen, Sean, and I will soon be leaving Kuwait. But we're not sure if we will be coming home. We're seriously considering going to Egypt. As I sit in this solitary study tonight, listening to the angry waves of the Bay of Kuwait below, I wonder whether this venture, returning to the Middle East, has been worth it. The Arab world is angry and is in confusion and tumult. In about forty-eight hours, I'll probably witness an event that could become, for the Arab people, one of the most important events of this century. The Arab states are about to impose an oil embargo against the United States. What is significant about the embargo is that these militarily weak and economically vulnerable oil-producing Arab states would even dare contemplate imposing an embargo against the most powerful nation in the world. For the Arabs, it will be a daring move, though conceived in the heat of passion and without weighing the consequences. Yet I find the prospect at once exhilarating and frightening.

"I find it exhilarating because the Arabs seem to want to emancipate themselves from their own crippling fears. I find it frightening because the embargo itself will no doubt solve nothing. It might even hurt many innocent people, including the Arab masses. Our mighty government may do something foolish, like using force."

Thafer puts his pen down and begins to reflect.

What if President Nixon, with all his domestic problems over Watergate, should decide to distract the American people and embark upon a military adventure in the Middle East? He won't get away with it. Thafer remembers Kathleen saying that she wouldn't mind giving her life for her dad's homeland. That's why Mary Pat didn't want me to come back to the Middle East, he muses.

"As you found out during your visit here," he continues writing, "the Middle East is still unstable. The war rages on. The last few days have witnessed a reversal of the early successes of the Egyptian and Syrian forces. There's a fierce argument going on between the Egyptian and Syrian political and military commands, which has become public. What concerns me more than anything else is that this war has had quite an effect on Kathleen and Sean. Neither will be the same again. Kathleen has even expressed a desire to stay in the Middle East and not return to the United States. Sean has expressed similar thoughts. Both have made me think more about the offer from the Alexandria law school."

He puts his pen down again. Kathleen wants to become a freedom fighter, and Sean wants to join the training camps of the PLO in Egypt. We would be like the Israelites living in exile in Egypt, awaiting the return to the promised land. We will watch the waves wash the shores of Alexandria, hoping they might one day carry us all to see your grandmother. "The world is so small these days," he writes, "that even halfway around the globe is not such an impossible distance."

I know that you too will soon come to join us, he thinks again. We'll all be together. That's the only way. Once upon a time, I fell in love with Mary Pat, your mother, and for that I lived in the United States for more than two decades. Now I'm in love with a Palestinian woman who shares my love for the homeland, who feels my pain and understands my anguish. She's waiting for us, and we must go. The time for leaving is getting near. I can't wait much longer. Your brother and sister will go with me now, and you'll join us later. We'll all wait for the day of return to the homeland. We'll all plan the wedding Suhaila and I have been dreaming about, the wedding in Jerusalem. And you'll all come to the wedding. Suhaila's two sons will come too.

"Do you know who's going to benefit the most from the imposition of the Arab oil embargo on the United States that is about to take place?" he writes. "Probably the United States. American oil companies will still make large profits at the expense of consumers everywhere, including the American consumer, who will be bewildered and angered by the embargo. In oil-producing countries, the embargo may mean more income for the corrupt and feudalistic sheikhs and monarchs of the Middle East. Until the United States reaps the maximum benefit from the embargo, it will make no effort to have it lifted, but Israel will continue to occupy Arab lands, including Jerusalem. Nationalism in its traditional form is changing. The small and poor countries of the world don't want only independence; they now want more income and a higher living standard. The Arab states are no match for the United States. By imposing this embargo, they might even be impeding progress toward raising their low standard of living. They have always been suspicious of the United States. Last year's U.S. dollar devaluation, twice in a row, didn't help. Helping Israel win this war is now the last straw."

He decides to write something hopeful.

"Yet all countries want oil. Maybe this conflict will have a positive outcome. Maybe discovering in a dramatic way how badly we need each other will teach us more about compromise and cooperation. And so I better conclude on this note. Love, Dad."

XXXVI | October 17, 1973

"What do you think the American response will be, Thafer?" Mahmood asks. He and Thafer are riding in Mahmood's car to the Emergency Conference of the Council of Arab Oil Ministers.

"You mean if they go ahead with the proposed embargo?"

"That's right. I know the Americans aren't the only ones who'll be affected, but they are the most important."

"We live in a unique era, Mahmood. I agree that if they do go ahead with the threat and impose an oil embargo, the effects will not be confined to the United States and to the Netherlands; they're bound to spread around the world."

"Do you think the United States might retaliate militarily?"

"It will make noises, but I doubt seriously that it'll take military action."

"And of course it can't use Israel now because Israel is exhausted. It may still try to encourage the shah of Iran to stir the Kurds against Iraq again or to carry out some mischief against Saudi Arabia or Egypt."

"I don't think that the shah will bite. He has good relations with Egypt and with Saudi Arabia."

"I know he does, but if his American masters pressure him to make an adventure, I bet he'll be overthrown by his own people. The Iranian people are very anti-American, Thafer. I don't need to tell you that."

"I don't think that the real threat is military. The real threat is economic."

"What can the Americans do? Our people's living standard is already low. The Americans can't deprive us more than they already have. It's their high standard of living that will be endangered, and God knows it should be. Didn't they attain it at the expense of the poor and hungry nations of the world, like ours?"

Thafer feels the tension in his friend's voice and decides to be quiet.

"The United States, Thafer, will only lose a little prestige if the Arabs go ahead with the embargo because the Americans don't need Arab oil that badly. What the Americans will be faced with is not economic hardship, which they may or may not undergo, but the fact that a militarily helpless country like Saudi Arabia would dare defy it—if, of course, Saudi Arabia doesn't get cold feet and back down at the last minute. This is what I meant when I asked my question about American reaction. Do you think the United States could tolerate this challenge from a country as weak as Saudi Arabia? If Saudi Arabia and the other Arab states get away with challenging the United States and do in fact impose an embargo, then who will be next to challenge the bully? The shah of Iran?"

Thafer does not answer.

"Maybe the shah himself won't, but Iran may," says Mahmood, answering himself in frustration and anger. "But mark my words, the world will wake up one day, and the shah will be no more. This is the tragedy of the United States. It has no sensitivity to the vicious violations of human rights perpetrated by the ruthless and repressive regimes it supports. Sooner or later, if the annals of history are a guide, these out-of-date despots will be taken to the gallows. You know who else is going to be taken with them?"

"Who?"

"The Israelis." Mahmood's face is full of anger. "One day, the Palestinians will have the bomb, and they will demand justice for their people. Who will blame them?"

"I know we're both angry, Mahmood, but going back to the embargo, any country that withholds its products from the market is itself likely to lag in the race. Let's discuss the economic implications of an Arab oil embargo for the Arab world itself."

"Are you against an oil embargo, Thafer?" Mahmood asks with irritation. "Are you upset? Virtually all countries want and need oil. The United States consumes about twenty-five million barrels a day."

"Don't you think the price of crude oil will go up if the embargo is imposed? Wouldn't that provoke the consumers?"

"This isn't about the price of crude oil. It's about justice. It's about the arrogance of the United States and its callous disregard for the rights of others. The small people and the poor people of the world are very agitated. They want not only political equality, but economic equality, Thafer. And they know that they will not attain economic equality as long as the United States of America controls more than half of the resources of the globe. Its population is less than 5 percent of the more than five billion human beings who live on earth, but it controls more than half of the resources of the world. This is the grave injustice and inequity that the embargo might dramatize."

"What if the embargo should turn out to be more beneficial to the United States and more harmful to the poor and de-prived nations of the world, including the Arab states?"

Mahmood squints.

"I just wonder if the Arab states are a match for the United States," Thafer says. "That's all I am trying to say. I'm not wish-ing for any military or aggressive move by the United States."

"I know you aren't, and I never said that the Arab states are a match for the bully, but even if the embargo does impede progress in the Arab world, even if it invites American retali-ation or American military action, it must be carried out. Politically, it is necessary. The United States should know that enough is enough. Look at last year's 20 percent U.S. dollar devaluation! And now the United States comes to the aid of Israel, supplying it with the most lethal and sophisticated NATO weapons, when all we're trying to do is liberate our lands from Israeli occupation. Anyone can see the injustice in the behavior of the United States."

"I'm not questioning that, but, forgive me, are the Arab states a match for the United States?"

"I know they are not, and that's why we must acquire the bomb, Thafer. When we do, the United States and Israel will stop blackmailing us."

"That won't happen. It's a difficult and dangerous process."

"I know it's difficult and dangerous, but it will happen. Then maybe the United States will begin to see that it's better to find a way to be fair and honest with people than to shoot and risk being shot at with nuclear weapons. Sooner or later, we *will* have nuclear weapons."

"In the name of God, the All Compassionate, the All Merciful," says the Algerian oil minister, opening the Emergency Conference of the Council of Arab Oil Ministers, which is being held behind closed doors in the Conference Hall of the Kuwait Hilton on October 17, 1973. "My brothers, let's all stand for a moment of silence in honor of the martyrs on the battlefield."

Everyone in the Conference Hall is on his feet instantly, with head bowed, in what seems like eternal silence.

Well, Thafer thinks, this is going to be quite a session, one I'll never forget.

What's the matter, Thafer? It's still too early. It isn't even six yet. . . . I just hadn't realized that after living so many years in the United States, married to you and having four lovely Yankee children, I would still have these passionate feelings about my homeland and my people. . . . I get nervous every time the plane speeds down the runway, but I get over it when we are airborne. . . . What matters is one's character and one's code of conduct. . . . At the end both sides must grow beyond that . . . must come to realize that neither an Israeli victory nor an Arab or Palestinian victory can ever be a victory for mankind.

"This Emergency Conference of the Council of Arab Oil Ministers will now come to order," says the presiding Algerian, breaking the gloomy silence. "My brothers," he continues in a strained voice, "we are gathered together today, united by God's will." He looks at the hushed delegations in front of him, then turns his face toward the window as though his mind has wandered hundreds of miles away. "My brothers," he resumes, still not looking directly at his audience, but lowering his voice this time, "the moment of truth is at hand. We must act decisively and in unison. There is no other way." He turns to his attentive audience and clutches the gavel in his trembling hand. "The enemy is not only Israel," he shouts in anger, his face suddenly turning red. "The more dangerous enemy is the United States of America." He pauses, then looks at his astonished audience again. "Our action should reflect this basic fact, my brothers," he says in a low voice, then sits.

A short and angry opening statement, Thafer thinks. It's alarming. I'm afraid the rage might escalate. He looks at the solemn faces of the delegates gathered in the silent auditorium and is humbled.

"Mr. President," says the elderly Egyptian oil minister, rising to his feet, his sad eyes conveying the humiliation he must feel over his country's part in the war. "Mr. President, I am sure we are all angry." He pauses to survey his audience. "These are anxious moments for our Arab nation, my brothers. Some of our gallant men have made the ultimate sacrifice, and have paid with their lives. Some still face a fateful struggle that will go down as one of the most important in our national history. I know that there have been some mistakes on the battlefield, but I agree with our brother, His Excellency the oil minister of sisterly Algeria, that the United States is the more dangerous enemy. This is not to underestimate the treachery of Israel. Yet were it not for the strong military and economic support of the United States, the operational pause of our forces in Sinai notwithstanding, Israel would have been defeated. It would not now be occupying our lands. There is no doubt about that. Were it not for the political backing of the United States, Israel would be unable to continue its oppression of our Palestinian brothers in Israel and in the occupied territories. We must, therefore, continue to face Israel on the battlefield, but we must, from now on, confront the United States on the economic battlefield. We must deliver a crippling economic blow to the United States that will paralyze it so that it will be unable henceforth to aid Israel while it occupies our lands and oppresses our people. My brothers, we have often spoken of the so-called 'oil weapon.' Our people have been demanding the use of this economic weapon for a long time. The United States, Western Europe, and Japan have been anticipating it with dread for a long time. The United States has now put our backs to the wall. We have no alternative but to use our last and most effective weapon—oil. There will be threats of invasion. There will be other threats. Yet we must stand firm and united. We must be prepared to blow up our oil fields and destroy all our storage facilities should the United States carry out the expected threat of invading our lands. We must shut off the supply of oil to the United States, Western Europe, and Japan. We must also shut off oil supplies to any country that might sell it to the United States. But we must never act unilaterally. We must always act collectively. Thank you, Mr. President."

"The chair recognizes His Excellency the oil minister of sisterly Saudi Arabia."

"Mr. President," starts the Saudi oil minister as he faces the Algerian oil minister. "My brothers," he says, turning to the assembled Arab ministers. "I stand before you with a heavy heart, humbled and perplexed. I am humbled because in prior conferences, in this hall and in others, the kingdom of Saudi Arabia has always assumed the good faith of its friend and ally, the United States of America, and often defended its policies against your wishes. I say that I am humbled because the kingdom of Saudi Arabia has reluctantly reached the conclusion that its prior defenses of the policies of the United States regarding our region have been misguided. I am perplexed because I find it difficult to understand how the United States of America could do to a friend and ally what it has done to the kingdom of Saudi Arabia, after all that Saudi Arabia has done to support the United States. You all know that on July 6, 1972, sisterly Egypt ordered the withdrawal of all Soviet experts from its territory. That order was made at the urging of His Majesty King Faisal, who was promised by President Nixon of the United States that if His Majesty could attain the withdrawal of all the Soviet experts from Egypt, then the United States would bring about the withdrawal of all Israeli forces from Sinai. Before sisterly Egypt ordered the Soviet experts to leave Egypt, the United States made a commitment to bring about the withdrawal of all Israeli forces from Sinai. After the departure of the Soviet experts, His Majesty tried resolutely to press the Americans to honor their commitment to him. He pressed the Americans very hard to make some move. He emphasized to President Nixon what an awkward position he personally found himself in because the United States was failing to honor its commitment to him. He explained to President Nixon that even before the United States made its commitment, which His Majesty had already conveyed to President Sadat, our Arab brethren often blamed the kingdom of Saudi Arabia whenever the United States did anything that harmed Arab interests. His Majesty pleaded with President Nixon and said that the Russians were now gone from Egypt, which the United States had asked His Majesty to accomplish, and therefore the American excuse for inaction was gone. President Nixon had told His Majesty that it was the presence of Russian troops in Egypt that created the risk of a global confrontation. But the United States, as we all know, has not only failed to honor its commitment to the Kingdom of Saudi Arabia, it has demonstrated its determination to help Israel even though Israel occupies Arab lands. The United States can no longer claim that its strategy is directed against the Soviet Union. It has demonstrated to the whole world, not only to us, that its policy is to help our principal enemy. That policy is contrary to the interests of the kingdom of Saudi Arabia and must be opposed by the kingdom with all the resources available to it."

The Conference Hall is hushed as the delegates' attention is concentrated on the Saudi minister of oil.

"My brothers," the Saudi minister resumes. "Oil is a strategic economic commodity. It is not, in and of itself, a weapon. By itself, therefore, oil can never win a war, but it can be used as a political lever. We all know that oil has always played a vital part in the politics and diplomacy of our consumers. We and the consuming countries have known this for a long time, so there would be nothing new if we were to make political use of this vital resource of which God has availed us. Yet, my brothers, we should be careful not to make enemies of the innocent consuming countries. If we supply this strategic commodity to a country that in turn will supply us with another strategic commodity, such as the armaments we need for our defense, the flow in both directions must be assured, whether we are engaged in a war with Israel or not. If a consumer withdraws the arms from us, then we must withdraw our oil from that consumer. We must also take note of the attitude of other countries and conduct ourselves accordingly. If they oppose our attempt to liberate our lands from Israeli occupation, we must take a stand against them. We have a right to expect Europe to support us and certainly not to show hostility toward us while we liberate our lands. We should expect Japan to do the same. At the very least, we should expect both Europe and Japan to exert pressure on the United States to cease and desist from inflicting harm on our armed forces while we struggle to liberate our sacred lands. This is the policy of the kingdom of Saudi Arabia."

The Saudi minister pauses, then looks at the Egyptian and Syrian ministers. "I want now to address our two brothers, His Excellency the oil minister of sisterly Egypt and His Excellency the oil minister of sisterly Syria. I know that I speak for all of us in this hall, indeed for the entire Arab nation, when I say that you have made us all very proud. As our king has said, in the past we could not lift our heads. Now we can. Our big sister, Egypt, and our beloved sister, Syria, have done their duty and have suffered in doing it. Their cities have been destroyed. The least the rest of us can do is to help them financially, politically, and militarily. Our help is not charity; it is our solemn obligation. Mr. President, Saudi Arabia proposes the immediate suspension of all supplies of oil to the United States and to any country that opposes our effort to liberate our lands from the grip of Zionist tyranny. We recommend, however, that oil supplies continue to Western Europe and to Japan, provided that no harmful action is taken by either against our Arab nation. I propose that this embargo be effected immediately, Mr. President. I also propose that we issue a warning that any country that takes actions harmful to our two sisterly states, Egypt and Syria, or to our Arab nation will invite an embargo in so doing. Thank you, Mr. President."

"The chair recognizes His Excellency the oil minister of sisterly Syria."

"Mr. President," starts the youthful Syrian oil minister, bowing his head to the Algerian minister of oil. "I stand before you, my brothers," he says, turning to the assembled ministers, "gratified and humbled. I am gratified by the voluntary financial assistance pledged by sisterly Saudi Arabia. I am humbled by its courage in proposing an oil embargo against those who have acted in a manner hostile to our Arab nation, notably the United States of America, the bastion of Zionism and of international intrigue. My brothers, there is a lot more we can all do. We can and must take other and more effective economic measures against the United States. We must nationalize all American assets in all our countries. We must make direct arrangements between our producing states and our consumers in Western Europe and Japan, thus eliminating any role for the United States. We must boycott all American products. We must appeal to all our friends—especially the Conference of Islamic States, the Eastern block states, and the nonaligned nations of the world to join in this economic boycott. Above all, my brothers, we should sever all diplomatic relations with the United States. I am certain, my brothers, that the overwhelming majority of mankind is sympathetic with our endeavor to liberate our sacred lands. I am equally confident that most states will respond sympathetically to a friendly request by us to isolate the United States economically for its treachery in helping the oppressor against the oppressed. The oil embargo proposed by sisterly Saudi Arabia will put us on the correct path. I am confident that we will be joined in this embargo by all the Arab oil-producing states. If we can enlarge it to include other friendly states, we can deliver a stronger blow to the United States in retaliation for its evil deeds in helping Israel harm our armed forces and destroy our cities."

The Syrian minister of oil turns around and faces his Iraqi counterpart. "My brother," he says, "your noble and brave men have defended Damascus. They have defended it well. I want to say thank you to our fallen Iraqi martyrs, but I want also to say that the grateful people of Syria share the grief of their loved ones. By spilling their blood and mixing it with the blood of Syria's sons, the martyred sons of Iraq have bestowed upon Syria and its people an honor that future generations will always carry as a symbol of Iraqi bravery, sacrifice, and brotherhood. Thank you, Mr. President."

Thafer is moved. He looks at the Algerian minister; his head is down, and he is rubbing his eyes.

"The chair recognizes His Excellency the oil minister of sisterly Iraq."

"Mr. President," says the Iraqi minister. He then looks at the flushed face of his Syrian counterpart. "My brothers, I did not intend to begin my remarks on an emotional note. I find myself, however, compelled to do so, having heard the eloquent concluding remarks of our Syrian brother. I want you, my brother, to convey to our brothers and sisters in brave Syria our deepest sympathy for the loss of life and for the destruction inflicted on our people in our beloved Syria. Your sorrow, my brother, is the sorrow of every man and woman, young and old, throughout our Arab nation. Your sacrifices and losses are deeply mourned and felt by all Arabs everywhere. Yet these losses, these sacrifices, my brother, shall not be in vain. If there is a God in Heaven, and I am certain that there is, then those in the United States and in Israel responsible for the bombing of civilian targets will one day pay for their crimes."

The Iraqi minister's face is grim, his eyes steady. He turns to the Algerian oil minister. "Mr. President, perhaps this time our efforts have not been successful. Perhaps the treacherous United States has been able to block our noble effort to liberate our lands and restore justice to our Palestinian brothers, but this cannot go on indefinitely, I assure you. The day will come when the people of the world in unison will condemn those who have helped the strong against the weak, the oppressor against the oppressed, and the occupier against the occupied. When that day of reckoning comes, God help the United States. The Almighty God, my brothers, works in His own ways. He does not throw bombs. He uses neither warplanes nor missiles. In His own wisdom, when the time comes, He renders justice. Of this I am sure."

The Iraqi minister then turns to the assembled ministers. "My brothers," he says, "Iraq commends sisterly Saudi Arabia for her brave and honorable stand. We are sure that it has not been easy for sisterly Saudi Arabia to propose these bold but inevitable steps. Iraq salutes sisterly Saudi Arabia and its brave king for this unifying and courageous initiative. Iraq will stand by its sister, Saudi Arabia, should the imperialists decide to take risks or begin adventures. Iraq considers any attack against Saudi Arabia an attack against Iraq. We will, my brothers, fight any aggressor with all our might. Finally, Mr. President, Iraq wishes to make the following motion: We move that all the Arab oil-producing countries immediately cease all exports of oil and its products to all countries that have acted in a manner hostile to our Arab nation, notably the United States of America and the Netherlands. We further move that all the Arab oil-producing countries immediately but temporarily reduce their output by 25 percent. We further move that the Arab oil-producing countries guarantee to the remaining Western European nations and to Japan the continued flow of oil as long as they refrain from acting in a manner hostile to our Arab nation. Should the United States of America succeed in convincing Western Europe and Japan to form a united U.S.–Western Europe-Japan front hostile to our Arab nation, then this embargo shall immediately apply to Western Europe and to Japan as soon as such a hostile united front is formed. Thank you, Mr. President."

"The chair recognizes His Excellency the oil minister of sisterly Saudi Arabia."

"Mr. President, I am honored to second the motion made by His Excellency our brother the oil minister of sisterly Iraq."

"Are there any points of discussion or amendments?" asks the presiding Algerian minister.

There are none.

"My brothers," says the Algerian oil minister, exhilarated, "a motion to impose an embargo against the United States of America and the Netherlands, and others who have acted in a manner hostile to our Arab nation has been made and seconded. Those in favor, please raise your hands."

All the delegates raised their hands.

Thafer looks at the grim faces of the delegates as they prepare to adjourn. He remains in his chair, his head in his hands.

Well, well, well . . . Thafer Ayoub Allam . . . I want you to go in the next room and take off all of your clothes . . . Turn around. . . . We're not going to admit you, Mr. Allam. . . . I really need to see my mother. She's an elderly woman, and I haven't seen her since 1959. . . . I'm a citizen of the United States. . . . I've never been involved in any military activity in my entire life. . . . You won't get away with this. . . . I promise you, you won't get away with it. . . . What does it take to construct a clean bomb. . . . Why should we be concerned about building nuclear weapons when some of our people are still barefoot and hungry. . . . Only when we acquire nuclear weapons will we be safe. . . . O Yee, O Yee . . . God willing our liberation is near . . . Looloo loloo loowee. . . . Look at the blue Mediterranean, Thafer. . . . I'll wait for you. . . . Will you also wait for me? . . . These past few days have made me dislike my own country. . . . Perhaps He's preparing another Ayoub Allam for the march to Jerusalem.

XXXVII

Thafer and his two children are packing their suitcases for their journey to Alexandria in Egypt and are about to make their final departure from Kuwait. Unsure whether he should accept the offer he has received the week before from the Alexandria law school, he is torn between his love for his native land and his desire to return to his adopted country. His indecision is a source of worry for his children. He sits in his study, his head between his hands, and broods.

Thafer's elderly cook announces that a woman and a young boy are waiting at the outer gate. "She's wearing a black Kuwaiti robe, trying to look like a Kuwaiti woman, but she really isn't," says the cook. "She wants to talk to you, sir."

"What does she want, Dad?" asks Kathleen, looking concerned.

"Did she say what she wanted, Haji?" Thafer asks.

"She wants to talk to you, sir. She's now inside the gate, in the garden."

"I'll go see who she is," Thafer says. "Are the lights on, Haji?"

"I turned them on when she rang the door bell. After I said you were home, she asked if she could come into the garden. When she came inside the garden and I closed the gate, she asked if I could turn the lights off. I did. She is very nervous, sir."

Thafer goes down the stairs, his two children following. He goes out and walks to the gate, where a tall woman in a long black gown stands at the entrance, her back to Thafer's house. She is clutching a young boy by the hand.

"Can I help you?" Thafer asks.

Still holding the young boy's hand, the woman turns around, pulls the black gown from her head, and faces Thafer.

"Joan, what's the matter?" Thafer asks, astonished.

Tears rolling down her fair cheeks, Joan walks toward him, momentarily letting go of the young boy's hand, and embraces him. "I need your help, Thafer."

"I'll do what I can," he says. "Where's Hamdan? What's upsetting you?"

She lets go of Thafer, rests her head against the iron gate, and cries quietly.

"Won't you please come in?"

"Let's talk here."

"Joan," Thafer says, taking her son's hand, "I'll do everything I can to be helpful. What is it that's troubling you?"

"I just can't live with Hamdan any longer," she says. "I want to go back to the United States and take Jaafar with me. I need to get Jaafar's American passport from the American embassy in Kuwait and go to the Kuwait airport tomorrow."

"Is Jaafar a U.S. citizen?"

"He has dual citizenship," she says, beginning to regain her composure. "I haven't got his U.S. passport. I entered Kuwait on my U.S. passport, but he entered on his father's passport. We arrived today from Saudi Arabia. He's registered at the American embassy as a U.S. citizen here in Kuwait, where he was born."

"Does the embassy know about this?"

"They do, and they'll issue him a passport, but they don't want this to become an international incident, especially with all that's happening now with the war and the embargo."

"Where are you staying?"

"We were at the Hilton with Hamdan," she says, beginning to cry again. "I don't want to go back there."

"Come in, Joan," he says, leading the desperate woman into his house. "These are my two children, Kathleen and Sean."

"Hello, hello," she says. "I'm so sorry to meet them this way."

"Hi," says Kathleen.

"Your father is a wonderful man."

"Yes, I know," says Kathleen. "I'm glad to meet you."

"Hi," says Sean. "I'm Sean."

"Hello, Sean. I'm sorry to put your family through this, Thafer."

"Don't worry about it. Kathleen, take Mrs. Mishaan to Colleen's room upstairs, sweetheart."

"Sure."

"Sean, carry Jaafar's small handbag upstairs."

"Will do."

"Come down when you're ready, Joan, and we'll talk in the living room."

"Thank you, Thafer."

"Who's this woman?" Kathleen whispers.

"She's the wife of a former colleague, sweetheart. She and her husband are having marital problems. She wants to go back to the United States."

"She said her husband is Arab."

"Yes, he is."

"She seems like a nice woman," says Kathleen. "The little boy is scared out of his wits. That's so sad."

"Yes."

"How do you get yourself involved in these things, Dad? I hope this doesn't turn nasty."

"It won't, dear."

"Is she American?" Sean asks.

"Yes," Thafer says. "She and her husband had a nice reception for me at their home when I arrived in Kuwait. She knows the dabkah, the Palestinian dance I was telling you about."

"She really does!?" asks Kathleen.

"Where's Jaafar?" Thafer asks, as Joan enters the living room.

"He just went to bed," she says. "He's very tired. He'll sleep with me in the same bed. He's very quiet once he goes to sleep."

"How are you going to get us out of Kuwait, Thafer? I'm sure Hamdan will report me to the police as soon as he reads the note I left him."

"What did you write?"

"I just said I've had it, that Jaafar and I are going back to the States, and that I'll call him from there."

"There'll be no problem in your leaving Kuwait, Joan. The problem will be when Jaafar exits. The Kuwaiti emigration people at the airport are going to wonder how he entered Kuwait."

"That's right. The American consul at the embassy mentioned this, but she knows someone in the Kuwaiti Ministry of Interior who's going to stamp Jaafar's passport as though he entered on it."

"Very good," he says. "Your plan is to go to London from Kuwait, then to New York, but maybe you should go to Alexandria with us. From Alexandria you can go to London, then to New York."

"Why?"

"A lot of Kuwaiti residents, including Palestinians, go to Alexandria every day, and the flights are very congested. The scrutiny has become quite sloppy. The traffic to Europe is far less congested, and someone could be at the airport expecting you to go to London or to Paris to catch a flight to the United States. No one expects you to fly to Alexandria. We have to plan this to minimize the possibility of a confrontation."

"I like the idea of going to Alexandria, then to London."

"Would you mind traveling dressed like a Palestinian woman?"

"Of course not."

"My older daughter left a lot of Palestinian garments behind, figuring that it would be easier and less expensive for me to ship them to the United States through OAPEC. I can get Palestinian clothing for Jaafar from my relatives."

"What if the emigration people speak Arabic to us?"

"I'll be with you. We'll board the plane to Alexandria together. All of us. I'll pick up Jaafar's passport from the embassy tomorrow. Do you want me to change your tickets and make them for Kuwait to Alexandria, Alexandria to London, London to New York?"

"Yes, please."

"The flight from Kuwait to London is at 10:45 in the morning, but the flight to Alexandria is at 6:00 in the evening."

"Does that mean I have to stay overnight in Alexandria?"

"All of us will."

"We'll go to Alexandria, then to London. That is safer. Will you go to London with us?"

"I haven't decided yet."

XXXVIII

As they prepare to leave the next day, Joan puts on a handwoven white linen Palestinian dress, embroidered with red and pink

silk, over her cotton dress. It is the dress given to Colleen by
Mama Adla when Colleen first arrived in Kuwait. Joan adds
Colleen's Palestinian necklace, a chain with six more chains
suspended from it. She wears a white veil over her head. On
her wrists she wears handmade silver Palestinian bracelets and
on her ankles a pair of anklets. Thafer gives her Colleen's
white cotton purse with the wooden handles.

"Now let's dress Jaafar. I brought a boy's Palestinian robe
and white headcloth," says Thafer.

"I'm sure that'll work. We'll wrap the headcloth around
his face to protect him from the dust," says Joan.

"Good."

"Can you tell me about this lovely purse?" Joan asks.

"It's cotton, made in Hebron."

"What about the dress?"

"It is known as the white rumi dress and is worn by
women in the Ramallah region. The necklace is called saba
arwah, which means 'seven lives,' and it's made in Bethlehem."

"They're lovely."

"The white veil is called Bourkou. You'll notice the four
colors—blue to ward off the evil eye, pinkish red for healthy
children, orange for prosperity, and amber for good health.
The anklets are called Khulkhal, and are given to a Palestinian
girl by her parents. Don't they look authentic?"

"They do. They're beautiful."

"You don't have to wear any of this, Joan."

"I'll wear everything."

"Now, we should be leaving in a couple of hours. Would
you and Jaafar like to have something to eat before we leave?"

"I'm sure they'll feed us on the plane, but I'd like to go
upstairs for a little rest with Jaafar before we go. I'm a little
down, Thafer."

"I'm sorry," says Thafer. "You'll be all right."

"I hope so," she says, holding her son's hand. Then she
takes the young boy upstairs.

XXXIX

It is a hot, dusty evening. Wearing a white Arab robe and white headcloth, Thafer drives Joan, her young son, Kathleen, and Sean to the Kuwait airport in the small white car he's been driving around Kuwait. The visibility is poor.

"I didn't know you had this jalopy," Joan says.

"I'm going to leave it here at the airport for Saeed. He was thrilled when I told him he could have it."

"That's great. No one would expect this."

"Joan, when we get to the airport, Sean and I will hold Jaafar's hand, and we'll walk just a step ahead of you and Kathleen. I'll do all the talking to the customs inspectors and to the passport people. Don't look at anybody, just look down. Kathleen will walk with you as though she's your own."

"She is my own. What if they ask me any questions?"

"Just appear shy and timid, say nothing, and don't smile. I'll answer whatever they ask."

"Thank you, but I'm a little nervous."

"Of course you are, but you're going to be OK. Just try to relax, though, Joan, as if nothing is bothering you. This is important so that you don't appear worried. It's going to be all right, I'm sure."

"I hope so." Her voice is trembling.

"It'll be all right, Aunt Joan," says Kathleen.

"Thank you, Kathleen. You're so sweet."

They walk into the airport. It is congested, and the heat is unbearable. Thafer wears his sunglasses and covers his mouth with the headcloth to protect himself from the dust. He covered Jaafar's mouth earlier. Sean, dressed like his father, covers his mouth too and clutches Jaafar's hand.

Egyptians, Kuwaitis, Syrians, Lebanese and Palestinians—men, women, and children swarm around the ticket counter.

Thafer proceeds to the emigration window, clutching Jaafar's hand, Sean beside him, Joan and Kathleen a step behind.

"Arab Americans?" asks the emigration officer.

"Yes," says Thafer, his voice slightly strained, "Palestinian Americans."

"You're all going?"

"That's right, sir, we're all going."

"You're all set," says the emigration officer, handing Thafer the five stamped passports.

The five of them walk into the hot and humid waiting room crowded with mostly Egyptian travelers.

"I think we're safe now, Joan," he says.

"I hope so. My whole body is shaking, Thafer."

"We'll all board soon. It won't be too long now."

"How long, Dad?" asks Kathleen.

"About five minutes."

"You be sure to come and see us in Connecticut when you return to the States, Kathleen, won't you?" says Joan.

"Yes, I will," says Kathleen.

"You too, Sean."

"Thanks, I would like that."

"How long will you be in Alexandria, Thafer?"

"We're not sure."

"Give me a call when you get back in the States, won't you?"

"I'll do that."

"My parents would like to meet you, especially my father," she says.

"I would like to meet them," he says.

"Flight 501 to Alexandria is ready for boarding. All passengers please proceed to the airplane and identify your luggage."

Thafer walks out of the waiting room, holding Jaafar's hand tightly and taking Joan's arm as the five approach their plane. Thafer identifies the five suitcases and climbs the stairs of the plane behind Joan and his two children, still holding Jaafar's hand.

"Thank you, Thafer. You can't possibly know how grateful I am."

"A taxi will meet us at the airport in Alexandria and will take us to the Alexandria Hilton. Then he'll pick you up in the morning and take you to British Airways."

"Thanks again, Thafer. Be sure to call me when you return to the States, won't you?"

"I will." He takes her arm and walks with her into the plane. He seats Jaafar next to her. He and his two children sit together.

"She's really an amazing woman, Dad," says Kathleen. "I like her a lot. If she's forced to do this, her husband must be dreadful. Is he, Dad?"

"These family differences are always tragic, Kathleen. Her husband is not an easy man."

"I felt bad for the little boy, Dad," says Sean.

"I did too," says Kathleen. "He didn't say one word while we were at the airport. I wonder how he'll remember this when he grows up."

Now, there's something noble about what you've done, Thafer says to himself. You've gallantly exposed yourself to the risk of a dangerous confrontation by responding to the pleas of poor Joan. Why did you do this?

I'm confused, he admits to himself. When I first arrived in Kuwait, the dance with Joan, sweet daughter of my adopted land, awakened the most tender memories of my youth, stirring within me deep yearnings for my homeland and my kin. What could she know of this? Now it has fallen on me to save her from a brother.

And my beloved Suhaila, daughter of our cherished homeland! Sharing your longings and your hopes has brought life to a part of me that had despaired. You have soothed me and dressed the deepest wounds in my heart. Our homeland unites us; yet for its sake we are scattered like seeds far and wide.

Yes, I am torn.

And I am lonely.

"What are you thinking about, Dad?" asks Kathleen. "You've been engrossed in deep thought. I could even hear the wheels grinding in your head."

"Yes, Dad," asks Sean. "Why are you so quiet?"

"I'm just wondering whether we've done the right thing. I feel badly for Joan and for her family."

"I feel good about what we've done, Dad," says Kathleen. "She seems to be a wonderful woman."

"So do I, Dad," says Sean. "I really like her."

"That's good," Thafer says quietly.